SEDITION

TOM ABRAHAMS

A POST HILL PRESS book

ISBN (trade paperback): 978-1-61868-997-9
ISBN (eBook): 978-1-61868-998-6

Sedition copyright © 2013
by Tom Abrahams
All Rights Reserved.
Cover art by Jason Farmand
Edited by Felicia A. Sullivan

Post Hill
PRESS

For an interactive experience with downloadable documents please visit *www.tomabrahamsbooks.com*

For periodic updates, information about appearances, and new releases, please email tomabrahamsbooks@gmail.com

For my co-conspirators: Courtney, Samantha, & Luke

PROLOGUE

"We learn from history that we learn nothing from history."
--George Bernard Shaw

For a man known to make noise literally and figuratively, Dexter Foreman's death was remarkably silent.

He was alone in his office.

Foreman liked to have one half hour of office solitude each morning to read the paper and drink a cup of fully caffeinated coffee. He often joked coffee was a drink that, without caffeine, served no godly purpose.

It wasn't just the sense of quiet, the newsprint, and the Arabica he enjoyed in his office. A student of architecture, Foreman loved the neoclassical style of the room; the two-foot rise of its domed ceiling, the niches inset into the curved walls. He admired the Eighteenth Century sentiment.

He and his wife had chosen to honor the office's first occupant with green accents throughout. The subtle pea green of the rug complemented the alternating white pine and walnut flooring.

The matching curtains and valances on the windows were muted with cream sheers. It was colorful but tasteful. Historians loved the homage to an earlier time. Despite the office being more ceremonial than practical, Foreman loved his time there.

He was reading *The New York Times,* a below-the-fold article about his efforts to enhance Public Law 107-56, an act initially designed to "provide appropriate tools required to intercept and obstruct terrorism". He'd not gotten past reporter Helene Cooper's byline.

The moment the artery blew within his head, he felt a sharp lightning bolt of pain as the blood exploded into his brain.

The last image he saw was the portrait of George Washington hanging in its gilded frame above the white marble fireplace across from his desk on the north side of the room.

He lost focus. The portrait dissolved to black. His eyes fixed.

His face dropped onto the thick English oak, cracking the bridge of his nose. Blood pooled resolutely around his head, sticking to the gel in his styled salt and pepper hair. It leeched onto the corner of the *Times.*

Had it not been for a planned meeting in his office just three minutes later, his body might have gone unnoticed for a half hour. But because of the meeting, his senior aide knocked on the northwest door of the office just forty five seconds after the vessel popped.

That aide knocked twice, as was the custom with Foreman, and then opened the thick door from the hallway outside. The young man's head was down as he entered the room. He lifted it to meet Foreman's eyes with his. But instead of the expected nod from his boss, he

saw him slumped on the desk across the room.

His mind flooded with confusion and panic. At first he wasn't certain he was processing the scene correctly. There was a bright diffused light from the triplet of south facing windows directly behind the desk. It backlit Foreman's body and made it difficult for the aide to focus. And what the aide saw before him appeared surreal: a cup of coffee, a newspaper, and an unconscious, bleeding Dexter Foreman.

He hurried to the desk, lifted his wrist to his mouth, and spoke hurriedly.

"Bandbox respond. Boxer is down. Boxer is down."

Two other doors swung open into the office from the rose garden outside and from an adjacent smaller room. Men in dark suits rushed to the desk, their fingers on the DAK triggers of their drawn .357 Sig Sauer P229 side arms.

"Sir?" The aide touched Foreman's shoulder, not expecting a

response.

Regardless, he repeated himself as three more suited, armed men ran into the office. This was not the meeting on the schedule.

"Mr. President?" The aide's voice was shaky. He swallowed hard past the thick lump at the top of his throat, focusing on the empty distant gaze in Foreman's eyes. His own welled.

Steam rose from the cup of coffee to Dexter Foreman's right. It was inches from his hand, untouched and black.

The president was dead.

PART ONE
THE CONSPIRATORS

"A conspiracy is nothing but a secret agreement of a number of men for the pursuance of policies which they dare not admit in public."
–Mark Twain

CHAPTER 1

Matilda Harrold winced at the slight squeal of the struts on her government issued Smokestone Metallic Ford Fusion. Auto mechanics was one of two areas in her life which she neglected. The other was her social calendar. Both needed overhauls they were unlikely to receive.

Fifteen miles south of Baltimore, Matti was avoiding the main gate to her building. After showing her green identification badge to a series of M16 armed military police officers, she wound her way across the 5400 acre Fort George G. Meade toward the eastern side of the campus. Normally, she would have taken the "official" route, but today she felt like a change.

It was a random choice she'd spontaneously made on the short drive to the office.

Matti was taking baby steps.

Security at Ft. Meade was at its standard post 9/11 level. Outside of the Oval Office, nobody yet knew of the president's death.

Matti turned the steering wheel as she approached her facility, a pair of high rise, green reflective glass buildings. She parked and retrieved a small black, soft leather Coach briefcase from the floorboard of the front passenger seat. The 29 year old code breaker checked her watch and walked toward the headquarters for the National Security Agency.

For nine years now, she'd driven to work on a secured base, pulled out her green (fully cleared) identification badge and slipped it over her head on a beaded neck chain. She invariably reported to work exactly fifteen minutes early. It could take a quarter hour to clear security on some days. Matti approached her entrance and slid the badge into an access control terminal. She punched in her personal identification number and opened the temporarily unlocked door.

Once inside, she waded through three checkpoints and was searched at each one. Her bag was checked for weapons, cameras, phones, iPods, and a host of other items banned by the Agency's M51 Physical Security Division.

There were two distinct areas within the NSA headquarters: Administrative and Secure. Matti worked in a Secure area, and as such she was privy to classified material.

She reached her fourth floor office exactly on time. It was small and she shared it with three other analysts. On her desk were a computer, a notepad, and two telephones. The gray telephone was a secured line. The black phone was an unsecured line. Whenever a black phone was in use, the others in the office were alerted and they refrained from speaking aloud.

She placed her bag on the floor next her to her desk and sat down, and was adjusting her seat when the black phone rang.

"Harrold." She always answered last name only.

"In my office," said a man's voice.

"Yes, sir," Matti replied and hung up. She immediately stood and left her office for the unscheduled meeting with her supervisor. It wasn't often he contacted her directly.

What did he want?

* * *

Sir Spencer Thomas stirred the Chivas Regal Royal Salute with his left pinkie then sucked the rare liquid from his finger.

He'd saved the fifty year old scotch since 2003 when it was gifted to him at the celebration of the fiftieth anniversary of the coronation of Queen Elizabeth II. Now was as good a time as any to self-medicate with a $10,000 bottle of Strathisla malted scotch.

From his high back, brown leather chair in his suite at the Hay-Adams Hotel, he could see the White House, the Washington Monument, and the 52-inch LCD television alit with coverage of President Foreman's sudden death. The news was minutes old and already the spin doctors were talking succession.

The body isn't even cold yet, he thought and crossed his legs.

He took a sip from the leaded glass and listened to the commentary on television.

"What complicates matters so much," opined the pundit on the screen, *"is that the president's death comes so soon after the prolonged illness and death of the former vice president. It leaves us with a bit of a constitutional crisis. The replacement nominee is confirmed, but hasn't taken the oath. Does this mean the speaker of the house becomes president? Does she take the reins only until V.P. nominee Blackmon is sworn in? Who is in control right now?"*

At the bottom of the screen flashed a crawl of announcements. Sir Spencer muted the television as he read the information moving from right to left across the screen.

Wall Street trading suspended after sharp 900 point drop. Mourners gather outside 1600 Pennsylvania Avenue. Cabinet meets in emergency session in White House. Leadership vacuum not a concern, says Speaker Jackson. Doctors say Foreman's last checkup revealed no health issues. Aneurysm suspected in President Foreman's sudden death. Autopsy is scheduled for late tonight with results tomorrow.

Sir Spencer took another sip. The scotch was smooth and it finished with a creamy taste. He stood from the chair, using his left hand to balance his six-foot-five inch frame as he rose. It was a simple task that had become increasingly difficult with age and indulgence. Sighing, he stepped to the window overlooking the People's House and thought about the incredible opportunity fate had chosen to bestow upon him.

The possibilities!

The knight was a man for whom manifest destiny was a deep belief. It did not end with his adopted country's purchase of Texas, as some historians suggested. It did not end with the imperialism so many believe the U.S. employed in Iraq and Afghanistan.

It was, for him, the idea that America's place as the world's foremost military, economic, and social power was ordained in perpetuity. Sir Spencer believed the death of a president and the ensuing uncertainty might be exactly what was needed for America to regain her authority and rightful place in the hierarchy of nations. *This is what we've waited for. This is our opportunity.*

Sir Spencer reached into the inside breast pocket of his blue, combed cashmere Kiton jacket. He pulled out his Sigillu encrypted cell phone and punched a series of numbers with his thumb, pressed send, and slipped the phone back into the pocket.

"A Deo et Rege," he murmured as he again lifted the glass to his lips. *From God and the King.* He could smell the strength of the scotch.

* * *

For American University undergraduates not prone to rise early, the news of President Foreman's death was as much an excuse as it was a reason to miss class.

Professor Arthur Thistlewood knew this, but he did not excuse from class the few who showed up for his American Government survey. Instead he found it to be the perfect teaching tool.

"The order of succession for the presidency," he started. "Who knows what it is?"

"Vice president," offered a pimply boy in the fourth row. "Then speaker of the House."

"After that?" asked Thistlewood with his back to the auditorium. He wrote on an overhead projector. Most teachers employed computerized versions of the display. They used PowerPoint and other software to share their chalkboard musings. Thistlewood was bourgeois.

"The cabinet?" a young woman in the back of the room.

It always amazed Thistlewood that students would actually pay to sit in the back. If he were a rock star or a standup comic, they'd shell out big money to sit in the front. But in college, they paid their $50,000 a year to sit in the back.

"Not yet," responded the handsome professor, rubbing the white scruff on his chin, eyeing the robust blonde in the third row. He paused and then counted with his fingers. "The President Pro Tempore of the Senate is next. He or she is followed by the cabinet: the Secretaries of State, Treasury, Defense, and the Attorney General. Then it's the Secretaries of Interior, Agriculture,

Commerce, Labor, Health & Human Services, HUD, Transportation, Energy, Education, Veterans Affairs, and Homeland Security."

"What happens if they all die at the same time?" the boy in the fourth row asked with all seriousness. It drew some snickers.

"Good question," Thistlewood pointed at the boy as he turned toward the class. "And that is virtually impossible."

"Why?"

"One of those in line must always be separated. For example, when Barack Obama was inaugurated in 2009, Defense Secretary Robert Gates was the 'designated successor'. They sent him to an undisclosed location. Had something catastrophic happened he would have survived to provide what's called a 'continuity of government'."

"Why are the cabinet members after the Speaker and the president of the Senate?" A third student was now engaged. Thistlewood could hear the rusty gears turning slowly in his students' heads. He eyed the third row blonde again and imagined her wearing far less than a sweatshirt and jeans. *Maybe next semester.*

"Favoritism," Thistlewood responded. "By having elected officials at the top of the succession list, it prevents the president from essentially handpicking all potential successors. It was a key point of the 1947 Act of Presidential Succession.

"Some constitutional scholars would argue the placement of the Speaker of the House and the Senate President Pro Tempore ahead of any cabinet 'officer' is unconstitutional," continued Thistlewood. "But that's how the law is written."

Thistlewood scanned the classroom, trying to catch the expressions of the few dozen students seated in front of him. He saw mixed interest and then felt a vibration against his hip.

"Tell you what," he reasoned aloud while checking his pager. He refused to carry any kind of newer device to class. A simple numeric pager was good enough for the professor while he taught. His encrypted cell phone was on his desk in his office. "I am going to leave a notebook up here for each of you to sign. Everyone who attended today gets ten points added to the next quiz."

After looking up from the series of numbers displayed in dot matrix on his 1998 Motorola, he again surveyed his students. A few sat up straighter. Some nodded and smiled at the student closest to them. Thistlewood knew how to enthuse.

* * *

Matti Harrold sat across from her supervisor's desk, stunned as much by what he was asking of her as she was by the president's sudden death.

"Do you understand what your assignment is?" he asked without a hint of expression.

"Yes sir," she replied, refocusing. "Though I *am* somewhat confused."

"By what?" He was looking down at his desk, tapping on a closed 8 ½ x 11 folder. It was stamped "Secret" at the top left.

"Well, sir," she said hesitantly, "we don't deal in human intelligence. We protect American systems and information. We collect adversarial signal intelligence only. Executive Order 12333 prohibits gathering or sharing information about U.S. citizens. Isn't this out of the realm of what we do?"

She'd often impressed teachers and superiors with her ability to rattle off long streams of text or complicated sets of numbers. Technically, she was an *Eidetiker*, the name given to the estimated one in a thousand adults with eidetic memory. It was a gift that had faded with age as it did with most eidetic children. But she still possessed a significant ability to mentally retain detailed images for long periods of time.

Her memory was not truly photographic, but she could filter out the clutter and focus on particular images and structures. Hers was a rare ability that rivaled even some of the more well-known Eidetikers such as Kim Peek, the autistic upon whom the movie *Rain Man* was based. Doctors estimated he could remember 98 percent of everything he read and had thousands of volumes of text available for instant recall.

Matti knew there were always skeptics who thought photographic or eidetic memory was a farce. The legendary artificial intelligence expert, Dr. Marvin Minsky, wrote in his book *Society of the Mind* that eidetic memory was a myth. Others in the field thought it was little more than a mnemonic trick in which Eidetikers could associate images with words to enhance their recall.

Even her own therapist, who'd helped her through the darkest days of her adolescence, doubted Matti's ability until she'd recalled to him the verbatim details of police reports and eyewitness accounts from the night her mother died. They were pieces to a code she'd never been able to crack. But her memory wouldn't let her let go of it. It was a gift and a curse. And at the moment, she knew her boss was cursing it.

"No, Harrold." Her supervisor lifted his gaze to her without lifting his head. "There are many things we do here at NSA which are outside the realm of 'what we do'. The Eric Snowden debacle should have made that clear to you. You've read the classified briefs on what that traitor did and did not reveal."

"Yes sir," Matti said. "I read the Snowden briefs, and saw the news accounts."

"And if you recall," he continued, "that same order 12333 directs all departments and agencies to share the responsibility of gathering intelligence."

"SIGINT," he offered without averting his glare, "is what the Congress asks publicly of us. But there are cases in which it is better we ask forgiveness than permission. This, Harrold, is one of those cases. Are you up to this? "

"Yes, sir." Matti didn't care for the lecture.

She understood the CIA, under the direction of the NSC, was the lead for human intelligence. Anybody who'd paid attention knew that in October of 2005, the CIA and the office of the director of National of Intelligence developed a plan to create the National Clandestine Service.

The NSC became a special branch of Central Intelligence and was responsible for the coordination, de-confliction, and evaluation of all clandestine operations across the entire spectrum of intelligence gathering agencies. But its primary intelligence gathering job was human intelligence (HUMINT).

Leading that charge was the CIA director. He delegated the acquisition and collaboration of HUMINT, reporting only to the Director of National Intelligence. Even under the 21st century version of the U.S. intelligence community, NSA was not publicly mentioned as having anything to do with HUMINT.

Matti wanted to remind her boss the NSA was an agency born from a single memorandum in 1951. CIA director Walter Bedell Smith wrote to then secretary of the National Security Council, James Lay, that 'control over, and coordination of, the collection and processing of Communications Intelligence had proved ineffective'. The memo suggested a detailed study of communications intelligence, which was approved and completed by mid-1952.

But here she was now with all of that history shoved into a box marked "irrelevant". Tradition did not matter; this was about the future.

"Since 9/11," her supervisor instructed, "we have found ourselves stepping on the toes of every acronym you can name." He was leaning back in his chair, his hand still on the closed folder. "It is a painful dance amongst competing agencies that keeps us safe. To that end, our 'responsibility' is not limited to SIGINT."

Matti wished she'd never challenged her boss. It was unlike her to question authority. There was an order to things that she always accepted. But this assignment puzzled Matti. It was out of order. It didn't follow the prescribed rules. *Maybe*, she thought, *that was why I questioned the validity of the charge.* She rubbed her elbows with her fingers.

"So," her boss nodded slightly, "we have an asset who has alerted us to a scenario which may require drastic action on our part. You will be the primary contact. You will handle all levels and types of intelligence from this asset and keep me informed of what you learn. We are on a tight timeframe here. I need real, actionable information." He pushed the file folder across the desk to Matti and waved his hand to shoo her from his office.

She picked up the folder and stood to leave. As she reached for the handle of the door, she stopped and turned.

"Sir?" She wanted crystal clarity.

"Yes?" He'd turned his back to her and was beginning to punch numbers into his gray phone.

"I report to you alone? I await contact from the asset? I do not initiate, correct?"

"Yes to each of your questions. Gray line only. Nothing emailed.

Period. And nothing written unless it is sent to me alone."

"Why me, sir?" Matti ran her fingers through her hair and tilted her head slightly. She was unclear why a mid-level SIGINT analyst had been chosen for such an unusual, high-level assignment. It didn't fit the pattern.

"The asset requested a woman handler," he replied. "We obliged." He stopped dialing and turned to look her in the eye. "There is additional ongoing surveillance. You will have access to what I determine you need. And as it states in the guidebook, which I am sure you've memorized, everything is 'Need to Know' only."

"Understood." She assumed that was why, until that moment, dealing with human intelligence as an NSA analyst had never entered her mind.

Until now she'd never needed to know.

CHAPTER 2

The Hanover-Crown Institute was in a nondescript limestone, iron and glass building on South Street in Georgetown, halfway between Wisconsin Avenue and 31st Street, NW, just a block from The Shops at Georgetown Park.

It stood three stories tall, not including a below-grade basement garage for employees and special guests. On the flat roof of the brownstone-style structure, hidden by the façade, was a pair of small satellite dishes. One of them received television signals and the other uplinked them.

The Institute was a nonpartisan think tank that had neither the prestige nor financial prowess of The Brookings Institution. It resembled a European institute in that its research was heavy on opinion while being somewhat light on number crunching and measurable analysis.

Hanover's gem was a small production studio it used to showcase its higher profile opinion-shapers. One of them was former Attorney General Bill Davidson. He was a legacy politician, whose father had served two presidents in varying capacities. While not much of a success as A.G., Davidson knew Washington politics. He knew where the deals were made and where the bodies were buried. In that capacity, he was valuable to Hanover-Crown.

The cable networks loved Davidson. He was always good for a sound bite or an unfiltered opinion of whatever was happening inside the beltway.

Because the networks loved Davidson, Hanover-Crown loved

him. The Institute's media department built the small television studio with an adjacent office and storage room *for* him. The Institute's website had a section titled "Bites with AG Bill." Every time he appeared on a talk show or news program from that studio, the hits and page views for the Institute's site skyrocketed.

There were deep furrows across his lengthening brow. His tightly curled brow hair was combed forward to make it appear fuller. His eyes were sunken and puffy; the skin beneath his brow was melting onto the lids. He lamented the sky blue surrounding his pupils had long ago faded to a soft gray, as though the life was slowly leaving them.

Davidson's strong jaw and chin were diffused by the skin and fat surrounding them. His ill-fitting bridge made his gums smack when he talked. Given his high profile, he knew it was ridiculous to live with bad dental work, but there was something comforting in the familiarity of the old bridge.

Almost everyone saw him as a famous statesman and pundit, but Bill Davidson couldn't get past the aging, sad man staring back at him in the reflective glass above the sink. He was a good actor.

He would call on that skill for the next three hours as he prepared to sit in the studio as a guest on various cable news programs. They all wanted his take on the constitutional questions surrounding the president's death.

As he applied a light powder to his forehead to reduce shine from the studio lights, there was a knock at the bathroom door.

"Attorney General Davidson?" It was the studio coordinator. "We have about five minutes and I need to get you wired up, sir."

"Okay," replied Davidson through a face stretched to apply makeup in the right places. "I'm on my way."

Davidson shook the makeup brush free of light chocolate powder and placed it in its plastic sleeve. He was slipping it into his pants pocket when his Blackberry vibrated against his hip. He pulled it from the clip attached to his belt and saw he had a new text message. Davidson pulled open the bathroom door with his right hand as he pressed the text icon with his left thumb. He saw the text was from "Caesar", and stared at the numbers on the screen deciphering them quickly in his head:

3 1 20 15 0 19 20 18 5 5 20 0 16 21 2 0 100 1 13

He looked at his watch and sighed, knowing it would be a late night. He then pulled from his coat pocket a small blue journal. It was a diary of notes he kept with him everywhere he went. It was useful for thoughts and appointments.

A habit he first acquired in law school, it had stuck with him. At home in a file cabinet, he had stacks of small journals, each of them filled with almost indecipherable numbers and notes. He pulled a ballpoint pen from the same pocket and yanked off the cap with his teeth. He quickly jotted the series of numbers onto an empty page, recapped the pen, and put both items back in the pocket.

Davidson slid into the studio and sat in a low back leather chair, rubbing his palms along the brass nail heads on its arms.

* * *

George Edwards flipped open his cell phone and cursed at the series of numbers on the screen.

"I hate these damn codes," he grumbled, running a yellow light at the corner of 10th and L Streets. He was heading East on L and had just passed the Washington Convention Center. He was late for a meeting at a local reception hall on the corner of 16th and L. The hall doubled as a gallery at which he was premiering some of his latest work.

Edwards was a digital sculptor. He used his computer to enhance/alter iconic portraits or designs, and they were in very high demand. His manipulated "sculpture" of the painting *Declaration of Independence* by John Trumbull sold for $105,000.

Edwards called his version of the painting *What Really Happened.* He played off of the fact that the scene depicted in the iconic representation of a nation's birth never actually happened the way Trumbull painted it.

Instead of Charles Thomson standing directly across from Thomas Jefferson on the right side of the canvas, Edwards inserted a free-floating dartboard with the face of King George III. On the left side of the piece, Edwards altered a standing, cross-armed William Paca, putting a dart in the right hand of the Maryland lawyer. Thomas Jefferson held a pint of ale instead of a page of the declaration. The entire painting was colorized with shades that differed from Trumbull's original, making the work appear almost lifelike.

They were sophomoric enough changes that most would dismiss the work as a joke. But it was that which *wasn't* so obvious to the casual viewer that made Edwards' offerings so prized. Much as caricaturist Al Hirshfeld was recognized for hiding his daughter Nina's name in his drawings, Edwards was revered for his ability to hide messages in some of his digitally re-mastered works.

Hidden amongst the signers of the Declaration in Edwards' parody was the phrase, *"The modern bourgeois society that has sprouted from the ruins of feudal society has not done away with class antagonisms."* The words were a direct translation from Karl Marx's *Communist Manifesto.* Lithographs of the digital sculpture were amazingly popular on college campuses throughout the country. They were third in sales at the Harvard "Coop" behind a poster of Moe kicking a football off of Curley's head and Salvador Dali's *The Persistence of Memory.*

Edwards knew he needed to decode the text message quickly. There was limited street parking around the convention center but he saw a blue BMW pulling out ahead of him. He quickly pulled into the parallel spot to park.

He left the keys in the ignition and kept the engine of his Audi A6 running. It hummed quietly at a low RPM as he leaned over to open the glove compartment. Inside, he found a small court reporter's notebook and an uncapped Bic pen. Still strapped into his seatbelt, he sat the pad on the front passenger's seat and scribbled a circle on the paper to make sure the pen still worked. It did. He sat his phone on his left thigh as he copied the numbers on the pad.

3 1 20 15 0 19 20 18 5 5 20 0 16 21 2 0 100 1 13

Edwards stared at the numbers. It was a "Caesar Cipher", in which letters of the alphabet were replaced with numbers. Sometimes the numbers were shifted, sometimes they were not. This time he knew they weren't. Off the bat, he knew the zeroes were spaces between words. If there was a shift, the zeroes would be multiplied to signal the shift. "00" would indicate a shift of one. "0000" would indicate a shift of three. "0" meant no shift. 1=A, 2=B, 3=C...

Three separate zeroes meant four words. He knew three or four digit numbers were times of day. The "100" third to the last in the sequence was 1 o'clock. The "1 13" following the time was A.M. He had a meeting at 1:00 A.M.

"Great," he muttered. "Just what I need right now." Begrudgingly, he deciphered the rest of the code to determine the location of the clandestine get-together.

* * *

The Cato Street Pub was a bar in the 2100 block of Pennsylvania Avenue, NW. It was a favorite for politicos; dark, cheap, and served call brands for house prices.

The red brick two-story building was squeezed between a drug store and a Vietnamese restaurant. It had the look of an 18th century London home. The two windows on the second floor were twelve panels with white paint on the trim. There were sheer white draperies drawn on the inside.

On the first floor the large, solid wood doors at the entrance were painted a glossy red. A large engraved brass plaque affixed to the brick, just to the left of the doors, bore the pub's name and its hours of operation.

The pub's interior was wall to wall hickory. The twenty-foot long bar was lacquered rosewood, as were the dozen four-seat round tables scattered across the dining portion of the first floor. Directly opposite the bar, which sat to the right, was a series of four red velvet booths.

On the walls were black and white photos of famous politicians who'd sidled up to the bar aboard the brass and leather stools. From Tom DeLay and Tip O'Neill, to Strom Thurmond and Robert McNamara, the powerful had haunted Cato Street for decades.

And yet, unbeknownst to the even the most connected Capitol Hill broker, the bar and its upstairs apartment served as the place where the self-described disenfranchised would meet to talk treachery.

The owner of Cato Street was Jimmy Ings. He'd purchased the bar in his early twenties as a place to commiserate and imbibe with friends. He lived in the upstairs apartment alone. Over the years,

Ings used his profits to buy a nearby butcher shop and a coffee house. The coffee sales were good; the meat profits were non-existent. Both were primarily cash businesses.

He was a thin man who drank more than he ate and sucked down two packs of Camel unfiltered regulars a day. His thinning hair was white and tinged with yellow from cigarette smoke. The skin on his cheeks and nose was reddened from a severe case of aggravated rosacea.

He was an unhappy man with a dry wit and a penchant for the television show *Jeopardy!*. He was particularly good at historical and political categories.

Ings was also a founding member of the underground Datura Project, a virulent offshoot of the Tea Party movement that formed during President Barack Obama's early days in office.

The "Daturans", as the small group's members were called, had met each other at Tea Parties in the Metro D.C. area. But they'd found the group's ideology too naïve and not quite radical enough.

Jimmy Ings quickly grew impatient with the "all talk/no action" mentality of the movement. A Senator from Kentucky and one from Texas weren't enough to actually do anything. A few members of Congress sleeping in their offices "to save their constituents money" was window dressing.

And so, despite a massive Tea Party membership boom in its first years, Ings and some compatriots decided to form their own group and act.

They first met in Ings' upstairs apartment as a group of four and soon added a fifth. The group determined that half of a minyan was large enough and stopped recruiting. They called themselves the "Datura Project" in honor of the poisonous plant certain Native American tribes would diffuse into a hallucinogenic tea during rites of passage.

The Daturans knew what was best for their country, and they believed they could best affect change with swift action. But meeting after meeting their leader, Sir Spencer Thomas, convinced them the right opportunity had not presented itself.

Most of the group appreciated that. Ings complained they were no better than the chatty "Tea Baggers", who had a bully pulpit on cable television and talk radio, but who'd failed to exact any sort of real course correction.

Maybe that will change now that the president is dead.

With chatter of the president's death on the flat screen behind the bar, but nobody in the seats, Ings decided to close up early. He sent his barkeep and cook home with a few extra bucks, locked the front doors, and climbed the stairs into his apartment. The rest of the group would be there in a few hours and he needed to be ready.

Plus, *Jeopardy!* was on Channel 8 and he didn't want to miss it. It was "College All-Stars" week. He hoped it wouldn't be preempted by news coverage of the president's death.

* * *

Standing in the Cox Corridors on the House side of the U.S. Capitol, Felicia Jackson's mind was swirling with the possibilities. She was transfixed by the large mural above her in the Central East-West Hallway. The corridor, with its sixteen murals focusing on the short history of her nation's democratic folly, was called The Great Experiment Hall.

Felicia was standing directly beneath the large mural depicting the inauguration of George Washington. It was breathtaking.

She was somewhat saddened she'd never taken the time to appreciate the work in the past. But with the halls eerily quiet as everyone on the Hill busied themselves behind office desks and in front of televisions, she had the perfect chance to reflect and admire.

It was a 1973 oil on canvass by Allyn Cox, a New Hampshire artist known for his murals. Felicia, who was stealing time on a day in which she had none, stared at Cox's interpretation of Samuel Otis holding the bible as Washington faced left towards the chancellor of the State of New York, Robert Livingston. Otis was wearing the same shade of green President Foreman had chosen for the Oval Office. Washington was in a muted brown, his right hand raised as he took the oath.

Felicia rubbed her neck as she kept her gaze upward. As Speaker of the House, she knew she might be the next American to take that oath and inherit the green office.

She'd asked her staff for a few minutes of privacy as she took the short walk from her first floor office to the Cox Corridor murals. She'd been in high level, classified meetings all day. Her people were fighting for her to assume the presidency, while not-yet-sworn-in Vice President John Blackmon was staking his own claim.

Her case was open and shut, she'd thought. But Blackmon's attorney had quickly filed an injunction in U.S. District Court in D.C. He claimed her ascension to the presidency would cause irreparable injury for which no damage award could compensate. He also contended his case, on constitutional grounds, was in the public interest.

While the district judge considered the case, she was temporarily stopped from taking office. Nancy Mayer-Whittington, the Clerk of the Court, had told her lawyers the injunction was filed along with her team's response and that the judge would decide on its merits the next morning.

Mayer-Whittington had called just before the office closed at 4 P.M. They were short staffed already, and Felicia imagined this case would only further stress the Clerk. She pictured lines of reporters banging on the Constitution Avenue entrance, all of them asking for copies of the filings.

It was a nightmare as far as Felicia was concerned. By waiting overnight, the judge was effectively granting the injunction and giving Blackmon's legal team time to better formulate their argument.

To make matters worse, she was about to deliver a joint address with Blackmon to assure the American people the government was in good hands as both parties worked together to stabilize what was a precarious situation.

She envied George Washington as she looked at him with his left hand on the bible. He didn't have injunctions. He didn't have 24-hour cable news. He wasn't battling two wars and a financial meltdown.

Speaker Jackson shifted her gaze to the mural's left. It depicted the beginning of the nation's judicial system. It was the same system that was enjoining her from becoming the nation's first woman president. She sighed and straightened her Brooks Brothers silk linen bamboo jacket, tugging on the ends.

The "People's Business" had been good to Speaker Jackson. A school teacher, school board member, and county commissioner turned Member of Congress, she'd been on the fast track. She was witty and politically savvy. She had a handsome face and physique.

Felicia Jackson was, as some cable pundit once put it, Mensa's answer to Sarah Palin. She didn't boast the folksy charm of the former Alaska Governor, but she did have the wink, the smile, and the concealed handgun permit.

Felicia was a Stanford graduate with a Master's Degree in Education from the University of North Carolina. Her husband was a well-known neurosurgeon, who'd given up active practice to support his wife's rocketing political career.

She won the seat in South Carolina's first congressional district by a staggering fourteen points over a six term incumbent. Leaders from both parties started courting the strong-willed moderate the moment her brown leather Cole Haans hit the baggage claim at Reagan National.

Over the course of four terms, the black-haired, blue-eyed shark had amassed a casino-full of favors. When her party narrowly won the house in a mid-term coup, she'd cashed in her chips for a leadership position. She was named Majority Whip, and then Speaker.

She wasn't the first woman to slam the gavel, but she whacked it the loudest. Every favor she'd amassed, every handshake and smile from across the aisle she'd garnered, disintegrated with the squeeze of her iron fist.

If Felicia were a man, she'd have been considered shrewd and opportunistic. As a woman, though...she became the very personification of a variety of misogynistic terms used to diminish the perceived power of headstrong women. It put Congress in a bad light. National polls indicated the lowest levels of support since July of 2008 when approval dropped to 14 percent. She was less than a year into her first term as Speaker and there were rumblings all over the Hill that she would not keep the post another term. She'd heard them.

Yet here she was with the possibility of ascension to the highest office. There were three years left in Foreman's second term, a political eternity. It was plenty of time to change her image. But standing in the way was a litigious ass who wanted to skip his way from the Cabinet to the White House.

Felicia spun on her three-inch heels and plodded her way to the Rotunda to address the nation. She prayed she would be the one speaking first. It wouldn't look good, she knew, to have the Secretary speak first. She needed to look like the leader, the one in command. Blackmon would have to take the back seat.

* * *

Matti hurried down the hall to her office, still confused about the conversation with her supervisor.

What was the NSA really? What intelligence did they truly seek? How long had they been spying on Americans? Was she working for the good guys?

Of course I am, she convinced herself. There were white hats and black hats and she knew the difference.

She thought she knew the difference.

She didn't look at the file in her hand until was she was at her desk. On the top of the front page was the title "DATURA PROJECT". She'd never heard of it. In the pages that followed she learned of what NSA believed to be a fringe group bent on producing some level of anarchy.

The group, she learned, was an offshoot of the nationwide Tea Party Movement which began in Chicago in early 2009. There were Tea Party derivatives in every major city across the country. But the "Daturans" were displeased with the group's lack of action and futile attempts to elect sympathizers, and had spun off.

The NSA believed the initial, informal meeting was during a "Tax Day" protest at Lafayette Park in the District. There were transcripts of what looked to be cellular conversations amongst members of the Datura Project. Matti also found evidence of intercepted text messages. Most were encrypted, and the contents unknown, but a few of the numeric codes were deciphered. They contained meeting information and alerts to larger, non-Daturan rallies or protests.

Matti puffed her cheeks. She let out the air in an exasperated sigh and ran her hand through her hair. She was reading secretly recorded voice intelligence.

These are U.S. citizens on these tapes!

She was familiar with the Bush administration's legal contention that the Fourth Amendment of the Constitution, which guarded against unlawful search and seizure, did not apply to NSA activities. And in times of war, search and seizure was reasonable on U.S. soil, even if the "enemy" was not foreign.

The Department of Justice asserted warrantless communications targeted at the enemy in times of armed conflict were traditionally acceptable, arguing the NSA's signal intelligence was included in that exception. Lawyers went so far as to suggest the NSA was a domestic military operation.

Toward the end of the second Bush term, the Office of Legal Counsel backed off the assertion but never fully denounced it. Some suspected the government was essentially spying on its own citizens. Matti sat with the proof right in front of her.

The NSA had an estimated annual budget of fifteen billion dollars. It was a small part of the sixty-six and a half billion spent on intelligence across all agencies and the Department of Defense. It was double the amount doled out pre-9/11.

Fifteen billion, Matti thought. *And we're chasing a bunch of loons who named themselves after a poisonous, hallucinogenic tea?*

There were twenty pages of short, clipped conversations between various members of the group. She flipped past the logs to the short biographical pages of the suspected conspirators.

One was a college professor; a second was an artist; another was a local businessman who owned a meat shop and a bar. Matti flipped through the black and white surveillance photographs snapped of the various alleged plotters. She made mental notes of the names and faces. Then one caught her attention.

"Bill Davidson?" she whispered. "The former Attorney General?"

It clicked. This wasn't some ragtag band of Ron Paul or Debra Medina sympathizers crying about the Fed and property rights. The Daturans had the support and backing of a former cabinet member.

Davidson was connected. He was well-known. He used to run the Department of Justice, and he had the ear of policymakers and financiers. He was the star of a D.C. think tank and was on television nearly every week. Bill Davidson could make things happen.

She'd met him once at B. Smith's restaurant at Union Station. In between alternating sips of Low Country Creole Stew and swigs of ice water, Matti had noticed the Attorney General walk in and command the room. He'd been tall and friendly and seemed to stretch the thirty-foot ceilings of the historic room.

The dining room was in fact called The Presidential Suite. Matti had read in a magazine it was built in the early 1900s as a safe room for presidents awaiting their trains. It was once sparsely decorated for security reasons. In 1939 it was upgraded to welcome a visit from the King and Queen of England.

B. Smith's was a national landmark. Matti visited there frequently, and often saw dignitaries dine there. They were generally guarded and unapproachable.

Davidson was the contrarian. Though it was just before nine o'clock on a Thursday night, the U.S. Attorney General had made a point to say hello to every person dining.

Matti had stood, her napkin falling to the floor as she did, and had thanked the A.G. for his leadership. He'd thanked her as well, looking into her eyes as he did, and then moved to the next table.

Matti remembered she'd been dining with a potential suitor. It had been their one and only date. She'd liked the man; he'd told jokes and she'd laughed. He'd complemented her and she'd demurely accepted it. And then it soured, just as quickly, when he'd asked about her family. He'd never called again after dinner that night.

Now years later, she sat alone at her desk and suddenly understood the file with clarity. Bill Davidson. *He* was why and how the NSA got involved. *He* was why national security was an issue and why this was a new priority given President Foreman's sudden death.

Any potential threat, especially one with a D.C. insider, needed serious oversight. Matti was reading about Davidson's lesser known post-A.G. proclivities when her gray phone rang.

* * *

Art Thistlewood stared at the paper on his desk. He'd scribbled the translation to the Caesar Code sent to his pager during class and couldn't believe he was summoned to a meeting in the middle of the night.

"One o'clock?" he whined in his small office. It was on the third floor of the Ward Building on the campus of American University and overlooked the north end of the Quad from the window next to his desk.

It was a typical professorial lair. Three of the cream colored walls were essentially held up by cheap, imitation wood grained bookshelves. The shelves were stuffed with texts and novels and essay collections. Thistlewood claimed he'd read everything on those shelves. Nobody believed him, though some young coeds often played to his ego.

Every term, he found himself embroiled in a weeks-long affair with a woman at most half his age. He told them up front it was not forever. They usually obliged with a lack of interest beyond the posting of their final grades.

Professor Thistlewood was a good looking man. His thick mop of white hair dropped over his ears and collar. His habit of fingering back his bangs off of his forehead was an unintentional turn-on to the girls who sought out his extra credit.

Aside from women, he loved art by politically motivated artists. His small Embassy Row apartment boasted several collected pieces by artists Shepard Fairey, Robbie Conal, and Trek Thunder Kelly. He especially loved Kelly's *IPod Ghraib*. It was a shocking pink canvas with the dark silhouette of a thin Iraqi prisoner under hood and cloak at Abu Ghraib prison, electrodes attached to his fingers as he stood with his arms extended outward and his feet on a box.

In Kelly's work, the electrode wires were replaced with ear bud cables attached to a pair of I-Pods. It looked similar to the popular Apple advertisements on which a music listener's dark profile was highlighted by the use of the digital music player. Thistlewood thought the piece to be magnificent and had purchased it directly from Kelly at the artist's Venice Beach studio. As much as he enjoyed the juxtaposition of commercialization and torture, his love of the work fell second to the only piece of art hanging in his office at work.

On the wall directly behind his desk was a large color lithograph of Thomas Jefferson, James Madison, and Andrew Jackson. The three former presidents stood beside an oversized unplugged ATM emblazoned with the Great Seal of the United States. Jefferson covered his eyes. Madison covered his ears. Jackson covered his mouth.

The work was titled, *We Three Kings*. It was a social commentary on the failure of the Federal Reserve and the three men who first opposed its initial creation in the late eighteenth century. In the lower right of the poster, just above the frame, it was signed.

The inscription read, *"To Art: A patriot who understands the hallucination. A Deo Et Rege, George Edwards."* It was written in black marker.

Thistlewood shifted in his chair. He gazed out the window to his left, through the thin slats of the metal mini-blinds that covered the pane. He thought of the meeting that night and the possibilities that lie ahead.

He'd not allowed himself yet to process the implications of the sudden change of power. It was something he had experienced only twice before in his lifetime. The first time, when President Kennedy was assassinated, he was too young to understand what it meant to his country's course.

And when Richard Nixon resigned under the threat of impeachment, Thistlewood was excited for what the future might hold. Gerald Ford was the salve a wounded nation needed.

But now, only hours after a president dropped dead onto the Resolute Desk, he wasn't prepared to contemplate how he and his fellow ideologues might use the days ahead to alter public opinion. He assumed that would be the agenda at one o'clock in the morning. It was a meeting that didn't quite accommodate a 7 A.M. lecture on the Separation of Powers.

Thistlewood was a tenured associate professor at American University. For a time, he served on the Advisory Committee for the school's prestigious Center for Democracy & Election Management. It was a labor of love to spread true American idealism and freedom to other parts of the world. But America, as he saw it, was changing.

He rolled his chair out from behind his desk and over to his office door. He closed it, locked it, and rolled back to the desk.

There were evening plans to change. He picked up his desk phone and dialed.

A bespectacled 24-year-old grad student with fantastic lips would have to wait to taste the tannin of a dusty 1996 Oregon pinot noir.

Thistlewood was an oenophile who often told the same wine joke at parties. With a glass cradled in the fingers of his swirling right hand, he'd laugh and lick his lips. He'd protest mildly before someone cajoled him to continue with the joke most of them had heard before.

"Okay..." He would roll his eyes in false modesty and then barrel through the joke. "A dinner party of different international ambassadors arrived at a restaurant. They each ordered a glass of wine, but when the wine arrived they noticed each of the glasses had a fly in it. The Swede demanded new wine in the same glass. The Brit wanted new wine in a new glass. The Ukrainian drank the wine, fly and all. The Spaniard picked the fly from the glass and drank the wine. The Chinese ate the fly but left the wine. The Jew caught the fly and sold it to the Chinese. The Italian drank two-thirds of the wine and asked for new wine. The Norwegian took the fly and went to fish for cod. The Irishman ground the fly and mixed it in the wine, which he then donated to the Brit. The Scotsman grabbed the fly by the throat and roared: 'Now spit out what you swallowed!' The American sued the restaurant for five million dollars, claiming mental anguish."

The long, over told joke always drew a polite laugh, most heartily from the young, beautiful woman on his arm. This term, she was tall and lean and whip smart. Thistlewood smiled as he thought about her.

She'll understand, Thistlewood promised himself as he waited for her to answer her cell phone. He would miss her legs as much as those of the pinot.

CHAPTER 3

Sir Spencer Thomas' dietician had warned him of "emotional eating", but the knight found himself consciously ignoring her expensive advice in favor of stress relief.

He'd requested the daily menu from the hotel's restaurant, The Lafayette, and was weighing the emotional benefits of the offered items. The menu was not typical private dining fare, but the hotel was incredibly accommodating to its more frequent guests.

Sir Spencer picked up the phone and dialed the operator, who in turn connected him with room service.

"Yes, Sir Spencer," a woman's pleasant voice answered. "How may I be of service to you?"

"I am ready to order an early supper." He'd made his selections without regard to calorie or wheat restrictions.

"Please, sir. Go ahead with your order."

"I'll begin with the Steamed Jumbo Green Asparagus and Diver Scallops. And I would like additional ginger mustard vinaigrette on the side." He was emotional.

"Yes sir. And for the main course?"

"Pan Seared Maryland Jumbo Lump Crab Cakes with extra pesto."

"Of course."

"And your exotic fruit plate. Is that available?"

"Yes, sir it is. Chef Schaffrath will attend personally to your order. Anything to drink?"

"A large bottle of Fiji and two glasses of ice."

"Yes, sir. The total charge is sixty-four dollars plus a delivery charge. The Fiji is complimentary. Your order should arrive within forty-five minutes."

He thanked the woman and hung up the phone. It was late afternoon and he needed to write an outline for the meeting he'd called.

Though none of the Daturans had responded to his text message, he knew they would attend. There would be no more important meeting in the history of their confederacy.

He walked over to the small table positioned between the dining table and a pair of sofas in the living area of his suite. Already on the table was a pad of yellow legal sized paper and a pen.

The pen was a jet black Mont Blanc Meisterstuck Rollerball. It was a gift to Sir Spencer from José Manuel Durão Barroso, former Prime Minister of Portugal and president of The European Union Commission.

Barroso sent the pen to Sir Spencer on the occasion of the birth of his third child, Francisco. The boy's initials, FdSUDB were inscribed on the shaft of the pen. Sir Spencer thought it much better than a cigar.

The yellow legal pad had no such ancestry. Sir Spencer picked it up at a FedEx-Office on his way to the hotel along with some Post-It notes and a box of paper clips. He hadn't anticipated needing the supplies for a Daturan meeting, but had procured them as he always did during business trips.

Sir Spencer Thomas was a world traveler with friends on every inhabited continent. He knew captains of industry, politicians, warlords, bankers, arms dealers, clergy; anyone who pushed the world to spin on its axis.

Still, Sir Spencer was an enigma to most of the power brokers from whom he sought favor. He was known well enough to be invited to their functions, but he was also the one in group photographs whose name nobody could quite remember.

Sir Spencer liked it that way. It was easier for him if the conversations always dabbled in light politics and stormy weather. Even Barroso knew very little about his friend. The knight was a colorful shadow.

Nobody was certain about how he made his money, though they

knew he had a lot of it. Some of it was inherited, most of it was earned. Sir Spencer was a man whose "advice" was often sought at great expense.

His ancestry was only slightly royal (one branch of his family tree included a Marquess Douro), but he was a real knight. Queen Elizabeth II honored Spencer Thomas with an offer to join the Order of The British Empire in 1998. Sir Spencer and investment banker Nathaniel Charles Jacob Rothschild, 4th Baron Rothschild, were the only ones offered knighthood that year.

As was tradition, the Queen relied on the recommendation of the Secretary of State for Foreign and Commonwealth Affairs. At the time it was Robin Cook, a "fan" of Sir Spencer's work who suggested he was worthy of recognition for "superlative civil efforts on behalf of the Queen and The Empire".

Cook resigned his post five years later in protest over the Iraq war and then died suddenly from a heart attack in 2005. Sir Spencer attended the memorial service at St. Margaret's Church, Westminster. The epitaph on Cook's headstone at Grange Cemetery in Edinburgh read, *"I may not have succeeded in halting the war, but I did secure the right of parliament to decide on war."*

As evidenced by his arms-length relationship with Cook, Sir Spencer was not a warmonger. He'd advised President Reagan against Operation Urgent Fury in 1983. Sir Spencer's opposition was echoed loudly by the United Nations and by Great Britain. But President Reagan had disregarded Sir Spencer's advice and invaded the Caribbean Island of Grenada, quickly deposing its military government.

Sir Spencer was not a pacifist either. The year before, he'd opposed the Grenadian conflict, and he'd supported British action against the Argentinean insurgency in the Falklands.

For all of the things he was not, Sir Spencer *was* a lover of freedom and democracy. Though not a U.S. citizen, he privately thought of himself as one. And had it not been for his knighthood, he'd have renounced his British citizenship and become a naturalized American.

But Sir Spencer knew the greatest empire in the world needed a nudge in a new direction. It was a potentially violent nudge that went against the knight's more refined inclinations. As a willing martyr for his beliefs, though, Sir Spencer Thomas saw no other way. He picked up the pen and began making notes.

* * *

The asset seemed uncomfortable and uncertain about playing both sides of the fence. Matti could tell that from the moment she picked up the gray phone at her desk.

"Harrold," she answered as she pulled the handset to her ear.

"You don't sound like a Harrold." The voice on the other end was distorted. The caller had attached a portable voice changer to a cell phone. It connected to the phone through the mini-plug headset jack and included two high pitch and two low pitch options. Should the recordings of the conversations ever become public, Matti assumed the asset wanted some level of deniability.

"Then who do I sound like?" Matti knew this was her contact.

"I don't know," the voice was low and robotic. "I assumed Harrold was a dude."

"Not a dude," she didn't want to talk too much. Though she was inexperienced in HUMINT, she approached this as any salesman might confront a tough sell: the first one to talk loses the deal. Her mother had taught her that.

"Got that."

Matti said nothing.

"So, you are my handler?"

"Yes," she replied and picked up a pencil.

"What do you want to know?"

"What do you want to tell me?" Matti flipped to the front page of a small notebook.

"There is a meeting tonight."

"Tell me more," she was taking notes now.

"It's a strategy session."

Matti pulled the pencil to her mouth and bit on the metal ferrule that attached the vinyl eraser onto the wood shaft. It bent slightly.

"I think there is some big plan in the works to make a statement. The president's death has the group anxious, I think."

Matti spun the pencil and she lightly chewed. It was a stress habit.

"They've talked about it for a while," the robot voice droned. "You know, doing something that would make a statement about our cause."

"And what is your cause?" Matti decided to prod.

"That's complicated," the asset paused. "But I am sure you spooks know all about it."

"Spooks are CIA," Matti corrected.

"Funny."

"Not intended to be," Matti didn't like being compared to CIA.

"So, as I was saying, there is a meeting tonight."

"Details, please." She was doing her best to seem as though she'd done this before. She wished she could distort her voice.

"I am under the impression there'll be some sort of plan discussed at the meeting. I think the president's death has sped up the plans for action."

"What plans?"

"I've discussed some of this with people at your agency in the past. I've given them generalized information about the group's intentions. It should be in some sort of file, right?" The asset sounded irritated.

"I have a file," Matti didn't want to reveal too much about what she already knew.

"Well, I think the action, whatever it is, will involve violence. Or at the very least it may include the threat of violence. I think it will happen soon," the asset continued without prodding, "because the opportunity to have influence would diminish greatly once President Foreman is buried and the new president, whoever it is, settles in."

"So are you thinking weeks?" Matti stopped nibbling and was again taking notes. She knew that, despite her supervisor's insistence on secrecy, the agency was recording every second of it, cataloging it, transcribing it, analyzing it, and filing it. But she wouldn't have access to the final version for hours, maybe days. It was important that she have notes at her desk.

"No," the robotic voice couldn't have had less intonation. There was a pause.

Matti stopped scribbling and waited for the rest of the answer.

"We're talking days. A week at most."

"Okay," she responded as though she was unsurprised. "Then

I'll need a debriefing after tonight's meeting. Where did you say it is?"

"I didn't."

"Okay then," she sighed in a way that conveyed frustration.

"I am certain your people know where it is. I will call after the meeting. I am thinking by 4 A.M. maybe. Will you be at work?"

"Yes." Matti's day had just gotten a lot longer.

There was a click. The conversation was over.

Matti hung up and then picked up the black line to call her supervisor. She hesitated. Looking back over her notes there were some things that bothered her. What stuck with her most was the first thing said when she answered the phone. The asset expected a man named Harrold. Even through the electronic alteration she could sense the surprise. Yet her supervisor told her she was chosen for the assignment because the asset requested a woman.

Had her boss lied? Was he trying to keep something from her?

She was a great SIGINT analyst, but it struck her as unbelievable she'd been handed the responsibility of deconstructing a violent act of terrorism just days from execution. Maybe her boss knew she was never one to shy away from a challenge. She'd spent much of her adult life trying to piece together her mother's final moments. She'd poured through the forensic photographs, she'd flown to Richmond and talked to the bartender who'd served her mother into a stupor; she'd even found the junkyard hiding the truck which had crushed her mother's skull beneath its front tire. But there were so many questions she could not answer: *Why was her mother at a bar so late at night? Why was she run over and left for dead in the gutter of a downtown street? Why was there cocaine in her purse? Was it an innocent night out with clients? Was it something else?* She couldn't decode the death of her own mother. What would make her boss think she could handle this?

Matti slipped the notepad into her desk drawer, locked it, and stood. She had questions for her supervisor and she couldn't wait for the answers.

* * *

Davidson stared into the camera. In his right ear was a custom molded earpiece used to listen to what television people called "IFB".

"Interrupted Fold Back" was what allowed on-air television talent to listen to a program while, at the same time, letting producers and directors "interrupt" the program so they could issue instructions to the talent.

He was a guest on the cable program *Constitution Avenue* and was awaiting his turn in the live guest cue. As he waited, he listened to the current discussion between the host and a political reporter for the website PLAUSIBLEDENIABILITY.INFO. It was a site that reported Beltway news with a TMZ sensibility. The reporter's name was Dillinger Holt.

"Our sources are telling us the president will be buried at Arlington National Cemetery and that his public viewing will be within the next three days. He'll lie in state at the Capitol, and there'll be some sort of memorial there. Then the burial will include cabinet members and Foreman's family. There's no word on when or how long the public viewing will be."

"Dillinger," asked the show's host Vickie Lupo, "I am curious. I know it's early. We shouldn't speculate, but are Capitol Police already preparing for the hundreds of thousands likely to show up and pay their respects?"

Dillinger was framed on the television in a box to the right of the screen. "Well, I don't know about hundreds of thousands. Maybe. I mean, when President Reagan was memorialized in June 2004, there were an estimated 200,000 who funneled through the Capitol to see his casket. And that was the first state funeral for a former president in, like, thirty years. So, I don't know we will see that many here. We could, given that Foreman was a sitting president, but I'd be surprised."

"Dillinger Holt," the anchor jumped in. "With the wildly popular website, PLAUSIBLEDENIABILITY.INFO. We thank you for your insight."

Davidson couldn't see the screen, but he could hear the program as music began to grow louder. Vickie started talking again.

"When we come back to *Constitution Avenue* we are joined by a D.C. insider with a unique perspective on the president's death.

Former Attorney General Bill Davidson is up. You're gonna wanna hear his take. I'm Vickie Lupo and we're back in two minutes."

Davidson heard the percussion crescendo again before the commercial began. He pulled out his pen and journal and made a quick note about Dillinger Holt's interview.

"Bill, I need a mic check from you." The voice in Davidson's head was an audio technician in the show's control room.

"Okay," replied Davidson, "One, two, three, four, three, two, one. Is that good? Do you have your check?" He put the journal back in his pocket but held onto the pen. It was a good prop.

"Got it. Thanks."

"Bill?" It was the producer's voice this time. She was the woman who made certain the show's segments stayed on time and kept moving.

"Yes?" He was adjusting his tie, running his thumb along the black 50-ounce silk tipping along its backside. He'd already checked for the dimple under the knot; it sat perfectly.

"We've got four minutes for your segment, though I am going to try and keep it to three and half. So when I give you a wrap, I need you to finish your thought and stop talking. Cool?"

"As a breeze." Davidson was a pro. He was relaxed and comfortable on camera, and got right to the point of any conversation.

"Ten seconds," the producer gave her final warning to Davidson the show was about to return from commercial. The music restarted and then Vickie Lupo, with her bottle blonde hair and large white teeth, began her introduction of the segment.

"Back on *Constitution Avenue* now!" She squinted into the camera and feigned concern as she acted the script on the Teleprompter in front of her.

"Joining us with some perspective on this sadly historic day is D.C. insider Bill Davidson. He is a current fellow at the Hanover-Crown Institute, a political think tank here in Washington, and he is a former Attorney General."

"Bill, thanks for being with us." Vickie Lupo leaned on her right elbow and gestured with her left hand.

"Thank you, Vickie." Davidson nodded and smiled almost imperceptibly. He ran his tongue across the bridge in his mouth.

"Bill, you have a unique insight here as the former top cop. Explain why we don't have a new president yet? Shouldn't Speaker Jackson already be in the Oval Office?" Vickie leaned into the camera as she folded her arms and waited for a response. Her head was tilted slightly.

"It's not that simple," he began. "The constitution is a living, breathing document open to interpretation. There are fundamental questions being raised here. The 25th Amendment is clear that the vice president 'shall' become president should the sitting president be unable to perform his duties. And the Act of Presidential Succession of 1947 provides that, should both the president and vice president be unable to serve, then the office falls to the Speaker of the House upon resignation of his or her Congressional seat."

"So the office belongs to Speaker Jackson?" Vickie interjected.

"Not so clearly," Davidson raised his hand. "In testimony before the United States Senate Committee on the Judiciary in September 2003, Miller Baker, a lawyer who focuses on constitutional litigation, made the strong contention the 1947 act is unconstitutional."

"We have some of that testimony," Vickie again interrupted. "Let's put the text on the screen for our viewers."

Davidson couldn't see the text, but he'd discussed this with the producer beforehand and so he had notes on the excerpt in his journal. He began to read aloud.

"He testified, Vickie, that 'The 1947 Act placing Congressional officers in the line of succession is probably unconstitutional and is certainly unwise policy...because it appears that the Speaker of the House and the president pro tempore are not 'Officers' eligible to act as President within the meaning of the succession clause.'" Davidson paused and then looked back into the camera.

"Now," he restarted, "this is followed by Baker's legal argument that the line of succession is a constitutional mess once we get past the vice president. There are others who agree."

"Like who?" Vickie, Davidson knew, was playing the devil's advocate. "I mean, Bill, c'mon. Aren't these just conspiracy people bent on anarchy?"

"Hardly, Vickie." He shook his head and his brow furrowed slightly. "These are well respected scholars. For example," he cited, "Akhil Reed Amar is the Sterling Professor of Law and Political

Science at Yale University. He teaches constitutional law there. And he sat on a panel about a month after Baker's testimony that dealt with this very issue. It was a popular topic in the aftermath of 9/11. He talked about the problems with succession. I was there in attendance and I think I sat next to Senator John Cornyn of Texas. And Amar, who's also coauthored a paper on this, talked about the 1947 Act's misinterpretation of the word 'officer' as it relates to succession. The Framers, he said, essentially meant that officers were cabinet members and they weren't intending to include members of the legislative body. That is part of the argument examined in a 2004 Congressional Report prepared by Thomas Neale, dealing specifically with succession legislation. Again, this was a thoroughly examined issue in the thirty-six months following 9/11."

"Is that the basis for Secretary Blackmon's lawsuit then?" Vickie was reading a piece of paper on her desk as she asked the question. When she finished speaking, she raised her eyes to the camera while only slightly lifting her head. Davidson thought it gave her a judicial appearance.

"It could be," Davidson nodded. "We haven't seen the emergency request yet. But it likely will fall into the realm of the validity of the 1947 Act. And that opens another can of worms."

"How so?" Vickie tilted her head again.

"If Blackmon wins the constitutionality argument, it still doesn't guarantee him the office. He was never sworn in. It could be that his fight drops the job into the lap of the Secretary of State."

"So, Bill, where do we go from here? What is going on inside the White House tonight? How is what's left of the administration coping and moving forward?"

Vickie Lupo came across to the former Attorney General as crass and tacky and he had read somewhere that she was paid $600,000 a year to be that way.

"Vickie," Davidson chuckled, "I'm not sure that's the right question to ask. Or even the right series of questions. But I will say in response to you," he was trying to talk his way through her verbal diarrhea, "that this is something that has not happened since John Kennedy was shot and killed in Dallas in 1963. It's the first time since Richard Nixon's resignation in 1974 that we've had no time to process the loss of a leader.

"It's not something that is easily moved past. Members of the Foreman administration are mourning his loss. Without thinking about what's next, they are consoling one another tonight."

"But, Bill," Vickie had shifted her weight to the other elbow and was now pointing her red Sharpie at the screen, "I can't believe there is no politicking and scheming. There is a country to run. Right? And these are professional people. I have to believe the people's business is a part of the discussion tonight in the West Wing."

"Sure." Davidson remained the statesman the country believed him to be. "You are right that there are series of emergency meetings this evening. We know there are some legal issues delaying the official transition of power. But as the Chief Of Staff deals with the reality of serving whoever takes the oath, he is hurting. The staff is hurting. And I can tell you that amidst the planning inside the White House and Executive Office Building next door, and aside from the politicking that's going on up on the Hill tonight, there is sadness. We are a country in mourning, and I think we need to take a moment to embrace that grief.

"To that end," he continued, without giving Vickie and her high-definition-friendly Ellen Tracy cardigan the chance to cut him off, "I would suggest the previous guest made suppositions about the viewing, memorial, and funeral for President Foreman that are inappropriate. And I think—"

"Bill," Vickie interrupted. "Bill, I am sorry to interject. But," she continued joyfully and breathlessly, "we need to get our viewers and friends straight to the Capitol Rotunda where we are expecting a joint statement from Speaker of the House Felicia Jackson and Secretary John Blackmon. Blackmon, as you know, was confirmed late last night as the next vice president. But he has yet to take the oath of office."

Davidson was no longer on camera. The producer got in his ear and asked him to stand by. He agreed and sat listening intently to Vickie and the impending speech. He opened his journal again, flipped to a new page, and scribbled into it.

"There we are now." Vickie was no longer on the screen, and instead there was a stationary shot of an empty lectern in the rotunda. "We are looking live at the rotunda where, in an unprecedented move, television cameras are allowed on the floor. I've never seen this before."

"Just an incredible night, folks," she continued. "And I am told we have just a few seconds until we hear from the two people who, I think it's fair to say, are fighting it out to be our next president. I for one, am incredibly anxious to see who speaks first. That should tell us a lot about the behind-the-scenes machinations. Who is the wizard pulling the strings right now and who is left to click their heels?"

* * *

One hundred and eighty feet beneath the dome of the Capitol Rotunda, Felicia Jackson walked with purpose to the lectern, the microphone, and Secretary John Blackmon. In front of her was a wall of television cameras stretching almost the entirety of the 96-foot diameter of the symbolic heart of the Capitol.

She looked every bit the ambitious legislator as she took her place between statues of George Washington and Thomas Jefferson and next to Secretary Blackmon toward the southern facing edge of the room. She smiled at him and shook his hand with both of hers. She appeared magnanimous but was fuming that the Secretary had arrived before her. The Speaker leaned in to feign a kiss on his cheek when he whispered in her ear.

"I think I'll just say something real quick, then let you have the rest of the time." He pulled back and smiled. Without waiting for her response he slipped forward to the microphone.

He'd outmaneuvered her.

How could this have happened?

He was getting a chance to speak first. He was the one appearing presidential. She was the "woman behind the man".

Felicia glanced up at Washington's statue and imagined he would be displeased with the spectacle. She silently apologized to him for having earlier been jealous of his revolutionary circumstances. The Speaker then affixed her gaze on the opponent of the moment and his tall, thin frame. From behind him she noticed his regal carriage and broad shoulders. Blackmon was well-kempt and polished.

For the sake of propriety, she nodded and stood a step behind him to his left. She appeared to the right of the screen on television, remaining close enough to him that even if the cameras zoomed in to a tight shot, she'd be in it.

"I would like to begin tonight with just a few words before handing the microphone to my colleague from the House, Representative Felicia Jackson of South Carolina."

He is smooth, Felicia thought. He was reminding the country she was from the weaker side of the Hill. He did not mention she was the Speaker of House, as protocol would dictate he should.

"For those of you who don't yet know me," he continued, placing his right hand over his heart, "I am confirmed vice presidential nominee and Secretary of Veterans Affairs, John Blackmon. On behalf of your elected leaders, I would like to express our condolences to the family of President Foreman and to you, the people who make up our grieving nation."

Felicia suddenly felt nauseous. Blackmon was stealing the job and the power she coveted. He was doing it in front of the entire nation and she had to watch silently.

"I know I speak for both of us when I say that despite the loss of my friend, Dexter Foreman, this country is in good hands. There is no absence of strong leadership. Congressional leaders and President Foreman's staff have been meeting much of today, insuring a smooth transition to the next administration.

"To our friends around the world, we say thank you for your prayers. To our enemies we warn you our nation and its foundation are as strong today as they have ever been. May God bless President Foreman's soul and may God Bless America."

John Blackmon spoke for less than a minute. He was calm and forthright. And he was, Felicia hated to admit, presidential.

She slid to her right as he stepped back. It was her turn. She knew she needed to strike the same tone Blackmon had so effectively engineered.

"My fellow Americans," she began after adjusting the microphone downward slightly. "We stand with you as your humble public servants asking for your help and guidance in these coming days."

She was not using the Teleprompter in front of her. She felt the sudden urge to improvise.

"I can tell you that Secretary Blackmon and I are working together with the administration to continue the work important to President Foreman and to the nation. We promise to keep you informed of all developments with regard to a plan for succession. And as we learn more about the memorial and funeral for President Foreman, we will share those details with you."

"Right now," she paused and bit her lip for effect, "we can tell you that all Americans will have the chance to honor the life of the president, as there are plans for him to lie in state right here in the Capitol Rotunda. I think it's best we keep this brief, so we can get back to the business of the people, but I will be happy to entertain a couple of questions." She pointed to a reporter from *The Washington Post*.

"Speaker Jackson," asked the man as he poked his head above the row of cameras in front of him. "Please comment on Secretary Blackmon's court filing that prevents you from taking the oath of office. And please tell us if you have plans on resigning your Congressional seat to become president."

"Well," she smiled falsely, "I think the suit is better addressed by Secretary Blackmon. But I will suggest it is better for our nation to move forward as quickly as is possible. A prolonged fight predicated on personal gain is not what's best for our democracy."

It was a nice little stab.

"As for the second question," she continued, "there is some issue, my attorney advises me, as to whether or not I need resign my seat to assume the Presidency. The constitution may not require that. For me to resign that position right now would leave the nation in an even more precarious position. Should the court take a prolonged time to determine the proper succession in this most serious matter, it would be better that I continue to serve as Speaker of the House. Given that there is currently no president and no vice president, I am the highest ranking officer in the line of presidential succession according to the 1947 Act. That act requires eligible successors must have taken their sworn oaths of office. I have done so."

"So you are suggesting the current situation is precarious?" the

Post reporter chirped in an unapproved follow up.

"Only in that we are mourning. We are distracted as a nation, and rightfully so. President Foreman was a good man and a good leader. We miss him." She felt a gentle hand on the small of her back. She turned her head to her left and saw Blackmon was moving in toward the microphone and was physically suggesting she move aside. Felicia stiffened against his touch and only moved when he began speaking without the microphone directly in front of him. She could not appear to be rude.

"I think, as Representative Jackson recommended, I should address the reporter's first question." He moved squarely behind the lectern as the Speaker finally ceded her position. "It relates to my request that we take a moment before rushing into a Presidency which may, indeed, violate the terms of the document upon which our freedoms are based. There has long been concern about the constitutionality of the current line of succession. While I'll refrain from making a legal argument here tonight, I will suggest to you the public interest is best served by reflection and a thorough examination of our laws."

He was a lawyer. The Speaker knew she hated him for a reason.

Felicia stood slightly behind him, looking at his profile as he spoke. She was convinced he could have defined "is" for Bill Clinton and the former president couldn't have argued with him. It was killing her. She despised lawyers in a town filled with them.

"We have nothing to lose here," he continued. "Our nation and your neighborhoods are in capable hands. We have strong leadership in all three branches of government. I am certain," he raised his index finger and looked back over his shoulder into Felicia's eyes. "I am certain," he repeated looking back into the cameras in front of him, "our good servant, Felicia Jackson, feels as I do that the Presidency is too awesome a responsibility to treat without such pause and regard."

He thought he'd left her no opening. But she saw one. She raised her hand and began speaking as she moved back to the lectern, forcing Blackmon to step aside.

"My colleague is so right," she began, looking directly at the *Washington Post* reporter. "It is the constitution that I swore to uphold and protect when I took my oath of office as Speaker of the

House." There was silence in the rotunda. By the time the assembled reporters had refocused and were jumping to ask questions, Felicia had turned to Blackmon, put her hand on his back and began to lead him away from the lectern. She was ending the press conference. She was taking control. He may have had the first word, and a few pointed ones in the middle, but she'd had the final word. Reporters continued to call after the two politicians as they made their way out of the rotunda and toward Statuary Hall. Her office was nearby. A pair of security guards followed them. As a member of House leadership, Felicia always had a security detail with her.

Once they'd cleared the sight of the reporters gathered in the Rotunda, she stopped and turned to face Blackmon.

"I don't know what the hell you think you're doing," she lectured as she stuck the manicured, polished nail of her index finger into the Secretary's chest. "This is the biggest piece of self-serving crap I have ever seen."

Blackmon stood still. He took the abuse and appeared to delightedly watch the Speaker implode.

"You were never sworn in," she reminded him. "We've been without a vice president for months. Even though the Senate confirmed you, you are not first in line to succeed Foreman. As the Secretary of an insignificant department, you are second to last on the list. You know this. Hell, three weeks ago nobody south of Newport, Rhode Island even knew who you were."

"Are you finished?" Blackmon said smugly.

"Yes." She folded her arms in front of her.

"You know as well as I do that there is a constitutional question about the legitimacy of your claim. Everyone who was here post 9/11 knows this. I was twenty-four hours away from being sworn in. I have a case." He took a breath. She was scowling.

"And for the record, Madame Speaker," he started to turn and walk away from her as he finished his thought, "insignificant Secretary or not, Foreman picked me. He could have picked you. He didn't." He didn't turn around as she called after him.

"You are making a mistake, John. The country will not forgive you for this." She stood there watching him walk away from her.

She immediately regretted her decision to attack Blackmon. She accomplished nothing but revealing her own insecurities. The little Rhody had, for the most part, bested her in the rotunda on national television, then he'd beaten her in the hall. For a woman with such power, she worried she was revealing incredible weakness. She needed to circle the wagons and get a handle on this "constitutional question". The Speaker knew her attorneys were awaiting her return to the office.

Felicia tugged on the bottom of her jacket and turned to her security. They followed her heel clicks out of the hall without acknowledging any of what they'd just seen and heard. They were headed to office H-232.

* * *

George Edwards was walking out of the Washington Sports Club on Wisconsin Avenue, NW when his cell rang. He was turning left onto Calvert when he looked at the number displayed on the phone. It was a restricted number. Edwards knew who it likely was and pushed the button to answer.

"Hello?" The phone felt heavy as he lifted it to his ear. His bicep reacted as though he was beginning another set of curls.

"Hello my friend!" The accent was what the British called "the Received Pronunciation". The dialect was formal, almost pretentious, and socially helpful to a man or woman with ambition. It carried a certain historical prestige in England and Wales, and was most often the voice of the aristocracy.

Edwards knew the voice; Sir Spencer. He was careful not to use his name. "Sir, how are you?"

Sir Spencer had just finished his supper and was perched on his bed, Kiton jacket hung on the door, pants unbuttoned. "Well, I was wondering about your thoughts. It might be good to gather an idea or two together before we decide on anything."

"I am on my cell phone," he said, unaware that the call was encrypted on Sir Spencer's end.

"I am fine with that."

"Okay then." Edwards turned right onto Tunlaw Road, NW. "Do you have any thoughts?"

"I was going to look to you for that." Sir Spencer used his

tongue to suck a seed out from in between his teeth. "You are, after all, the artist."

"I have some thoughts." Edwards arrived at the front door to his building. He lived at the Archstone Glover Park Apartments, just north of Georgetown and west of the park. It was a seven-story red brick building that resembled a warehouse conversion. His one bedroom provided plenty of room for his work, a futon, and a 52-inch wall-mounted LCD television.

Edwards walked into the lobby of his building through the double glass doors. To either side of the unoccupied security desk were sitting areas with identical modern green chenille sofas, sand-colored chairs, and mailboxes that resembled the kind found in a post office.

He moved to the left as the door closed quickly behind him, and he sat on the green couch. The cushion sank beneath his weight.

"My ideas involve something with Czechoslovakian flavor." He was being intentionally vague. "The dish would be served to a large gathering. It's a messy recipe."

"I see," said Sir Spencer, sounding surprised but pleased.

"It's the only way to feed the people," Edwards wasn't giving up on the metaphor. "But we'll need to acquire the ingredients."

"I think I can help there."

Sir Spencer was a man of means. He'd told Edwards of his access to instruments of violence. He'd specifically mentioned "magic marble" in the past, Edwards remembered this. How better to accomplish the goal than with a "poisonous cocktail", so to speak? They were Daturans, weren't they?

This could be the perfect chance to start a fundamental rebellion. They could stop the increasingly invasive government "anti-terrorism" programs of post-9/11 America. Edwards rationalized it as a modern day French Revolution, and he imagined that Sir Spencer did as well.

"Then let them eat cake," he said with a laugh. "We will talk later." He hung up the phone, stood from the sofa, and rode the elevator up to his fourth floor apartment.

The apartment was 750 square feet with wall-to-wall parquet flooring. The galley kitchen was newly renovated and was awash with white cabinets and appliances. It had a minimalist feel that appealed to the young bachelor. He enjoyed living a Spartan existence, aside from the indulgence of his Audi A6.

Edwards walked into the apartment, through the kitchen, and into the dining area. There was a small round glass table onto which he tossed his gym bag and keys. He then dropped himself onto a large wooden framed futon and picked up the television remote, pushing the "On" button.

The television was already set to a cable news channel. On the left side of the screen was the ever-present Vickie Lupo, and on the right side was Bill Davidson, the former Attorney General. He smiled and turned up the volume .

"...not at all surprising to see the two of them staking their claim." Davidson was referring to the somewhat awkward joint address from Secretary Blackmon and Speaker Jackson.

"I mean, here is the Speaker, who is in a historic position to be the first non-vice president to ascend to the Presidency—"

"Not to mention the first woman," interjected Vickie Lupo from the left side of the screen.

"Which is why I didn't mention it," sneered Davidson.

"But it is significant!" Vickie pointed her finger straight into the camera.

"On some levels, of course it is, Vickie." Davidson rolled his eyes. *"But I'm talking about the constitutional significance of this. Long after we've had our first woman president, the effects of this succession will impact our democracy."*

Vickie Lupo conceded Davidson's larger point with a nod and slight frown of understanding. Edwards watched the exchange with amusement. He turned up the volume slightly.

"The big deal here is that our line of succession is now in the hands of the court. This is a sheer cliff on which we are now perched. Washington has become a place where, far too often, the politics of the individual are placed ahead of the country's best interest. Judges legislate from the bench. We spend trillions of taxpayer dollars putting bandaids on the gushing arterial wounds of banks and automakers. Am I the only one who sees the irony here?

"We bypass the courts that are intended to help failing

corporations and choose to spend our grandchildren's money to help them. We are essentially throwing out good money after bad."

"Bill..." Vickie Lupo was trying to interrupt, apparently sensing the digression. She was unsuccessful.

"Let me finish, Vickie!" Davidson pointed his finger to the camera and kept talking. *"And yet we choose to use the courts here, where they are only a hindrance to good government. This is no different than the election in November 2000 when lawyers and courts helped determine the outcome. A court is going to decide our next president."* Davidson released the rest of the air from his lungs.

"So, Bill," Vickie started, *"are you siding with the Speaker on this? Are you contending that the line of succession, as was written in 1947, is constitutional?"*

"No." Davidson shook his head. *"I am not siding with the Speaker. I am merely lamenting our use of the courts. It seems we use them now for political and legislative purposes far more than we do for legitimate legal issues. I don't know how the district court will rule. I imagine whichever way it goes, there will be an appeal. It's headed for the Supreme Court."*

"So this is not a quick fix?" Vickie was taking notes on the left side of the screen.

"No." Davidson was calm again. *"It will be several days. There is a good chance that President Foreman will be buried before we know his successor."*

"And to that end," Vickie was now the only one on the screen, *"we have just received some limited information about President Foreman's funeral and memorial."*

Edwards sat back as he watched the screen fill with blue and the words "Breaking Developments" fly from right to left across his television. Vickie Lupo was still talking.

"We have confirmed from the White House the information that we reported earlier today. President Foreman will be buried at Arlington National Cemetery. And we know that in two days his body will lie in state at the Capitol Rotunda. We do not yet know the exact timing or the logistics. Our sources cautioned us that this is dependent on the speed of the autopsy and the return of his remains to his family. But that is the latest news there. Also we

know that...."

Edwards turned off the television and set the remote on the futon cushion. He leaned his head back against the black cotton that covered the futon mattress, chewing on the inside of his cheek. A conspiracy to change the course of American history *and* a gallery opening in the same week were enough to test the nerves of any patriot.

* * *

Matti's supervisor was unsure of how much information he should share with the mid-level SIGINT analyst who, against protocol, stormed into his office demanding answers. He simultaneously regretted his decision to choose her for the assignment and congratulated himself for picking someone with nerve.

He knew about her obsessive quest to find out what had happened to her mother. He knew that her father had closed himself off to anything more than idle conversation once his wife had died. He was aware that Matti had done everything she could to please her father; following the rules; maintaining the necessary emotional disconnection in order to survive. But he thought her to be someone who fully believed in good versus evil, in white hats and black hats. He thought she could see no gray. Maybe, he pondered as he sat across from someone who he was sure now doubted his veracity, he'd underestimated her. He watched her unconsciously rub the bend of her elbows with arms crossed in her lap.

"If you are going to trust me to handle this asset," she leaned forward and ran her hand through her hair, another tic, "then you should be able to trust me with truth as to why you selected me."

"Okay then," he stopped typing and folded his hands on the desk in front of him. He looked at the young, ambitious woman in front of him and smiled. "The asset didn't ask for a woman. I picked you."

"Why, sir?"

"Separation, Harrold." He leaned back and dropped his hands into his lap. He twisted his seat back and forth as he talked. "I need separation on this. There are a lot of levels to this investigation. The asset cannot become too comfortable with knowledge of how we do business. And, ultimately, I don't need that instigator from Wikileaks, Julian Assange ,screaming *my* name from his virtual rooftop."

He could tell from her body language, how she was closed off to him, that she didn't like or even believe the answer. Would she push that point?

"Sir," she pressed, "another question."

"Of course," he turned back to his computer and placed his hands on the keys to type. He used a modified "hunt and peck" method of typing; using his two index fingers and his thumbs. It was an odd but efficient technique.

"The asset alluded to the fact that our agency would already know where tonight's meet is taking place. Why is that? And why would I not have that intelligence in the folder you gave to me?" Matti, her supervisor could tell, was beginning to figure out that there was a lot more to this "investigation" than he felt *she needed to know*.

"As evidenced by the photographic and biographical intelligence you received about the group," he kept typing, "you are not the only analyst working this effort."

"Clearly, sir...but if I am to be effective at this then—"

"Wait there," he stopped typing and leaned his elbows on the desk. He swiveled back to her direction. "Effective?"

"Yes."

"You are being *effective* by passing along the information this asset gives to you. You are to gather HUMINT and give it to me. I, in turn, give it to those who need to know." He was beginning to lecture again. "You have been with this agency long enough to understand how we work. You are to do as you are told; gather, analyze, and pass along. This job is no different. Should I rescind my offer and find someone else?"

"No sir," Matti said. "I understand."

"Now go back to your office, process the HUMINT gained from the asset's phone call. Forward the information to me and then await your next contact." He shooed her away with his right hand and turned his attention to his computer again.

Matti got up and left the office knowing that something was not right, but that she'd pressed her luck far enough. Given the paramilitary nature of the NSA, she decided to follow orders.

Matti surprised even herself with her doubt. Since joining the agency, she'd only occasionally asked questions beyond the scope of her work. When met without answers to those questions, she generally shrugged and went about her work unfazed. Matti needed to believe in people and things and ideas long after most had given up.

She could define and describe the differences between frankincense and myrrh at age five, but was 13 when she accepted the non-existence of a living, breathing Santa Claus. An anatomical whiz in elementary school, she could name all 206 bones in the human body, but she left bedtime notes for the tooth fairy until the last of her baby teeth fell out.

Before her mother's death, Matti's parents always appreciated the "little girl" in their daughter. They did everything they could to facilitate her youth as long as possible. When the principal of her elementary school suggested that Matti skip second grade, her parents refused. They also discouraged her participation in organized activities intended for older children, choosing instead, to stimulate her intellect with extracurricular learning. She took part in museum youth programs and studied piano.

Matti's mother traveled a lot as a regional makeup sales representative. Her father worked at the high School and was often not home until after dark. She was a 12 year old latchkey child who learned how to pick the lock on the back door on the days she forgot the key. She learned how many holes to poke in the cellophane covering boxed macaroni and cheese after burning it too many times. Though she was sometimes lonely, Matti was happy.

And then her mother died.

Matti remembered her mom wearing a floral print top with a cream-colored skirt when she left for the trip. She'd smelled like peaches.

"I'll be back in three days," Matti remembered her mother telling her. "Just a quick trip to Virginia and back. I'll call tonight and we'll say prayers." She never called.

The next day, the phone rang and her father wailed. The vision of him sinking to the kitchen floor, the phone spinning as it dangled from the wall was embedded in Matti's flash drive of a mind.

Hit and run. Killed instantly. Closed casket. No suspects. Toxicology. None of it made sense to either Matti or her father, and nothing was ever the same after that.

The two coexisted. Though Matti's father was home a lot more after her mother's death, she was more alone than she had ever been.

At night, as she lay awake, she would hear her father calling out for her mother in his dreams. He was at the other end of the house, but she could clearly hear his subconscious cry for answers. She was resolved to try and find them. Maybe they would help her father sleep. Maybe they would make the two of them a family again.

"I don't want to know," he told her one night over a take-out pizza. "It doesn't matter."

"It *does* matter," she reasoned. "If I can figure out what happened it will help. If I can get us answers, maybe you can sleep."

"I sleep just fine." He shook his head and tore a piece of pepperoni from a slice. "And you're no Dick Tracy. Let it rest. Let *her* rest." He rubbed his temples below his rapidly receding hairline

Sixteen year old Matti picked at her plate. She knew her father wanted the answers every bit as much as she did, though unlike her, she thought him to be afraid of what she'd find. Matti knew there had to be a clear cut answer somewhere. She reasoned that every puzzle had a solution and every code had a key. That is, until her boss gave her an assignment too good to be true.The NSA prided itself on allowing its employees to 'move around within the agency' and experiment with different elements of the intelligence game. But this was an unusually rapid transition with no merit. Of that, she was positive. There was more to this "asset" and this "investigation" than her supervisor wanted her to know. It was as if she'd caught her mother hiding Easter eggs.

* * *

Jimmy Ings was in a foul mood when *Jeopardy!* was preempted for network television coverage of the president's death. He understood it, but he didn't like it.

He watched the embarrassing rotunda performance of the two

would-be-presidents. Ings was on the verge of feeling sorry for them as they bowed and curtsied their way in and out of undeniable truths.

Our country, Ings thought as he watched, *is in need of serious change. At least when there's an election, I get a* choice *between the lesser of two evils.*

He leaned heavily on the high ball of his Berry Brothers & Rudd concoction, alternating breaths with gulps of the light colored whiskey. The yellow labeled, green glass bottle was never far from his reach.

Ings had bragged during the years that should they ever conspire to actually *do* something, he could get the immediate aid of a couple of dozen people. Until now that need had never arisen; not during the end of King George W. Bush's reign of secrecy and deceit, not while Barack Hussein Obama taxed and stimulated his way to nationalized health care and double digit inflation.

They'd failed to act when the Republican party so clearly lost its way that it picked a deaf radio host and a bottle blonde, hate spewing author to draw its platform. They'd sat on their hands as the Democrats picked on small business and middle income wage earners while slowly socializing everything but the board game Monopoly.

For years Ings felt as though he was living in the final days of Rome. He saw gladiators prepared to fight, only to have oppressors chain them to the coliseum floor so that lions could devour them. He believed 9/11 hadn't been a big enough wakeup call.

The attacks had forced little more than privacy invasion, religious intolerance, and debt inducing war. Ings wholeheartedly believed the empire was burning. It was on fire and in need of a suffocating, oxygen depleting blow. He knew, as he believed the others did, that a single act, with purpose, could galvanize the country in a way it had not seen since World War II.

He wondered what Sir Spencer was devising. Would it be full page ads in every major newspaper and magazine as they'd once discussed? Might they purchase television time to produce a slick message? Maybe they would storm a television studio and take over the airwaves. Or perhaps they could stage a disruptive protest with sympathizers outside of the Capitol. Whatever it was, he knew it would be big. He knew it would be good.

The rotunda event ended without the television returning to an abbreviated broadcast of *Jeopardy!*, and Ings decided to brood with a good book.

One of the bar's patrons, knowing Ings' love of history, had loaned a dog-eared copy of an interesting five hundred page book, *The 100: a Ranking of The Most Influential Persons in History.* While not inclusive of a post 9/11 perspective, Ings enjoyed the book as both a primer on world history and as food for thought from the book's author, Michael H. Hart.

Ings was on page 471 of the text and was reading about Queen Elizabeth I, ranked 94th. *"Elizabeth's greatest shortcoming,"* wrote Hart, *"was perhaps her reluctance to provide for the succession to the throne. Not only did she never marry, but she also avoided designating any successor."* Ings licked his finger and turned the page to continue reading. *"Whatever Elizabeth's reasons for not naming a successor, had she died young...England would probably have been plunged into a civil war over the succession."*

Ings' mood brightened as he read. He smiled at the historical parallel.

* * *

Professor Thistlewood lived on Davis Place, NW in a two bedroom, one bath apartment that cost him $2,200 per month. He paid another $250 for parking and $75 to rent a storage room. It was a lot of money for a 900 square foot apartment, especially since the Embassy Row building was built in 1939. But its character was attractive to him and to the women who frequently slept over.

In fact, his addiction to women and wine had disabled his ability to cancel his date that night. And so there she was in the apartment, Oregon Pinot cupped in her hand, while Art admired the breasts cupped underneath the sheer cashmere of her light sweater.

They were in the main living area, a warm environment with large overstuffed chairs and a single love seat. Throughout the space there were books and artwork. On the wrought iron and glass coffee table there was a large book about art.

He stood behind her and lightly touched the right side of her neck with his lips. She purred and giggled before moving away.

"What's that one about?" she asked, tipping her glass to the wall before swirling the wine and taking a small sip. She held it in her mouth, rolling it over her tongue. He had taught her well.

"That's my favorite piece. It's called *IPod Ghraib*. It's a social commentary on commercialism and politics. See the iPod in the hands of the Iraqi prisoner? Those replace the electrical wires shown in the original photograph."

She swallowed the wine. "Who's the artist?"

"Trek Thunder Kelly." Thistlewood moved in again, placing his hands on her denim hips. They were only slightly wider than her girlish waist.

"Who?" She took another sip with her left hand and placed her right hand on his. She wrapped her fingers around the tips of his and pulled them to her belly, leaning back into his chest.

"Trek Kelly." Thistlewood moved his left arm around her waist to clasp his hands around her from behind. He squeezed slightly. "He's a California artist who actually ran for Governor in 2003. That's the year Arnold Schwarzenegger won the recall election. Anybody in the state could run if they paid the registration fee or gathered enough signatures. Hundreds of people ran. Trek's platform was legalized drug use. He theorized that if you legalized certain drugs and taxed them, the state would eliminate its budget problems. T had its merits..."

"Sounds a little unusual." She took another sip. The glass was almost empty. It was her second.

"Maybe," Thistlewood chuckled. "Trek was in the midst of his 'Blue Period', where he wore the same shade of blue, head to toe, every day all year. Performance art."

"Hmmm," she raised her glass to the adjoining piece on the wall. "Did he do that one too?"

"Yes." The professor moved his hands back to the small curves just above her hips. He loved that part of her body. He slipped his fingers underneath the cashmere to lightly touch her skin. "Another social commentary. This one is, again, about the war in Iraq."

The piece was a manipulated photograph titled *Target Iraq-Fallujah Battle*. It depicted three U.S. soldiers crouched near a stone building. Each was holding an M-16. But instead of their typical desert camouflage uniforms, they were outfitted in red uniforms patterned with white Target store logos. It was one in a series of six.

Thistlewood was opposed to the Iraq war and how the Bush administration had chosen to mislead the American people into believing national security was at stake. He hated that it had diverted attention away from the war in Afghanistan.

The pieces spoke to him because of their raw attitude. Kelly was unafraid to speak his mind and challenge established thought.

"Very interesting," she turned from the picture to face Thistlewood and wrapped her arms around his neck. The glass of wine was still in her hand and it hung just above and behind Thistlewood's head. Her reading glasses fell on the bridge of her nose. She looked like a naughty librarian. "You like interesting things, don't you, Professor?"

He found her interesting. She was 24-year old graduate student at American University. But he hadn't met her in class, surprisingly enough. They'd met at a funeral some months prior.

The deceased was a longtime friend of Thistlewood's. His funeral service was at a small parlor owned by the coed's father. She was there handing out service programs to the guests. The professor was immediately attracted to her.

"I'm Art Thistlewood," he had offered, extending his hand. He couldn't take his eyes off of her full and exquisite lips.

"I'm Laura Harrowby," she had replied while shaking Thistlewood's hand. Her fingers were long and slender. "My father owns the place."

Harrowby's Funeral Home & Chapel was among the more established mortuaries inside the Beltway. In three generations it had established itself as a place of kind service and great discretion, both valuable attributes in a political town. Harrowby's had handled the preparations for a long list of notables.

Thistlewood and the coed had exchanged telephone numbers. They met for brunch the following Sunday and had been dating since.

Standing in his apartment, her arms wrapped around his neck, Laura pushed against him and kissed his lips gently. Thistlewood could tell she was preoccupied with the scruff on his upper lip.

"You didn't shave today," she whispered.

"Long day," he replied softly, "with the president's death and all." He leaned in to kiss her again but she pulled back.

"Oh, I almost forgot to tell you!" Laura said excitedly. "I think my father may handle the preparations for President Foreman's funeral."

"Really?" Thistlewood asked in surprise. "How did that happen?" He wasn't really that intrigued by the development but he humored her.

She stepped back. She was standing a foot in front of him, though Thistlewood's hands were still holding her. "He'll probably just handle the casket and flowers. The White House called to ask about the logistics before I came over."

"That's fascinating," Thistlewood said, dismissing her apparent excitement in favor of his. "Now where was I?"

Laura pointed to the spot behind her right ear. His thumbs rubbed against her skin just above her hips. Thistlewood gently pressed his lips to her neck.

"Mmmm," Laura spread her fingers and ran them up the back of the professor's head. "Now aren't you glad I talked you into *not* cancelling tonight?"

Thistlewood nodded without speaking as he breathed softly into her ear, tugging on the lobe with his teeth. The small mantle clock chimed eleven times. He had little more than an hour until he needed to leave for his meeting. It would be enough time, he thought, as the pair slid onto the love seat.

* * *

Felicia Jackson was pacing in her office as a team of exhausted aides sat in chairs, three-ringed binders and reams of paper on their laps.

"Look, people," she directed, "I am not a constitutional scholar. I need the basic information here. I have to know *what* we're doing and *what* we're fighting against. Don't give me legal mumbo-jumbo."

The more experienced attorneys were busy elsewhere formulating her case, and a young attorney on loan to her from a powerful D.C. law firm spoke up

"Madam Speaker," he offered, "let's get down to brass tacks here."

"Good!" She stopped pacing and pointed at the young man. She noticed that he was still in his three piece suit, tie knotted to the top button.

"The line of presidential succession is mentioned in the Constitution in two places. The 25th Amendment provides for the ascension of an able-bodied vice president. That element is essentially moot here because there *is* no current vice president."

"Won't they make the case that Blackmon is the VP?"

"Yes. But the 25th Amendment probably won't come into play. We have to concern ourselves with Article 2, Section 1."

"Which says what?" She asked the question as she turned her back on the lawyer and walked to her desk, half standing, half sitting on the desk's edge with only one foot on the floor.

"It reads," the attorney looked down at the paper stack on his lap, "'Congress may by Law provide for the Case of Removal, Death, Resignation or Inability, both of the president and vice president, declaring what officer shall then act as president, and such officer shall act accordingly'. We argue," he continued without looking up, "that you are the 'officer' at the top of the succession order. Though, you must first take the oath before you can assume the duties and authority of the office."

"So," Felicia said, mulling over what the lawyer was saying, "this is nothing different from what I was told earlier. I am still *not* clear on why Blackmon has any case at all. He never took the oath."

"That is true, Madame Speaker," the attorney replied. "But their case is about the constitutionality of *your* place in the line of succession. This will center on the Succession Act of 1947."

The lawyer picked up the stack of papers from his lap and placed them on the floor in front of his chair. When he bent forward, Felicia noticed the small circular bald patch on the top of the young man's head. She felt sorry for him. He couldn't be more than 30 and already he was losing his hair.

"Here's where we make our case," he said, sitting up straight in his seat. "United States Code Title 3, Chapter 1, Section 19 lays out the 'officer' eligible to act as president should both the sitting president and vice president be unable to perform their duties. In subsection A1, it clearly states that 'the Speaker of the House of Representatives shall, upon his resignation as speaker and as representative in Congress, act as president.'"

"Then what's the problem?"

"Well, Madam," the attorney paused, "they will point to the same U.S. code subsection E. It reads, 'Subsections (a), (b), and (d) of this section shall apply only to such officers as are eligible to the office of president under the Constitution.' And they will argue that you are not eligible."

"On what grounds?"

"On the grounds that you are not 'constitutionally'," he used his fingers to indicate a set of quotes, "an officer."

"Why not?" She hated air quotes. It was evident in the altered, derisive tone in her voice. The other aides in the room recognized it and simultaneously shifted uncomfortably in their seats. Had this been Rome, the Speaker would have shot the messenger.

"It's an argument that predates the 19th century," he answered. "In 1792, when Congress first developed the Act of Succession, there were politics involved."

"Aren't there always?" the Speaker sneered. Her aides snickered in subservient agreement.

"Yes, Ma'am," the lawyer agreed. He cleared his throat, adjusting his collar with his index finger. "In this case, Thomas Jefferson was Secretary of State. His opponents did not want him atop the list. They bickered over who to place on top. It was decided that the President Pro Tempore should be immediately after the vice president. The Speaker of the House was next. James Madison, one of the authors of the Constitution had a big problem with it. He wrote a letter to another founding father, Edmund Pendleton, in which he expressed concern over the Act."

"What does the letter say specifically?"

The lawyer bent over to the stack of papers on the floor and pulled out a single sheet of paper highlighted with yellow. His bald spot, which now glistened with little beads of sweat, was irritating Felicia. Everything was beginning to irritate her.

"The letter reads in part, 'On another point the bill certainly errs. It provides that in case of a double vacancy, the Executive powers shall devolve on the President Pro Tempore of the Senate and he failing, on the Speaker of the House of Reps. The objections to this arrangement are various. 1. It may be questioned whether these are *officers,* in the constitutional sense.'"

"So? It's a letter. It's not the law," the Speaker opined.

"Yes," agreed the attorney. "But it is potential evidence. It was written by one of the Constitution's authors. The point is salient enough that in 1886, the President Pro Tempore and Speaker of the House were dropped from the line of succession in favor of the president's cabinet officers."

"I imagine," countered the Speaker, "that was political too?" Her aides snickered again as she stood from her desk and walked around it so as to sit at the high back leather chair behind it.

"It was in deference to the emerging power of big business," explained the lawyer. He pulled a handkerchief from his breast pocket and dabbed his forehead, then his bald spot. "The thought was to reward appointed officers as opposed to ambitious politicians."

"Regardless," the lawyer loosened the knot in his tie and unbuttoned the top button of his shirt, "your position was removed for six decades. It wasn't returned until 1947, as you know, when the Speaker and President Pro Tempore switched positions atop the line of succession. They will make these points. They will argue the lack of constitutionality based generally on these grounds. The court will listen."

The Speaker was silent. She watched the lawyer organizing the papers in front of him. He lifted them onto his lap and Felicia leaned forward on her desk. Her elbows were on the marble topper, her hands touching as if in prayer. She tapped her chin with her index fingers, trying to determine if his charcoal suit was summer weight wool or gabardine.

CHAPTER 4

Matti palmed the mouse to the right of her computer. On the screen was a digital supplement to the file that her supervisor had given her. It detailed the history of a group of men who called themselves "The Daturans".

The group was initiated by a man named Spencer Thomas. The agency seemed to have quite a bit of information about him. He was a childless bachelor who was well-connected and wealthy.

The agency put Thomas' known and suspected assets at somewhere around $275 million. He had accounts in New York, Switzerland, The Bahamas, Andorra, and Liechtenstein. There were surveillance photographs of Thomas exiting banks in Geneva, Andora la Vella, and Vaduz.

There were also copies of deeds to homes in Frankfurt, Messina, Odessa, Greenwich, and Kensington. He had rental agreements for three other properties in Riyadh, San Francisco, and Houston.

For decades, Thomas had befriended whoever was politically expedient. The agency knew that he'd advised President Reagan and Prime Minister Thatcher in the 1980s. He was a Nelson Mandela confidant during the mid-1990s. Egyptian President Hosni Mubarak asked for Thomas' advice on closing the Rafah border-crossing when Hamas took control of Gaza in 2007.

He was knighted in 1998; it seemed to U.S. intelligence, as a repayment for helping Tony Blair lead the Labor Party to victory in 1997. He had connections to Saudi royals that were not entirely understood, though he owned large amounts of stock in U.S. and British held energy companies.

Incredibly, the NSA noted, sixteen months before the company filed for bankruptcy, he sold 13,000 shares of Enron stock at $90 each. Thomas had attended art museum parties in Aspen with the late Enron CEO and Chairman Ken Lay.

And on a humid Houston Saturday in June 2003, he sat on a wooden courtroom bench in the federal courthouse when Enron accounting firm Arthur Andersen was convicted of obstructing justice. There was a wire service photograph of Sir Spencer standing behind the attorney at a press conference outside the courthouse after the verdict was announced. His name was not in the caption.

Matti was certain that if anyone had the means to pull off an action that might threaten national security, it was Sir Spencer Thomas.

* * *

Sir Spencer lumbered into a cab outside of the Hay-Adams and told the driver where to go. He sat in the right rear passenger's seat. It was a cool night after what had been an abnormally warm day. The driver had the windows down and the radio turned up just enough to hear it over the whistle of the wind passing by the car. Sir Spencer recognized the music as Irish, likely from the collection of Thomas Moore melodies. It was an odd choice for a cab driver, Sir Spencer thought, but he appreciated it nonetheless

The driver turned left onto I Street, NW and drove slowly to its intersection with Pennsylvania Avenue. The distance was less than three-quarters of a mile. Sir Spencer easily could have walked it; his dietician would have recommended it. But given the hour, Sir Spencer Thomas thought it better to take a cab.

"This is it. Cato Street Pub on the left across the street." The cab driver didn't turn around as he spoke. "That's four dollars." He pointed to the red meter on the dash.

"I was in your cab for two minutes!" complained Sir Spencer, reluctantly fishing a five dollar bill from the money clip in his jacket pocket.

"Three dollars to get in the cab, and a quarter for every sixth of a mile. Not my rules." The driver turned as he reached back to take the cash from Sir Spencer.

"It's robbery, whether it's your rule or not," Sir Spencer grumbled and pulled on the door handle. He opened the door and got out at the curb. He shut the door and looked across the street at the Pub as the cab drove off. It was as he remembered it, not having been there in about a year. The red doors almost glowed against the faint yellow coach lights to their side and gave the pub the look of a den of iniquity.

Sir Spencer looked across Pennsylvania Avenue. He waited for a dark sedan to pass and then crossed. He could not see the camera pointed at him through the vehicle's darkly tinted windows.

As he crossed the street he noticed two men approaching the door from the east. He recognized them as his compatriots.

"Gentlemen," Sir Spencer nodded in their direction as he stepped onto the curb in front of the bar. "Good to see you." He extended his hand to Art Thistlewood.

"And you, Sir Spencer," replied Thistlewood as he took his hand, "are looking as smart as ever."

"Kiton," replied Sir Spencer, looking down at his jacket.

"Good to see you too, Sir Spencer," George Edwards chimed in. Sir Spencer nodded, smiled, and put his hand on the young artist's back as they walked toward the red doors.

"Splendid to be with you again, George."

It was Sir Spencer who had brought Edwards into the fold. After an initial introduction from Thistlewood, Sir Spencer was impressed with Edwards' intelligence and political bent. He seemed creative and extreme. Sir Spencer saw himself in the artist and liked him.

The old Brit watched Edwards try to open the locked doors to the pub. When Thistlewood took his turn pulling on the brass handles, the dark sedan passed again.

The men did not notice. Nor did they pay attention to the jacketed bum leaning against a trashcan a half block up the street. They were too far away to hear the rapid clicks of his camera's shutter.

"Let's see here," offered Sir Spencer. "I think we might rouse Mr. Ings if we knock loudly." He rapped on the doors.

* * *

The surveillance photos of James Ings were unflattering. Generally dressed in jeans and a plaid flannel shirt with a cigarette in hand, there was nothing remarkable about him. Matti thought he looked like a bar owner.

Ings was not particularly flush with cash, though he had plenty of assets. In the expanded intelligence on the computer screen, it listed his other real estate holdings. He owned the building in which his bar was located. He also owned, mortgage free, "The Light of Bean" coffee bar and "Meat Up" butcher shop. Matti laughed at the names. Ings had a sense of humor she appreciated. He was an alcoholic chain smoker, but he was witty.

There was a vague indication that the butcher shop was a front for something illicit. It was a money loser and yet Ings kept it open. The intelligence suggested that the business merely cleaned cash for a dubious import-export supplier. Ings generally paid far more than market value for Argentinean beef and wrote it off as a loss when it didn't sell. The import-export business, called Grosvenor Square Importation Company, was a Delaware licensed limited liability corporation.

The agency knew Delaware was a state with favorable ownership laws, allowing for the creation of certain businesses without identifying directors or owners. Neither the agency nor the Internal Revenue Service had been able to pin anything on Ings.

Overpaying for beef was not a crime. But it was a cash business; so was the bar. Matti knew that the accounting for those types of businesses were often easy to manipulate. She could tell from the recent spike in intelligence regarding "Meat Up" that her cohorts were just beginning to sink their teeth into that angle of the investigation.

The agency started tracking Ings' activities after a Tea Party event in 2009. He was the "star" of a YouTube video that went viral in the days following the public event at Oregon Ridge Park in Baltimore County. In the video, he was using a bullhorn and chanting "Heads on a stick!" Behind him was a large poster with caricatures of then-Speaker of the House Nancy Pelosi and then-House Majority Leader Harry Reid. Their grossly exaggerated "bobble heads" were drawn atop painted spring coils and sticks. Beneath the drawings were the words "HEADing in the Wrong Direction!"

There was nothing unusual, as far as Tea Party videos were concerned, with the chanting or the sign. But off screen, a band started playing on stage at the rally, and a fairly drunk Ings began dancing in such a way that nearby paramedics thought he was having a seizure.

EMTs attempted to help Ings, but he refused their offer and started running from them. The video captured Ings running in a circle around the confused paramedics for more than a minute before he collapsed from exhaustion and was carried off to a cooling tent. Matti watched an embedded copy of the video on her computer, and she couldn't help but laugh.

How did I miss this?

She loved scouring the internet for humorous videos. It was a guilty pleasure she indulged late at night with a pint of Blue Bell Homemade Vanilla ice cream. She'd sit at her desk, face glowing blue from the screen, and spoon small tastes into her mouth.

Occasionally she'd invite over one of her few girlfriends from college to share her guilty pleasure. They'd connect the computer to her television and watch the embarrassments on a 37- inch LCD. Matti shared the ice cream and occasionally some Kahlua and coffee.

She enjoyed her friends. They were a break from the world of code breaking. They didn't judge her. They didn't expect her to be a hero. She could relax.

Despite believing she had seen every viral video from the Evian roller skating babies to the grape stomping newscaster and the 2007 Miss Teen South Carolina map disaster, she'd never before seen this particular drunken embarrassment.

Ings, she learned, was an unwitting internet clown for weeks. He unknowingly caught the attention of the federal government, which already had its concerns about Tea Party activism. But as Matti filtered through the details of Ings' life, she couldn't find any indication of violent tendencies. He was a lonely addict bent on living in a fog. She thought him to be more personally self-destructive than anything else.

* * *

Jimmy Ings walked down the stairs from his apartment, yelling at the front doors of the pub as he braced himself against the banister.

"I'm coming!" he shouted. "Stop your knocking. I'm coming." Ings reached the front doors and leaned on them with his left forearm. He cradled his head in the crook of his arm as though he were counting to ten in a game of hide-and-seek.

"Are you there, Mr. Ings?"

Ings recognized the voice as that of Sir Spencer Thomas and was pleased to hear it.

"I'm here." Ings stood and went through the motion of brushing himself off. His Wranglers and plaid long sleeve shirt were wrinkled beyond a fix. He opened the door, surprised to see two other compatriots with Sir Spencer.

"Art, George. Good to see you men." Ings reached out to shake their hands and then ushered the trio inside. As they disappeared inside the building, he checked quickly to see if anyone was watching and then shut the door.

Ings was happy to have the men there. They could finally get down to business. He stepped behind the bar to grab a couple of bottles off of the top shelf and then tripped up the steps after the others.

Ings surveyed the men in front of him as they settled themselves in his upstairs living room. He saw Sir Spencer look at the couch and grimace as if he'd smelled something foul.

Prima donna, he thought. Aloud he said, "Just brush it off, Sir Spencer. It ain't gonna kill you to sit on my couch."

"No," agreed Sir Spencer, his nostrils still flared, "but it may well ruin this jacket." He pulled a linen handkerchief from his Kiton breast pocket and laid it out flat on the cushion before sitting.

Ings laughed as he walked to the adjoining kitchen. He opened the oak cabinet next to the refrigerator and pulled out a trio of glasses, holding them with his thumb and forefingers. His other hand was grasping the two liquor bottles from downstairs.

His hands and arms full, Ings walked back over to the group. Thistlewood was next to Sir Spencer on the couch. Edwards sat by himself in a brown leather and wood grain laminate Eames knock-off, his feet on the ottoman. Nobody appeared thirsty.

"Okay then," Ings put the glasses and bottles onto the coffee table. "The drinks are here if you want some later."

The barkeep rubbed his palms on his thighs and then took a seat in an antique gold La-Z-Boy Amity recliner. The flared arms were peppered with cigarette burns, most of the nine buttons in the tufted cushion back were popped, and the reclining handle was damaged. But Ings didn't care, he loved the chair. It often served as his bed.

He'd drifted off to a light sleep when he was awoken by Sir Spencer's knocking minutes earlier. He sank into the seat again and swiveled toward the couch.

"Fellas, what's up?" He smiled his crooked smile and thumbed his hands on the chair's arms. "We got a lot to talk about and none of you seem up to it."

"I'm still adjusting to the odor, James," Sir Spencer finally offered. "You seem to have let the place go in the past year."

"It has been a year, hasn't it?" Ings thought back to their last meeting at his place. It hadn't been a good one.

"I'm sick of not doing anything!" he remembered yelling at the others. *"How can we do anything if nobody knows who we are and we have only five members? That seems insane to me."*

Sir Spencer had assured him that political success did not always depend on numbers or volume, and that often it was about timing and strategy. If they chose the correct moment in time and executed the perfect plan, they would be effective. On the other hand, Ings recalled Sir Spencer informing him that a loud persistent voice was bound to be ignored eventually.

"We don't have a voice," Ings had countered. "We're invisible. We are wasting our time."

They'd tried to affect change through back channels and lobbyists. The conventional cheating hadn't worked and neither had funneling money to sympathetic candidates. It all seemed almost pointless.

"Inaction can be the best action," counseled Sir Spencer. "We need to talk and meet and discuss so that when the time comes to act, we are ready. If you choose not to be a part of that, so be it." Sir

Spencer had hoped Ings would calm himself. He valued Ings for too many reasons to see him quit.

The group had disbanded and didn't correspond for three months. After years of discussion and organization, the Daturans were done. Ings thought for certain his discontent had regrettably ended the project.

Then, out of the blue, George Edwards sat down at Cato Street and ordered a drink. Ings poured it himself and spent time talking to the young artist. During their conversation, Ings learned that Edwards and Sir Spencer were in constant contact. They still believed in the plan to affect a New American Order, and they needed Ings' ideas and resources to make it happen.

Reluctantly Ings agreed to give it another go. Sir Spencer subsequently stroked Ings' ego and pocketbook just enough to make the partnership hold together.

Ings now sat in his La-Z-Boy on the eve of action, reflecting on the water under the bridge, and he was again impatient.

"What are we going to do? I thought we were here to act." "We are here to act, good man," said Sir Spencer, his lips curling like a pair of salted slugs in what resembled a smile. "I have the perfect plan. But I think maybe we should wait for the Attorney General."

* * *

Bill Davidson was running late. He sat on the side of the bed, slid his steel Omega Constellation onto his left wrist and looked at the time.

"I'm late," he said without turning his head.

"Better you than me," purred the woman in bed behind him. She arched her back, stretched her arms and reached across the sheets to run her finger lazily down his back. She laughed at herself. It was a deep laugh; throaty and sensual.

Davidson smiled. He got the joke. He loved her laugh. It seemed genuine.

"You're not yourself, Bill." She poked his back with her long red fingernail.

"Just preoccupied..." He took his journal off of the nightstand next to the bed and wrote down a reminder.

"You and that little book of yours," she said, sounding more judgmental than curious.

"What about it?" Davidson was being overly sensitive and he knew it.

"You're always writing in there. Is it about me?" she purred.

"Not this time."

"Is it the president?"

"Remotely." Davidson stood and was pulling on his pants. "I have a meeting to attend. Remember, I told you about it? It's with a group of politically likeminded friends." He closed the buckle on his belt without first putting on his shirt. He turned to look at her.

She pulled the sheet down to her navel, revealing a small diamond piercing, but Davidson's attention was held somewhat higher on her body. Her alabaster skin appeared flawless. His eyes moved down to the piece of expensive jewelry he'd purchased for her.

"Are you sure it's not another woman?" She smiled and then closed her mouth to lick the front of her teeth.

Davidson laughed her off and went to the desk chair to grab his shirt, slipped on each sleeve, and then buttoned it. He left it untucked from his pants as he slipped on his loafers, placing a hand on the chair to balance himself. It was dark in the room, except for the light from the small window that shone onto the bed, and her red hair looked almost black.

"Just checking," she said. She rolled onto her side and pulled her knees up to her chest into a semi-fetal position as she watched Davidson finish dressing. "When will I see you again?"

Her arms were stretched on the sheets toward the headboard. There was a small tattoo on the inside of her long bicep. It looked like a blue upper case "H". It was her astrological sign; Aquarius. Davidson thought it suited her. He'd read once that Aquarians were physically magical and prone to experimentation.

"I don't know."

He adjusted his jacket and stuffed his silk tie into an interior breast pocket. He grabbed his keys and some change from the desk.

She slinked over to the edge of the bed and sat up, hanging her legs off the side. Her feet barely touched the floor. Davidson went over to her and touched her face. She looked at him, exposed, and smiled. She closed her eyes and stood to kiss him. He slid his hands from her shoulders down to her waist as she rose to meet his lips. He kissed her without closing his eyes, inhaling her scent. She smelled like an intoxicating mix of cinnamon, chocolate, and fruit.

"You like the way I smell?" she asked, her lips still touching his. "It's Bond Number 9 Coney Island."

Davidson pulled away and kissed her forehead. "You smell edible. But I have to go." He walked to the door and left without turning around, knowing that if he looked at her again, he'd never leave.

As the door automatically shut behind him, she walked over to the desk and saw five one hundred dollar bills fanned out next to the phone.

He always paid in full.

Twice a week they met in the same room at the same place. He was a creature of habit, her best and most regular client. They'd met through a mutual friend. It was pleasure for him, business for her.

Sometimes, she imagined that Bill pretended they were a couple. He'd give her occasional gifts. She'd accept them and purr about how sweet he was to think of her.

He'd often talk about his work and ask her about things that *didn't* relate to her work. She was a student of history and he enjoyed engaging her in philosophical debates. But she never pried too much. It would be stupid to ruin a good thing over a false curiosity.

Davidson took the elevator down to the first floor and exited to the right into the large lobby. He pulled his shirt collar to his nose and inhaled. It smelled like her.

He took another right to avoid the front doors of The Mayflower Hotel, slipped through a side door onto DeSales Street and hailed a cab.

"2100 Pennsylvania Avenue, please," he told the cabbie. Davidson pulled out his cell phone and pressed a number saved in his speed dial. It rang twice.

"Hello?"

"It's Bill," he spoke softly.

"Hi, Bill," she whispered back. "I thought you had a meeting?" She was already dressed and was pulling on her red leather heels.

Her finger was stuck between her heel and the strap.

"I do," he answered. "But, look. About next time..."

"Yes?" She was smiling. He could hear it through the phone. She freed her finger from the shoe and stood from the bed, cradling the phone cradled between her ear and neck.

"How about later tonight? After my meeting." He was addicted.

"Wow. That's a change. Are you sure you won't be otherwise entangled?" She picked up her large purse and walked toward the door to the room.

"I'll make sure that I'm free if you do."

"Okay," she giggled. She told him that she wasn't sure of her schedule but that she'd make arrangements to be available. She turned around to put down her bag and sat back down on the bed.

"See you." Davidson ended the call. He needed the stress relief. For three years she'd been good for that. He picked his journal from his pocket and made note of the appointment.

Davidson had never married. As he aged, his ability and desire to play the dating game had diminished. He didn't want rejection. He wanted to cut to the chase.

Discretion was important. He didn't use traceable payment and he always stuck with the same woman. Nonetheless, it was a calculated risk.

He worried that someday he'd be outed for paying a prostitute. He knew that former Louisiana Senator David Vitter always believed his secret trysts were safe until the feds busted Deborah Palfrey, the "D.C. Madam."

When that happened, all hell broke loose. People of power throughout the District lost their jobs and the respect of their peers. The Madam threatened to expose thousands of D.C. insiders who used her services. If a complicated service like Palfrey's could get caught, then the A.G. knew his potential exposure in a far less sophisticated business was enormous. But he couldn't help himself.

An unseen photographer caught his exit from the cab on Pennsylvania, and followed him from the Mayflower as it had twice a week for nine months, completely unbeknownst to him.

Davidson paid the cabbie and exited the vehicle, then walked up to the twin red doors and knocked. He checked the Omega on his wrist. It was 1:30 in the morning.

* * *

Matti didn't spend much time on Bill Davidson's dossier. She knew most of what there was to learn about him, including his penchant for hookers. Instead, she was intrigued by the handsome, womanizing professor from American University.

Arthur Thistlewood didn't look like a domestic terrorist. Then again, Ted Bundy didn't look like a serial killer.

But the professor had a deep interest in politically controversial artwork and so he was watched. The government knew about his trip to visit Trek Thunder Kelly, an artist whose work was definitively anti-Bush. There were pictures of the two men standing outside of a single-story red building in Venice Beach that appeared to be Kelly's art studio. There were additional photographs of Thistlewood and Kelly walking on the beach.

Matti noted that Kelly had "disappeared" in the fall of 2009. In a note to friends he revealed that he was selling everything he owned and was "dropping off the grid". Then in 2012, he spent much of the year traveling the country in search of "good". He had a website and a blog, but Kelly never did anything suspicious other than advocate the legalization of drugs.

Maybe he believed the government was watching him.

Thistlewood traveled frequently to both Los Angeles and to northern California where he visited friends at Stanford and at the University of California Berkeley. There were dozens of pictures and reports detailing meetings with various professors and educators, none of them remarkable. Matti thumbed past them with little attention until she found a tidbit that sparked her interest.

While Thistlewood was clueless about the current surveillance targeting him, Matti assumed it wouldn't have surprised him. He knew he was on the government's Consolidated Watch List during the final years of the Bush administration.

Art Thistlewood was publicly critical of what he considered constitutional violations. He talked about those concerns during a graduate lecture that was televised on campus closed circuit television and then posted to the web.

Not long after, he was denied curbside check-in for a flight from

Phoenix to Reagan National. According to the intelligence report on Matti's desk, Thistlewood was allowed to fly home, but not before a strip search and a thorough examination of his baggage. His only checked suitcase was "lost" during the nonstop flight.

He wasn't preaching hate or violence, so she wondered how the administration could consider him a threat. Even though something didn't smell right, she'd always known she was working for the good guys. There was no reason to doubt the integrity of her mission, she assured herself.

Continuing to read, she learned that Thistlewood was removed from the list after filing a complaint through the D.H.S. Traveler Redress Inquiry Program. He filled out a three page form, detailing his experience and personal information, and then mailed it to a facility in Arlington, Virginia. After a few months and a handful of phone calls, he was removed from the list. The surveillance, however, did not stop.

She felt somewhat less sorry for the man as she read more about his predilection for short term relationships with long legged coeds. One after another was photographed with Thistlewood. Some were blonde, others were brunettes. All of them were attractive.

Matti read about his current love, a graduate student whose father ran a local funeral home and mortuary. Her family was well-connected but held little influence. They gave money to both parties and a variety of charities. Matti wondered what the girl would think about her "boyfriend" being involved in an anti-government conspiracy.

You never really know people. Their codes are too complex.

Matti had lived with that idea for so long. And try as she could to let it go, she couldn't. She needed to believe that every mystery was solvable, that books were told by their covers. But slowly, she was beginning to find that not to be the case.

Maybe everything was gray.

At the end of the report on Thistlewood, she saw the connection to the fifth member of the group: George Edwards. Matti rubbed her eyes and looked at the clock on the lower right portion of the computer screen. It was nearly two o'clock. She couldn't believe it was already that late.

Sometimes she believed that the same people who designed casinos in Las Vegas were in charge of constructing offices for NSA analysts. Once inside there was no sense of time. A day could slip by without taking note of just how much time had passed.

Matti needed a break. She wanted caffeine.

* * *

"Now that Bill is here," began Sir Spencer, "we can begin." He glared at the former Attorney General. It was obvious to everyone in the room that Sir Spencer was irritated by the delay.

Bill Davidson leaned against the pony wall that separated the small dining area from the living room where the other men were seated. Standing was his self-imposed penance for being late. He ran the tip of his tongue along the back of the bridge affixed to his gums.

"I am of the opinion that we can effectively induce radical change in the country," Sir Spencer said, leaning forward on the couch, his eyes scanning the room. "Given the peculiar constitutional predicament in which we find ourselves," he continued, "there is a window of opportunity for us. We can, I think, significantly alter the political direction of this wayward government. I know our feeble attempts of the past have failed. Money isn't worth what it once was to these heathens running around the bowels of the Capitol. We underestimated that. This time, we must fully commit. If we do, we will succeed, my good men."

"How is that?" Ings asked between drags on his unfiltered Camel.

Sir Spencer struggled to stand against the depth of the sofa, but managed. He adjusted his jacket and pulled each arm down to ease the wrinkles, then leaned toward Edwards. "I think George has some ideas about technique. Then I will further explain the process by which we take control. George?"

Thistlewood's eyes darted between Sir Spencer and Edwards, his brow furrowed. Given the proximity of their Georgetown apartments, the two had shared a cab to the meeting, and on the way, Edwards had said nothing to Thistlewood about a plan. He folded his arms across his chest and waited to hear what the artist had kept from him.

"Well..." Edwards began slowly, "I think the answer is Semtex."

* * *

Matti's coffee break was short lived, but it was enough to push her through the remaining pages of intelligence.

She learned that the artist George Edwards was roughly her age. He'd studied political science and art history at the University of Virginia in Charlottesville and never held a traditional job.

Edwards and Thistlewood originally met during a small showing of the artist's work at the Katzen Arts Center on the American University campus. There were pictures of the two men walking with each other on Ward Circle near the Metro bus stop. They were a little grainy and taken at a distance, but Matti could clearly see the two men engaged in a deep conversation. Both of them seemed to be talking with their hands.

According to the information in the file, Thistlewood brought Edwards into the Datura Project. There were lists of dates and meeting sites at which Thistlewood and Edwards met with Thomas, Ings, and Attorney General Bill Davidson.

Whoever had compiled the intelligence seemed to be convinced that the men were conspiring. If not, the report asked, why meet in secret? Why use encrypted phones? Why use codes to communicate? The codes, Matti thought, were basic and easily decipherable. But they were codes nonetheless. She now had the same questions.

What were *they conspiring to do?*

* * *

"Semtex?" Davidson asked. "Why Semtex?"

"It's an explosive," Edwards said, looking at the knight as he spoke.

"I know what Semtex is, George!" Davidson snapped. He *was* once the head of the Justice Department. He knew that the plastic high order explosive was developed in 1966 in Pardubice, Czechoslovakia. A combination of Semtin and explosive, it was

TOM ABRAHAMS

originally produced in large quantities for use during the Vietnam War but had since become a weapon of choice for paramilitary groups around the world.

The Pan Am Flight 103 explosion in 1988, the bombing of the U.S. Embassy in Nairobi and the World Trade Center attack in 1993, and the 2008 Irish Republican Army attack on Irish police were all accomplished with the help of Semtex.

The explosive came to be known as "The Magic Marble of Pardubice". After the Cold War, much of the product disappeared. Czech soldiers sold the product for as much as $500 per kilogram. Of course Davidson knew about Semtex.

"What I mean," Edwards elaborated, "is that we will use Semtex to alter the Presidential succession process."

Davidson didn't like where this was going. "Are you talking about killing people?" he asked. "I don't know about this. I don't think I am up for murder."

Sir Spencer interjected, "Were the founding fathers murderers? Were they terrorists? Or were they men for whom death was a small price to pay for freedom and democracy?" Sir Spencer sat down to let Edwards continue. "Listen to the boy. Give him his due." "Bomb sniffing dogs cannot detect Semtex," Edwards explained. "At least, not the older stuff. The newer plastics have an odor inserted into them, but the original compositions are perfect for our purposes. If we can find a way to get the plastic into the midst of the president's funeral or memorial..." Edwards let his thought trail off.

"You're insane," quipped Davidson.

"It's an impossible task," Thistlewood said. Apparently he didn't think it was achievable either. They'd failed at lesser plots with fewer risks.

"I must be drunk," added Ings, "because I thought I just heard you say you want to bomb the president's funeral."

"You *are* inebriated, James," confirmed Sir Spencer, "but your ears are sober."

"It can be done," Edwards insisted. "With the people we have in this room, we can get the Semtex where it needs to be. When President Foreman is memorialized or buried, most of the line of succession will be there."

"Not everyone will be there, George," Thistlewood piped in. "There's always a holdout. They always keep at least one person in the line of succession separated to ensure the continuity of government."

"I know," replied Edwards. He looked past Sir Spencer to nod at Thistlewood. "But we don't need to get *everyone*."

"How do we get our hands on Semtex?" asked Ings, eliciting nasty looks from Thistlewood and Davidson. "I mean, if we needed it."

"It's irrelevant, Jimmy." Davidson shook his head. "I am not going to resort to violence. That's just going too far. How can any of you be okay with this?"

"Bill," Sir Spencer said, holding up his hand to calm the former A.G., "think about this rationally."

"I am the only one in this room who *is* thinking rationally."

"Okay then," reasoned the knight, "think about it *ir*rationally."

Davidson ached to write down his thoughts in his journal, but it would have to wait until after the meeting when he was on his way back to the hotel and his woman-by-the-hour.

"We have watched silently," continued the knight, "as administration after administration has thumbed its nose at the foundations of our society. It's either a secret CIA torture program okayed by a vice president or a taxpayer bailout of an automotive industry too bloated to wipe itself after a bowel movement. We have been fleeced. The Patriot Act stole a little bit of our privacy," Sir Spencer preached. "The war in Iraq happened without ever receiving Congressional permission to declare war. The list of atrocities – real and imagined – is endless. We are Gomorrah. The only way to save this nation is to act swiftly and decisively. If that act calls for violence, so be it."

"I don't see it..." Davidson had worried before the meeting that the group might want to resort to violence given their earlier failures, and was not surprised that his fears had been justified.

"You don't see what?" Sir Spencer sounded condescending. "You don't see that the children of this nation are strapped with a debt so deep they'll never recover? You don't see the dollar shrinking against the euro and the pound? The middle class is disappearing, Bill. Our borders are a joke. Our deficit exceeds the gross domestic product. The Federal Reserve is driving us into stagflation. It is only a matter of time before states begin to go belly up and the feds step in to save them as they did banks and the auto industry. The sovereignty of the states is a natural disaster or a fuel shortage away from disappearing. What is there *not* to see, Bill?"

"You keep saying *we, us* and *ours*, Sir Spencer," Davidson remarked. "*You* aren't an American."

"You are right, Bill, I am not an American citizen. But I *was* born here, I own homes here. I *am* a citizen of the world. And the world needs a strong United States to lead it." Sir Spencer stood and walked slowly over to Davidson as he talked. He was pointing his finger at him. "What do you politicians like to call it? The shining city on a hill? Something like that?"

Davidson stood quietly, ruminating on the points Sir Spencer had made. He thought about the colonists who'd risked their lives and fortunes on an idea that government could be better. They conspired, they stole, they maimed and killed. Two centuries later they were heroes, their names and actions synonymous with patriotism. Maybe Sir Spencer and Edwards had a point.

"I will hear you out, George," Davidson offered, "but I am not complicit in this yet."

"I still want to know how we're gonna get the explosives," Ings said, easing the mounting tension in the room. The others laughed with the drunk before Sir Spencer answered his question.

"I have enough," he informed them, and the room quieted. "I have roughly 28 kilograms of Semtex, which converts to about sixty pounds."

"Where did you get it?" Ings asked though a burp.

"Let's just say that the French are very generous."

Sir Spencer was tipping his hand to Davidson. It was known in intelligence circles that the French had long used a decommissioned facility to store Semtex. The storage house was a 19th Century fort at Corbas near Lyon. In July 2008, a thief had stolen 61 pounds of Semtex and packages of detonators. After the break-in, the French admitted they'd left the fort unguarded.

"*You* stole it from Lyon," Davidson said in sudden realization.

"The issue," Edwards said, taking the floor, "is that we face a couple of obstacles. The first is access. How do we put the Semtex where it needs to be? Our plan is to use five pounds. It should be more than enough. But certainly, getting it into the right place is the primary concern."

"Maybe not," Thistlewood, who had been quiet until that point, cut in.

He was not thrilled with the idea of violence, though he suspected that it might be the only way forward. It challenged the core of who he thought himself to be.

But Thistlewood was not strong enough to dissent. He'd listened to Sir Spencer's diatribe about patriotism and appreciated its point. He knew that the founding fathers, if viewed objectively, were terrorists every bit as much as Al-Qaeda or the Palestinian Liberation Organization. He taught in his classes that early Americans fought against a British throne that they thought was oppressive and unjust. They used guerilla tactics. The Sons of Liberty, well chronicled groups of pre-revolutionary patriots, began committing acts of violence as early as 1765, a full eleven years before the colonies declared their independence from Mother England.

In fact, Thistlewood taught his undergraduates that the Sons of Liberty operated as groups of cells in a manner similar to Al-Qaeda. Being a patriot and a terrorist were not mutually exclusive propositions.

He knew that if they proved successful, they could begin a new movement. They could succeed where Tea Party-backed candidates like Senators Rand Paul and Ted Cruz had failed to significantly change policy despite winning seats on Capitol Hill, where the GOOH – *Get Out Of Our House!* – movement had failed to dump every member of the House and elect true citizen legislators. He also wanted badly to please Sir Spencer. Given the relationship George Edwards had apparently forged with the knight, he felt the need to prove his worth.

"I think I can help get the Semtex into the right place." He said it quietly, almost hoping nobody would hear him.

"Really?" Sir Spencer turned to Thistlewood and slapped the professor on his knee. "How so?"

"George, you say the explosive doesn't have a smell?" Thistlewood asked. "I mean, we could hide it and security wouldn't find it?" Edwards nodded. "I have a friend who may have access to President Foreman's casket."

"If it were hidden in the lining of the casket it would be undetected," Edwards said, almost breathless with excitement. "The casket itself, whether wooden or metal, would be the shell of the bomb."

"Fantastic!" Sir Spencer was giddy. "Do you believe, Arthur, that you can rely on that friend to help you?"

"I can make it work," Thistlewood said confidently. He was sure that he could get Laura Harrowby to help him unwittingly. "But I have a question."

"Go ahead," Sir Spencer nodded.

"Let's assume we are successful in this endeavor," Thistlewood said, leaning forward to look at each of the conspirators. "How do we change anything? The American people will hate us."

"Yes," replied the knight, "but we'll be in power. Everyone in the line of succession, save one, will be nearby when the bomb explodes. Whoever lives is the president."

"How does that help us?" Thistlewood said. "We're just five men."

"No," Sir Spencer shook his head. "We are six."

"Six?" asked a suddenly re-engaged Ings. "Who's the sixth?"

"A friend who has asked that I withhold their identity," Sir Spencer said coyly.

"Even from us?" Davidson asked.

"Especially from *you*," Sir Spencer shot back. "The sixth member has been with us since the beginning, but needed to remain physically disconnected until the right time."

"And now is the right time?" Edwards asked.

. "Now is exactly the right time," Sir Spencer said smugly. He straightened his back and raised his chin slightly.

"So who is the sixth man?" repeated Ings.

"The sixth Daturan, my good men, is the successor *not* there when the bombs explode." Sir Spencer paused to appreciate the silence of the other men in the room. "The sixth will be our next president."

PART TWO
THE PLOT

"Our own Country's Honor, all call upon us for a vigorous and manly exertion, and if we now shamefully fail, we shall become infamous to the whole world."
–George Washington, 1776

CHAPTER 5

On the top floor of the Wooster & Mercer lofts, in a modern 2500 square foot condominium, Felicia Jackson couldn't sleep. On most nights, the Arlington, Virginia escape was a place of solace for the Speaker. She was in love with the park views, the hardwood floors, and the high-end Wolf and Subzero appliances. The three bedroom, two and a half bath condo on Clarendon Boulevard was her home away from home. But after the day she'd had, Felicia was not enjoying it as she normally did.

She had underestimated Blackmon's drive and acumen. He was a formidable opponent. She wondered what his real end game might be.

Even if he won the court case, he was unlikely to become president. His own argument against her constitutional right to the office did nothing to help him. Unless he was trying to somehow stall long enough to take the oath of vice president, it just didn't add up. She believed that the Chief Justice of the Supreme Court wouldn't be so bold as to administer the oath to Blackmon, when she'd been respectful enough to let the succession issue play itself out.

A weary Felicia walked up the wrought iron staircase to the second floor catwalk/balcony which ran the length of the space directly above the kitchen. She stopped at the top of the steps to run her hand along the exposed brick in the corner. She loved the brick.

She turned to her left and leaned on the balcony railing, gazing through the picture window opposite her when her cell phone rang.

She looked at the caller I.D. It was her Chief Of Staff. Apparently he couldn't sleep either.

"Yes?" she answered, even though she did not want to talk.

"I just wanted to see how you're doing."

The Speaker liked surrounding herself with ambitious back-biters who went beyond the pale to please her. She wanted young, energetic politicos who hoped to accumulate power and large Blackberry address books.

Her employees were typical of the young Capitol staffing corps, but they were better at the game than most. They were intensely loyal. Felicia Jackson was their ticket and they knew it.

"I'm fine." She wasn't. "I just wish I'd been more in control tonight. I was too emotional."

"You're passionate about this," he countered.

"That's one way of looking at it." Felicia paced at the railing along the balcony. "Tomorrow will be better. I'll be less passionate, if that's what it takes. Do you think we need to hit the morning shows? Should I make myself available?"

"That's why I'm calling. I've already arranged back to back interviews with a few of the morning shows."

"Network or cable?"

"Both," he replied. "We're in a studio from five to nine o'clock tomorrow morning."

"Don't we need to be in White House briefings? Shouldn't we be available for court?" She was rethinking strategy. "Aren't there a dozen other things I could be doing that are of more importance than spin and public perception?"

"We'll have a couple of staffers at the White House, and our attorneys will be in court. I think it would appear either presumptuous or desperate for you to be in the West Wing tomorrow, and showing up in court makes you seem defensive."

He made good points, she conceded.

"The best thing you can do," he continued, "is to talk to the people. You're telegenic. You can handle the talking heads. I'm telling you, it will be great. It'll give you a chance to..." he paused.

"Appear presidential?"

"Yes."

"What's Blackmon doing? Have any of the shows booked him

too?" She certainly didn't want to be blindsided.

"I'm getting a handle on that," he said apprehensively. "Some of the bookers are evasive on that question."

"Find out!" She snapped back. "I don't want to be unprepared."

"I got it," he said. "I will have talking points for you before the first interview." "What time?"

"Be there at 4:45," he advised. "That will give you enough time to get some coffee, go over the notes, and then be on the air. I'm told they'll hit your interview at about five after. I will text you the location."

"I'll do my makeup at home. If they need to fix it they can." She touched her hair subconsciously. "I'll see you there."

"Good night."

"Good night." She hung up and held the phone in her palm. She looked at the time displayed on the screen and figured she could sleep for forty-five minutes. That would be enough to recharge and refocus.

The Speaker walked back down the steps, having forgotten why she'd gone upstairs. She plopped herself onto the sleek, uncomfortable sofa in the living room. It was contemporary, white, and not meant for relaxation. But in this case, with minutes to sleep, it was perfect.

Felicia set the alarm on her phone, placed the device on the glass coffee table in front of the sofa, and leaned back. She was half sitting, half reclining when she closed her eyes. It felt good to rest.

* * *

Jimmy Ings was standing at the bar of his small kitchen, sipping instant coffee from a Styrofoam cup. He looked over at Sir Spencer, who still sat on the sofa long after the others had left.

Ings singed the tip of his tongue tasting the coffee and winced.

"You could use a small piece of ice to chill the coffee," suggested Sir Spencer. He could tell from the grimace on Ings' face, that the drink was too hot.

"Good idea." Ings turned to grab a piece of ice from the freezer atop his refrigerator. It was an old cooler that didn't have a door mounted ice maker, so Ings kept a torn-open bag of ready-made ice cubes in the freezer. He cracked off a piece and dropped it into his cup where it quickly melted.

"So, James," began the knight, "we have some items to discuss." Ings nodded. "I figured. Money or bombs?" He took another sip and smiled. The ice had apparently worked.

"Both," the knight said. "You haven't paid for the most recent meat shipment. And I need access to the Semtex."

"Not a problem on either end." Ings shook his head. "I've got the cash downstairs. Three thousand, right?"

The knight nodded. The money was cleansed in small amounts so as not to raise suspicion. He didn't like paying taxes. It was not, he believed, among his patriotic duties.

The money, usually cash, was deposited into a foreign account. From the foreign account it would find its way to beef producers, who then delivered the product to the knight's Delaware-based import company, which in turn would provide cash to Ings. He was an unlisted officer of the company. His "salary" was shown as profit from his bar and coffee shop, and he used that cash to "overpay" for the beef.

That money was, in turn, returned to the import company. The company paid its other unlisted officer, Sir Spencer Thomas, who then moved the money to other bank accounts.

It wasn't a classic example of how to launder money but served its purpose by creating a tangled web of cash flow. If nothing more, it would at least complicate any I.R.S. investigations, and give the knight time to react.

He began the scheme within weeks of Swiss bank UBS revealing to the I.R.S. the names of certain account holders. The tax agency had subpoenaed the bank in 2008, seeking the names of 52,000 account holders. After a year-long dance, USB agreed to pay $780 billion in fines and to reveal the names secretly attached to forty-four hundred accounts.

The U.S. government believed the bank was encouraging U.S. citizens to cheat and hide their assets, and the accounts mentioned in the settlement were worth $18 billion. As part of the deal, the U.S. would ask the Swiss government for the specific information regarding those accounts, the Swiss would then ask UBS to release the information within nine months.

The knight was not an American citizen and was not subject to all of his income being taxed, but the money earned from American sources was taxable. The amount was great enough that he needed a way to hide it.

Had UBS not gone soft, Sir Spencer Thomas never would have entered into such an arrangement with a drunk like Ings. However, the bar owner had proven reliable and loyal during the course of their agreement, and Sir Spencer assumed the nice stipend he gave Ings was enough to keep him honest and quiet.

"And the Semtex?"

"Yeah," Ings nodded. "All of it is in the cooler at the meat shop. All boxed up and marked. It's good to go."

The Semtex arrangement had preceded the money laundering. It was, in fact, the use of the meat shop as the storage facility that first gave Sir Spencer the idea to funnel his cash through the failing business. After the theft of the explosives, Sir Spencer needed somewhere to store the goods. He wanted it kept at arm's-length, should anyone of importance ever discover it.

Ings never asked to know the intended use of the explosives. He never questioned Sir Spencer as to why he was in possession of them. Ings had seen enough handshake deals in his bar to know when ignorance was bliss. As long as the money was right, Sir Spencer could have stored dead women or live boys inside that freezer for all he cared.

"So were you planning this all along?" Ings asked.

"Yes and no, James," replied the knight. He stood from the sofa and started walking toward the kitchen bar. "I saw an opportunity to acquire the Semtex and I took it. At the time, I had no use for it."

"I guess we're just lucky then," Ings chuckled.

"Ah, James, my friend," the knight was not laughing, "a Roman philosopher once said, *'Luck is when preparation meets opportunity.'*"

"I like the quote," replied Ings. He'd turned his back to pour some more coffee into the small cup. "But I thought Neal Peart said it."

"No," the knight said, amused. "It was Seneca. Who is Neal Peart?"

Ings was incredulous. "Drummer and lyricist from Rush. You

know...the rock band – Rush? *Tom Sawyer?*"

"*Tom Sawyer* is Mark Twain," Sir Spencer corrected.

"No, the *song.*" Ings sounded as though he couldn't believe he was having this argument.

"Never heard of it," Sir Spencer said smugly. "I'm not acquainted with Rush or Mr. Peart."

"Oh my dear sir," Ings said, mocking Sir Spencer's accent. "You are missing something. *Tom Sawyer* is a political ballad."

"Really?" Sir Spencer was unimpressed.

"*A modern day warrior, mean, mean stride,*" Ings began half singing the lyrics:

"*Today's Tom Sawyer, mean, mean pride.*
Though his mind is not for rent
Don't put him down as arrogant.
His reserve, a quiet defense.
Riding out the day's events."

"I am surprised," offered the knight as he leaned on the bar opposite Ings. "I thought you a bit old to be an aficionado of rock and roll."

"I own a *bar*, Sir Spencer. How can I tend bar without hearing the music of the day over and again? It's been that way for decades. And I appreciate the drums. There's something soothing about a jungle rhythm."

"I underestimate and misjudge you then," conceded Sir Spencer. "But I insist the quote is Roman and not the work of a modern day warrior." The two laughed at the absurdity of their discussion before the knight asked Ings to call him a cab.

"Have it pick me up across the street please," he cautioned. "Give the dispatcher that address." He began inching his way to the door that protected the stairwell. "I will see you later."

"Sounds good, Sir." Ings toasted the knight with his cup and pulled out his cell phone to make the call. He had Diamond Cab saved in his speed dial and hit the button as the knight disappeared down the steps. Before he went to bed, Ings flipped on his computer. At the knight's suggestion, he needed to learn how to build a bomb.

* * *

"Harrold," Matti answered when the gray phone rang. She looked at the clock on the computer screen. 4:15 AM.

"You're there?" the robotic voice asked in surprise.

"I told you I would be." Matti cradled the phone in her neck so she could pull out her notepad and pencil. She popped the ferrule into her mouth and started spinning it between her teeth. It made a soft rattling sound.

"A spy who keeps her word," said the caller, the sarcasm evident even without inflection. "How paradoxical."

"Especially for a non-dude, non-spook," Matti countered in an attempt to lighten the mood. She'd done a poor job of that during the first conversation.

"Touché," droned the asset.

"So how was the meeting?"

"Done with foreplay?" It sounded odd through the cell phone voice distorter. "Straight to the action."

Neither Matti nor the asset spoke for a moment. Then the asset shattered the silence.

"It will be violent. People will die," the soulless admission hung uncomfortably in the air. "The goal, as I understand it, is regime change."

Matti ran her hand through her hair as she took notes. She was both appalled and intrigued. 'Regime change' was a phrase reserved for the deposing of dictators. It was an odd choice of words.

"It's already in the planning stages. It'll happen soon."

"Okay. Can you give me more? Location and method?" Matti pushed.

"There's an exhibit opening tomorrow night."

"Is that where the violence will happen?"

"No," answered the voice. "But I think you should be there."

Matti thought about the request before answering. At first, she was confused, but then recalled reading about George Edwards' new exhibit. The information was in his file.

"What's the benefit?"

"All of the players will be there," the asset responded. "You'll get a chance to see them in person, gauge their personalities a little more thoroughly than you can from reading information in a file."

"And?"

"And what?" *Coy.*

"What is *your* benefit?" Matti knew the asset wanted to gauge her personality a little more thoroughly.

"Why do I have to have a benefit? Why does this have to be about me? It doesn't. I am just a messenger as far as you are concerned."

"Understood, but you came to us. You are working for us. You are helping stop what amounts to a terrorist attack. So what is the hesitation? Why not tell me everything you know?"

"Well, I don't know everything about the plan, so I can't tell you everything. It's not entirely true that I came to you. We're both pawns you know."

"No, I don't know." Matti didn't like the implication.

"You talk about this being a terrorist attack. That's a matter of opinion isn't it? You have to look through the eyes of the group."

"Why?"

"The founding fathers were heroes to us and terrorists to the British. The man convicted of blowing up Pan Am Flight 103 was a terrorist to us, but when the Scottish released him from prison, the Libyans rejoiced in the streets. Eye of the beholder, right?"

"Not sure I agree with that," Matti said, getting a better sense of the ideology. These Daturans thought of themselves as patriots. The reference to the Lockerbie flight was peculiar.

Why choose that example?

Matti typed "Lockerbie + 103+ terror" into her browser and hit search.

"You don't have to agree with me," the asset said matter-of-factly. "But you should be at the exhibit."

Matti was half listening as she quickly scanned the results. *270 dead. Worst airline attack against U.S. prior to 9/11. Abdelbaset al-Megrahi convicted. Abdelbaset al-Megrahi released after serving 8 years. Explosive in cargo hold. Semtex in tape recorder.*

"Can you tell me where and when?" Matti was stalling. She typed in "Semtex". It was a guess. She didn't assume the connection to be Libyans or airplanes.

"I think you can find it."

Matti quickly scanned information about the plastic explosive: *odorless; small amounts were effective; often used or suspected in terror attacks.* She remembered reading at the time that investigators believed the bomb was hidden inside a cassette recorder.

It was dripping with irony, given that the NSA had actually invented the precursor to the first cassettes in the 1960s. No American crypto-spies, no cassette recorders, no such hiding place for a plastic explosive.

"You're using Semtex," she threw it out there.

Just a hunch.

"What did you say?" Even through the altered voice, Matti could hear the surprise.

"Semtex," she repeated. "The plan involves blowing up something with Semtex. Am I right?"

There was silence at first.

"Yes," the asset admitted. "Semtex." There was an audible click and the line went dead.

"Hello?" She asked, not quite believing that the asset had hung up on her. "Hello?" She waited a second or two and then hung up her receiver.

It was late and Matti had been at work for nearly twenty hours. Yet she was invigorated. She'd handled the asset perfectly. Scribbling dashes and lines – shorthand – onto the notepad, Matti considered the conversation.

It was fruitful. She'd pushed the asset to reveal more than anticipated. Maybe she had a talent for this HUMINT stuff after all. Matti wondered why the skill had never translated into her personal life.

She wasn't "needy" professionally or socially. But by trying to make everyone around her happy while adhering to a rigid morality, she sometimes neglected her own desires or missed out on opportunities.

Matti hadn't gone to her senior prom. Instead, she had stayed at home and finished Larry Ragle's *Crime Scene: From Fingerprints to DNA Testing - An Astonishing Inside Look at the Real World of C.S.I.* She'd been hoping it would reveal some sort of knowledge that might help her piece together disparate clues in her mother's death. It hadn't. Neither had a lengthy phone call with the detective on the case nor the fifty-dollar bribe she'd paid the owner of the junkyard where she found the car that hit her mother. Matti refused to accept that she might never know what happened.

There *had* to be an answer. She had to find it, to piece it all together.

Matti put down the mangled pencil and flipped back through her notes. She organized her thoughts and began the business of typing a report for her supervisor.

She'd learned about a clandestine meeting; she'd familiarized herself with all five Daturans while determining that their myopic view of the world was violent and self-aggrandizing; her asset had revealed to her the vague outline of an imminent deadly plot involving untraceable explosives; and she now believed the ultimate goal of that plot was to gain attention for a particular ideology.

Not bad, Harrold!

It would be another long day ahead. Between the lack of sleep and a conspiracy to help unravel, she would have to pace herself. She would need to find a way to connect more of the orphan dots floating around in her mind.

Matti reopened the thick file on her desk and spread out the pictures of the five men. Which of them was the asset? Was it the artist? At first it seemed reasonable to assume that, however, Matti determined it would be too revealing for him to invite her to his own show.

Was it the wealthy politico, Sir Spencer Thomas? He seemingly was the leader of the group. At least that was Matti's impression. He had the heft and experience to coordinate an ideological movement.

But why would he sabotage his own gang?

Maybe it was the handsome philandering professor. Matti presumed, from his dating carousel, that he was an insecure child of a man. He might have been jilted by the group and decided to retaliate. He may have figured that resorting to violence wasn't his style. He was a possibility.

Bill Davidson was possible too, she theorized. He was a popular man who was deeply connected to the Establishment. Fringe-thinking was one thing, she reasoned, but fringe-violence was something else altogether. The A.G. might be the turncoat.

She didn't figure it to be the drunk bar owner. He didn't seem savvy enough to play both sides of the fence. Matti discounted him as the possible asset as quickly as she had the knight and the artist.

She settled on two viable possibilities: Bill Davidson and Art Thistlewood. She would go to the art opening and see them in person. The asset was right; it would help. Matti knew, however, she would first need to convince her boss.

CHAPTER 6

The E. Barrett Prettyman Federal Courthouse was one block west of the U.S. Capitol building, sandwiched between the intersections of Pennsylvania Avenue, 3rd Street, C Street, and Constitution Avenue. Its main entrance faced the spot where Pennsylvania and Constitution merged.

It was a large complex that, to one side, sat on the edge of John Marshall Park. The park, named after the former Chief Justice of the Supreme Court, was part of a major redevelopment of Pennsylvania Avenue in the early 1970s.

In front of the building on Constitution was a beautiful marble statue of Major General George C. Meade, the same Meade for whom the Southern Maryland Army Base was named. That base, Ft. Meade, was home to the NSA.

The power of the statue, however, paled in comparison to the force wielded within the halls of the courthouse. Article III of the U.S. Constitution provided for the establishment of the Supreme Court and all inferior federal courts. It gave them the power to interpret and apply the law.

Unlike federal criminal cases, in which defendants usually went to trial within seventy days of arrest, civil cases could take months or even years to resolve. There was no such promise of a speedy trial in civil disagreements.

Blackmon's case against Speaker Jackson was to be handled with lightning speed. It was a constitutional question that could not be shelved on some future docket. Unfortunately for the judge who received the case, he'd "won" the random drawing used to assign equal caseloads among the district's twelve active judges.

Even before the sun peeked over the dome of the Capitol to the east, the judge was at work. He knew his opinion would draw immediate and loud reaction worldwide. While he would not rule until after both Blackmon's and Jackson's attorneys made their arguments later in the morning, he needed to be ready with questions for both sides.

It was a complicated. Should the Speaker of the House be second in the line of presidential succession ahead of the cabinet officers? On the surface, the answer was yes.

But as the judge looked at previous versions of the Succession Act, and as he read the argument that James Madison made to Pendleton, he understood the argument against the constitutionality of the current Act.

He read with interest the case that Blackmon's team of constitutional lawyers made for the "irreparable harm" that would come to his client and to the nation should Speaker of the House Jackson be allowed to take the oath of office.

"The question might be asked as to why the Plaintiff has not taken the oath of office for the Vice Presidency," the attorneys reasoned in the brief. It was a moot point on two fronts. The line of succession according the Article III, Chapter 1 of United States Code, automatically applied when there was a simultaneous presidential and vice presidential vacancy. Taking the oath subsequent to the president's death would not place the Plaintiff atop the line of succession.

However, the 25th Amendment to the United States Constitution required no such oath. It read: *'Whenever there is a vacancy in the office of the Vice President, the President shall nominate a Vice President who shall take office upon confirmation by a majority vote of both Houses of Congress.'*

The judge reasoned that, according to Blackmon's interpretation of the Constitutional amendment, the vice president automatically assumed power once both houses confirmed the nomination. It was, the judge noted, an unorthodox, but potentially effective argument.

It answered the question why Blackmon had not tried to outmaneuver Jackson with a quickie oath. By his own attorneys' assessments, the oath either didn't matter or wasn't necessary. The key was to stop Jackson from becoming president, not speeding up Blackmon's ascension. The judge thought it was a brilliant strategy.

The response that Jackson's legal team had filed was straightforward and clean, but uninspired. It relied primarily on the current Act signed in 1947 and on existing U.S. Code. It did not make a constitutional argument, given that no mention of the Speaker of the House was made in the document as it related to succession.

The only two places, constitutionally, that discussed succession were the 25th Amendment and Article II Section I. Those both directly named the vice president as successor. Article II Section I did discuss "Officers", but Jackson's lawyers thought it better to avoid that question until arguing the definition before the judge. It was an outwardly simple case that was in fact incredibly complex.

The judge knew that regardless of how he ruled later in the day, the case was headed a few blocks north and east to the Supreme Court. There was no way around it.

* * *

Professor Thistlewood had the feeling that he was being watched. He'd sensed it from the moment he left Cato Street some hours before.

He'd convinced himself that he was just paranoid, assuming anyone would feel that way after having the kind of discussion he'd just had.

But the more he thought about it, the more he was sure that he was only trying to validate his concerns. When he turned left out of the bar's front doors, he was certain that the bum sitting a block away had snapped a picture of him. There was no flash, but as Thistlewood glanced over his shoulder and to his right, he caught the glimpse of something shiny hidden underneath the man's coat.

When he got into the taxi, he was sure that the black sedan three cars back was following him to wherever he was headed. Thistlewood told the cab driver to take him to his office on campus rather than to his apartment. He'd be safer there, he thought. Plus, he had less than four hours until his 7 A.M. lecture.

Once in his office, he sat at his desk looking pensively out the window, trying to identify the sixth Daturan.

There were seventeen possibilities, including Speaker of the House Felicia Jackson and Secretary of Veterans Affairs John Blackmon. Thistlewood had no clue as to who their coconspirator might be.

He was relieved to know, however, that their efforts would be rewarded. For quite some time he had been unsure how any action by their small band could be effective on a large scale. If they had an insider on their team, the game was changed. He could feel his heart beating with excitement. Or maybe it was nerves. Either way, Thistlewood felt alive.

He took a deep breath and exhaled, looking to the north end of the Quad. Below, he could see the crisscrossing asphalt paths that split the grass along the stretch of green space. His eyes moved from left to right and back, looking for anything unusual. It was empty, except for the occasional custodian. The sun was just coming up and it was still hard to make out shapes.

Then he saw it. Next to a large oak, something was moving.

His eyes focused and he could tell the shape behind the tree, on a bench, was human. It was someone in dark clothing, trying to hide behind the trunk of the massive tree. The figure moved out from its position two or three times, and the professor thought he caught the reflection of light flickering toward the top of the figure.

Binoculars!

Thistlewood's heart skipped a beat and he could feel the blood pumping in his neck. He sunk down in his chair and leaned back out of sight of the window.

His breath was quickening and getting shallow as he slid onto the floor. On all fours he crawled over to the door on the right side of the office. From a kneeling position, he reached up with his right arm to flip the light switch. He snagged the top of the switch with his middle finger and pulled down, cutting the light.

Thistlewood let out another deep breath and sat on the floor with his back against the door. He could feel the sweat beading on his forehead and on the back of his neck. He rubbed his temples with his hands.

Thistlewood leaned forward onto his knees and crawled over to the window. When he reached the sill he gripped it lightly with his fingers and pulled himself up. He rose just high enough to see the spot where the figure was hiding. He pulled the tree and bench into focus. Nothing. Thistlewood rubbed his eyes with his left hand and looked again. Still nothing. And then he heard rapping behind him. Someone was at his door. It nearly stopped his heart.

Who was it? Was the figure confronting him? Was he about to be arrested?

Another bang on the door. Three hard knocks.

"Who is it?" Thistlewood was still on the ground next to his window. He felt the sweat roll from his temple to the side of his jaw and rubbed it dry with a shrug of his shoulder.

"It's George."

George Edwards? What was he doing here?

"Uh," Thistlewood struggled to his feet, "okay. Hang on, George. I'm coming."

The professor stepped to the other side of the room and flipped up the light switch before turning the lock and opening the door. The fluorescents were still flickering when Edwards stepped into the office.

"Are you... sweating?" Edwards looked at Thistlewood with a puzzled expression

"A little," Thistlewood admitted. He wiped his forehead with his fingers and extended his arm to guide Edwards to the chair across from his desk. He didn't want to explain his appearance. "Why are you here so early? The sun's just coming up."

"I have something I need to discuss with you." Edwards crossed his legs and placed both hands flat on the arms of the chair.

"Okay, go ahead," Thistlewood said, walking around the desk to his chair and taking a seat. "What is it?"

"I think we're being followed."

"Why?" Thistlewood shifted in his seat, leaning in toward Edwards.

"I don't know if you saw it," Edwards was looking out the window as he talked, "but as we left Cato Street this morning, I think we were being watched."

"I know," Thistlewood said, surprising George. "The bum."

Edwards looked relieved. "You saw that too?" He smiled

uncomfortably at the professor. "I thought maybe I was going crazy, you know? Like I am suddenly getting paranoid."

"That's why I'm sitting here in a cold sweat, George." Thistlewood ran his hand along the back of neck, feeling the cool dampness of his skin underneath his hair. "I thought I saw somebody out in the Quad."

"What do you mean?"

"I was here in my office with the light on, looking out the window there." Thistlewood pointed to his left. "I saw a figure sitting on a bench behind that oak tree in the dark."

The sun had risen enough that the tree was now clearly visible. The grass on the quad appeared dewy. There were small groups of students starting to cross the paths on their way to early classes.

"I think he had binoculars."

"So what'd you do?" Edwards looked back at Thistlewood, who was now gazing blankly out the window.

"I turned out the light and tried to get a better look at the guy." It was evident from his voice that the professor was still on edge. "Did you see him?"

"No." Thistlewood snapped out his trance and turned back to Edwards. "He was gone. And then you knocked."

"So how do we handle this? Should we start avoiding each other? I mean, we have my opening tonight. Should we skip it?"

"I don't think so," Thistlewood said, shaking his head. "If we are being followed, we don't want them to know we suspect it, right? So we should go about doing what we do. But we do need to be more careful about where we talk about things."

"So you'll be at the exhibit tonight?"

Thistlewood thought that Edwards sounded like a son looking for Dad's approval. "Of course," he smiled. "I wouldn't miss it."

"And afterward?"

"Afterward I take a visit to my friend's family business," Thistlewood said. "When will you get there?"

"That depends," replied Edwards. "If the casket is ready and available, then it'll be pretty quick. If it's not ready, then we may have some problems to work out."

"Let's hope it's ready."

"Let's hope," agreed Edwards.

"I think I should send Sir Spencer a heads up about being watched, don't you agree?" "I don't know," Edwards cautioned. "We don't know who is watching us. What if we're wrong?"

"*I* think we're right," Thistlewood insisted emphatically. "We both suspected the guy outside the bar, I believe I was followed in a car too, and then there's the man outside with the binoculars. We need to inform the rest of the group. We should be prepared to avoid any surveillance. There's nothing wrong with a little paranoia."

"Yeah," Edwards shrugged. "You're right. I can text Sir Spencer a coded message to let him know and he—"

"No," Thistlewood cut him off. "I'll do it. You worry about the opening tonight and what you need to do afterward. The whole deal hinges on what you do."

"Okay, you win."

"I've got a class at seven. I'll see you tonight, okay?" Thistlewood stood from his chair and pulled a thick binder from the desk, tucking it under his arm.

"Sounds good." Edwards stood as well. "By the way, I love the piece on the wall there." He pointed to the work directly behind the desk as he walked with Thistlewood out of the office.

"Yeah?" Thistlewood laughed. "I know the artist. I could probably get you a deal." He patted Edwards on the back and the two went in opposite directions down the hallway.

Neither of them turned around as they went their separate ways, but Thistlewood was troubled as he walked to class. Something was not right with his friend George Edwards.

Edwards didn't seem particularly bothered by the idea that someone might be following them. It was as though he'd confessed his suspicions to gauge the professor's response.

Thistlewood's suspicions were further tweaked by Edwards' desire to not share the development with their cohorts. There was no reasonable explanation for that, as far as Thistlewood was concerned.

He considered how envy might be clouding his judgment. He knew that Edwards' burgeoning relationship with the knight was a sore point, and he was self-aware enough to recognize it.

The professor couldn't control his own puerile coping mechanisms, much like he couldn't control his pubescent libido.

Thistlewood knew he was an emotional man. The same thing that made him a passionate lover of politics and women, of art and wine, also made him unable to dispassionately separate himself from reality and fiction. He walked into his classroom thinking that he was being unfair to so quickly judge his friend.

In front of him there was a classroom full of students ready to learn more about the Separation of Powers. He needed to refocus. It wouldn't be easy.

* * *

"Good morning to you, Joe," said Speaker of the House Felicia Jackson. She was on her fourth live interview. In the previous three, she stayed on message. She was retaking control of the debate.

Felicia was sitting in a room outfitted for remote television interviews. In front of her was a television camera with a small monitor directly underneath the lens. She could see herself and the anchor with whom she was speaking by looking just beneath the camera.

Behind her was a large oak bookshelf containing a handful of books and a potted plant. The bookshelf sat over her right shoulder, screen left. To the right of the screen there was a large corn plant, which added some depth and color. The lighting was excellent. The Speaker looked fresh and awake.

She was wearing a slate colored sateen suit. The slight shine of the fabric caught the lighting of the studio in just the right way. The long lapels of the jacket blended seamlessly into the straight lines of her pencil skirt. It was flattering to her thin figure. She appeared conservative and strong, chic and feminine.

A strand of small, cultured Mikimoto pearls hung around her neck. She'd debated the jewelry and decided a classic, understated accessory was good. Her matching pearl earrings were hidden behind her black hair, which fell onto the tops of her shoulders.

She wore foundation, plum lipstick, and soft gray eye shadow. The camera was high-definition, and her media consultants had taught her not to overdo the makeup in HD. Less was more. They suggested she needed just enough to prevent shine.

It didn't hurt that Felicia Jackson had a fine plastic surgeon who'd masterfully erased the stress of aging. Her face hinted at wisdom but preserved the youthful beauty she'd long relied upon as a political ice breaker. Viewers at home never would have guessed she'd slept only forty-five minutes since the president's death.

"Madam Speaker," the newsman said in an incredibly affected anchor voice, his delivery nasal and pompous-sounding, "we all know Secretary Blackmon was confirmed by both the senate and by the legislative body you lead. So you, yourself, are okay with him becoming vice president. Why not step aside and allow him to become president? Why put the country through an extended, painful court case? Why not do what's best for a grieving country and allow it to move forward?" It was more a statement followed by a series of opinions than it was a question. The Speaker handled it with aplomb.

"Joe, that's more than one question to answer," she laughed and looked down to the right before answering. It was a tic she'd adopted from former President Barack Obama, who always affected the same reaction to questions he did not like. "But I will be happy to address each one," she continued, her smile intact. "As for 'stepping aside' that's not really a decision for me to make. As a believer in our constitution and U.S. Code, I am required to follow the laws set forth by my predecessors. I would be derelict to ignore them."

"You also asked," she added, the smile waning, "why I would put the country through a painful court case. I am not the one who filed the injunction. That question might be better suited for Secretary Blackmon. Though I suggest it's a question laced with opinion, and probably not fair to ask him either."

"And finally," she said, her eyes bright and knowing, "without repeating your question, I will tell you that I *am* helping our great nation move forward. My fantastic team, along with those of Secretary Blackmon and President Foreman, are in constant contact. We are doing the business of the people, and while we grieve our loss, our government is in good hands."

"Okay, Madam Speaker," Joe said, placing his hands on the news desk and leaning in, "but you didn't answer my question as to why you oppose the Secretary's claim to the presidency, given that the House and the Senate voted in favor of his confirmation. I mean, seriously, Madam Speaker, we're talking about a technicality here. Had President Foreman lived twelve more hours, Secretary Blackmon would have been sworn in, right?" He smirked and then sat back to await her answer.

Felicia kept her cool despite wanting to jump through the screen and backhand the smug, blow dried goober of man. "Actually, Joe, you *didn't* ask me that question. You merely stated it as fact without asking me to respond. Instead you asked me three other questions which I answered directly and succinctly. Once again, you have stated what you believe to be the facts, and have asked me an unrelated question."

The Speaker paused to gauge whether or not the anchor would interrupt her. When he didn't, she continued. "If President Foreman were still alive, we wouldn't be having a conversation about anyone assuming the office."

"So let's shift gears slightly," the anchor countered, failing to press the point. "Why would you make a better president than Secretary Blackmon?"

"Wow, Joe," her eyes widened as she considered the question. "That's a surprisingly inappropriate question. But," she reasoned, "it's irrelevant. My colleague and I are not running for office. We are on the same team. The question is who, constitutionally, should take the oath. It's a legal question and not a political one. I think the American people feel the same way. I don't presume to know the collective thought of our citizens, but I do know that President Foreman was beloved. I do know he is missed. Questions about who should succeed him are best left to the courts."

"Point taken, Madam Speaker," the anchor acknowledged. "But I do want to know why the American people should feel comfortable with you at the helm. What can you do to assure them that you are qualified?"

Again, the Speaker felt the bile rise in her throat, sickened by his persistence on this point. He wanted her to bash Blackmon. He was trying to goad her into saying something inflammatory. She would not oblige.

"Qualified?" She looked down and laughed again. "That's the easiest question you've asked me today, Joe."

"How is that?" His eyebrows furrowed and he pursed his lips.

"I am a natural born citizen of the United States. I've lived here for at least fourteen years. I'm at least 35 years old, though I beg you, Joe, to not press me on my exact age." She smiled as she ratted off the presidential qualifications as they were listed in Article II Section I of the constitution.

"All right, very good, Madam Speaker," the anchor conceded. "If you don't want to answer my questions then..." He was about to end the interview when Felicia determined she'd had enough of his rude asides.

"Wait a minute, Joe," she interrupted. "What questions have I failed to answer?"

"You don't want to tell the American people why you're a better fit for the office," he stated. "You can't tell us why you're qualified."

His nasality was incredibly annoying to the Speaker. She had a nearly overwhelming urge to shove an endoscope up his nose and clean him out without the use of anesthetics.

"Joe," her tone softened, "maybe your earpiece is malfunctioning and you can't hear me. Can you hear me, Joe?"

"Yes, Madame Speaker, I can hear you." His smug grin had disappeared.

"Good," she leaned to the camera and slowed the cadence of her speech as though she were speaking to someone who could not easily follow English. "My quali-fi-ca-tions and those of Se-cre-tary Black-mon, a-side from our a-ges and na-tion-al-i-ty are not at is-sue. This is a con-sti-tu-tion-al ques-tion. I know the American people agree with me on this. We are not campaigning, Joe. We are preserving the continuity of our government."

"Thank you for the civics lesson, Madam Speaker." The anchor rolled his eyes on camera and then turned to face another camera in his studio. Felicia was no longer on camera when he thanked her for taking the time to appear on the show. "Next on the program this morning, we will hear from the other politician at the center of this debate, Secretary of Veterans Affairs John Blackmon."

The Speaker glanced down at the monitor beneath the camera to assure she was no longer on camera and summoned her Chief of Staff with a wave.

"Is this mic off for now?" she asked nobody in particular. "How long before the next interview and how many more do we have?"

"Five minutes before our next and last interview," replied the aide. Someone behind the camera informed the Speaker the microphone was off.

"Two things," she said, pointing at the Chief of Staff as she spoke. Her voice was barely above a whisper but she may as well have been screaming. Her hand was pressed against her lapel to dampen the microphone's ability to pick up her voice, just in case.

"One," she instructed, her facing reddening, "I will not do another interview with that man. Never! Do not book me. Do not ask me. I can handle tough questions. I can handle fair questions. That was a hose job. Understood?"

The chief nodded and whispered, "Yes." He took a pen to the scheduling sheet he was cradling and made a note of her directive.

"Two," she continued with her finger just inches from his face. "I thought I told you to make sure we knew who was getting Blackmon. You didn't give me that information. Not good. Are we recording him so we can respond to his points if necessary?"

"Yes," replied the chief. "We're recording the entirety of all of the morning shows. We'll have copies of everything. I've told staff to transcribe your interviews and any conducted with Blackmon." He stepped back out of range of her finger.

She dropped her hand to her side and turned to look at herself in the monitor underneath the camera. It helped her primp between segments. A makeup person was standing by to refresh the powder on her forehead, nose, and cheeks.

"C'mon man," she said without turning back to the chief. "This is politicking one-oh-one. You know this. If you can't keep up, I need you to tell me now. Can you keep up? Is this too much?"

"No," he responded. "I mean, yes I can keep up. No it's not too much."

"Good, then," she replied and pressed her lips together. "Turn my mic back on please. Let's do this last interview and move on with the day."

* * *

"Harrold, this is good." The supervisor was leaning back in his chair with his left leg crossed over his right. He was reading the report she'd generated from her phone interviews with the asset. "What made you assume the mechanism is Semtex?" He peeked over the top of the document.

"It's there in the report, sir," she half nodded toward it. "I detailed the conversation."

"Yes," he leaned forward and uncrossed his leg, his tone agitated and almost whiny, "but what made you draw the conclusion? It's quite a leap."

"That's somewhat complicated, sir."

"Try me." He dropped the paper onto the desk and squared himself to face Matti.

"I began by making certain assumptions," she exhaled. "First, the asset was clear people *would* die. That's a very careful choice of words. So that rules out, in my mind, hostage situations or anything that involves the possibility of targeted survivors."

"Go on..."

"Then there was the short rant about patriotism and terrorism. I thought that was somewhat revealing in that terrorists tend to use high powered weapons and/or explosives. There is the possibility of poison or gas, as was the 1995 case with the AUM Shinrikyo attack on the Tokyo subway. They used sarin in that case." *The pieces were fitting together.*

Matti sucked in another breath and continued. "But the mention of the bombing of Pan Am flight 103 was an unusual reference point, so I quickly checked information on that attack. I found the suspected explosive used was Semtex." She gauged her supervisor's expression. It was blank almost, as though he were still processing what she'd said.

"Hmmph," he leaned back and pulled the papers from the desk. "Interesting."

She could tell he wasn't going to give her any additional credit. Matti drew the conclusion he was actually *disappointed* in her ability to exceed his expectations.

"Is there anything you did not include in the report?"

"Yes." Matti cleared her throat. "He invited me to an art exhibit opening tonight."

"What do you mean?" He dropped the papers again and his eyes narrowed.

"As you know, one of the conspirators is an artist. He has an opening tonight," she sat up straight, her hands folded in her lap. "The asset suggested I might be better able to assess the threat by attending the event. All of the players are planning to attend."

"How would this help you?"

"This is HUMINT," she reasoned. "I am better off analyzing what the asset reveals about the plot if I'm able to observe the conspirators' interactions with one another."

"And they can observe you."

"I suppose," she conceded.

She watched him think about the pros and cons of the proposal. Were the potential gains mitigated by the possible losses? He folded his arms and swiveled in his chair and didn't speak for several minutes.

"Okay," he nodded. "For observation only. Do not engage the subjects."

"Yes sir." Matti tried to conceal her excitement, resisting the smile creeping from her lips.

"Before you go," the supervisor cautioned, "get some sleep. Buy a dress. You look like hell."

"Yes sir," she said, offended at his insensitivity but too pleased with his decision to let it sting. She stood and thanked him again before leaving.

As soon as she'd shut the door behind her, the supervisor was on his secured line dialing a series of numbers. He tapped his hand on the desk as he awaited an answer.

The supervisor was hurried. There were developments. There were arrangements to make.

* * *

Bill Davidson wasn't much for watching television. While he was often on the tube, he rarely found the time or inclination to participate as a viewer. But when he received a "Breaking News Alert" email from the *New York Times*, he decided to find the nearest set and watch the developments. It happened to be inside the lobby of the Capital Hilton, two blocks from the White House.

Given the hotel's proximity to the seats of power in central

Washington, D.C, Davidson had imbibed frequently at the Statler Lounge inside the hotel. He loved its private, orange curtained seating areas. The bar was a tribute to the hotel's original name, The Statler Hotel. It was built in 1943 and was historically significant in that it was one of the few hotels built during World War II.

He walked past the doorman and straight to the television mounted on the wall near the concierge. The volume was low, but he could hear it as he approached.

"The District Court has sided with Secretary Blackmon's case and has granted the injunction," explained the reporter standing outside the Perryman Courthouse. *"This means that Speaker of the House Felicia Jackson is stopped from taking the presidential oath. Her team has already responded with an appeal. It is a foregone conclusion this is headed for the Supreme Court, should the justices agree to hear the arguments. It is most likely they will, given the constitutional implications on each side of this case."*

Davidson checked his phone again. It was buzzing against his hip. Another "Breaking News Alert". This one was from the "editors of *PlausibleDeniability.info*" and also reported the District Court's ruling. He looked back at the television.

"We've also learned," the reporter said breathlessly, lending to the sense of urgency he was trying to manufacture, *"President Foreman will lie in state in the Capitol Rotunda beginning tomorrow afternoon until his burial the following day. His memorial service will be that evening. The public will have a chance to pay their respects after the memorial."*

That doesn't give us much time, Davidson thought. They would need to accomplish all of their objectives within one day. It seemed impossible. He felt a sense of relief. Maybe they wouldn't have to go through with it.

He turned to leave the hotel and was about to pull his journal from his jacket pocket when he was stopped cold, startled to see Sir Spencer Thomas standing in his path, dressed in a Brioni navy and black Birdseye suit. The drape was flawless. He wore a bright yellow silk pocket square and a Robert Talbott maize and blue striped beige twill dress shirt. His shoes were a light brown, Barker Black brand Ostrich Cap Toe. It was the knight's casual look.

If clothes made the man, then Sir Spencer was well made. He

spared no cost to present himself as the well-heeled quasi-aristocrat his ancestry bestowed upon him.

From five thousand dollar custom suits, to thousand dollar pairs of shoes, and ten thousand dollar watches, he bought whatever he liked. People noticed. Kings and queens, prime ministers and presidents saw it. Even a former attorney general recognized the knight's style.

"Sir Spencer?" Davidson said in puzzlement at what he thought was a coincidence. "What are you doing here?"

"I'm here to see you, my good man," he winked. "We have many things to discuss and not much time in which to discuss them."

He stepped to Davidson and placed his arm around the A.G.'s shoulders. His massive right hand guided Davidson as a ballroom dancer would lead his partner.

"What do we need to discuss?" Davidson asked, sensing something untoward in the knight's tone and demeanor. Against the woody musk of the knight's Bois Rouge cologne, he resisted slightly.

"The Capital City Club and Spa are here in the hotel," the knight explained. "I am part of what they call their 'Presidential Wellness Plan'. Between you and me, it is just a fancy name for their most expensive membership. I play along and act as though I'm impressed with their astounding commitment to *my* health. It's quite exclusive and relaxing for a hotel spa. Rather convenient. I have a locker here. They have a wonderful sauna." The knight was still guiding Davidson toward the spa entrance. "I'd be delighted to have you join me."

"Oh, I couldn't," Davidson said. He didn't understand he had no choice.

"No, Bill," Sir Spencer stopped walking. He stood next to Davidson and leaned in to his ear. "I insist," he said. "This will be good for us. You and I will benefit from some time together. Just you and me, good man. No interruptions. I think we'll be able to clarify our positions."

Davidson said nothing.

"And I have to tell you, Bill," offered Sir Spencer, "the sauna here is a wonder. It will clear your head, I assure you."

His cheer was disconcerting to Davidson It reminded him of the kiss a mafia don offered a man whose execution he'd already ordered. Davidson resigned himself to the inevitability of the sauna and nodded.

CHAPTER 7

The asset was conflicted. Cooperation with the government was essential to personal survival, but every time the asset thought about the group and what would happen to them, the feeling of guilt was almost overwhelming. The depth of the betrayal was bottomless. The men had bared their souls and agreed to share the risk for what they believed was a high calling. And even if there was reluctance to employ violence, all of the Daturans understood it was a means to an end. The death of a few was a fair price for the freedom of many.

The asset sat in a booth at Androphy's Delicatessen, hands cupped around the warm, wide ceramic mug on the table. It was a glazed white mug with 'Androphy's' scrolled across the face in brown cursive writing. It was the kind of lettering one might find on an old baseball pennant.

On the plate next to the mug were the crumbs from a toasted 'everything' bagel with butter and a crumpled paper napkin. The asset's attention was focused upward and across the restaurant to a large flat screen television along one of the walls opposite the succession of booths. The volume was turned down, but the closed captioning was on, revealing the on-screen conversation in black rows featuring white lettering. The letters appeared as if typed onto the screen, rolled up a row, and then disappeared as new words appeared beneath them. It wasn't the optimal way to watch television, but it served its purpose.

His phone rang.

"Yes?" the asset said softly and waited for the voice on the other end to respond. "No, I'm not busy at the moment." *As if that mattered.*

A waiter came over and motioned to the plate on the table. He didn't want to interrupt the phone call, but wanted to remain attentive to his customer. When the asset nodded, the waiter removed the plate and walked off toward the kitchen.

"What about the analyst? Does she know we're communicating?" That part of the equation hadn't added up yet. "Risky, isn't it?" The asset was told not to ask questions above pay grade. Given the pay was nothing, the asset had no room for interrogatives

"Fine," the asset huffed. "I'll head over there in a minute and I'll check in later."

The waiter was back again. He had the check ready. "Can I get you anything else?"

"Yes, actually. I'll take a fill up on the coffee. And toast, please."

"Sure." The waiter took out his pen and scribbled on the check. "We have white, wheat, sourdough, rye…" He trailed off as though the list was longer, but that he didn't want to make the effort to recite it.

"Wheat is good. Two pieces please, butter on both."

The waiter nodded and scurried back to the kitchen to place the order. The asset lifted the mug and drank what was left of the coffee. It had cooled but wasn't cold. He glanced around the restaurant. There were young couples laughing together between bites of granola and fruit. Old men sat alone with newspapers and bowls of oatmeal. Some tables paired business-types in suits. They drank coffee and ate egg whites with Canadian bacon on the side. They did not know of the psyche-altering blitzkrieg that awaited them. The asset could have told them, and imagined running from table to table announcing the plot.

"What do you mean terrorists?" they would ask.

"How could this happen?" they would question.

"But I thought the government had us protected!" they would assume.

"Oh no," the asset would tell them. "The government isn't protecting you. It's protecting itself." The asset laughed at their naiveté and how their view of the world would shatter as they learned a table at a time, what civilization was really about. The asset knew the secrets of powerful men and the crooked thrones upon which they sat.

"Excuse me?" The waiter was standing next to the table again. He noticed the asset was deep in thought. "Hello?" He waved his hand in front of the asset's face.

"Yes?" The asset snapped to attention, blinking and then turning to look up at him.

"Your toast," the waiter used his left hand to place the plate in front of the customer. He then poured more coffee with his right. "Is everything okay?"

"I'm good," the asset said, pulling a new napkin from the stainless steel dispenser on the table. "Thanks."

"Okay then." The waiter thanked his customer again, placed the check on the edge of the table upside down, and floated off to another guest.

* * *

Felicia Jackson's Capitol Hill suite was in an unmarked corridor between Statuary Hall and the Rotunda. She was standing just outside of the offices on the balcony overlooking the National Mall, her eyes aimed west toward the Washington Monument. It was a spectacular view. She often used the outdoor space to entertain small groups of colleagues or lobbyists. The location usually made for great conversation, but not as she listened to her attorneys explaining their morning loss in district court.

"This is a nightmare!" She would not turn to face the men as she stood, arms folded, with her back to them.

They didn't respond. After explaining to her that the granting of the injunction was expected, that they'd planned an appeal, that the case was headed to the high court, and that none of this was anything about which to worry, they stayed quiet and listened.

She finally turned to face them. "I am *this* close," she said, holding up her hand and pinching her thumb and index finger together. "Do you know only one Speaker of the House has ever become president? Did you know that? I bet you didn't. Only one. James Polk. Do you know why? Because *he* didn't have to rely on lawyers."The Speaker began pacing with her arms folded. She was looking at her feet as she walked. She would not look the attorneys in the eyes.

"I bet you Joe whatever-his-name-is, that news guy from this morning, is rejoicing. I'm going to guess he has a copy of the ruling in one hand and is masturbating into it with the other." She stopped pacing momentarily and eyeballed the lawyers. "Really!" She was pacing again now, and simulated manual stimulation her left hand. She looked like was shooting craps.

One of the attorneys snickered. It was incredibly amusing to hear the Speaker of the House resort to masturbatory humor. He immediately regretted his lack of judgment and lost the smile on his face.

"Is that funny?" She walked up to the lawyer and got inches from his face. He was taller than her, but she was commanding his space and he shrank. "It's not funny to me! It's embarrassing. We have the U.S. freaking Constitution on our side. We have U.S. Code on our side. We have the 1947 Act of Succession on our side. And *you* can't win. Why is that?"

She backed off of the attorney far enough to look at the group as a whole.

"You, the one in my office last night," she pointed at the young attorney who'd explained the case to her the previous evening, "you seem smart. You're balding a little early for someone so young, but you're knowledgeable, so explain this to me." She was as mean as a snake when she felt cornered, and her rattle was often followed with a bite.

"It's not so much that we lost, Madam Speaker," he began, "it's that they won."

"Oh good lord!" Felicia put her hands on her hips and threw her head back. "Are you kidding me?"

"No," he continued, but not before he self-consciously touched the back of his head with his hand. "There is a difference."

"Go ahead," she said, dramatically dropping her chin and looking directly at the young lawyer.

"This is a constitutional question, pure and simple. The judge is going to err on the side of caution," he spoke calmly, charming the snake. "We knew, as I tried to explain last night, that this would happen. If for some crazy, unforeseen reason we'd won this morning, Blackmon's attorneys would have filed an emergency motion and appeal as we did. We know the Supreme Court ultimately will hear the argument. We've lost nothing."

Felicia opened her eyes to look at the attorney. She took in a deep breath and then exhaled again slowly.

"I still don't like it," she said, her tone slightly less poisonous. She rubbed her neck, slipping the fingers of both hands beneath her hair. "I still think you guys are full of it."

Tired of standing outside, she ushered the team back inside and followed them into the suite.

"You men do whatever it is you need to do," she said without turning around. "I have business to attend to."

The men continued out of the office and past the statue of Stephen F. Austin into the hall. Felicia walked alone into her private office. She shut the doors behind her and locked them. Her hands stayed on the door while she thought about the exchange she'd just had with the lawyers. She hated lawyers.

She walked over to the loveseat that framed one end of the room and sat. Whether it was the stress, the anxiety, or the loss of a president, she wasn't sure, but as she sat there, tears welled in her eyes. They were followed by a thick, dry, painful lump at the base of her throat. Felicia held it in as her lips and chin quivered. It was all too much. The tears poured down her cheeks as she buried her face in her hands. She was weeping and shaking uncontrollably.

An aide knocked on the door and tried the handle. "Are you okay, Madam Speaker?"

"Yes," she sobbed. "I'm fine." As quickly as the emotions had overcome her, they receded. She felt purged.

Felicia stood and puffed out her cheeks then laughed at herself. She was a mess. She walked to her desk and pulled some tissues from a box, then dabbed the corners of her eyes and her nose.

A woman in power had such an unfair balance to maintain. Toughness and femininity were contrary attributes; compassion and leadership were difficult to manage simultaneously

Publicly she chose the tough, impervious persona, which cost her both politically and personally. Many of the friends she accumulated on her way to the top abandoned her when they found her methods too prickly.

Was it too late to swing the pendulum the other direction? Regardless of the outcome of the court case and the presidency, she wondered if it was possible. Could she soften her image and still lead effectively?

Felicia considered the viability of this as she wiped the mascara from her face. She needed to blow her nose, but kept sniffling instead. She laughed at herself. The thought of an anchorman masturbating to a court filing really *was* funny.

* * *

The air in the sauna stung Bill Davidson's nostrils. The combination of simmering birch leaf and eucalyptus was almost overpowering, but the odor wasn't the real cause of his discomfort.

"You may know, Bill," Sir Spencer started amiably, "the Finnish have a saying about the sauna."

"What is that?" Davidson said, not at all interested in the answer.

"They say," he continued, "and this is loosely translated, '*If drink, tar, or sauna cannot help you, then the illness is fatal.*" The knight laughed. Davidson smiled weakly.

The two men had the sauna to themselves. Sir Spencer had arranged it that way. They both sat on thick cotton towels, and Davidson also had a towel wrapped around his waist. Sir Spencer was nude; unclothed as much for the comfort of it as much as it was to disarm Davidson.

"Let's talk plot," the knight said, not wasting any more time. "I get the impression from you, Bill, you're uneasy about our plans. Am I wrong about this?"

"No," Davidson said honestly, "you're not wrong. I am uncomfortable with violence."

"Why is that, good man?" The knight knew the answer but asked regardless.

"I don't like the idea of killing fellow Americans." Davidson's jaw was clenched as if it were wired shut when he spoke.

"Bill," the knight clapped his hands together mockingly, "I applaud your sanctimoniousness. Really, good man, it is honorable.

But you and I both know that what those in power choose to call terrorism is in fact the only effective weapon of the weak against the strong."

"Didn't Gaddafi say that?" Davidson asked. "Are you quoting Muammar Gaddafi?"

"Think of the reward, Bill," Sir Spencer said. "You help me and I help you. Very rarely does somebody get two shots in the cabinet. James Baker, Caspar Weinberger, Elizabeth Dole... you'd be joining elite company."

"Who are you working for, Spencer?"

"For whom am I working?" He leaned back. "The American People, Bill. I am working on behalf of the American people."

"Is it the Saudis?" Davidson paused. "The Iranians?"

"Bill, before you go and do anything rash, I ask you this: What did you *think* was going to happen? How did you *think* we would be able to affect change? You cannot be that naïve, my good man. I refuse to entertain that notion. We all knew from the beginning that violence could spring from the well."

Davidson shifted his weight on the towel and placed his hands palm down on the cotton. His elbows were locked and his body language spoke volumes.

"Just think about it, Bill." Sir Spencer stood and stretched languidly. "I just want you to take some time alone and think. No need to be so rash. We've spent years planning for this and you seem ready to disregard all of that work over some misplaced morality." The knight moved to the door and put his hand on the carved wooden handle. "You have until morning to decide. I need the information you can provide ahead of everyone else, otherwise it becomes too complicated. We don't need any additional complications. You give to me the little bit of innocuous factual information I want and I give back to you the power and prestige you covet."

The knight lowered his voice. "We both know, William, that you, my good man, are a self-loathing hypocrite. Anyone can see it if they choose to look. You never lived up to your father's billing. You were essentially an impotent member of the cabinet. Despite the rank afforded your position and your public, radical grandstanding, your president never lent you his ear. He chose you because you were a pedigreed, biracial lawyer who satisfied the melting pot. No more cable appearances, during which you offer meaningless opinions. I can take you from the chattering class to the ruling class. I know you haven't lost your desire for power, Bill. You know you haven't lost that taste," he stepped over to Davidson and patted his knee. "But it is up to you. I'll be in touch."

Sir Spencer left his towel on the wooden bench and walked out of the sauna naked. The door slammed behind him. Davidson sat alone in the dry heat knowing that everything the knight had said was true. Every last, painful word was on target.

He inhaled the sauna fumes and flinched, questioning how he had allowed himself to become entangled in a treasonous, violent plot. Was he making an even bigger mistake by trying to undo what was already done?

It was more than 200 degrees in the sauna, but as Davidson thought about all of the eventualities he faced because of his shortsightedness, he shivered.

He shifted his weight to stand when the door suddenly opened again. He stopped his forward momentum and sat back, his attention squarely on the door.

"Bill, are you here?" It was a woman's voice.

Davidson was momentarily confused. He recognized the voice, but he couldn't process quickly why she was there in the sauna.

"What are you doing here?" He stood up, holding his towel around his waist to ensure it didn't fall.

"Well, hello to you to sir!" She eased over to him, surprised at his modesty. "I'm a member here." She dropped her own towel, revealing her thin, deliciously pale body. The diamond in her navel sparkled. Her auburn hair was pulled back in a ponytail.

"O-okay," Davidson stammered and smacked his bridge. She leaned into him, wiggling her body between his knees. "But how did you know I was here?"

"I saw you walk in here with that big, heavy dude. I was getting ready to go for a swim, but I waited. When he left, I thought I'd pop in and surprise you." She tickled both sides of his chest with her fingernails. The temperature in the room was dramatically hotter for Davidson.

"You surprised me."

"So how was your meeting last night?"

"Long."

"Did you enjoy catching up with your friends?" She moved from between his legs and sat on the bench next to him. "We didn't get to talk much when you got back to the hotel," she giggled. "After you showered, we were otherwise engaged."

"Aren't you worried someone will walk in and see you?" "No. Are you?"

"A little," he admitted. Davidson was not nearly as comfortable with his physique or his sexuality as she seemed to be. "You left before I woke up."

"I had things to do. You know, Mr. Davidson, you're not the only one with a busy agenda and clandestine meetings." She rubbed her left hand across his head, dragging her nails on his scalp.

"So regular time tonight? At The Mayflower?" She asked, leaning on a towel with her palms flat against the bench.

"A little later." He covered her right hand with his left. "I have a gallery opening to attend."

"Oh, your artist friend, right? I forgot about that. You mentioned it before."

They sat quietly for moment and then the door swung open. Davidson jumped and moved his hand into his lap. She was unaffected.

"Oh my," said Sir Spencer. He had draped a new towel around his waist and seemed embarrassed at the scene in front of him. "My apologies, young lady. Bill, I am dreadfully sorry."

"It's okay." She smiled at Sir Spencer, almost flattered by the old man's inability to avert his eyes. Davidson noticed this and felt a rush of anger.

"What do you want?" he asked, glaring at the knight.

"That's my towel." He pointed to the towel on which the woman was sitting. "But given your state of undress, perhaps I will find another."

"You're wearing one already." Davidson pointed out. His companion giggled demurely.

"Oh am I?" Sir Spencer looked down at his waist. "Yes. There I am, aren't I? Wasn't thinking. Just remembered leaving the towel in here and thought I'd retrieve it."

"Goodbye," Davidson said, decidedly more aggressive than he'd been just minutes before when the knight emasculated him.

"Goodbye." The knight nodded at the woman, never turning his eyes to Davidson. "Again, my apologies." He backed out of the small room as though leaving the presence of royalty.

"That was odd," she laughed.

"Yeah."

"Who was that?" She turned toward Davidson on the bench.

"A dangerous man."

"Why?"

"He wants to run the country and rule the world."

"Doesn't everybody?" She laughed again, as though she didn't take him literally.

Davidson turned to look at her. At first he was stone faced and expressionless, but when he looked at her face his tension eased. He smiled before talking about their third delicious tryst in twenty-four hours.

* * *

Shopping for clothing was a duty for Matti Harrold. She was utilitarian and never had succumbed to the Madison Avenue-pushed trappings like so many women had.

Matti was undoubtedly feminine. She was arguably catwalk ready without a stitch of makeup or a crunch of her abs. She loved handbags, especially Coach. But she was not a fashionista. If anything, she was the antithesis.

Most women, Matti had long ago observed, shopped like feeding sharks. They would enter a store and circle the perimeter. Then, as their taste narrowed, they would work inward. Brushing against fabrics and tugging on price tags or labels, they would eventually find the target. The entire event could take hours to play itself out.

The process repeated itself infinitely in each section of the store. Even when shopping for their men, most women would attack the racks with the same method. They overbought with the full intention of returning most of the goods. The process was complicated further by signs perched above the clothes. "SALE", "BOGO", "1/2 OFF!"

was the equivalent of bloody chum in the water and only served to aggravate the huntresses.

Matti was certain she'd somehow missed the shopping gene, which she knew was the product of natural selection. Instead, she shopped like her father. Her technique was a reconnaissance mission. She was in and out of the store along the shortest line possible. Her bounty most often included cotton and/or denim. Rarely was anything shiny or smooth, strapped or strapless. She knew very little of labels or thread count. To her, satin and sateen were the same thing. Other than Coach, she recognized only designer Kate Spade because she was the sister-in-law of one of her favorite comedians, David Spade.

So when she entered the chic women's clothing store at The Westfield Montgomery Mall in Bethesda, Maryland she was a fish out of water. She needed a pretty dress or skirt, a pair of non-functional shoes, and some accessories. Matti spent the thirty-five minute drive considering what colors would look best and decided that whatever she chose should be black or navy.

"May I help you?" asked the pixie-like blonde who greeted her at the store's entrance.

"Yes, I need something for an art exhibit opening tonight, please." Matti pulled her black leather purse strap a bit higher onto her shoulder.

"What size are you?"

"Six, I think." Matti wasn't entirely sure. "I usually buy something with an 'S' or an 'M' on it, but I think my jeans are usually a six."

"Are you looking for a dress? Or would you like a skirt with a cute top?" The girl waved her into the store and to the left.

"I'm not sure. What do you think would be appropriate?" Matti had her own ideas of appropriateness and assumed the girl's definition would be starkly different.

She was pleasantly surprised when the pixie showed her a rack of clothing that included very simple black dresses. Matti looked at the pricing sign above the rack.

"This is good." She was excited. She hadn't betrayed her shopping sensibilities. One store, one salesperson, one dress, and Bingo!

"I think we have this in a four and a six. I don't see an eight."
The girl pulled two dresses from the eye-level bar. "Why don't you
try these first? If they're no good, then I can look in the back for an
eight. Okay?"

Matti nodded and followed her to the dressing stalls in the back
of the store. They weren't as private as she'd have liked. The girl
slipped a key into one of the pink doors and opened it for Matti
then hung both dresses on a hook inside the door.

"Let me know if you need the eight."

Matti closed the door and began undressing. As she slipped out
of her clothes and into the dress she thought about the meeting
she'd had with her supervisor only an hour earlier. While she was
certainly thrilled that he'd agreed to her attending the art exhibit, she
was beginning to question his motives. She knew better than to take
anything at face value.

She was, after all, working for an agency that was never above
suspicion for its actions and motivation. Most of what it did, and
why it did it, was secret and confidential. Occasionally some of the
subterfuge was known publicly.

Matti remembered a report in the *Baltimore Sun* when she was
in college. It detailed how the NSA had conspired with a company
called Crypto AG to alter encryption machines. Crypto AG sold the
machines to as many as one hundred twenty different countries. For
years, the article alleged, the NSA secretly rigged the machines so
that U.S. intelligence analysts could easily break their foreign codes.
The NSA could, without much effort, detail the daily activities of
government agents from all over the world.

Nobody knew when the rigging began or what specific
encryption machines were involved. Crypto denied the allegations,
shrugging them off as ludicrous claims by disgruntled former
employees, but the newspaper reported that it had evidence of NSA
employees meeting with Crypto to discuss machine design. It cited a
litany of other examples that all pointed to an American-born
conspiracy to perpetuate consumer fraud on a global scale.

Matti recalled being somewhat put off by it, but she chose to
think of the Crypto affair as one that had ended long ago under a
different administration. That was her naiveté at work. It was her
long held desire to create a clear separation between the good and

the bad, the black and the white, that kept her from fully embracing the shadowy, ethically-blurred world of her employer.

Looking at herself in the mirror she reached an epiphany of sorts. What the asset said to her about terrorists and patriots made sense. Everything was in the eye of the beholder.

Standing there in a simple, clean cut dress that accentuated every feminine part of her body, she realized that playing by the rules was fruitless. The only way to get ahead was to inch one's way outside the lines. It was evident to her, as she processed the previous thirty-six hours, that she was a tool. The asset told her she was a pawn and it was true.

Her supervisor was using her for something. He knew it, the asset knew it, and countless other agents and analysts who "needed to know" knew it. What that "something" was remained irrelevant to Matti. What mattered was finishing what she started.

Though she considered playing by the rules as she always had, Matti ultimately decided otherwise. She couldn't allow the limits that her supervisor placed upon her to govern how she approached her mission. She would engage the subjects despite his admonition not to do so. She would talk to them and flirt with them and gain as much information as she could. The dress was the first step.

Matti turned to the side and put her left hand on her stomach as she looked at her profile and her posterior. She needed a second opinion. She turned the handle on the door and stepped into the store. She was barefoot and didn't want to go searching for the pixie so she called for her. The girl heard her and rushed to get a look.

The girl's jaw dropped when she saw her.

"What?" Matti looked down at herself and panicked. "Is something wrong?"

A huge grin spread across the pixie's face, revealing impossibly white teeth. "Not at all. Where were you hiding that body? I am so jealous."

Embarrassed now, Matti crossed her arms high across her chest. Maybe the dress was too much.

"Put your arms down and let me look!" The girl took Matti's hand and extended her arm. "Perfect." The girl kept looking at her, nodding her head.

Matti wondered if it was a sales job. She'd never known women to be complimentary of one another.

"Are you just trying to sell me on this?"

"What?" The pixie looked at Matti as though she'd discovered a third eye. "No! Girl, if I was trying to sell you, I wouldn't pick *that* dress. We have some more expensive numbers I'd be pushing on you if it was just a sales job. If you'd like, I could try."

"No," Matti shook her head. "That's okay. I'm just surprised by your reaction." She did feel good in the material. It clung just enough without appearing as though she'd been sewn into it.

Growing up, Matti had taken longer than most girls to outgrow her baby fat. She was a cute but chunky tween who was more at home on the sidelines of her dad's football practices than shopping at the mall or talking on the phone. Boys never paid her much attention until the summer before her junior year. Matti grew an inch and lost ten pounds, and her physique caught up with her intellect. The opposite sex started to notice Mattie and she was completely oblivious. It was her lack of physical self-confidence that led the boys, and even other girls, to think of her as aloof and untouchable.

The pixie folded her arms and drew one hand up to her chin. "Now we need to get you some shoes, maybe a necklace. And yes, on those items, I *am* trying to sell you."

The two laughed and Matti felt good about herself. She would use the advantages the good lord had so generously, if not belatedly, bestowed upon her to help with the evening's work. She felt a little bit like Jamie Lee Curtis in the movie *True Lies*.

A half hour later she walked out of the store with a pair of shoes, a necklace, and the size four dress. She only had a few hours to get home, get ready, and make her way back into the District for the event.

CHAPTER 8

Jimmy Ings unlocked the walk-in cooler that held the cache of Semtex. He'd closed the store for the day and paid his two employees to go home. They didn't know what their boss kept in the smaller of the shop's two walk-ins. He'd instructed them upon being hired that they should not ask.

Ings mumbled as he puffed on the cigarette that hung from his lips. He didn't enjoy paying people not to work, but he knew he had no choice in the matter. He slipped the ring of keys back in his pocket and wiped his hand on his flannel shirt.

He held the only key to the cooler and had no duplicates. Ings was good at keeping secrets. Despite his penchant for good drink, unfiltered smokes, and conspiratorial conversation, he never allowed any of them to compromise the deals he'd made with Sir Spencer.

He took a final long drag off of his Camel and tossed the butt onto the cement floor of the shop. He was in the back of the building in an area behind the meat counter and through a door. He stepped on the still smoking cigarette and rubbed it into the floor with the toe of his shoe. He knew better than to mix a lit cigarette with high order explosives.

Ings was about to step into the cooler when he heard a knock on the glass door at the entrance to the shop. He was expecting help and emerged from the back room to see George Edwards standing on the sidewalk holding a backpack by its strap.

Ings waved and walked around the counter to the front door.

He turned the lock and opened the door. Once Edwards walked past him, he closed the door again and relocked it, then reached up and pulled down a cheap vinyl roller shade to cover the glass.

"Hi, Jimmy," Edwards extended his hand. "You ready?"

Ings shook Edwards' hand. It was soft but muscular. "I just unlocked the cooler. Come take a look." He led Edwards behind the counter and into the back of the shop, pulled the large metal latch on the cooler door and opened it. He reached in to the right and flipped on a fluorescent overhead light which hummed and flickered to life.

"It's impressive in there," Ings said. "You ever seen sixty pounds of explosives?"

Edwards shook his head. He'd looked at some pictures on the internet but he had no concept of scale.

The two men walked into the large 10x10 space. Edwards noticed it was significantly cooler inside the box, but it wasn't as cold as he thought it would be. He looked to the right and noticed a long table and a couple of plastic fold up chairs.

He scanned left and saw a large grouping of yellow-orange bricks wrapped in a thin cellophane-like material. The individual packages were unlabeled and they looked to him like blocks of sharp cheddar cheese. The stack rose from the floor to waist level and stretched half the length of the cooler.

"That it?" Edwards motioned toward the cheese with his head, careful not to stand too close to it.

"Yep."

"Looks like cheese."

"Yeah, it does." Ings walked up to the stack. "This is the old stuff. There's absolutely no odor. The manufacturer didn't add little metal pieces to the mix. They did that with the newer stuff so that metal detectors and x-ray machines could pick it up more easily. You know, for tracing. This stuff also decomposes real slowly. The newer plastic supposedly goes bad after three years. Not these babies." He gestured at the stack. "This is the nasty Semtex."

"That's why I suggested it," boasted Edwards. "A little research on the matter made me think this was the most viable tool."

"Smart boy," Ings remarked. He wasn't really impressed, but he didn't want to hurt Edwards' feelings. "You bring the phones?"

"Everything we need is in here." He held up the backpack and then slung it over his shoulder. "Did you study the instructions on how to put all of this together?"

"Yep."

"Let's get to work then."

The two men sat down at the table and Edwards unzipped his backpack. From it he pulled four older model Nokia 6210 phones, four pieces of plywood cut to measure 6"x6", a small cardboard box containing inch long Phillips head screws, a screwdriver, a bundle of black plastic zip ties, six packages of AA alkaline batteries, a spool of thin copper wiring, wire cutters, a hand crank drill with an 1/8 inch bit, a plastic wrapper full of double-ended alligator clips, and four packages of model rocket sparkers. Edwards made sure to arrange all of the materials neatly on the table.

He read the instructions aloud while Ings took apart the cell phones. When disassembled, each of the phones contained five major parts. With Edwards's help, Ings located the small vibrators on the lower right portion of an internal board.

"Do the vibrator motors work?" Ings asked. "These are old phones."

"Yes, I found the parts online and I replaced both of them. They also have newly refurbished batteries that have full charges. They can last one hundred twenty hours on standby. That should be plenty of time."

Ings used the wire cutters to notch out a small hole in the shell of the phone next to where the vibrator sat. He then reassembled the phones and inserted two small pieces of copper wire that Edwards had cut for him.

The men set the phones aside and each pulled out the pieces of plywood. First Edwards and then Ings used the hand crank drill to bore eight holes in each of the boards.

"Can I have the zip ties?" Ings asked, holding out his hand. Edwards passed him a handful, which he used to strap his phones to the left side of the board; Edwards followed suit with his phones.

They used two additional ties to strap four batteries to the right side of each board. Between the phones and the batteries the men affixed two screws, one atop the other.

"Clips?" Ings asked, as though he was a surgeon asking a nurse for a scalpel. Edwards obliged and handed them over.

Ings took one alligator clip and attached it to the batteries and snapped its other end onto the top screw. He then took a second clip and attached it to the bottom screw but left its opposite end unattached. A third clip was clamped to the batteries with its partner also unattached. The two open clips were then connected to the model rocket sparker.

Edwards completed the same tasks on his board but took somewhat longer. He was more meticulous than Ings. When he was done, he scrolled through the menus of each phone, setting them to vibrate. Ings took the two small copper leads which ran from the vibrator through the opening of the phone and attached one to each of the screws on the boards. The detonators were ready.

"Let's test the numbers." Edwards handed Ings a small card that contained the phone numbers. Ings pulled his cell from his pocket and dialed the first number.

As soon as the first phone rang, the end of the model rocket sparker popped and ignited for a brief second. They repeated the process with the three other phones and got the same results.

"Tell me about the numbers," Ings requested. He was concerned about law enforcement's ability to trace the calls to the detonators.

"We're covered," Edwards replied. He started picking up the wrappers and excess wires from the table and put them in his backpack. "First off, I was able to purchase a month's worth of coverage with a prepaid credit card. Then I went to another service provider and paid cash for four prepaid phones. Those are the numbers you dialed. I set those numbers to automatically forward to the detonator phones. The accounts are temporary and have no names attached."

Ings stood from his seat and placed his hands on his hips. He took a deep breath and thought about the complexity of their assignments. It all seemed so simple on the surface: make a phone call, change a democracy. But he knew that it was more than that.

"How do we know when to trigger the bombs?" He asked.

"I think that's the information Bill is providing. He's supposed to get the inside scoop of the exact timing of the day's events. He knows somebody who knows somebody." Edwards stood and stretched. "That's why we're using remote detonation instead of the phones' internal alarm clocks. We need to make sure they go off at the right time. If something gets delayed, we can adjust."

"How do we know where to put the two extra bombs?" Ings felt like he was out of the loop. There were questions to which he thought he should already know the answer, and it bothered him a bit that Edwards seemed to have all of the information. Why was Sir Spencer so much more open with the artist? After all, Ings was the one who'd cleaned all of the money and stored the explosives. He was the loyalist beyond reproach. What had Edwards done?

"Sir Spencer will figure that out. Again, maybe Bill has the answer to that."

Edwards was too focused on packaging the detonators so they could be transported to sense the rising resentment in Ings posture or tone. He did find himself surprised that Ings hadn't asked why they needed two additional bombs or for whom they were intended. Unless Ings asked, Edwards wasn't going to tell him.

* * *

Standing just above the south bank of the Tidal Basin, the asset knew that the NSA was keeping tabs. Two blocks away there was an agent drinking coffee, reading a paper, and pretending not to be who he was.

Ever since the NSA first made contact, the agency was like a sexually transmitted disease. It might hide for a week or two, but then it was back and irritating.

If given a choice, remaining a blind Daturan sympathizer would have been the most appealing. But given the temerity of the feds to essentially blackmail cooperation, the asset knew there was no choice. The NSA and the FBI made that abundantly clear. They knew the asset's activities, associates, financial situation, and emotional baggage. They would use it if they didn't get the help they needed. It was a dangerous game, in which there were likely no winners. Either people would die or people would go to prison. Maybe both. There were no other options.

After spending part of the morning with a paranoid conspirator, the asset needed to engage in some stress relief. A trip to the

Jefferson Memorial was always calming. Even if there was a spook keeping watch.

Regardless of one's upbringing or profession, it was hard living in D.C. without knowing a little bit of American history. Maybe it was because the asset visited the Memorial as a child that it held a special meditative quality. Perhaps it was because the architect, John Russell Pope, had modeled the structure after the Pantheon in Rome that it seemed so grand and yet so intimate. Regardless, it was the perfect place to go when the weight of democracy fell heavy upon the shoulders. Only a memorial to Atlas might have seemed more soothing.

Once inside the building, the asset looked up at the five ton bronze statue of the third president. It was 19 feet tall and gazed out from the interior of the Memorial to the White House. The intention of the sculptor, Rudolph Evans, was to represent the Age of Enlightenment and Jefferson as both a philosopher and statesman. Along the walls of the Memorial surrounding the president were noted quotations that best symbolized the principles to which historians believe he dedicated his life.

The asset stared at what was called Panel Four, reading the ninety-four words excerpted from an 1810 letter that Jefferson wrote to historian Samuel Kercheval. Part of the passage seemed particularly prescient for the present times: *"We might as well require a man to wear still the coat which fitted him when a boy as civilized society to remain ever under the regimen of their barbarous ancestors."*

Did it mean that democracy was a living, breathing animal not confined to the laws of the past? Did it mean that the Constitution should be considered a reference point rather than the law upon which all others were based?

Whatever Jefferson's intended meaning, the asset took it to convey a sense of governmental evolution. He was a man who believed the people should rule above all else. Wasn't that exactly what the Daturans were doing? Weren't they seizing control from a misguided government? The asset became agitated, standing there in what was normally a place of solace.

It was time to leave. There was no respite. There was no break from it. The NSA made sure of that. They knew it was only a matter of time before the Daturans grew bold enough to act. They'd latched their hooks at just the right time.

Walking from the inside of the Monument toward Ohio Drive, the asset noticed the spook was gone. Maybe they'd gotten what they needed. Maybe they were somewhere hidden. It didn't matter. This would be over soon enough, one way or another.

* * *

"The Supreme Court has agreed to hear the case," the sixth Daturan said, wondering what effect, if any, it might have on Sir Spencer's plans.

"I know." Sir Spencer was in his suite at the Hay Adams. He was on his encrypted Sigillu cell phone, a modified consumer-grade Nokia that Sir Spencer purchased directly from the encryption company.

Sir Spencer knew that the data from wireless communications could reveal the date, time, and duration of any given call. Any eavesdropper could also determine the geographical location from where the call was placed, not to mention the identity and location of the person receiving the call. The company assured him that decryption of his calls was impossible. Even the mathematicians who created the encryption technology were incapable of decrypting a call. The software, which converted voice information into encrypted data using a constantly changing mathematical equation, was developed by an Israeli security company. Sir Spencer believed that if it was good enough for Israeli needs, it would serve his purposes.

Because the technology required that both phones involved in a call must be Sigillu equipped, Sir Spencer had provided each of the Daturans with an encrypted phone. But he often needed to remind the others that when answering a call from him, they needed to hit the "C" button before answering. If not, they needed to inform him that they were not secure. In this case, the call was secure.

"Does that change anything? I am in a very vulnerable position here."

The sixth Daturan could not afford for anyone to learn his identity.

"Why would it affect anything, good man?" Sir Spencer said

condescendingly. "What the Supreme Court chooses to do or to not do does not change our mission. It does not change our plans. If anything it's a distraction and affords us time. Everybody is so bloody focused on this court nonsense that they can't see the forest for the trees."

"I assume that's supposed to make me feel better."

"I don't care how it makes you feel," the knight retorted. "What I care about is you maintaining your focus here. The others all have jobs to do before the transition. Yours will begin immediately afterward. That's when the heavy lifting starts on your account."

"So the others—they're all on target then?"

"Yes," Sir Spencer hedged. "Well, I should say yes, but one of them is a bugger."

"Bill Davidson?"

"Yes. I paid him a visit this morning, I think he'll come around. You know I can be quite persuasive."

"Quite."

"So we're quite good then."

"Do they know who I am?"

"No." The knight was sure they didn't know. He'd not even told George Edwards, who'd become his confidant of late, or even Jimmy Ings, the most trustworthy of the bunch. "They can assume you are a cabinet member and the Secretary of Something. They know you are in the line of succession. But other than the knowledge that you are not the beautiful and talented Felicia Jackson, they have no clue."

"How do they know I'm not the Speaker?"

"I referred to you as a man. And there are...what...just three women to consider, regardless?"

The sixth Daturan was irritated. "So they know I'm not Jackson and that I'm not the Secretary of Education or HUD."

"They also know you're not any of the three hundred million Americans living outside the greater Metro area. What's your point? In two days everyone in the world *will* know who you are, when you're sworn into office."

"True." There was less irritation. "I'm a little sensitive about this. I have the highest profile in this, the most to lose."

Sir Spencer appreciated the secretary's egocentrism, but he

didn't like it. The secretary may be the eventual face of the invisible revolution, true, but he didn't have any more to lose than the rest of the conspirators.

The knight had hand-picked the sixth Daturan. At that moment he was wondering if he'd made the right choice. There were others who'd have joined the movement. The cabinet was full of ambitious men. It was always those closest to the seat of power who coveted it most.

He'd settled on his choice because of the man's desire for change. He was often a contrarian in cabinet meetings. President Foreman regularly told him to bite his tongue. It was thought, for a period of time during the first term, that Foreman would replace him after forcing a resignation. However, other matters were more pressing, and given the burden of a bitter campaign for reelection, Foreman chose to keep as many of his original cabinet members as was possible. His loyalty to dissenters and his affinity for making appointments from both major political parties won him a lot of favors. Only the resignation of the Secretary of the Interior and the death of his vice president forced Foreman to make second term nominations for his inner circle.

He stuck with the loudmouth. By the time he dropped dead in the Oval Office, President Foreman had grown quite fond of him.

Sir Spencer was fond of him too, which is why he befriended the secretary and appealed to his vanity. He pulled the strings perfectly. The knight whispered the things that made the secretary puff his chest. He told him of how things could be, given the right chain of events. Within months, he had the secretary on his team as the final cog in the wheel.

He couldn't necessarily blame the secretary for his ego, but he certainly could try to keep it in check. He could remind him who really was in charge of the operation. He could suggest that everything was subject to change if need be.

"You know, Mr. Secretary..." the knight began and then paused.

"What?"

"Have you ever heard of Narcissus?"

"Yes."

"What do you know about him?"

"He was a handsome man unable to love anyone but himself,"

The secretary responded, confused by the digression.
"Yes. Did you know that he died because he was unable to pull
away from his own reflection?" "What's your point?" The secretary
was in the back of a Lincoln Town Car. He was alone, though he
could see the driver outside of the car, leaning against the driver's
side door.
"Country first, my good man. Look up from your own
reflection."

* * *

Felicia Jackson's nubuck leather covered heels clicked on the
English Minton tile flooring. Her steps echoed as she crossed the
room to a large round table. She looked up as she walked, admiring
the cast iron railing that ran the length of the second floor balcony.
She'd never been in the Indian Treaty Room before and it was
as exquisite as she'd imagined. The detail was astounding. She loved
it.
The room was on the top floor of the seven-story Eisenhower
Executive Office Building across from the West Wing of the White
House. The treaty room was the most expensive to construct of the
building's five hundred fifty three original rooms.
The EEOB, as it was known, was initially built after the civil war
to house the Departments of State, War, and Navy. Unlike most of
the more conservative architecture that dotted the district, the
EEOB was a flamboyant example of French Second Empire design.
It took seventeen years to build.
The room was in the Navy Department's wing of the massive
structure and carried a nautical theme. Carved within the railing that
the Speaker so admired were dolphins and shells. Stars on the
ceiling represented navigation. On those Minton tiles was a compass
at the center of the room. The light hanging from the ceiling of the
Indian Treaty Room was the only original fixture remaining in the
entirety of the EEOB.
The space had originally been a library and reception area, but
in 1955 Dwight Eisenhower held the first ever televised presidential
press conference from that very room.
For decades it served as an extension of the White House,

housing the Office of the Vice President among other key administration officials. It was refurbished in the mid-1980s and had since served as a room for meetings and receptions. Given its size, the Foreman administration felt it was the most appropriate location to discuss the details of the president's procession, memorial, and burial.

Attending the meeting with Foreman's senior staff was the entire cabinet, the First Lady's senior staff, and members of the Congressional Leadership. That group included Speaker Jackson, the House Majority Leader, the House Whip, the Senate Majority Leader, and the minority leaders for both houses of congress.

Also present were several representatives of the Ceremonials division of the Office of the Chief of Protocol. The Ceremonials employees worked under the authority of the State Department. They were in charge of special events; inaugurations, joint sessions of Congress, and funerals.

The large table would accommodate twenty-five people. The rest would have to stand. The room was filling quickly and Felicia decided it was time to find her seat.

She nodded at colleagues, shook some hands, and expressed condolences to those closest to President Foreman. The Speaker was doing her best to appear genuine. In reality, Felicia had no interest in attending this meeting.

Her mood was still sour from learning that the Supreme Court had agreed to hear the merits of Blackmon's case. Despite her attorneys' repeated forewarning of that eventuality, she wasn't emotionally prepared for the reality of it when they broke the official news.

The Speaker was just leaving her office when her legal team found her in Statuary Hall. She didn't lambaste them as she had on the terrace earlier in the day, but neither was she friendly. They assured her that they were preparing an outstanding case for the high court and that they knew they could win.

She asked the young, follicle-challenged lawyer what he thought about the case. He was surprisingly positive. It was encouraging to the Speaker, but not mood-salvaging as she climbed into the back of her black Chevy Tahoe and rode to the EEOB.

Trying her best not to sulk outwardly, she found a seat at the table and slid into the chair. To her left was Foreman's Chief of Staff and to her right was an empty seat that she noticed was reserved for John Blackmon.

"That man is the bane of my existence," she mumbled under her breath. She caught the eye of the Secretary of Defense and forced a quick nod and smile. She looked around the room for Blackmon and didn't notice him at first. After a group of men parted on the other side of the room she saw him. His head and shoulder were bent to his left as he listened to a trailing aide. He wore a dark suit and white shirt that essentially matched the attire of every other man in the room.

Brooks Brothers must have had a sale.

On the table in front of each seat was a glass goblet. Each was filled with ice water and was sweating. Felicia used a small cloth napkin wrapped around the goblet's stem to wipe it dry before taking a sip. As she did, she heard the clanging of a spoon.

Across the table, a mile away it seemed, a man the Speaker didn't recognize was holding a teaspoon in one hand and his goblet in the other. He was attempting to gain everyone's attention. It worked; the loud rumbling of voices softened.

"Everyone, please take your seats. We are ready to begin." He clanged the glass again. "I know every soul here has a tight schedule so let's get on with the meeting please. Take your seats."

Felicia watched Blackmon move toward his seat. As he neared, she turned away so as not to let him notice her gaze. She felt his left hand on her right shoulder.

"Felicia," he said cordially. "How are you?"

"Fine, John. And you?"

"Okay, considering the circumstances." He pulled his hand from her shoulder and took his seat. "I know we're all still in shock over Dexter's death. This whole thing is just surreal." He spoke softly enough for only her to hear him, smiling and waving at others across the table. "And this whole ordeal in court," he continued as he pulled in his chair. "It's so draining."

She said nothing.

"I'm sure it's been tough for you," he said, baiting her. He adjusted his red satin power tie against his waist. "I know it's been tough on me, so I can only imagine..." He let his false empathy hang.

"You probably can't imagine," Felicia said. She leaned to the right from her hips, close enough to Blackmon so that she could whisper. "That would require the use of the right side of your brain, Mr. Secretary."

John Blackmon laughed without looking to his left. Instead he pulled his own sweating water glass to his lips and toasted the Speaker before taking a drink.

"Good for you, Felicia," he offered as he put his drink back on the table. "You still have some fight left in you."

Felicia rapped on the table with the knuckles on her right hand. It was balled into a fist. She said nothing; knowing that to engage Blackmon any further would only lead to an embarrassing scene. He was pushing her; she couldn't allow herself to fall for it. She was saved by the man at the opposite end of the table, who still held the spoon in his hand.

"Hello all, my name is Phillip Taylor. I'm with the First Lady's staff. I've been asked to be the timekeeper for this meeting. We've got two hours, so let's get started."

Taylor was a tall, thin man who stood six and a half feet tall. He had a boyish face that belied his beltway experience. He held a clipboard and a stop watch.

The Speaker was relieved to know that the misery of the meeting was time limited. There were a million places she'd rather be. All of them were a long distance from Secretary Blackmon.

The first part of the discussion dealt with security and road closures. The main disruption to traditional traffic would occur on Constitution Avenue. It would close the next evening, to prepare for the following morning's procession to the Capitol Rotunda.

The route was relatively simple, in which Foreman's coffin traveled the length of the National Mall. It would ride in a hearse from 33rd and Constitution, just north of the Lincoln Memorial to 16th Street. There, the hearse would stop and the coffin would continue its trip to the other end of the Mall aboard a horse drawn caisson. The caisson would consist of six horses, all of the same color, and three riders. A separate horse would carry the section from the Old Guard Caisson Platoon. One additional riderless horse would follow the casket. As the procession passed Fourth

Street, twenty-one F-22 fighters would fly over in tribute to the Commander in Chief.

Once in The Capitol Rotunda, hundreds would attend the televised memorial service. After the service, the flag draped casket would remain for public viewing until the following morning, at which time it would leave for burial at Arlington National Cemetery.

It was an extraordinarily short time for a president to lie in state. Reagan's casket was available for viewing for thirty-four hours; President Ford's casket was in the Capitol Rotunda for forty-eight hours. He also lay in repose outside of the House side of the Capitol as a tribute to his time in Congress. Of the roughly dozen presidents to lie in state, Foreman was to be there for the shortest amount of time. Additionally, there was a break with tradition in that the president would not lie in repose at the White House.

Typically, presidents who died while in office lay in repose in the East Room of the White House. That was not to happen. Foreman, a sitting president, was essentially receiving the procession of a former president. There was no explanation as to why, other than that the wishes of the Foreman family precluded it. Nobody in the meeting questioned the departure from protocol.

A severe looking woman from the Ceremonials division announced the various members of the cabinet who had speaking roles at the memorial service. The woman was dressed in black with a small red brooch at her collar. She had her yellow hair pulled tight in a bun against the back of her head. She appeared to Felicia as though she were plucked straight from the beaverboard of Grant Wood's *American Gothic*. The Speaker had seen the work in person at the Art Institute of Chicago during a campaign fundraising event for an Illinois Senator several years earlier. She'd long wondered whether the artist intended to honor hardworking Midwesterners or poke fun at their stereotypically rigid morality.

Felicia had spent time researching Wood after seeing the work in person, trying to find out his real intentions. She had no McCarthy-esque motive, but rather a real desire to understand Wood's sense of things. Felicia, for all of her many faults and judgments of others, was one who loved loyalty. She considered patriotism the highest form of it and hoped Wood's *Gothic* intended a conveyance of love of country and not a subtle mocking of it. She never figured it out definitively, though she long remembered what Wood said about the sum of his work, just before his death in 1942.

"In making these paintings," he admitted, *"I had in mind something which I hope to convey to a fairly wide audience in America -- the picture of a country rich in the arts of peace; a homely, lovable nation, infinitely worth any sacrifice necessary to its preservation."*

"A homely, lovable nation worth any sacrifice necessary to its preservation," she'd often repeated to herself while compromising and cajoling legislation into law.

She sat in the Indian Treaty room learning the details of the memorial, recalling that Wood once earned money by sketching promotional flyers for a mortuary. It was ironic that he should come to mind as she passively listened to presidential funeral arrangements.

The gothic administrator told the room that Felicia was to begin the service with a short welcome address. She was also to end the ceremony with a brief thanks. Foreman's speech writers would provide her with a script from which she was told not to deviate.

She felt good about the assignment. Upon hearing of it, Felicia subconsciously found herself liking the dour Ceremonial worker. She noticed the flattering, natural color in the woman's cheeks and the pale blue of her eyes. But the brief affair was over when the woman revealed Senator Blackmon's role. It was inconceivable and it incensed the Speaker. She felt slighted and snubbed.

John Blackmon was the designated successor. Meaning, he would not attend the memorial service in the event that the unthinkable happened. His absence was to ensure governmental continuity. He was told to expect presidential-level security and that he would be taken to an undisclosed location until the end of the funeral service at Arlington. At the point that the majority of successors were no longer in the same location his life would return to normal.

It was a tactical decision without any political gamesmanship brought to bear. But Felicia took it as such. She viewed it as a message to the public, and to the Supreme Court, that he was the one worth keeping alive. He was the one needed to carry on in the event of mass casualties.

It was difficult for Felicia to sit still. She was biting the inside of her lip, internalizing the perception that everyone in the room was staring at her.

Blackmon, she learned, would be one of only two cabinet members not in attendance. The other was the Secretary of Energy. His absence irked her too. He'd already agreed to appear as a political analyst for one television network's coverage of the service. Despite his reluctance, Foreman's widow asked him to do it so as to help control the message. He was low on the list of succession, but Felicia was still irritated. She was beginning to believe there was some sort of conspiracy to stop her from becoming president.

She tried not to look over at Blackmon; she could feel that he was looking at her. But she couldn't help herself and slowly turned to look at him. His head was already turned in her direction, as she'd suspected. Blackmon leaned into her and spoke softly, so that nobody else could hear him.

"Practice makes perfect."

He was such an ass.

* * *

It was dusk when Matti slinked out of her cab in front of The Washington Post building on L Street between 15th and 16th. She'd taken the Red Line from Maryland to the Metro Center stop and then hitched a ride.

Matti didn't like driving into the District. She usually parked at a Metro station, rode mass transit into the city, and then walked everywhere she went. Tonight, in her three-inch heels and new dress, a cab was the better choice.

She carefully stepped from the taxi onto the sidewalk. Her inexperience with uncomfortable shoes made her look comically similar to a newborn giraffe taking its first steps. Once she was standing, Matti gripped each side of her dress at the hips and gently inched the bunched fabric downward toward her knees. She unsnapped her black sequined clutch, pulled out a folded ten dollar bill and handed it to the driver.

The Post was a half block from the reception hall where George

Edwards' new collection was featured. She walked to the entrance of the two-story concrete façade, noticing the red-vested valet assisting the chattering class out of Town Cars and Cadillac limousines. She was glad to have exited the cab out of their sight. This was not her crowd. She expected odd looks and judgments.

She'd gotten a lot of those looks after her mother's death. *Cocaine.* It was the red herring that had left her father and her alone.

As a child, Matti never asked her father about the whispers she'd heard. She was too afraid to bring it up. Years later, however, the detective assigned the case told her that there was cocaine in her mother's bloodstream and in her nasal membranes. She also learned that the autopsy indicated her mother had used the drug multiple times. It was a piece to the puzzle for which Matti did not want to find a place.

Was the drug related to her death? Did a dealer run her down? Did she owe someone money? Did her father know about the problem and keep it from his young daughter?

Following her father's rules of compliance and solitude had done nobody any good, except that it had instilled into Matti a drive to find answers; a need to separate the black from the white.

Rules are there for a reason.

Maybe she'd be better off obeying her supervisor's order to not mingle. Maybe the rules *were* there for a reason. Matti struggled against her nature, ultimately pushing through it.

Damn the rules.

This was as good a time as any to take the leap and blur the lines.

Matti let out a breath, turned back around, and walked past the doorman into the building. She remembered the clothing store pixie's advice to hold her shoulders back and her neck up to elongate her body. Matti moved into the gathering crowd and worked it. She could feel the men and women watching her as she walked past them. It felt surprisingly good. The apprehension she'd felt just minutes before had evaporated. It wasn't that she hadn't come to realize how attractive others thought her to be; she'd just never felt comfortable embracing it.

Strutting with uncharacteristic confidence, she walked to the bar at the far left end of the large open room. The floor was a black and white veined marble, the walls white plaster lined with Edwards' digital sculptures.

At the portable bar she ordered a ginger ale with ice and then turned to survey the room with more acuity. Most of the men were in what she imagined were their business suits minus neckties. The women wore cocktail attire in muted tones or black. Matti estimated there were already about one hundred to one hundred twenty-five people in attendance. She looked for familiar faces and saw none.

She scanned the walls, observing the small groups gathered around various pieces on the walls. Some waved their arms and pointed with their wine glasses as they discussed the genius of the work. Others stood near the art but didn't seem interested.

From Matti's position in the room she couldn't see any of the pieces clearly. Absent the conspirators, she decided to take a look at some of the art for herself. Hanging on the wall opposite the bar, on the far end of the room, was a piece that resembled Leonardo Da Vinci's *Vitruvian Man.*

The *Vitruvian Man* was among the most recognizable drawings in the modern world. Drawn in 1487, it was Da Vinci's attempt to illustrate the relationship between man and nature, between science and religion. It depicted a nude male with his arms and legs extended at two different angles, superimposed upon one another. The man was within a circle within a square.

From a distance, Matti couldn't see the modifications Edwards chose to make, but as she approached the canvas, she saw the differences clearly. Where the man's left legs should have been there were none. They were amputated at the knees, wrapped in cloth. The man's right arms, instead of being fully extended, were bent at the elbows. At two different angles, the arms and hands were placed in salute. On the man's head, instead of a Renaissance mop of hair, there sat a helmet. On the helmet's front there was the drawing of an American flag. The chin strap was undone and hung from the ears.

The canvas was yellowed to mimic Da Vinci's work. Above and below the circle there was script, as there was adorning the original. But instead of the "mirror writing" that Da Vinci employed to explain the mathematical proportion of man and architecture,

Edwards' wrote in Arabic. It appeared to Matti that the text was repeated multiple times:

‏.□□□□ □□□ □ □□□□□ □□□ □ □□□□

Though not fluent, she'd learned to read bits of Arabic. It was the second most popular alphabet in the world behind Latin. Her supervisors had recommended a rudimentary ability to read and write at the very least.

Her fluency in multiple romance languages did little to help with her study. But she managed. She looked at the script from right to left and slowly worked out the sounds in her head.

"We came. We saw. We conquered," she murmured.

It was an adaptation and pluralizing of the Latin phrase, "Veni, Vidi, Vici". Julius Caesar was said to have announced his victory in the battle for Turkey in 47 B.C. by telling the Senate, "I came. I saw. I conquered."

She didn't understand the meaning until she looked at the small white placard to the right of the work:

Cannons of Iraq, 2010
George Edwards
Digital Sculpture, 36 x 36

Matti got it. A lesser known name for Da Vinci's popular ink drawing was *Canon of Proportions*. It was a simple but profound message.

Brilliant.

"Amazing isn't it?" The voice came from behind Matti's right shoulder. She turned, not sure if the question was intended for her. Standing behind her was George Edwards. She pretended she didn't recognize him.

"Yes it is. It's very angry though." She was still facing the wall but opened her stance toward his body.

"Angry?" His eyes widened and eyebrows arched as he looked into her eyes. "How so?" he said, his tone flirtatious more than defensive.

Matti considered her response before answering. She folded her arms and took a sip of the ginger ale then motioned toward the canvas by tipping her glass.

"An amputated leg, a sarcastic salute, the sardonic homage to Caesar. It's angry." She was pleased with herself. "I'd say the artist has some serious issues."

"Hmmm." He stepped back from Matti. "Quite the critic, aren't you?"

Edwards slipped his hands into his pockets. He was wearing chinos, a long sleeve, sky blue linen shirt and a dark blue single-breasted blazer.

"You asked." Matti pulled the glass to her lips but didn't drink. She hinted at a smile and blinked. "I answered."

"True." He inched closer again, admiring the curve of her shoulders. They were covered only by the thin straps holding up the dress. Edwards liked black on her. Upon further inspection, he would have liked anything on her. Or not on her. "So what are the serious issues?"

"Well, I am no psychiatrist."

"But...?"

"But," she continued, laughing as she explained herself, "a lot of the pieces here are angry. They're politically clever and insightful, but sometimes the brilliance is lost in the grievance. It's too much."

"You know, I'm the artist." She said nothing as he extended his hand. "I'm George Edwards."

"I know." She shook his hand. He seemed so much more charming than she'd imagined from his dossier. But then again, she reminded herself, Bashar al-Assad had a cult of personality.

"Oh," he feigned offense still holding her hand, "*that* makes it easier to take the criticism. Even if you aren't a shrink."

"I'm sorry." She wasn't. "I do think you're incredibly talented, and I understand why you are so successful."

"Buttering me up now?" He'd let go of her hand, still holding her gaze.

Matti knew that her supervisor didn't want her engaging the conspirators. But she also knew there was something he was keeping from her. The rules, as far as she was concerned, no longer applied.

* * *

Professor Thistlewood watched Edwards from across the room.

He didn't recognize the young woman with whom Edwards was talking. He couldn't take his eyes off of them, even with his girlfriend standing right next to him

The girlfriend, Laura Harrowby, had her arm looped around Thistlewood, but she was turned away from him talking with another couple about wine. She lovingly popped him in the ribs with the back of her hand.

"Art," she asked, "what is that joke you always tell about the foreigners and their wine?" She looked up at him adoringly and then back at the couple. "This is so funny. Go ahead, honey. Tell them."

The professor obliged and shared his joke. The couple laughed politely and after a few more minutes of small talk they excused themselves. Once they'd left, Laura pressed her body into Thistlewood's side and wrapped her arms around him, still holding her drink in one hand.

"Do you know that girl talking to George Edwards?" Thistlewood motioned with his head and spun so that Laura could get a better look through her glasses.

"No." She squinted. "Should I?"

"Probably not." He placed his hand on the small of her back and kissed her on top of her head. "I'm going to walk over and introduce myself." Thistlewood now was suspicious of everyone and everything.

Laura released her hold on Thistlewood, but grabbed his hand and followed him over to Edwards and the mystery girl. They sidestepped through the still growing crowd and reached the artist. His back was turned to them but Thistlewood and Laura could tell he was laughing.

The woman looked at them, momentarily directing her attention away from Edwards. She caught Thistlewood's eye and it seemed to him as though she recognized him. It was just for an instant. As quickly as the perceived recognition bloomed in her eyes, it vanished.

Thistlewood reached out with his right hand and put it on Edwards' shoulder, still holding Laura's hand with his left as Edwards spun around.

"George!" Thistlewood smiled. "This is wonderful." He held

out his hand to congratulate him.

"Art," Edwards said. He reciprocated and shook his friend's hand. "Thanks for coming."

"George, I am sure you remember Laura Harrowby." Thistlewood looked at his girlfriend and grinned as he introduced her.

"Yes," Edwards nodded. "Nice to see you." There was an awkward moment as the two couples stood smiling at each other.

"I'm Matti Harrold." She thought about waiting for George Edwards to introduce her, but then she realized she'd not yet told him her name.

"Oh! Sorry about that." Edwards snapped to attention, suddenly realizing his faux pas. "I wasn't trying to be rude. I have just met Matti here, and didn't know her name until now."

"I'm Art Thistlewood." The professor offered his name but not his hand. "Matti is it?"

"Yes."

"And what do you do?" Thistlewood didn't trust her. A beautiful woman sporting up Edwards on the eve of their plot just didn't fall within his idea of normal.

It wasn't that Edwards didn't occasionally date attractive women. Edwards, Thistlewood had learned, could be particularly successful in carnal matters on the night of an opening. But it was always with the same women; hemp-wearing, patchouli-basted free thinkers.

This woman, this Matti, seemed too corporate. She seemed out of Edwards' league. Something was off.

"She's an art critic," Edwards answered for her. "I've found in our very short time together here, that she has an eye. It's a destructive, soul-crushing eye, but it's an eye nonetheless."

"I'm not a critic," she admitted. "I just answered Mr. Edwards' questions when asked."

"So you're not a critic." The professor was not amused. "What do you do?"

"Art," scolded Laura, "don't be rude. You've just met her." She squeezed his hand tightly.

"It's fine." Matti looked at Laura and then at Thistlewood. "I'm a translator. What do you do?"

"I'm a professor at American University." He lifted his chin so that he could look down his nose at the translator.

"He teaches political science," added Laura, who'd had too much wine. "He's a brilliant teacher. Was tenured very young."

"What are your politics then?" Matti said, knowing she was pushing a button.

"Excuse me?"

"What do you think of the current state of affairs? What do you think of your friend's work?"

Matti was feeling bold; she thought it might have been the high heels. Not only was she disobeying a direct order by talking to these men, but she was baiting them.

Thistlewood, for all of his suspicions about this woman, was not about to pass up an opportunity to preach. By the time he'd finished his first sentence, she was already tuning out.

* * *

Over Thistlewood's shoulder, Matti noticed a woman with a large leopard print handbag. She looked to be in her late 30s to early 40s and was dressed in a taupe pant suit. Her mouse brown hair was short and parted to the left. The woman was relatively unremarkable. What made Matti notice her was the way in which she held the handbag.

It was off her shoulder and cocked at an angle almost perpendicular to the woman's side. To Matti, it appeared as though the woman was aiming the bag. And then it hit her.

"Excuse me, please," she interrupted Thistlewood, who had already bashed both Presidents Bush and Obama. "I'll be right back."

Thistlewood was stunned, his mouth still forming the end of the word he'd last uttered when Matti crossed the room with purpose. As she neared the pant suited woman, the woman saw her coming and began to walk away.

Matti caught her near the bar and lightly touched her arm. "Excuse me," Matti began almost breathlessly, "I don't mean to upset you, but could you tell me what kind of purse that is? I just love it." She exacted a fake smile and lightly rubbed her fingers on the bag's material.

"Uh," the woman said, caught off guard, "I'm not sure. It was a gift." The woman's lips curled up, not quite forming a smile. She pulled away from Matti and quickly moved into the crowd, and Matti saw her leave the building.

Any minutiae of doubt that Matti had about her boss' secretive intentions were evaporating. He was tailing her, watching her. That woman was snapping photographs or shooting video with that bag and Matti was certain of it.

As fashion-challenged as Matti thought herself to be, she knew that bag. It was a large Coach brand Ocelot Haircalf Brooke bag. It cost fourteen hundred dollars. Matti loved Coach, and had several of the brand's briefcases. She found the brand practical and durable, and maybe just slightly indulgent. She knew any woman who spent that much money on a bag would know the designer.

Matti walked toward the floor to ceiling glass window that looked out onto the sidewalk. She saw the woman on a phone standing next to two men in dark suits who were also on phones. A black Chevy Suburban pulled up to the curb and the three got inside. It was NSA, no question. Her agency was spying on her.

She was watching the SUV speed off when George Edwards stepped up next to her. He looked out the window with her, though he didn't know what she was watching.

"Are you okay?"

"Fine." She stared outside before turning to look at Edwards. "I'm sorry for interrupting your friend like that." She looked back to the spot in the room where they'd been talking and saw Thistlewood still standing there with his girlfriend. They were looking at the Da Vinci knockoff on the wall.

"I should go back and apologize to him." She started toward Thistlewood when Edwards stopped her.

"Don't worry about it. I have someone else I'd like you to meet."

There was something kind about Edwards. She didn't understand what it was, but he was charming and chivalrous.

Underneath it all, however, she could sense that something was off. He was definitely angry. Whatever he repressed in conversation and personal interaction was evident in his art. She wasn't kidding when she suggested that he had issues.

Thistlewood, she reasoned, was a poser, an academic who thought he was smarter than those around him. She could see it in the way he looked at her and the way he related to his girlfriend. His body language reeked of superiority.

Compensation for insecurity. She recalled H.L. Mencken: *"Those who can - do. Those who can't – teach."* Matti thought that comic notion applied specifically to a man like Thistlewood. As attractive as she'd found him in the file, she found him repulsive in person.

She and Edwards reached the bar. Standing there, whiskey in hand, was a tall, impeccably dressed man. Matti recognized him from the file. It was Sir Spencer Thomas, the Daturans' leader. She suddenly felt flush.

"Sir Spencer Thomas." He genuflected and offered his hand as he bowed his head to the vision in front of him.

"Matti Harrold." She took the knight's hand. It was thick and cold.

"Lovely." The knight brought her hand to his lips and gently kissed it. "Absolutely smashing."

Matti studied his face as he looked up at her. His lips were thin and looked to her as though two worms were pushed together. His eyes were not warm. There was a distance in them; a darkness Matti could not reconcile.

"George, good man," he said, keeping his eyes on Matti, "who is this beautiful creature?"

"We just met, Sir Spencer," Edwards said, sounding proud of himself. "I thought you'd like to meet her."

Sir Spencer leaned on the bar and took a sip of his whiskey. Looking at Matti, he was pleased he'd decided to attend. He'd considered the potential consequences of the Daturans all appearing in public at the same place, then he'd reasonably convinced himself that they were invisible. There were no indications that the government even knew they existed, let alone that they were plotting something spectacular. He'd come to the conclusion that if the government did know about the group, and they were under any sort of surveillance, changing their habits would only bring more attention to them.

He'd told all of the Daturans to make an appearance. Edwards was there, of course. Thistlewood and his piece-du-jour were there. Sir Spencer had seen Jimmy Ings come and go. The only one he'd not seen was Bill Davidson.

Davidson's misgivings about the plot were weighing on Sir Spencer. Having Matti Harrold stand in front of him in her well-fitting black dress was a nice distraction. "Matti had some interesting things to say about my work," continued Edwards. "She seems to think I have a lot of anger. She likes my take on politics but worries that I have 'issues'."

"I didn't say I liked your politics," Matti corrected. "I said that I thought you were talented. I essentially agreed that the iconography in your work is powerful. I didn't say I agree with your point of view. There's a difference between admiration and agreement."

"Quite the spunky one, isn't she?" the knight observed. She appeared genuine to Sir Spencer. He was oblivious to the fact that her beauty was clouding his judgment. A man of his experience and expertise should have seen what Thistlewood had. An alarm should have sounded. This woman was not the kind to like George Edwards.

CHAPTER 9

Thistlewood saw the woman with the large purse before Matti noticed her. He could tell there was something odd about the way she held the bag. He'd also noticed two other men who seemed out of place.

They were wearing dark business suits and seemed disconnected from the party. They stood alone and were observing people more than they were admiring art. Thistlewood imagined they were government agents.

When the suspicious translator abruptly left their conversation to approach the woman with the bag, he was certain that something was afoot. This wasn't paranoia, he assured himself. They were being watched.

"We need to go see Sir Spencer and George," he told Laura. He grabbed her hand and pulled her toward the bar. "I need to talk to them."

When they joined the group, Laura let go of her boyfriend's hand and got the bartender's attention. She wanted to take advantage of the open bar.

"I am sorry for being rude a few minutes ago," Matti said, reaching out to touch Thistlewood on the wrist. "I have been looking for that handbag everywhere! I am a huge Coach fan, and I can't find the purse anywhere."

"Was the woman helpful?" Thistlewood pulled his wrist away from her hand.

"No. She'd gotten it as a gift and didn't know where it was

purchased."

"How unfortunate." His tone was polite; the sarcasm was on his face. He looked up at the knight. "Sir Spencer, could I have a moment?"

"Of course, good man." Sir Spencer slapped Edwards' shoulder and bowed to Matti as he moved toward Thistlewood. The two walked away, leaving Edwards, Matti, and Laura at the bar.

"What is it, Art?" "I think we're blown."

"Really?" The knight was unmoved "What makes you think that?" He knew that Thistlewood wanted his approval, but he didn't think the man would try so hard.

"First," Thistlewood was counting on his fingers, "I am sure I was being followed earlier. When I left the pub this morning, someone was tailing me. I think they were watching me in my office too."

"Second?" The knight remained impassive.

"Second," parroted the professor, "I think there were at least three people here tonight who were watching us. They may have been snapping photographs of us."

The knight knew himself to be a perceptive man. He'd seen nothing. He said nothing.

"Third," Thistlewood held up three fingers on his right hand, "there's something unusual about that woman with George."

"The only thing unusual about her is her beauty."

"Look, Sir Spencer, I am telling you that there is a leak. Someone in our group is playing both sides."

The knight considered it and studied Thistlewood's face. He saw desperation and fear. Even if the professor was paranoid, Sir Spencer could tell Thistlewood thoroughly believed what he was saying.

The knight looked over at the beauty and George Edwards. Edwards was talking to her and, at first blush, she appeared to be paying attention to him. However, the closer he paid attention, the more he could see she was disinterested. Her eyes darted around the room. She was surveying the crowd. She wasn't looking *at* something in the crowd, Sir Spencer concluded, she was looking *for* something.

"What did she say she does for a living?" Sir Spencer kept his

TOM ABRAHAMS

eyes across the room.

"Translator."

"Hmm."

"What does that mean?"

"Translator is a typical job for CIA or even FBI operatives. NSA sometimes," Sir Spencer replied. He bit his lower lip. "They'll generally tell you they work for the State Department or the Department of Defense. Did she say where she works?"

"No." Thistlewood's head was on a swivel as he looked at the translator and then looked at Sir Spencer watching her. Was he right? Was she really a spy?

"Which one of us do you think is responsible, good man?" Sir Spencer shifted his weight from one foot to the other and clasped his hands behind his back. The button on his jacket pulled on the cashmere, stretching it unattractively against his gut.

"You mean the traitor?"

It was an interesting choice of words.

"Yes."

"I don't know." He was hesitant to tell Sir Spencer who he thought might be the double agent. "It's hard to say."

"Take a guess."

"Well, George was acting unusual this morning." He winced, waiting for the knight to immediately, loudly refute his theory. Sir Spencer said nothing; he was watching Edwards interact with the translator.

Edwards seemed too comfortable, the knight thought. He was too relaxed around this gorgeous woman. Edwards usually didn't have that sort of game.

The knight checked himself. Were his thoughts tainted by Thistlewood's ideas? He wasn't certain what to think. He needed more information.

"Why do you say that, good man?"

"He came to see me at my office on campus," began Thistlewood. "We both agreed that someone could be following us. When I suggested that we tell you about it, he was hesitant. It just seemed odd."

* * *

George Edwards was unusually comfortable around Matti. He sensed it within himself. Normally he wouldn't have the guts to approach a woman with such apparent class. But there was something about her that made him feel at ease. She seemed real and not at all pretentious like most of the people who attended his exhibitions.

More than that, it was the plot that had freed Edwards from his wallflower tendencies. The idea that in less than forty-eight hours he would engage in a massive act of domestic terror was liberating. His life, as he knew it, would probably end.

He accepted the fact that he would eventually be caught. It might take a week. It could take a decade. But from the moment the detonator triggered the explosives, his life would never be the same. So, what did he have to lose by flirting with a woman who ultimately would reject him anyhow?

"So where do you work as a translator?" he asked, leaning on the bar and into her.

"The State Department."

"I imagine that's an interesting job." He swirled the ice in his cranberry vodka. It was a feminine drink, but he liked the taste. He crunched a piece of ice between his teeth. "What do you translate?"

Matti hesitated and then answered, "Whatever needs translating."

"What languages?"

"Romance," she raised her eyebrows and blinked. Matti didn't know where her flirtatious inclinations were coming from, but she enjoyed surprising herself.

Edwards lifted his glass to his mouth and caught another ice cube in his teeth. He put the drink on the bar and used his thumb and index finger to wipe the corners of his mouth.

"Excuse me for just a minute." He raised his finger to hold her there at the bar while he walked over to speak with Sir Spencer and Art Thistlewood.

Matti turned to speak with Thistlewood's girlfriend, Laura.

"So you're Laura, right?"

"Uh huh." Laura was spinning the gulp of wine left in the bottom of her glass. She was drunk.

"So how did you two meet each other?" Matti knew the answer. She wondered how forthcoming the coed might be.

"A funeral."

"Really?"

"Yes." She nodded and took the last swig of merlot. It was bitter and she closed her eyes as she tossed her head back. "My father owns a funeral home. I was there helping. Art's friend had died and he was there to pay his respects. We saw each other and had this instant connection."

"Sounds romantic."

"Oh he is," Laura motioned to the bartender. He was hesitant to give her another refill until she shot him a look that pushed him to oblige. "You'd think the age difference would be a problem but it's the opposite. He's not immature like so many college boys. He's smart. He gets me. He's taught me so much about wine." She lifted her glass before taking the first sip of her fourth glass.

"What does your father think?"

She rolled her eyes. "Oh he doesn't care. He's too busy with work to notice."

"He works a lot?"

"Yes." Laura put her hand on top of Matti's and squeezed it. "Can I tell you something cool?"

"Sure."

"He's handling the president's funeral," she said above a whisper.

Matti looked around to see who was within earshot. Nobody. Even the bartender was preoccupied. "What do you mean?"

"My dad knows people." Laura cupped her right hand along the side of her mouth, as if she were telling a secret. "He's providing the casket and flowers for the president's funeral. Amazing, huh?"

"Yeah," Matti was floored. "Amazing."

She couldn't believe what she was hearing. Did the agency know about this? Was she the only one who knew that a conspirator was dating the daughter of a man connected to the president's funeral? She needed a moment alone to process that.

"Excuse me, Laura. I need to use the restroom. I'll be back in a moment." Matti asked the bartender for directions to the bathrooms and then walked off. Laura took another sip of her wine, not thinking twice about what she'd just revealed to a spy.

* * *

"So she works for the State Department," Edwards was rationalizing. "It doesn't mean she's a spy."

"No," agreed Sir Spencer. "But it is curious."

"I don't know..." Edwards was trying to convince himself as much as the others that his new friend was a legitimate fan.

"George," Thistlewood questioned, "why is she here? You've never seen her at an event before. Look around. Other than some old money patrons and some young peaceniks, who is here? I'm telling you. Something doesn't add up."

"I don't know that I agree..."

"What about us being followed this morning? What about the woman with the purse earlier tonight? Very odd. Plus, she told you that she doesn't really like your politics."

"Yeah, maybe."

"I think we need to talk to her," Thistlewood stated. He looked at both men for approval.

"I agree," said Sir Spencer. He was beginning to wonder about the woman. He didn't so much agree with Thistlewood's assessment of Edwards' complicity in leaking information, but he agreed that Matti Harrold did not fit the profile of a George Edwards fan. The incident with the pant suited woman was troublesome. There was too much at stake to risk it.

"How do we approach her?" asked Edwards.

"Politely, good man," Sir Spencer's said expressionlessly. "If that doesn't work we'll have to press her a bit. There's a room upstairs in the back. It's quiet."

The men silently agreed and then walked over to the bar where they found Laura standing alone. Edwards turned to look around the room. He didn't see her anywhere.

"Where is Matti?" Thistlewood asked Laura.

"She went to the ladies' room." Laura placed her hand flat on the professor's chest and rubbed, pouting. "Can't we leave? I've had a little too much to drink. We've seen George's work. Let's go."

"In a minute," he answered and moved her hand from his chest.

"We need to talk to Matti. Just wait here." The three men looked at each other and purposefully walked toward the bathrooms in the back hallway of the first floor.

* * *

Matti found the men's and women's restrooms in a hallway that ran along the entire back side of the first floor of the building. They were split by the stairs that led to the second floor, a water fountain, and about twenty feet.

She pushed on the door to the ladies' room. It was locked. She knocked. There was no answer. She walked back to the other end of the hallway, closer to the reception, and pushed on the men's door. It opened.

"Hello?" she called into the room. "Anybody in here?" No reply. Matti had to go. She slipped inside and turned the lock on the inside of the door.

After using the toilet she stood at the wall length mirror that sat above the trough of sinks. Above the mirrors were air conditioning returns blowing cold air into the room. She noticed little strings of dust flapping against the vents. They needed to be cleaned.

Matti washed her hands and stood in front of the mirror. She wondered what connection there might be between the president's funeral and the conspirators. It was too much of a coincidence.

She snapped open the latch on her clutch and pulled out a tube of lip gloss. Matti was rubbing the open tube against her bottom lip when she heard voices outside the door of the bathroom.

"How do we get her upstairs?" said a man's voice.

"We ask her first. Then we persuade." The second voice was British. Matti recognized it as Sir Spencer's. The talking continued but Matti couldn't discern what the men were saying as they walked farther down the hall.

She quickly replaced the cap on the lip gloss, slipped it back into her clutch and smacked her lips. She then quickly moved to the door, unlocked it quietly, and slowly cracked it.

Matti peeked around the door toward the women's bathroom. She could see Sir Spencer, Art Thistlewood, and George Edwards huddled at the door. Edwards stepped to the door and knocked.

"Matti?" He pressed his side against the door. They wanted her! Had they figured her out? Did she tip herself off by approaching the woman with the bag? *Rookie mistake*, she chastised herself.

"Stupid! Stupid! Stupid!" she murmured under breath as she watched the men try to open the locked door.

"Matti? You in there? Are you okay?" Edwards looked back at the other two and shrugged his shoulders.

It would only be a matter of seconds before they realized she wasn't in the ladies room. They'd come looking for her. She shut the door and locked it, scanning the room. Looking up at the air vent, she had an idea. She'd seen it in a late night movie as a teenager on a night when she couldn't sleep. She watched a lot of late night movies.

The lint was no longer blowing. The air conditioning was off. The vent was on the side of the room such that its ductwork might connect to the women's room on the other side. She pulled up her dress, slipped off her shoes, and climbed onto the sink trough. Balancing herself against the mirror, she pressed her cheek against the filthy vent.

"George, is that you? I'll be just a minute." Matti stood on her tiptoes and pressed her ear to the vent.

"Okay. I'll wait." She could barely hear him, but there it was. He could hear her. He fell for it and thought she was in the other restroom. It would buy her time.

She climbed back down and walked back to the door. The floor was damp and it disgusted her. This was reason enough never to wear impractical shoes again.

Matti opened the door again and peeked down the hall. Edwards and Thistlewood stood at the door with their arms folded. Sir Spencer stood behind them. Matti watched him reach down to his ankle and pull up the cuff of his pants. Around his calf was what looked like a thick black sock strap. She saw him pull a small silver object from the inside of his leg. It was a pistol! He held it behind his back. The other two were oblivious.

"Matti?" Edwards called again.

She shut the door, relocked it, and ran over to the sinks. She turned on all of the faucets and then ran to each of the three stalls and flushed each of the toilets. It was loud. Matti hiked up her dress and hopped back onto the trough. She cupped her hands around her mouth.

"I'm just finishing up. Hang on!" She then hopped down, adjusted her dress and grabbed her shoes.

Holding the straps in her left hand, she unlocked the door with her right and opened the door. She quietly stepped into the hall, trying to move past the corner and into the reception hall without the men seeing her.

She didn't make it.

* * *

Bill Davidson was late to the party. He walked into the main hall and started looking for the men. He peeked over heads and into the still gathered groups of people. He didn't see any of them. No Sir Spencer. No Art Thistlewood. No George Edwards. No Jimmy Ings. Where were they? He couldn't imagine that they would have already left.

Davidson mingled with people who recognized him. He was polite but brief as he shook hands and smiled while working the room to find the other Daturans. He checked his watch. He had less than an hour until he needed to meet his girl at the Mayflower.

Davidson found the bar and ordered a vodka tonic. He was nervous, given what he was about to tell Sir Spencer. He didn't want to be a part of the plot anymore. It wasn't that important to him. He took his drink and walked toward one of Edwards' new pieces. It hung on a wall at the back of the room near the rear hallway. It looked like a Norman Rockwell painting.

Davidson stepped up to the canvas and looked at the detail. In the foreground of the drawing were two servicemen. The taller was a marine in dress blues. He stood tall, head turned looking over his right shoulder. His hands were placed on the shoulders of a shorter soldier. The soldier was in his desert fatigues and turned to the side. He was looking in the same direction as the marine. The soldier held a small map. On the map, Iraq and Afghanistan were highlighted.

Both men looked back at a darkened profile of George Washington. Washington sat with his hands held together in prayer, a sword at his feet. Behind him and to the right of the canvas, an unseen man held the reins of a white horse.

A deep red tear was drawn down Washington's left cheek from his eye. He was in pain.

Davidson recognized the work as a famous Rockwell postcard. In the original, Washington sat in the same position praying. There was no tear. In the foreground, the two men were not military. They were a Boy Scout and a Cub Scout. Rockwell had designed the work as part of a series. The Boy Scouts of America distributed the prints during the 1960s and 1970s.

Edwards chose to keep the same name as the original painting. Davidson looked at the white card to the right of the canvas.

Our Heritage, 2012
George Edwards
Digital Sculpture, 11 x 14

He moved to his left to look at another piece. It was a large vibrant canvas titled, *Universal Health Care*. It was a nearly exact duplicate of Picasso's 1937 painting called, *Weeping Woman*. Davidson remembered speaking with Edwards about this piece and it was among his favorite.

Davidson knew that Edwards was very specific about the paintings he chose to digitally alter. The choice of *Weeping Woman* was not by accident. It was a painting Picasso created to communicate the pain visible on a human face. The blue, green, and yellow woman depicted in the work was actually a friend and collaborator of Picasso. Her name was Dora Maar. She was close to Picasso during the time in his life when he was most involved in politics. 1937 was also a year in which the United States entered a second depression. It was the year Social Security paid out its first monies and that unemployment insurance became a law in all fifty states.

Edwards had replaced the colors of Picasso's original with red, white, and blue. The tears were in the shapes of melting stars. The face was altered just enough to resemble Lady Liberty. She wore a crown.

Davidson admired Edwards' work. It was smart and relevant.

He wondered why a man with so much talent would decide to ruin it. He was about to go back to the bar for a refill when he heard a commotion coming from the back hallway.

* * *

Matti was about to turn the corner into the main hall and slip out of sight when she heard her name.

"Matti?" Edwards was calling after her. He'd seen her tiptoeing down the hall. "Matti? Is that you?" He was confused and looked back at the bathroom door. She looked back at him but didn't speak.

Quickening her pace, and almost losing her balance, she rounded the corner into the main hall. She could hear the men begin to run after her. When she entered the hall she saw Bill Davidson. He was looking at her bare feet as she scurried by him. She walked quickly past Laura at the bar and then to the front of the room. Matti reached the door and turned to see the men still following her. Edwards was leading the other two.

Matti could feel the crowd watching her as she pushed past the glass door and onto the sidewalk. She looked to her left and then to her right. It was dark outside now. She saw no taxis to either side. She decided to run left. As she sprinted down the sidewalk, Edwards shoved through the door, gaining ground quickly.

Matti saw a cab ahead. She held up her shoes and waved. The cab slowed at the curb right in front of her. She scrambled for the handle, pulled it, and threw herself into the back seat. Out of breath but full of adrenaline, she slammed the door. Edwards was within a few feet of her but stopped running as if nearing the edge of a cliff and watched the cab pull away.

"The Metro stop at Reagan National," Matti huffed. Her feet hurt and she wanted to get as far away from the men as possible. She knew she'd blown it. She might have jeopardized the entire operation. Her supervisor would be incensed. She considered that breaking the rules wasn't such a good idea after all.

Rules are there for a reason.

Matti turned around to see the three men still standing on the sidewalk. Bill Davidson had joined them. They weren't following her.

She leaned back against the blue vinyl of the seat. What had she done?

* * *

"What was that about?" Davidson didn't bother to greet his brethren. "Why were you chasing that woman?"

"She's a spy," Thistlewood blurted out.

"What?"

"She's a spook, Bill," Thistlewood said, talking with his hands. "We're being watched and followed. The gig is up."

"We don't know that, Arthur." Sir Spencer had slipped the pistol back into the ankle strap underneath his pants. None of the others had seen it. "She was suspicious. She's likely working for some agency, but we don't know that she's a spy. And we don't know what information she has or doesn't have."

"George is the problem!" Thistlewood snarled and pointed his finger at the artist.

"What are you talking about?" Edwards said in a raised voice. "Why am I the problem?"

"Lower your voices, men." Sir Spencer stood between Edwards and Thistlewood. "Let's go back inside and discuss this privately." He waved the men inside and they walked back into the reception hall. A small crowd had gathered at the door. They moved back as the men entered.

"Nothing to worry about," announced Sir Spencer. "We thought that woman may have tried to abscond with a piece of George's work as a souvenir." The crowd bought the excuse and went back to its conversation and drink.

The men walked back past the bar to the rear hallway. Thistlewood stopped to assure Laura that he'd be only a few more minutes. She accepted the delay as the men disappeared up the stairs and into a private room.

They feared the plot was in peril. There was distrust amongst the conspirators. They needed to clear the air. Edwards was the first one into the room. He found a plastic chair in the corner in which to sit. He was also the first to speak.

"So what was *that* about, Art?"

"Someone in this group is telling the government what we're planning!" He waved his hand loosely around the room at all three men, stopping at Edwards. "I think it's you!"

"Me?" Edwards pointed at himself with his thumb. "What are you talking about? You know me, Art. What would make you think I would ruin what we've worked so hard to accomplish?"

"You didn't want to tell Sir Spencer that we're being followed. You insist on holding this high profile art opening, even though we're thirty-six hours away from the biggest day of our lives. You could've canceled it and kept our profile low. You didn't. Then you spend time with this woman who is probably a spy. It adds up."

"First of all, I didn't think we needed to make Sir Spencer believe we're getting skittish or paranoid." Edwards was standing, despite his now-throbbing ankle. "Secondly, I couldn't *cancel* the event. And if we *were* under surveillance, changing plans would have only raised suspicion. You said the very same thing at your office this morning. As for the woman tonight, I have never seen her before."

Davidson stood silently, listening to the back and forth between the professor and the artist. He wasn't surprised. He knew that a conspiracy was destined to breed jealously and paranoia. It was all the more reason for him to pull out.

Sir Spencer also stood quietly, gauging the reactions and body language of the three men. He could tell from Edwards' genuine shock and defense that he was telling the truth. The artist was no turncoat.

The knight was certain that the professor protested too much. He was worried at Thistlewood's steep decline from normalcy to rabid paranoia. But Sir Spencer was sure that he too was clean.

He thought about Jimmy Ings. The drunk was too deep into the plot to spill the beans. That left only one person who might be responsible for a leak if one existed.

"Bill, my good man," Sir Spencer looked over at the former cabinet member with something just short of contempt. His lips were pursed as though he'd sipped sour milk. "What are your thoughts?"

"Wait," Thistlewood interrupted. "What about George here?"

He gestured toward the irritated artist.

"Arthur," the knight said, fed up with the whining, "that will be enough. If there is a traitor among us, it's not George. I suspect it's not you, and I doubt James Ings has the wherewithal to betray anything but his brand of liquor. I know *I* am not talking to the government. That leaves the good attorney general here."

Davidson understood the knight's suspicion but it bothered him. Other than his expressions of concern and his hesitancy to follow through, he'd given no indication he would go to the authorities. He was too close to it. It was far enough along now that he risked complicity even if he shouted the plot from the rooftops.

"I ask again," repeated Sir Spencer. "What are your thoughts?"

"I haven't talked about this with anyone." He tried to avoid sounding defensive but wasn't successful. "What would I gain? I am the highest profile person in this group. I would only sully my public reputation were I to reveal my affiliation with you people."

"*You people?*" Thistlewood didn't like that. "That characterization gives me the impression that you don't consider yourself a part of this."

"Quite right," Sir Spencer concurred.

Edwards stayed quiet, enjoying the spotlight being on someone else.

"Well, I *am* having trouble with this," Davidson admitted. "I'm opposed to the violence. I can't justify it. But that doesn't mean that I would set up some elaborate scheme to undo you. I am still hopeful we can achieve our goals without killing or injuring innocent people."

"Fair enough," said Sir Spencer. "But we are resolved to accomplish our objective in the most effective way possible. In war there is always collateral damage. This is a battle over the soul of this nation and its global positioning. I think you comprehend the gravitas, don't you?"

"Yes." Davidson pulled a handkerchief from his pants pocket and dabbed beads of sweat from his forehead.

"I need an answer from you by midnight," Sir Spencer said. "And I need the information you have promised. I will call you."

Davidson nodded. "Am I done here?"

"Yes." There were things to discuss about which Davidson

didn't need to know.

Davidson started to leave when Edwards stopped him. "Bill, wait a second. I have something for you. It's downstairs." Edwards told the knight and the professor he would return in a moment and they walked out.

"How can we pull this off even if we *don't* have a leak?" Thistlewood said, convinced the plan was ruined. "We can't explain that woman, Matti, or what she was doing here. It's just too dangerous now. Maybe Bill is right."

"Bill is wrong." Sir Spencer crossed the small room and sat in the plastic chair that Edwards had vacated. He sighed. "If our conspiracy is compromised, we will know it soon enough. We are too far along now to step on the proverbial brake."

"How is that?" Thistlewood asked doubtfully.

"If they know anything about us, they likely know everything. Or at least, they think they know everything. In either case, they won't stop us until we advance far enough with the plot to give them probable cause."

"They won't try to stop us until it's too late to stop us. Even if we are caught in the act, there are elements to this that they won't expect. We will be successful regardless. The only thing we risk now, if we have been exposed, is our own freedom." Sir Spencer wasn't looking at Thistlewood as he spoke. The knight's eyes were distant. "I am willing to sacrifice my life for the greater good."

"But if they know about us now, then they could stop us from placing the explosives. Or they could disarm the explosives," Thistlewood insisted. He believed that the knight wasn't facing the reality of these new developments. "They'll arrest us. It will all have been for nothing. Remember that guy in Dallas? He was a Jordanian or Egyptian on a personal jihad, trying to blow up a building in downtown Dallas. Somehow his plan got discovered and he unwittingly divulged everything to the Feds, who were working undercover to bust him. They gave him a fake bomb which he left in a garage. He thought he'd pulled it off when the Feds rolled in and arrested him. That could happen to us. It could be happening already."

"Ye have little faith, Arthur." The knight snapped from his gaze and looked at Thistlewood. "A wise man attacks the city of the mighty and pulls down the stronghold in which they trust."

"Proverbs. I get it."

"I mean to remind you, good man, that wisdom conquers strength. We must trust that our just cause will triumph. There is no proof that anyone has betrayed us or that Matti Harrold is anything more than a desk-riding bureaucrat who became spooked at George thumping on the bathroom door."

Thistlewood considered the rationalization. He said nothing in response.

"Now you have a job to do," Sir Spencer concluded. "Get your girlfriend and get it done."

Thistlewood turned to leave as Edwards reentered the room and hesitated; he was uncomfortable leaving Sir Spencer alone with him. worried he himself would be left out of the loop. But he knew that his role that night was critically important and so he turned into the hallway. He didn't acknowledge Edwards as they passed.

Sir Spencer hit the "C" on his phone and made a brief phone call for some last minute arrangements. Davidson, he knew, needed a push.

* * *

Bill Davidson was two blocks east of the Mayflower Hotel. He walked from the exhibit hall and turned right onto 17th. He was holding a small bag that Edwards had given to him, which contained a copy of *Henry David Thoreau: Collected Essays & Poems*. It was a heavy hardback edition squeezed between two other volumes in a boxed set, and its weight stretched the plastic handles of the bag.

Edwards had borrowed it weeks earlier to read some of Thoreau's political writings. He'd expressed particular interest in the famed, "Civil Disobedience" essay. Davidson had mentioned that he knew a copy of the book was in a storage room at the Hanover-Crown Institute, and he'd borrowed it and loaned it to the artist.

Davidson turned left onto DeSales Street off of 17th. He took the side entrance into the hotel and went straight into an open elevator to his left in the main lobby.

When the elevator door opened again, he stepped out into the hallway and knocked on the first door to the right. He heard the pull of the chain lock on the door and the turning of latch. He was anxious.

"Hello, sexy," she purred. She was dressed in a white cotton robe and nothing else, the belt at her waist looped but not tied. She pulled him into the room and locked the door behind him. She had a glass of wine in her hand. "I thought you'd never make it."

Davidson walked her to the bed and dropped the bag onto the floor. He kissed her on the neck and then whispered in her ear, "I missed you."

"I missed you," she replied. "Now go get changed." She playfully pushed him away from her and took a sip of the wine. Davidson noticed a room service tray with a bottle and another glass.

"Okay, I'll be fast." He walked to the bathroom near the front door of the room.

"Oh," she said in between sips of wine, "you left your little book at the gym today." He felt his breast pocket and realized it wasn't there. He turned around to see her pointing her glass toward the small desk. It was next to her purse.

"Really? I don't ever take it out of my pocket except to write in it." Davidson was bothered. He walked purposefully to the desk to pick it up and put it in its rightful place.

"Don't worry, silly," she cooed. "I didn't look at it. I picked it up because I recognized it as yours. Your secrets are safe."

His eyes narrowed as he looked at her. He wasn't sure what to think. But there were too many other more important things about which to worry. He relaxed his brow. "Okay. Thanks for finding it." He patted his breast pocket and walked to the bathroom.

Davidson flipped on the light and shut the door. It was false modesty but it was habit. He had started to unbutton his shirt when she called to him.

"I love the wine, Bill," she said from just outside the bathroom door. Thank you, sweetie.""I didn't order it." Davidson thought she was kidding. He sat on the edge of the tub to slip off his shoes. "I thought you bought it."

"No." Her voice came from farther away; he imagined she was looking at the bottle. "The card just says 'Enjoy'. It doesn't have a name or a signature. So who sent it then?"

"Probably the concierge," Davidson said, suspecting it was from the hotel; he spent a lot of money there. He stood from the tub's edge and unbuckled his belt, dropping his pants to his ankles. He heard a knock at the door.

"Hold your horses, gorgeous. I'll be out in a minute."

"No that's the room door, Bill. I'll get it." She peeked through the peephole and saw it was the same man who'd delivered the wine. "Room service again, I think."

Davidson heard her unlock the door and swing it open. Then he heard two hollow sounding clicks within a second of each other followed by a thud. He didn't hear the door shut, nor did he hear any voices.

He looked down to see wine seeping onto the bathroom floor from underneath the door. "Are you okay?" In his undershirt and boxers, Davidson stood and felt a rush of panic. His heart rate quickened and he gripped the door handle. He pulled it open.

Her body fell onto his feet.

There was a deep red hole in the center of her forehead. There was a red trail down the side of her face and leaking from the back of her head. It wasn't wine on the floor. It was blood.

He knelt to the tile floor where it met the carpet, cradling her head in his hands. He called her name. She wasn't responding. Her eyes were open and fixed with fear. The last thing she'd seen was her killer. Davidson saw a dark stain growing on the robe at her chest. She'd been shot twice.

He pulled her limp body from the doorway and into his lap. The door to the room automatically shut. Blood was everywhere. His mind was racing.

Why would someone kill her? Was it another john? Her pimp? Did she owe someone money?

And then as quickly as the silenced shots had changed his world, he realized who was responsible. Sir Spencer. Davidson knew it. It had to be him. He gently laid her head on the bathroom floor and stood.

With blood on his hands, Davidson picked up his pants to find his cell phone. He couldn't remember in which pocket he'd stuffed it. Then it rang. He found the phone, pushed 'C' and placed the phone to his ear but didn't speak.

"Bill?" It was Sir Spencer. "I'm assuming you've made up your mind?"

Davidson's jaw was clenched. The vein across the top of his forehead was pulsing against his skin. He was seething but said nothing.

"It had to be done, Bill," Sir Spencer said with no compassion. "You understand."

No response.

"Okay." The knight sighed. "Here's where we find ourselves. You need to provide to me the information necessary for our success. If you do, the dead prostitute vanishes. Your relationship with her vanishes. The whole bloody mess vanishes." He paused then laughed. "That pun was intended, Bill."

"And if I don't cooperate?"

"I think you know the consequences of that."

"If I lose either way, then why do I help?"

"Oh, Bill!" the knight said condescendingly. "Don't you get it? If you don't help me, someone else will. You will be a two time loser. Bill Davidson: the killer of a hooker and the Benedict Arnold of the 21st century. You are the brains behind this whole operation, right? I mean, you pushed us to this violence, didn't you? I assure you that is the truth that the rest of us will be telling the authorities if it comes to that." He paused for effect. "If you do as promised, you have a chance to save yourself, Bill. There is a possibility that you can keep whatever shred of dignity you have remaining. That is up to you."

Davidson contemplated his options; he had none. He knew that if he called the police, he'd be arrested. Even if they didn't have a weapon or a motive, he'd be ruined. If he helped the knight, however, there was a chance that he could go on living his life.

Desperate men do desperate things; Sir Spencer knew that. He exploited that.

"Fine. I'll give you the information you want. Give me a half hour. Then you need to get this cleaned up."

"When you call me with what I need, then I'll clean it up. So chop chop, good man." The knight hung up.

Davidson stood weak-kneed and turned on the shower. He needed to get the blood off of his body. While he waited for the water to warm up, he stepped over the body and into the room. He went to the desk where he grabbed her purse.

Davidson dumped the contents on the bed. It bothered him that she'd had possession of his journal. He wanted to find out if there was some connection between her and Sir Spencer.

On the bed, there was a pack of cinnamon gum, a small makeup bag, a cell phone, a large headset, some loose change, a set of keys, two condoms, a roll of cash bound with a red rubber band, and a small canister of pepper spray.

He picked up the phone and scrolled through the numbers. He didn't recognize any of them except for his. He tossed the phone back onto the bed and picked up the headset. Davidson thought it was somewhat large for a hands-free device. It almost looked like something a Time-Life operator would wear. He'd only seen her use a wireless earpiece in the past.

He picked the phone up again and plugged in the headset. It fit. He scrolled down her call list and then randomly picked one that had registered a lengthy call time. He pushed send and slipped on the headset.

* * *

Matti was opening the door to her office when the phone started ringing. She'd decided to skip going home and had headed straight back to work.

On the drive from the Metro park and ride, she'd thought about the troubles that lay ahead for her. There would be a lot of questions in the morning. She needed as much time as possible to organize her thoughts.

There were so many things she'd done to disobey her direct orders, including engaging the subjects and compromising the integrity of three agents.

But as she drove with the windows down and the radio off, she wasn't apologetic. For the first time in her life she was coloring outside of the lines. She had gained valuable intelligence. She'd gotten herself out of a potentially dangerous situation. Those were good things. And she began to realize that nobody was what they seemed to be. Everyone had shades of gray.

Even my mother.

The wind whipped around her in the driver's seat of her

government issued Ford, and Matti found that she was more afraid of being pulled off the case because of the rush it provided than because of the eventual career consequences. She reminded herself of that as she walked into the office.

"Harrold." She was still standing when she picked up the receiver.

"Who is this?" said a robotic voice. Matti recognized it as belonging to the asset.

"This is Harrold."

"Who are you? Who is Harrold?"

Matti listened to the voice. It was somehow different. The tone was lower maybe.

"I'm Matti Harrold."

"Matti Harrold? From the art exhibit tonight?" There was something tentative and confused in the asset's voice. "You were wearing a black dress?"

"Yes."

"Do you know who this is?"

"No," Matti sat down at her desk. Something was off.

"Do you recognize my voice?"

"No. It's the same robotic tone you've been using with that alteration device," Matti said. She reached into her desk, pulled out her notepad, and started taking notes.

"Where do you work?"

She noted there was hesitancy, as if the asset really didn't know the answer.

"You know where I work."

Matti was concerned now that whoever was calling her was not the asset. She heard a rustling sound on the other end of the line.

"Where do you work?" It was a man's voice now, the robotic quality gone. Whoever it was had disconnected the device. Matti found the voice familiar, yet she couldn't quite place it.

"I saw you tonight, running away from three men. They were chasing you. You had your shoes off and you looked frightened."

"You suggested I attend the event. You thought it would be a good idea. Don't you remember?"

"I didn't suggest anything. But I was there. I saw you run out."

Matti suddenly realized who it was on the other line. It was the only conspirator not chasing her. She'd seen him as she turned the corner to run out of the building.

"You're Bill Davidson," she said in sudden realization.

Davidson stood in his boxers and undershirt, finally beginning to grasp what had happened. "You work for the government don't you? CIA? FBI? Which is it?"

"Something like that," Matti said vaguely. "You're not my asset are you?"

"No." Davidson looked over to the dead body lying on the floor. He thought about his journal and how it had ended up in her hands. His mind raced through all of the things he'd told his girl in confidence. He edged on hyperventilating as he thought of the access she'd had to his written thoughts whenever he slept next to her or showered in the adjacent bathroom. He shuddered. Holding the phone in his right hand, he brought his left to his head.

He squeezed at his temples. "Your 'asset' is dead."

PART THREE
THE EXECUTION

"We must all hang together, or assuredly we shall all hang separately."
-- Benjamin Franklin at the signing of the Declaration of Independence

CHAPTER 10

The smell of death was a counterintuitive aphrodisiac for Laura Harrowby. The odor was more a mixture of embalming fluid and lemon-scented Pledge than the exceptional stench of putrefaction, but it was the scent she most associated with her father's funeral home.

The fact that the funeral home sexually stimulated her was as much an unspoken commentary on her "daddy complex" as it was on her relationship with the much older Professor Arthur Thistlewood. When she stumbled into the lamp lit office in the back of the building, she inhaled deeply and moaned, clumsily punching the four numbers on the alarm console to turn it off.

"Shhh!" Thistlewood was already on edge. He didn't want to alert anyone to their presence. He checked the door as he walked in and made certain it was unlocked.

"There's nobody here *now*, silly man," she said, tilting into him and burying her face in his neck. "Just you and me. And me and you and tea for two," she hummed as she flicked her tongue on his neck and sucked.

He put his hands on her shoulders and forcefully pushed her back to look her in the eyes. She was sloppy drunk and still attractive. He would oblige her, but not in the office.

"Didn't you tell me that you wanted to show me something as soon as we got here?" He reminded her. "You've been anxious about it for hours."

"Oh yes!" Her eyes widened from the reminder. She giggled.

"Yes! Follow me." She grabbed his hand and led him through a narrow hallway to a wide door. She opened it and reached inside to flip on a light switch.

The light revealed a set of stairs leading down a flight to the basement. She carefully negotiated the steps by bracing herself against the wall to her right and by gripping the circulation from Thistlewood's right forearm.

They reached the bottom of the steps and Laura flipped another switch which illuminated a large open room. It extended in front of them some twenty feet and another fifteen feet to either side. The floor was smooth cement. It appeared remarkably clean. Except for a wide doorway at the far left side of the room, the walls and ceiling were a series of crossing two by four studs separated by sheets of pink insulation. The room smelled like furniture polish and cedar.

In the middle of the room, on what looked like a gurney, sat a single casket. It was deep brown with hints of red.

Thistlewood could tell it was hand-rubbed mahogany. The fluorescent lights hanging from the ceiling reflected against the sheen of the polish. Along its sides were stainless steel support bars that ran the length of the large box. Its Dutch lid was open. Thistlewood could see that the cream colored satin lining wrapped the entirety of the interior.

"That's the president's casket," Laura said, holding the professor's right hand with both of hers. "That's what they'll put him in."

"So that's the coffin, huh?" Thistlewood was studying the wood box for more than one reason.

"Casket," she corrected him. "Not a coffin."

There actually was a difference. Modern caskets didn't come into use in the United States until the mid-19th century. The metamorphosis from the simple coffin to a more ornate casket was first widely recognized in 1885 when President Ulysses S. Grant was buried in a metal casket with a full plate glass top. There was no question about *what* was buried in Grant's tomb, even if the *who* was debated for more than a century.

Those in the profession of serving the dead were sensitive to the vernacular. Undertakers had become funeral home directors and coffins had become caskets.

"Sorry," he said, but he wasn't. "It looks heavy."

"Most of the wooden ones weigh about 100 to 150 pounds," Laura informed him. She released her hands from his and moved them gently to the area between his legs. "Any wooden ones here?" She laughed from her throat.

He flinched and smiled at her. "Okay, just a couple of minutes. I've never been in a room like this before."

"It's called a Reposing Room," she offered. "This is where the casketing will happen. You know, when the body gets put into the casket and arranged. It's where we keep the body until the funeral." Laura turned away from Thistlewood and leaned back onto him. She wrapped his hands around her waist as they looked at the casket.

"It'll get rolled to the dumb waiter over there and hoisted up to the main floor," Laura said, motioning to the right side of the room with her head. Thistlewood was surprised that he hadn't noticed the large elevator-like hole in the wall. There was an electric panel next to the hole with a pair of large buttons.

"Obviously the president isn't here. If he were, he'd be through the doors to the left. That's where the embalming room is. Usually that's where the body would be until after it's dressed."

"When does the president get here?"

"Mmm," she purred, "I'm not sure. I just know that my father said some other company was preserving and dressing the body. For security reasons or something. My father doesn't know who's doing it. I think it's some time tomorrow morning."

Thistlewood looked at his Timex. It was late. He knew the others had to be waiting for his signal by now. He lowered his head and placed his lips against her left ear.

"Should we move to another room?" he whispered.

"It's about time." Laura turned her head to the left to kiss her boyfriend. She found his lips and sighed. He could taste the bitterness of long ago consumed wine on her tongue.

She pulled away after a moment and then took his hand to lead him upstairs. She was still intoxicated and found the flight up a bit challenging. But she managed it and led Thistlewood into a small parlor at the far end of the hall from the back office. He left the door to the Reposing Room open.

Laura found her way to the chenille sofa and lay down with her head on the rolled arm. She motioned for Thistlewood to join her.

"Let me just turn my phone off," he told her as he locked the door behind him. "I wouldn't want to be interrupted."

"No, we wouldn't want that," her eyes were closed.

Thistlewood pushed 'C' on his phone before sending a brief text message and turning off the phone. He joined his girlfriend on the sofa. She would be preoccupied long enough for her desire to be satisfied and her trust betrayed.

* * *

Bill Davidson sat in his room at The Mayflower for what seemed like hours, the day's events running through his head.

His recollections filled only a few minutes, but time had slowed. He leafed through the pages of his small blue notebook. Dotting the lines were names, dates, and addresses. There were thoughts about the country, about each of his co-conspirators, and about the plot.

How much of it had his now dead lover seen? What had she told the feds? Was he implicated? If he hadn't been previously, he was now. He'd made the mistake of calling the handler. That handler had been at the art opening earlier in the evening. There was no coincidence there.

The girl had clearly told Matti to be at the opening. Matti so much as admitted it. This was bad and getting worse.

Davidson looked down at his lap and noticed blood on his pants. He stood and untucked his shirt. He looked disheveled, but it hid the stain. The A.G. looked around the room as if he expected the scene around him to have changed. It had not. Straight ahead of him, toward the door, were the legs and feet of a woman who, only an hour earlier, was sipping wine and making small talk.

He needed to take control of the situation. Somehow, he had to find a way out of the predicament where there seemed to be none.

He picked up one of the cell phones from the bed, pressed 'C' and dialed a familiar number.

"You have my information?" The knight said smugly with no greeting.

"Yes, I have it."

"I'm listening." The knight pulled his Meisterstuck Rollerball from his jacket pocket and jotted down the specific times of the various events planned for the procession, the Capitol service, and the graveside funeral at Arlington. He already had the information, but getting the exact times from two different people made him more comfortable.

"And the rest?" He was relentless. "I need the rest."

"I've arranged it," Davidson acknowledged. "The people at Hanover are prepared."

"Excellent, good man," the knight hissed. "That wasn't as bad as you thought it would be, was it? All you needed was a push."

"You're right. A push." Davidson looked again at the lower half of the dead body extending from his hotel bathroom. "That's all I needed." He started to push the button that would end the call when he heard the knight call his name.

"Bill?" Apparently the knight wasn't finished playing. "Bill, are you there?"

"Yes." Davidson was acting the part of a masochist, as he sometimes had more joyfully done with the girl now suffering from algor mortis.

"You should have known better, Bill. If you didn't have the stomach for a revolution, you would have been better off as the laughing stock of a politico you've been for most of your adult life." The knight was riding his high horse again. "You wanted so badly to become something you were never really capable of becoming. It's sad really. I pity you."

If Davidson hadn't convinced himself of the next necessary step before the phone call, he had now. The knight had done it for him. Davidson didn't respond. He disconnected the call and picked up the other cell phone on the bed. He redialed Matti Harrold to arrange a meeting.

* * *

Matti was about to leave her office when the door swung open. Her boss stood there blocking her exit. His hair was uncombed and the soft skin beneath his eyes was dark and swollen. He hadn't shaved in nearly twenty-four hours, though to Matti it appeared to have been longer that. He was dressed in a UCONN sweatshirt and tan Dockers. Most pronounced, she noticed, was a thick vein bulging vertically from his hairline to his brow

"Harrold, why am I here?" He was talking through his teeth while gripping the door knob such that his knuckles were white. "Why am I here at this ungodly hour?"

"Well, sir—"

"I am here because you have disappointed me." He'd let go of the door and folded his arms. His neck and cheeks were flushed, his jaw was clenched as he spoke. "You disobeyed direct orders. You failed in the simplest of tasks."

He was not wrong. Matti knew that.

"Sir," she began again, fully expecting to be cut off at the knees.

"What?"

"The asset is dead."

The supervisor's glare softened almost imperceptibly as his eyes darted around the room trying to visualize the words that flew from Matti's mouth. How did he not know this already?

"She was shot and killed in the hotel room of a conspirator. The conspirator claims he did not do it. He inadvertently called the gray line, using the asset's cell phone after her death."

"How do you know this?" The bulging vein in his forehead had shrunk, but the frown lines stretching diagonally outward from the edges of his nostrils were profound.

"The conspirator told me." Matti suddenly felt flush for being so green; she'd trusted the word of a man plotting terrorism. She fought through the doubt if only to convince herself. "I believe him. He was panicked."

"First of all," he was heating up again, the shock of the confession wearing off, "if she were dead, I would know it. I just spoke to her earlier today. And secondly, Bill Davidson is as capable of deceit under duress as anyone in Washington."

"I didn't say it was Bill Davidson who called me, sir."

"Gimme a break, Harrold. Who else would be with the whore? His relationship with her was the reason we went after her in the first place."

"*You* went after *her*?" That wasn't what her supervisor had led her to believe.

"Grow up!" He laughed at her question as though it was unworthy of asking. "We knew that Davidson was involved in some rogue group, but we couldn't get a hold on it. These Tea Party deals have been a thorn in our side for years now. Little splinter groups pop up and go away all of the time. When a former cabinet member gets involved, we have to pay attention."

"Why her?"

"She was the entrée into the group. We appealed to her sense of self-preservation. She either helped us or we made life very difficult for her." His anger softened as he talked about the ingenuity of the Daturan infiltration. "She didn't really want to help. We pushed. She'd give us tidbits here or there. We got names and meeting times. It helped with surveillance."

"How long has she been an asset?"

"Two years."

"So why bring me in now? Why get me involved?"

"She was clamming up, and we believed that something was about to go down. We thought a new voice, a woman, might help."

"Oh."

"But that's over. And you're done," his tone was firm. "You blew the cover of three agents at the art exhibit and jeopardized the mission by consorting with the targets. You've compromised everything. Go home. Take the rest of the week off. I don't want you here right now."

He didn't know whether or not to believe the asset was dead. He believed that Harrold thought she was. He could find out quickly enough. They had surveillance on The Mayflower.

"Sir, I do think I have some important information to share with you before I am dismissed."

"What is that, Harrold?" He pinched the bridge of his nose between his thumb and forefinger.

"One of the Daturans is dating a woman whose father owns a funeral home."

"And?"

"She claims the president's remains will be at that home."

"And?"

"I don't believe in coincidences sir."

"What are you saying, Harrold?"

"Could they be planning something large in scope timed to coincide with the cortege or the funeral?"

"That's exactly what they're planning," he said impassively. "We don't believe Thistlewood's girlfriend has anything to do with it. That's a coincidence, regardless of what you choose to believe. We have no intel that leads us to think that either she or her father is involved. Our intel does suggest the Daturans want to blow up Arlington to make a statement about the wars in Iraq and Afghanistan and about our continued involvement in the Middle East. We know they think our economy will recover only after we've left those two theatres. Those elements are well documented. You read that in the dossier, right?" The question was rhetorical.

"We know that a violent statement like that would swing foreign opinion and hurt our coalition," he went on. "We're already weakened throughout the region. The Arab Spring did nothing to help us. What you're telling me is something I already know." He was dismissive, bordering on mean.

Matti had things to say and wanted to counter his theory. As much as she'd grown in outward confidence in the past three days, she knew better than to challenge her boss. She nodded silently as if admitting defeat. It did not soften her supervisor.

"Now shut up and go home."

"Sir?" Matti had one more question. "You said you spoke with the asset today. Why was that?"

Her boss winced. He seemed caught off guard. He replayed the conversation in his head until he recalled having slipped. He nodded with recognition but said nothing.

"Why were you talking to the asset?" Matti was growing impatient. Her involvement in the operation seemed unlikely from the beginning. The fact that her superior was communicating with her asset without her knowledge seemed to bolster her theory that something was amiss.

"I had the asset leak to you the information about the opening," he admitted begrudgingly. "We wanted you there."

"Why?" Matti was confused.

"We needed the Daturans to be distracted. And I knew that with your..."

"With my what?" Matti's body language changed. She went from cornered puppy to pit bull in an instant.

"With your *charms*, we hoped to get additional intel from the other analysts attending the event. It was working. You had Edwards and Thistlewood and Spencer Thomas wrapped around your finger. Didn't you?"

Matti said nothing. She wasn't looking at her boss. Her eyes were directed at her desk, her sight aimed inward. She thought back to the way the men reacted to her at the art opening. She was a decoy. Her entire involvement, from the beginning, was a setup to help "real" agents get the intelligence they were lacking. Her boss never expected her to contribute anything to the effort other than a tight body and disarming smile. For all she had done at the agency, she was nothing more than a piece of ass. She looked up at her boss the way a daughter looks at a father when she first realizes her daddy isn't perfect.

She looked at him the way she looked at her father when he finally admitted that he'd known about his wife's cocaine problem and that he'd been unable to stop it. She didn't want to believe it. She couldn't believe it. Just as she refused to believe her boss was using her.

"Then you screwed up, Harrold. Now we've got what we've got – a plot to blow up a cemetery. Think about it. There's a Lockerbie memorial at Arlington right next to the spot where Foreman is to be buried. Lockerbie. Semtex. It adds up."

Matti fought hard to keep tears from welling in her eyes. She was a tough woman, but the revelation that she was nothing more than a wooden duck in a blind was almost debilitating.

"As for your future here," the boss was relentless now, "that's yet to be determined. Now do as I instructed. Go home."

* * *

George Edwards and Jimmy Ings were pleased to find the back door to Harrowby's unlocked. As soon as Edwards received the coded "NOW" text from Thistlewood, he and Ings mobilized into position.

Ings backed through the door first. He was rolling a small, rubber-wheeled hand truck loaded with three large cardboard boxes stacked atop one another. He cleared the threshold and turned around to wheel the cart from behind. He stepped quietly into the hall and waited for Edwards.

Edwards entered the office and quietly spun the knob as he shut the door. He knew Thistlewood was somewhere in the building with his girlfriend and he wasn't sure how close they might be to the office. He didn't want to alert Laura Harrowby to their intrusion. Edwards carried a large backpack across his left shoulder.

He met Ings in the hallway and squeezed past him to lead the way. Edwards winced when he moved by the drunk, his nostrils catching the rough mixture of Camels and blended scotch.

Edwards saw an open door to their left revealing a set of descending steps. He adjusted the backpack on his shoulder, pulled a small flashlight from his front pants pocket, and switched on a thin yellow beam. He aimed the light down the steps and motioned Ings into the doorway.

"Be careful, Jimmy," he said, placing his hand in the square of Ings' back as the drunk slowly backed the hand truck downward one step at a time. "And be quiet."

"I'm trying," Ings whispered forcefully, dribbling spit onto his chin. He grimaced and narrowed his eyes to slits, each time the wheels dropped from a step, past the return, and landed, bouncing slightly, on the step beneath. The weight of the task, both literal and figurative, was on the edge of being too heavy. Each man could sense it in the other. Neither said anything about it. Step by step they inched downward until they reached the floor.

Once they'd leveled the dolly onto the floor, Edwards swung the flashlight to where he thought he might find a light switch. He found one to his right and flipped it. The light illuminated a room much larger than either of them had anticipated.

"Big," opined Ings. He was sober enough not to have lost depth perception.

"Yeah," Edwards agreed. "Look at that casket. That's gotta be expensive." He approached the centerpiece of the room and rubbed his right hand along the mahogany. It was sealed in a thick lacquer and almost glowed in the fluorescent light hanging from above.

"It *is* the president, my good man," Ings said, affecting a knightly impression. He did not impress Edwards, who wouldn't acknowledge the joke at all. He was too busy scoping the target.

Edwards ran his hand lightly across the cool steel of the support bars and leaned into the opening of the Dutch lid to survey the satin lining. He knew getting underneath the lining to the metal frame without damaging the thinly woven fabric would be tricky.

He'd done his homework and knew that the metal frame could be adjustable so as to rest the body in varying positions. He also knew that the most common types of support frames were a set of L-shaped rails connected at the ends to form a rectangle. The shorter end rails were attached to the long rails with small fasteners. In between the end rails there were often additional supports. Running across the middle of the casket were more rails to support the middle of the body. They strengthened the overall integrity of the casket.

The parts that would provide the best camouflage for the explosive riggings were the thin, flexible metallic straps that extended from one end rail to the other and were attached at those ends with springs. They supported the length of the body. Edwards envisioned them as the mattress support of a cheaply framed metal bunk.

It was between those thin straps, underneath the lining and the body, that he believed they could effectively hide the metal components of the bomb assembly. No metal detector would distinguish the types of metal. And, from the intelligence the knight had gathered, there would be no X-ray of the casket anywhere along the route, at the Capitol, or at Arlington Cemetery. It was the perfect cover.

While Ings returned to the top of the steps to turn off the stairwell light and lock the door, Edwards set down the flashlight and began searching the lining of the casket for a seam. He was bent awkwardly at the waist, poking into the lining with his fingers.

He tugged gently at the fabric with his fingertips until he felt a loose edge tucked between the wall of the casket and its base. Wiggling his finger underneath the small gap he freed a three inch section from its place just below the hinges for the Dutch lids of the box.

"I think I've got the spot." He pointed to it when Ings rejoined him aside the casket. "Could you please hand me the small utility knife out of my backpack? I think I can pull the seam here and maybe remove the padding without damaging anything."

Ings unzipped the pack on Edwards' shoulder and found the small plastic knife. It was red and contained slide up blades that snapped off when dulled. It was cheap but effective. Within a few minutes, Edwards had managed to successfully remove the lining and thin pad, exposing the metal frame.

Between the lattice of the frame and the bottom of the box there were four inches of space in which the explosive mechanisms could fit. The trick was slipping them underneath the frame and then attaching them securely to the underside.

Edwards used a small hook on the handle of a rubber mallet to extend and then release the springs on one end of the casket. Once they were loose, access to the underside was improved significantly.

"Do you have the phones?" Edwards turned to Ings, expecting to see him just over his shoulder but he wasn't there. He was sitting on the steps, elbows perched on a step behind him, bracing his weight. His eyes were closed and his head bobbed up and down, twitching as his body reacted to the discomfort of falling asleep while sitting up.

Edwards rolled his eyes and walked over to the drunk quietly. He gently placed his hand on Ings' left knee. It was enough to wake up the barkeep.

"Huh?" He belched as he got his wits about him. "I'm awake. I'm up." He sat forward and looked up at Edwards. "Sorry."

"I need your help." Edwards walked over to his backpack and pulled out two 6"x6" pieces of plywood with the Nokia 6210s attached. He rested them on the edge of the casket as he checked the connections between the phones and batteries, the clips and model rocket sparker. He made sure the copper leads from the vibrators to the screws were secure then slipped them underneath the wire frame lattice and set them on the floor of the casket.

"I have the zip ties," Ings said from behind him.

Edwards took the plastic zip ties and looped them around the metal frame. He picked up each board and ran the ties through small holes at each corner of the plywood boards. He tightened the ties on all four corners, using a pair of small shears to cut the excess plastic from the ties. The boards were pressed up against the underside of the metal straps that ran the length of the casket and were placed such that they would sit underneath the shoulder blades of the body.

Edwards turned. "Now for the fun part." He motioned to the dolly and looked at Ings as if to say "Fetch!" He was irritated that Sir Spencer saw fit to team him with the member most likely to hinder the effort.

Ings retrieved three yellow-orange bricks wrapped in plastic, stepping carefully as if trying not spill vodka from a full glass. Edwards thought the care a little ridiculous, given how the drunk had been nonchalantly wheeling around three times the amount on a dolly.

"Should we remove the plastic?" Edwards asked Ings.

"I don't know if it matters," Ings remarked. "We probably should."

"How much do the bricks weigh?" Edwards took the first brick from Ings and then knelt to the floor beside the casket. He'd placed a thin visqueen sheet on the floor for the next phase.

"Twenty-four ounces."

"So..." Edwards quickly did the conversion in his head, "a pound and a half?"

"Yeah."

"Let's use three." Edwards knew they wouldn't need all ten bricks, but thought it better to be over prepared.

He took a large plastic knife that he'd slid from his backpack and pulled back the cellophane from the brick. He gently cut the brick into several thin slices, laying each slice onto the top of the metal frame, making certain the pieces were evenly spaced. He'd chosen a plastic knife to avoid any chance of it sparking with standard metal cutlery.

A thin layer of yellow powder coated the visqueen and plumed as Edwards squared another brick to cut on the plastic. It was a tedious but necessary step to ensure the secrecy of the material. There could be no hint of anything askew or the plot would be blown without any explosion. Edwards wiped the perspiration from his forehead with the back of his wrist as he cut the second and third pieces of Semtex.

"All finished, I think." He leaned up from the casket after positioning the detonators and looked across at Ings, who'd been watching quietly. "How much elapsed time?"

Ings looked at his watch. "Thirty-three minutes." Their goal was forty-five. They set about replacing the lining into the base of the casket to cover their handiwork. They knew they were on schedule. The professor's promised stamina and his girlfriend's alcohol-induced narcolepsy would buy them that long.

"I think we're good, Jimmy."

Edwards was on his knees, carefully folding the visqueen so as not to spill any of the residue onto the floor. He then slid it into his backpack and zipped it. "Do you see anything we might have forgotten?"

Ings was walking around the casket looking for anything amiss. "I don't think so." He got down onto all fours to scour the floor. The cement was cold against his palms. He found nothing. "We're clean. Let's get out of here."

"Agreed." Edwards slung the backpack over both shoulders for the trip upstairs. "Let me help you with this." He held one end of the dolly and walked backwards up the stairs as Ings shuffled forward.

The men quietly huffed up the steps in the dark until they reached the small platform inside the door. Edwards held the dolly with his left hand and reached behind himself to grab the doorknob with his right. He slowly turned it, leaned into the door with his backpack and stepped into the hallway to the left. He was backing up to help Ings into the hall when his heart stopped. He felt something press into the small of his back.

Edwards froze with Ings perched on the top step just inside the door. He didn't breathe. He didn't turn around. He was certain that someone was standing right behind him sticking the barrel of a gun into his back. He could feel breath on his skin just behind his ear.

"Is it done?" the voice whispered. "Is everything in place?"

He recognized the voice and spun around. It was Thistlewood with his finger cocked like a pistol and a big smile on his face. His cheeks were flushed. Even in the dim light of the hallway Edwards could see that. His heart resumed beating.

"Damn it, Art!" Edwards snapped in a fierce whisper, slapping at the professor's hand. "Why would you do that? You about scared the life out of me."

"Calm down, George," Thistlewood said, still smiling. "Laura's asleep and not waking up anytime soon." The professor had known what he was doing. He wanted to irritate Edwards, wanted to make him sweat.

"Whatever," Edwards snapped again, clearly not amused. "It's done. Everything is in place." He motioned for Ings to finish his trip up the stairs. The drunk was still standing at an awkward position in the open doorway. Ings said nothing as he stepped onto the landing and backed past the doorway. He and Edwards kept moving toward the office and the building's exit as Thistlewood followed behind them.

"Good then," said Thistlewood. "So we'll see each other tomorrow?"

"After the body's in the box," Edwards replied as he and Ings made their way from Harrowby's to their awaiting car. "We'll meet at Cato Street."

Thistlewood stood at the back door watching the two men load into the vehicle. The plan was working, he thought. His worries over what the government may know and which of his compatriots was betraying his trust were momentarily allayed.

Maybe, he thought to himself, *just maybe, we will pull this off.* He shook his head thinking about the possibility of success. This would be bigger than anything the Tea Party could ever have conceived. He was almost giddy as he shut the door and locked it. Thistlewood looked at his watch. He needed to get Laura and himself out of the building before the president's body arrived early the next morning.

* * *

"Do you want some dumplings?"

Felicia Jackson wasn't much for sharing, but Crystal Thai delivery was too good to keep to herself. And she had an ulterior motive.

"No thank you. I'm good with what I've got."

Her husband was not a big fan of dumplings. He assumed her

offer was based on that knowledge. Felicia, he knew, didn't concede as much as a dumpling without having first determined the cost/benefit. He loved her but knew better than to think she would freely give without expecting something in return.

"What did you order?" she asked even though she knew the answer; it was the green curry chicken.

"Green curry chicken." Felicia's husband looked up from his plate and smiled. "Would you like a bite?"

"If you won't eat all of it I'll take the tiniest of tastes." It was a courtship dance where she always took the lead. Of course he allowed her to lead. That was his way. He was the strong man behind the good woman. It was his idea to decompress for a couple of hours with their favorite take-out food.

Crystal Thai was an Arlington restaurant not far from their Clarendon Boulevard loft, that offered free delivery on orders over eighteen dollars. They were open late and the food was authentic. The Jacksons loved Asian food, and good Thai was a mutual favorite.

"You know," he offered after watching her relish the curry chicken, "it'll be okay no matter the end result." He'd thought better of saying anything until now. They were sitting at the small bistro table in the kitchen. The idea of the dinner was to ease the tension and help his wife relax, but he couldn't ignore the elephant in the room.

"What do you mean?" Her words echoed as she pulled a glass of ice water to her lips.

"Whatever happens with the presidency," he said. "Whether the court agrees with you or Blackmon, it'll be okay."

Felicia took a deep breath. She flicked her tongue across her front teeth to clean them before swallowing then pulled a napkin from the table and wiped the corners of her mouth. She couldn't look her husband in the eyes. She knew he was well intended, but she didn't want to hear it.

He was a typical man, offering a solution to a dilemma for which none was asked and none was required. Why couldn't he let her enjoy the momentary diversion of spice and curry?

"You know," she started slowly, pausing just long enough to intone displeasure with her husband's observation, "it won't be okay. Not for me, not for you, not for this country. Do you understand what constitutional ramifications exist should the court side with him?" She was revving up. "Do you follow how damaging this would be to the power I currently have? Not only would we be the laughing stock of the Hill, but my opponents would seize upon the snub to try and replace me as speaker. Losing the court battle would be like a no-confidence vote from Parliament." She stopped and took another sip from her glass.

"I don't think you can compare the two, really," her husband countered. He spoke forcefully but without much volume. "Losing the court vote has nothing to do with you. It's all about the law."

"You are so naïve!" she snapped, her condescension surprising both of them. "Of course it's about me."

She stood and snatched her plate from the table. Walking to the sink, she stopped suddenly and spun her heels on the wood flooring. She leaned into the black granite of the countertop.

"It's always about me. When they chose me to lead the party, it was about me. If they kick me out, it will be about me. If the court rules that a woman speaker cannot constitutionally assume the presidency because she is not an 'officer', it is most assuredly about *me!*" She turned her back on her husband and slammed her plate into the stainless steel sink. It rattled before the room was again uncomfortably silent. "Are you finished?"

"With my meal or with the conversation?"

"Either," she huffed. "Both." She reached the small table and was about to take his plate from him, when he reached out gently and put his hands on her narrow hips. He pulled gently and she shuffled to him. He could see that she was doing her best to stay angry. But the slightest sadness in her eyes told him she was weakening.

He could have fought her on the notion that everything was always about her. He could have argued the stupidity of comparing a no-confidence vote to a ruling on the constitutionality of presidential succession. But he spontaneously reasoned it pointless. His wife and best friend was hurting. She was a tightly wound ball of stress. Any disagreement with an irrational spouse would only serve to widen the emotional distance between them.

"I was wrong," he offered. "I know how invested you are in this.

I understand your passion. I won't bring it up again. Just know that I am here for you regardless."

He was good; she'd give him that. A lifetime together had taught him how to handle his powerful wife.

"I know that," Felicia said. She looked up at the ceiling and laughed, trying to fight back tears. "I know that."

He stood from his chair and wrapped his arms around her waist, his arms extending upward to her shoulders. She buried her head in his chest. He moved his right hand to the back of her head and gently stroked her hair. He knew indeed that if the court sided with Blackmon it would not be okay.

* * *

Bill Davidson was sweating through his shirt as he left the relative warmth of the Mayflower Hotel. The morning sun was just beginning to purple the sky along the horizon when he pushed through the exit onto DeSales Street. It was cold and cloudy outside. Despite the sun, Davidson thought it might rain. The dampness on the white cotton around his neck, under his arms, and in the middle of his back was uncomfortable. He'd had a busy couple of hours.

First, he'd called the front desk and arranged to book the hotel room connected to his. He then extended his stay for two additional nights and asked that he receive no maid service in either room.

He made a dozen trips to the ice machine down the hall and then, bucket by bucket, filled half of the bathroom tub with ice. It would slow the decomposition of the body and prevent an odor from alerting other guests or hotel workers.

After managing to pick up, drag, and then dump the body into the iced tub, he dead-bolted the lock and pulled the safety bar across the door to his room. Once he'd cleaned up as best he could, he locked the adjoining door and exited through the second room.

Davidson didn't trust that the knight would follow through with the clean-up and wanted to make it as difficult as possible for anyone to enter the room

He'd considered the altruism of calling the police immediately, damn the consequences. Ultimately he decided his country might be better served by him avoiding arrest and lengthy questioning in a holding cell. He had things to do and lives to save.

"South Street between 31ˢᵗ Street, NW and Wisconsin," Davidson instructed the cabbie as he opened the door and slid onto the black vinyl bench seat in the back seat of the taxi. He placed a bag on the seat next to him and then wiped the sweat from his forehead. He could feel his shirt sticking to his back.

The cabbie turned off of DeSales, south onto 17ᵗʰ Street, SW, and then left onto K Street. The trip was only a mile and a half, but given early morning traffic, it took 20 minutes to pull up in front of the Hanover-Crown Institute.

Davidson paid the cabbie, pulled his bag across the seat, and crawled out of the taxi. He stood on the sidewalk looking at the building in front of him. The bland appearance of the façade saddened him. The limestone, glass and iron were unwelcoming.

He'd never taken the time to notice it before, but now he saw the austerity of it. It was appropriate, he reasoned, that the bland, unimpressive entrance reflected the outward appearance of his own career.

There was good on the inside. There was passion and intelligence within the walls of the place. There was unreasonable hope for a grander future and the respect of peers. He smiled weakly at the coincidence of it and slowly made his way into the building with his head down.

Winded by the time he sat down in his office and swung the heavy bag onto his desk, Davidson leaned forward in his chair and pulled the boxed set of books from the bag. He slipped his index finger in between the box top and the spine of the center book.

He pulled the book onto the desk and flipped to Thoreau's essay on "Civil Disobedience, thumbed to part one, paragraph four, and then stopped. He read the words aloud: *"Can there not be a government in which majorities do not virtually decide right and wrong, but conscience? In which majorities decide only those questions to which the rule of expediency is applicable? Must the citizen ever for a moment, or in the least degree, resign his conscience to the legislator?"*

Davidson shoved the book away from him to make room for his elbows on the desk surface. He then leaned on the desk with his head in his hands and continued to read: *"Why has every man a conscience, then? I think that we should be men first, and subjects afterward."*

Davidson had always loved this part of the essay. But now it put a thick lump in his throat. It hurt to swallow against the dryness of it. He knew that Thoreau was arguing against patriotism and service to country for the sake of it. He understood that Thoreau believed conscience and moral compass should guide a man above the will of the majority. Thoreau was espousing a libertarian view that echoed well with both the Tea Party movement and the Daturans. He was at once against civil government's ability to oppress its citizenry and supportive of the few pragmatic taxes for needed social programs.

Davidson wished that he'd always followed his conscience above the will of the majority. His life and country may have been better for it. He ran his hand down the page a final time and closed the book. He slipped it back into the box between the other two books. One of them contained a collection of Thoreau's many politically-themed speeches. Among the addresses in that volume was one referred to as "Plea for Captain John Brown", a speech that Thoreau delivered at a Concord, Massachusetts town hall meeting in which he supported the actions of the famed, but violent, abolitionist.

"I do not wish to kill nor to be killed, but I can foresee circumstances in which both these things would be by me unavoidable," Thoreau contended. *"The question is not about the weapon, but the spirit in which you use it."* Thoreau, a noted pacifist, was advocating violence for the sake of revolutionary political change.

It was the book containing that speech which George Edwards had meticulously hollowed out so as to make room for a Nokia 6210 cell phone strapped to a 6"x6" piece of thin plywood and 8 ounces of Semtex. One quick phone call would wreak havoc on the written word and anyone within 100 yards of the blast.

Sir Spencer told Edwards that the explosive was meant to silence Davidson, if in fact he was the leak. If he wasn't the traitor, the knight suggested that Davidson was too weak regardless. The Daturan movement stood to suffer in the wake of the coup if Davidson's conscience ever got the better of him.

It was the artist's sense of irony that led him to choose that book over the one containing "Civil Disobedience". Edwards was more warped than anyone realized. Nobody ever really noticed it beneath his warmth and charm.

Davidson never noticed the criminal alteration to the boxed set as he walked to a storage room next to his office and replaced the books on the shelves from which he had taken them.

When he returned to his office he noticed a woman sitting at his desk. She was wearing dark denim jeans, a pair of brown Gore-Tex Merrell Sport shoes, and a plain cotton heather gray sweatshirt. Her hair was pulled back in a ponytail. It took Davidson a moment to realize she was the same woman he'd glimpsed rushing past him at the art opening the night before.

"Matti Harrold?" he asked and bit his lower lip. He was almost certain it was her.

"Yes," she stood from the chair and offered her hand. She recalled the last time she'd actually met the man and how different he seemed then. At B. Smith's restaurant all of those years ago, he was larger than life. But here, in his cramped back hall office, he appeared small.

Mattie always wondered what a shell of a man looked like, and now one stood humbly in front of her. His hand was thick but cold as he grasped hers.

"I'm sorry I was sitting in your chair," she said, gesturing behind her to the comfortable seat. "I am just so tired." She smiled with her lips pressed together.

"Oh," he waved it off, "no worries, Ms. Harrold. It's there for whoever needs it. And as you and I both are acutely aware, I won't need it much longer."

Matti wasn't sure how to respond to that, and in fact, felt rather awkward. Rather than respond clumsily to what she inferred, she chose to ignore it.

"So you wanted to meet with me," she offered as a change of direction. "You said you have something to share with me that might help."

"I do, yes."

Davidson stepped farther into the office, brushing past her, and sat at his desk. He rolled the seat to a beige file cabinet to the left of the desk, grabbed the handle on the bottom of three drawers, pushed an adjacent button with his thumb, and pulled. He reached into the drawer with both hands and withdrew a stack of small blue books. He spun back to the desk and set them down, then reached into a bag on his desk and removed a balled up sports coat. He unwound the ball, found the inside breast pocket, and removed another blue book, identical to the stack of five on the desk.

"Okay," he spun back around to face Matti and slapped his hand on the stack, "these are my journals. In these pages is everything you need to know about the Daturan movement: the people, the places, my thoughts, my fears, and the plot to secretly usurp the executive branch of the government for its own design."

Matti swallowed hard. She pulled her hands to her mouth before folding her arms in front of her chest. Her eyes danced between the books and Davidson as she considered the consequences of his gift.

"Given the generosity of my girlfriend," he continued, "you may already know much of the information they contain. I have no idea what she did or didn't reveal."

"Your girlfriend was pretty forthcoming with some things," Matti allowed. She thought 'girlfriend' a myopic description of the dead call girl, but she played along for the sake of expedience. "Not so much with other things. She was an unwilling asset for a while before I got involved."

"And how long have you been involved?"

"Two days." Matti looked at the floor as she said it.

Davidson recoiled his neck like a chicken about to peck, instantly reconsidering his decision to share the journals with someone so lightly invested in the operation.

"I'm an intelligence analyst," she offered quickly. Matti could sense the regret in his tone. He'd pulled his hands from the stack of journals and had folded them in his lap. She noticed his shoulders hunched as the air left him. He was deflating.

"I'm very good at what I do," she assured him. "It's because of my technical skill that my supervisors pushed for my direct involvement. They believed I could break through in ways other handlers could not." She didn't go into the sexist details of the reality of her involvement.

"Did you?" He was the one looking at the floor now.

"Did I what?"

"Did you break through?"

"Apparently not enough." She hesitated before offering any more to Davidson. "I'm off the team now."

Davidson's eyes narrowed and he cocked his head slightly.

"When you saw me at the art opening, I'd made some mistakes. My boss pulled me from the surveillance." She waited for Davidson to respond, and when he didn't, she added, "I compromised too much. They had to remove me."

He thought about revoking the offer of the journals. But he rationalized that she was the *only* one to whom he *could* give the journals. She was as on the outside looking in as was he. She was persona-non-grata at the NSA and he was the equivalent with the Daturans.

Matti Harrold was maybe the perfect person to whom he could hand over the information. It made sense. He chose the journal atop the stack and handed it to her.

"You'll need these," he said. "You are the only one in a position to really stop this. Your bosses may think they know what's going to happen but they don't. They have no clue." He pulled the other books to the edge of his desk and then piled them into Matti's arms.

"Ms. Harrold, I would suggest that you read the most recent one first. Everything is there." He pursed his lips and nodded at her. It was his signal to her that she should leave. He rotated his chair, facing his desk again and turning his back on Matti.

"You can't do that," Matti snapped. "You can't hand me some instruction manual when you could just tell me what they're planning." She pulled her shoulders back, adjusting her posture as she cradled the books in front of her. "We both know there is no time for games."

She was right and Davidson knew it. He couldn't just give her the books without an explanation. He couldn't expect she'd dutifully walk away without challenging him.

"They're going to blow up the Capitol," he said emotionlessly without turning to face her. "And they're going to kill everyone inside of it by lining the president's casket with explosives."

Matti stood motionless at first. The weight of the books was almost too much for her to hold. She backed out of the room slowly and then started an awkward jog down the hall and out of the building. They weren't planning to blow up Arlington on the day of the funeral, they were planning the attack a full day earlier. The Daturans didn't want to make a statement. They wanted to affect the country's leadership. They wanted to destroy a symbol of American strength.

She remembered people theorizing for years how the American psyche would have been affected if the 9/11 hijackers had succeeded in crashing a fourth plane into the Capitol dome. How much worse would it be now if homegrown terrorists did it? She didn't want to think about the possibilities. She couldn't let it happen. She couldn't fail.

Matti had to make a phone call; her supervisor needed to know. He'd passed along the wrong intelligence. If he'd listen to her, she could help him stop the pending attack and save hundreds of lives.

Matti needed redemption.

CHAPTER 11

Dexter Foreman was dressed in a Paul Stuart navy bead stripe suit. The worsted English wool and cashmere pressed cleanly at the lapels was buttoned once. The side vents of the jacket were stitched closed for appearance.

The blue, white, and navy fancy stripe shirt was accented with an Italian silk pin dot tie, carefully knotted into a double Windsor at the shirt's point collar. Foreman's wife chose the stripe shirt over traditional white, because she was concerned that the heavy makeup applied to her husband's face and neck might stain the collar and appear dirty. She planned an open casket for the memorial and wanted him looking clean.

His body lay in the casket in the basement of Harrowby's Funeral Home & Chapel after arriving an hour earlier. The casket was surrounded by the six soldiers prepared to carry the president once they reached the Capitol steps.

The soldiers were assigned to the Military District of Washington and the 3rd U.S. Infantry Regiment. Most people knew them as members of "The Old Guard". Since World War II, they had served as the official Army Honor Guard and the escort to the president.

On the shoulders of their uniforms were blue oval insignias with red borders. The Washington Monument was at the center of the design, along with a double-handled sword. The monument was emblematic of their area of responsibility. The sword symbolized protection. Their motto, in Latin *Haec Protegimus*, translated to

"This We Guard".

The War Department created the Military District to plan for any potential ground attacks against the nation's capital during the war. But its mission evolved over the decades to more of a ceremonial role. Its units eventually included the U.S. Army Band, known as "Pershing's Own".

Now the soldiers embarked upon their most solemn responsibility: they were to help bury their commander-in-chief. It was an awesome task.

Dexter Foreman would be the twelfth president to lie upon the Lincoln catafalque. It was a simple bier of pine boards nailed together and covered with black cloth, constructed hastily to accommodate the public viewing for Lincoln's casket. A century and a half later, it was still the same seven foot long, two and a half foot tall platform. While the cloth had been replaced several times, it was in the original style drapery used in 1865.

The soldiers were quiet as they checked the casket and tested its weight. The task of carrying more than three hundred pounds up the steps of the west front of the Capitol at the end of the procession was taxing. Even for six strong men, keeping the weight level up the steps and into the Rotunda was fraught with potential embarrassment. After a final metal detector sweep around the outside of the casket, the men practiced carrying the full weight of it in Harrowby's large basement.

Harrowby himself stood to the far left side of the expanse. When the soldiers finished their brief exercise, Harrowby helped them place the casket onto the lift, such that they could move it from the basement to the main floor of the building. He then followed the soldiers and a couple of other government types up the stairwell into the hallway. There was a group of Capitol Police officers, Metro Police, and uniformed Secret Service gathered in the crowded space. They were talking and laughing, a couple of them nursing cooling cups of coffee. Harrowby politely pushed his way through the grouping and made his way to the casket lift. Waiting next to the opening of the lift was a steel-tubed casket cart. Harrowby pulled open the lift door and a couple of his employees help him shift the casket onto the cart, resting it on the six small rubber tips that kept the heavy wooden box in place. The officers, who just a moment before were chatty, fell silent. They watched wide-eyed as Harrowby kicked the brake off of the rear left wheel. With help, he rolled the cart toward an exit and the awaiting hearse.

* * *

Sir Spencer sat on the edge of the bed in his room at the Hay-Adams. He was groggy after ninety minutes of sleep. He was dressed only in boxers and the expanse of his hairless white stomach obscured the cloth as he leaned forward into his hands.

The knight rubbed his eyes and stood slowly, feeling his age in his back as it tightened instead of stretching to help him rise. His knees cracked angrily at being asked to support the weight that the knight forced upon them. He grunted, gained his balance, and walked to the bar. Sir Spencer grabbed the remote to flip on the television and then retrieved the bottle of fifty year old scotch.

He poured three fingers' worth and stood against the bar, sipping the liquor and watching the presidential smotherage on television. He was amused. The knowledge of what was to come provided a shot of adrenaline to the old man.

"We've learned some brand new information here," chirped Vickie Lupo from the television set. It seemed to the knight that whenever he turned it on, she was there with her coiffed hair and sharp wit.

"We're hearing from our 'Avenue' sources at the wonderful little building just east of the Capitol dome," she smirked, the right side of her mouth curled higher than the left, "you know, the Supreme Court."

"She amuses herself above all others," mumbled the knight. If it weren't for the new information she promised him, he'd have turned down the volume. "She's insufferable," he scoffed and took another sip.

"Our sources are telling us," she continued bloviating, "and this is on good authority, mind you, that the Court will not render its decision until after the memorial for President Foreman."

"Here, here," toasted the knight. It was expected, but still he was glad to hear it. A decision favoring Speaker Jackson before the memorial would put a wrench into the works. He hobbled over to the pea green chair closest to him.

Sir Spencer sat down and his knees thanked him. After muting the volume on the television, he found his cell phone on the side table next to him and picked it up to dial.

He placed the phone to his ear and listened to the ringtone. It chirped once, twice, three times. Then an answer. The voice on the other end confirmed the call was secure.

"We have the location of the Secretary?" The knight was splitting his attention between the muted Vickie Lupo, and the overcast window view of the White House. "We know where Blackmon will be then?"

The response of the voice on the other end was certain and reassuring. The knight sensed no apprehension. He pressed the button to end the call. Everything was in motion. He pressed another series of numbers and awaited a new voice on the other end of the secured wireless line.

"Hello?" the sixth Daturan answered hollowly. He sounded tired.

"It's me, good man," the knight said, knowing his accent would be instantly recognizable. "We are as planned."

"Good." The sixth Daturan was smiling wryly despite his malaise. He had always known that Sir Spencer could facilitate what others might claim impossible. "You know I will be otherwise engaged during this afternoon's affair?"

"Yes." The knight stuck his pinkie into the remaining drop of scotch before sucking on it. "I am aware."

Sir Spencer and the sixth Daturan had known each other for years. For some time, the two of them had met privately without the knowledge of the other men in the group. The sixth Daturan wanted as few entanglements as possible. He once explained to the knight that discretion had no part of valor in the hands of a drunk, a has-been politico, a philandering professor, or a self-important artist. The knight had agreed and promised not to reveal the sixth Daturan's identity, or existence for that matter, until appropriate.

Together the two plotted the sixth's political path. Unlike others who refused to bow to Sir Spencer's influence, the sixth implored the knight to secretly bankroll his campaigns and political action committees. The knight privately discredited the sixth's opponents when he could and paid them off when he couldn't.

Through favor, coercion, and well played histrionics, the knight was able to help the sixth catch the eye of the Foreman administration. While the president's unexpected death hastened their work and turned their effort violent, the sixth knew that he was always intended to be the wizard to the knight's man behind the curtain.

It was kismet, they both agreed, that brought them together at such a time in the nation's history and provided them the opportunity to seize power. They were so politically myopic that they failed to see the pathology of their method. As the knight was so fond of saying, they were patriots in the mold of Adams and Revere.

"We will talk later," promised the knight. "When we've seen the outcome."

"When we've seen the outcome," parroted the sixth. "That's good."

Sir Spencer replaced the phone on the table next to the chair. He rubbed his knees, leaned back in the chair, and then he looked at the clock on the coffee table. He needed to get dressed. It wasn't long before he needed to be at the Cato Street Pub. There was more to do and he had another phone call to make.

* * *

Jimmy Ings took his seat aboard the 85 passenger bus, squeezing himself into an empty seat toward the back of the vehicle. He'd paid his $27 to the tour operator, pulled a ragged Washington Bullets ball cap down over his eyes, and worked his way past tourists anxious to see some of the nation's most significant buildings and monuments.

Underneath the seat in front of him, he slid a medium sized backpack. The space was just large enough that he could shove it completely from view. Ings was nervous, but he knew his task was of critical importance to the mission.

As the bus pulled away from the Lincoln Memorial and headed toward Virginia, Ings looked out the window. He exhaled and adjusted the brim of the cap, happy to have made it aboard the tour.

TOM ABRAHAMS

He was even happier to find it operational on the day of the president's procession.

Some of the regular stops along the mall and the northern part of the "American Heritage Tour" weren't available because of the blockages along Constitution Avenue. The southern part of the tour was still operational.

The bus chugged and hummed its way across the Potomac as a man's voice narrated the points of interest over a loudspeaker inside the cabin. Ings was too preoccupied to listen. The job that lay ahead was consuming him.

Before hustling to catch the bus, he was sitting alone in his second floor apartment watching a "College All-Stars" episode of *Jeopardy!* that he'd recorded the night before. The category was "Royalty". The clue was "This Kentucky poet laureate based *All the King's Men* on the life of former Louisiana governor Huey Long."

Ings had known the answer and was about to blurt it out between sips of scotch when his cell phone rang. Disgusted, he'd paused the DVR and picked up the phone. He'd pressed C and then answered.

"Who is Robert Penn Warren?" Ings had asked as he pressed the phone to his ear.

"James, what are you talking about?"

"You interrupted *Jeopardy!*. The answer to the clue is 'who is Robert Penn Warren.'"

"I see," said Sir Spencer. "So the clue was about poetry? Or was it about Cajun politics?"

"Cajun politics." Ings had taken another swig.

"And where is James Carville when you need him? Right, good man?"

"I didn't need him. I knew the answer." Ings had chomped on a piece of ice before sucking the sweetness from it. "What do you need, Sir Spencer? Are you coming over early?"

"No," the knight paused a beat. "I need you to run an errand. You likely won't be back in time for the meeting at Cato Street."

"Oh?" Ings had picked up the television remote, hit the OFF button, and sat up in his recliner. "Why's that?"

"As you well know, James, we may have been compromised last night at the opening. There's really no telling what the government

- 208 -

knows or does not know."

"But I thought you said—"

"Wait, just hold on."

"Okay."

"So, James," Sir Spencer had continued, "we need to create a little diversion. And in that effort I need your help."

"What is it?"

"There is a backpack behind your bar downstairs that contains an extra explosive. It's one of the four that you built with George."

"Uh huh..."

"The assigned number to that phone is on a card inside the small front pocket of the backpack. I need to you to take it somewhere for me and leave it unattended."

"Why?"

"I need you to do this," counseled the knight, "because a young man's ambition is to get along in the world and make a place for himself. Half your life goes that way, till you're 45 or 50. Then, if you're lucky, you make terms with life, you get released."

"That makes no sense to me."

"Aside from the point that this is your opportunity to release yourself from the chains of an ordinary life, and aside from the hope that your actions will enable to plot to move ahead as planned, it's a quote from Robert Penn Warren."

Despite his misgivings about the unexpected mission, Ings had dutifully gotten up from his comfortable seat, found the backpack behind the bar downstairs, and left a key under the front doormat for the men to find later.

Now he sat on a tour bus pulling up to the gate at Arlington National Cemetery.

* * *

Matti was nonplussed. She'd called her supervisor's direct line and his cell phone. She'd paged him and texted him. He'd not answered, replied, or called her back. She was sitting in the back of a coffee shop at 2300 Wisconsin, just north of her alma mater.

It was empty except for two baristas and an unkempt undergrad with an unshaven face, a pair of ear buds, and a large espresso. He was so deep into Uriah Heep and the latest issue of FHM that Matti thought him oblivious. This was as good a place as any to find relative privacy.

There was no time to head back to Ft. Meade. She needed to skim the journals for details so that when her boss called she could provide him with actionable intelligence.

Matti was nursing a latte while thumbing through the most recent Davidson journals. She scanned the center of the pages for relevant passages and notations, amazed at the breadth of the information. Matti now had a Daturan's perspective of the last several days.

"Sir Spencer tells us the end game is regime change," Davidson had written. "He tells us that the founding fathers were heroes to us and terrorists to the British. The man convicted of blowing up Pan Am Flight 103 was a terrorist to us. But when the Scottish released him from prison, the Libyans rejoiced in the streets. He contends that the line between patriotism and terrorism is all in the eye of the beholder."

The passage seemed familiar to Matti, as if she'd heard it somewhere before. She scanned her memory quickly. Then it hit her. She *had* heard it before. The asset used almost the exact same argument during one of their phone sessions. She must have taken it from the journal. Matti was more determined to keep reading the little books the A.G. had entrusted to her.

She learned more about the amount of Semtex available to the conspirators and how they'd obtained it. She knew how they planned to sneak the explosive material into the Capitol and the method by which they were to detonate it.

But most importantly, the young analyst was learning about the motive and the endgame. She was sure that as much as the NSA thought it knew about the plot, it knew little if anything about the reason. As Matti read through Davidson's notes about the plot, she had trouble believing it herself.

"Spencer Thomas," wrote the A.G. in a small, hurried script that hugged the lines of the pages, "is a megalomaniac. He has conceived this violent plot to overthrow a government he believes is ill-equipped to serve its people. I know that our path as a nation has strayed from one that is truly righteous and abiding of the constitution. But he is misguided."

"For years," his handwriting was like that of a man in a hurry; it was approaching scribble, "I have gone along with the idea that we could affect change at the very highest levels of government. Never did I envision violence. The greasing of palms and the quid-pro-quo of political favor was murky enough for me. I did not sign up for murder."

Matti made mental note of Davidson's assertion that an unknown conspirator was somehow involved in the plot, but she kept reading to finish Davidson's thoughts. It was the only part of the journal that she'd read so far, which was rife with personal opinion.

Her cell phone chirped, indicating she'd received a text message. She picked up her phone and checked the message. It was from her boss. Finally.

U R OFF THIS. I THOUGHT I MADE MYSELF CLEAR.

It was not the kind of reply Matti had been hoping to receive. She didn't want to leave a phone message or send a text that contained sensitive information. She flipped open the keyboard on her phone and typed.

I HAVE NEW INTEL. NEED TO MEET. URGENT.

She pressed send. The phone chirped again, confirming to her that the text was successfully sent. She went back to the journals.

Though Davidson was certain the Daturans would detonate the Semtex with cell phones, he did not denote which kind of cell phones they would use.

Her phone chirped again. Another text message alert was flashing on her the display. She marked her place in the journal and picked up her cell, hoping her supervisor had agreed to a meeting.

NO MEET. BUREAU HAS CONTROL. LEAVE IT ALONE.

Matti stared at the screen trying to process the text. She hoped that reading it more than once might change the words on the small screen.

Why would he not meet with her? Why would he NOT want new intelligence? She dropped the phone onto the table and pushed it away from her. She blindly picked up her coffee cup and sipped through the small slit in the plastic lid. The drink was still hot and singed the tip of her tongue. She touched it to the back of her teeth and winced.

Matti might have been naïve about the nastiness of her chosen profession, but she'd long known its shortcomings. She asked herself why her boss was so disinterested in potentially valuable information while instantaneously answering it in her head.

The FBI had taken over control of the investigation. That meant that the heat was off of the NSA and that her boss didn't feel the need to staple an addendum to the file. Her agency, she thought he'd have reasoned, did everything that was asked of it and kindly passed along all relevant information. Therein lay the most dangerous problem in American intelligence gathering.

Despite the debacle of 9/11, when the FBI had information about the hijackers that was never passed up or down the command chain to the appropriate people, the United States intelligence community never fully got used to the idea of shared turf.

While the prevailing wisdom was that legal walls prevented the sharing of information between agencies, Matti knew that perception was wrong. She'd read the 9/11 commission report that concluded there had been no legal reason why the information could not have been shared. She'd also read James Bamford's book about her own agency which argued that the lack of adequate information sharing was due solely to inter-agency rivalries.

The Department of Homeland Security was created to facilitate cooperation and information sharing. All it really did, many believed, was create a greater bureaucracy through which good intelligence was filtered from bad.

Nowhere was that more evident than in the aftermath of the attack at Ft. Hood, Texas in late 2009. A full eight years after 9/11, Army Major, Nidal Malik Hasan, was suspected of opening fire on dozens of unarmed soldiers and civilians in a medical clinic at a readiness center on post.

Hasan, an American born Muslim, and a practicing psychiatrist, killed thirteen and wounded another thirty people. In the aftermath of the mass shooting, the FBI revealed that Hasan was "on their radar" for months as a possible Al-Qaeda sympathizer. Matti remembered that FBI director Robert Mueller ordered an investigation into how the agency mishandled information about

Hasan, employing the help of a former director, William Webster, to get to the bottom of the communication breakdown.

In the midst of that investigation, a young Al-Qaeda trained Nigerian named Umar Faruk Abdulmutalleb was charged with trying to blow up a Northwest Airlines flight as it traveled from Amsterdam to Detroit on Christmas Day 2009. Matti recalled that he'd worn a chemical explosive in his underwear and managed to light it as the plane approached its destination. Had he been successful, he could have killed hundreds.

Matti remembered from news reports that the kicker was that the government had information about the suspect prior to his attempted attack and yet it failed to act. Intelligence suggested that, in the weeks leading up to Christmas, Al-Qaeda leaders had discussed a "Nigerian" being prepared for a terrorist attack. But that information was never passed along to the appropriate authorities.

What's more, the suspect's father had gone so far as to contact the U.S. Embassy in Nigeria to express his concerns about his son's radicalism and association with terrorists in Yemen. He met with the CIA and other agencies to discuss his assertions. A summary of those meetings was sent to CIA headquarters in Langley. The embassy cabled Washington with the information along with instructions to raise alarms if Abdulmutalleb applied for a visa.

It was discovered he already had a multiple entry United States visa and it was not revoked. Abdulmutalleb's name was put into a database of 550,000 people with possible ties to terrorism but he was never put on the no-fly list. So, according to the government, the radicalized Nigerian boarded a plane armed with chemical explosives.

President Obama admitted there were missed signals and uncorrelated intelligence that should have prevented the would-be bomber from ever getting on the plane. He said the nation's security agencies were guilty of "a mix of human and systemic failures".

Here she sat with her nation's security at stake *again*, finding out firsthand that nothing had changed. The imaginary walls still existed. Agencies were willing and ready to pass the buck to protect themselves rather than share vital intelligence.

Matti thought about a position paper she'd come across a few years back, written by a blogger and self-professed security expert named Bruce Schneier. She'd memorized the opening lines of his argument because they served as a reminder to her about the importance of her job.

"Security is both a feeling and a reality," Schneier wrote, *"And they're not the same. The reality of security is mathematical, based on the probability of different risks and the effectiveness of different countermeasures. But security is also a feeling, based not on probabilities and mathematical calculations, but on your psychological reactions to both risks and countermeasures."*

In this case, Matti neither felt safe nor had confidence in the math. The FBI would be too late based on the intelligence she believed they'd obtained from their own investigation and that they'd received from the NSA.

She knew the FBI would wait to thwart the plot. If they acted too soon, they risked losing evidence of intent. Their method of operation was to wait until the last possible minute to stop the detonation, if they even had the ability to do it.

Matti wasn't convinced the FBI knew about the casket bomb. She wasn't sure they had intelligence about the cell phone detonators. For all she knew, they were expecting a more conventional attack.

She could try to alert them through some radical, attention getting act. Getting arrested somehow might facilitate a meeting with the right people. But by the time authorities bought into her story and deemed her legitimate, it could be too late.

Matti's reasoned calculations were hijacked by a seemingly impossible notion. She tried to fight the ridiculous idea. But as she mentally played out the various endgames in her head the conclusion was always the same. Matti more carefully sipped through the foam in her latte as she convinced herself of the laughable. She would need to stop the attack herself.

* * *

Laura Harrowby's temples were throbbing with each pulse beat more excruciating than the one before it. Her tongue felt thick and her stomach uneasy. The acid of the merlot was scolding her for the overindulgence.

Laura was prone on the love seat in Thistlewood's Embassy Row apartment, a cool washcloth covering her forehead. She was still in the sweater dress she'd worn the night before. Her flats were on the floor, as were her pantyhose and bra.

"Are you feeling any better?"

Thistlewood was seated in one of the room's two overstuffed chairs. The mantle clock chimed. It was later in the day than Laura imagined it would be.

"No," she said in a gravelly voice. She cleared her throat. "How long before I can have something else for my headache?"

"I don't know," Thistlewood looked at the clock. "An hour maybe?" He was thumbing through the *Washington Post*, but he was only mildly interested in the content. He was killing time until it was killing time.

"Remind me of what happened last night?" Laura slipped the cloth off of her eyes such that she could see her boyfriend. "I know I drank too much wine. I know we went over to my dad's place. After that, it gets kinda fuzzy."

"Well," Thistlewood shifted his body to face Laura, "we had some fun. A couple of times. And then, because I didn't want to leave you alone at your place, I brought you back here. I've been nursing you back to health since you awoke." He smiled at her and winked with his right eye.

"You're too good to me," she cooed, her voice still raspy. "I'm so lucky to have you." She pulled the cloth back over her eyes. "You're such a giver." She giggled.

Thistlewood felt a tinge of guilt wash through him. He'd used her. He'd betrayed her trust. It wasn't right and he knew it. But the guilt, however sincere, was not enough to push him from the prescribed course. It was too important. It was greater than his relationship with Laura Harrowby.

"You know," he suggested, "you can stay here for the rest of the day. I've got to leave for a little while. You can hang out until you feel better. If you're here when I get back, we could head out for a late bite to eat."

She was quick to respond despite her funk. "I don't think I will feel much like eating today. At all. But I will take you up on your offer to stay here. I like being with you. Are you sure you have to go?"

"Yes, I have a quick meeting. Maybe a couple of hours or so, but I'll be back before it's too late."

She feigned a frown and moved a pillow to a more comfortable position under her head. She felt like she could vomit. Again.

"Do you mind if I watch some television?" he asked. "I'll keep the volume low so as not to amplify your headache."

"Whatever you want. I'll be fine." He could have asked her to stick her head inside a bass drum while he thumped it and she would have obliged. They both knew it.

He leaned forward in his chair and reached for the wrought iron and glass coffee table. Atop a large art book was the television remote control. He pulled it to him and turned on the 32" LED panel that hung from the wall amidst his Trek Kelly art collection.

The television glowed to life and an image of President Foreman's cortege appeared on the screen. Thistlewood adjusted the volume so that it was loud enough to hear it but soft enough to not irritate Laura.

"This is a sight," observed the commentator, "that we hope to never see. The memorializing of a sitting president. It is at once both majestic and heart-rending."

Thistlewood watched the screen as the president's casket was pulled from the hearse and placed onto the caisson. He looked at his watch and then at the clock. Time was crawling.

"This exchange would normally take place at the Pennsylvania Avenue entrance of the White House," offered the newswoman. "That is the protocol for a sitting president after his death, given that traditionally he would lie in repose in the East Room prior to the procession."

"She's quite the historian," quipped Thistlewood.

"Who?" Laura's eyes were closed and she wasn't listening intently to the television.

"The newswoman on T.V. What's-her-name from the political show. You know..."

Laura listened to the woman and then snapped her fingers. "I know her voice." It was on the tip of her tannin-thickened tongue.

"Who is she then?" Thistlewood turned to look at his girlfriend. For just an instant they were again a legitimate couple in his mind.

He'd not betrayed her. She wasn't merely a means to an end. It felt good for that moment. But when she answered him, and he turned back the television and the truth of the situation, the pseudo-euphoria evaporated.

"Vickie Lupo," Laura pointed at her boyfriend and then clapped. Her face was still covered in a damp cloth that was quickly acclimating to room temperature.

"*The Avenue* is her show, right?"

Lupo appeared on screen briefly before the "live" video of the procession replaced her. She continued her exposition.

"So we understand that from this point at 16th Street and Constitution in front of the White House South Lawn, the procession moves down Constitution at the other end of the Mall. Once it arrives at Fourth Street, military jets will fly overhead and assume a missing man formation.

"Now as we watch, the caisson begins its path to the Capitol," she continued almost breathlessly. "I want to take a moment to talk about tomorrow's funeral, and give you a sense of the history there."

"See," Thistlewood pointed at the screen in disgust. "What did I tell you? History professor Vickie Lupo."

"Are you threatened, baby?" Laura's tone was sympathetic. And it was obvious that she was joking. "Is the big, bad news anchor coming to take your job?"

Thistlewood knew that Laura was teasing him and he laughed. In reality, he was bothered that highly paid Teleprompter readers got to play the part of historian in front of such large audiences. He knew, and Vickie Lupo knew, that the information she was spouting was fed to her by a producer and a researcher. And they both knew that she was merely reading it from a script or from notes. It irritated him that a person of such little education, but with a flair for the dramatic, could command such attention

As a lover of history and politics, he should have been thrilled that anyone with a soapbox might deign to educate. Any discussion of political perspective was good and was needed. An informed electorate was the only path to a true democracy.

But Thistlewood was small and paranoid. And despite Laura's sense of humor, he knew that if someone like Vickie Lupo wanted a job teaching politics at a university, she'd get one. She had caché. She had a name, even if he had trouble remembering it.

Thistlewood was certain that was how Bill Davidson got his plush gig at Hanover. It wasn't because the former A.G. had some stout political mind, the professor surmised. It was because he had a name.

Everyone knew that Davidson was an ineffective lawyer at every level. But his name, or more correctly his father's name, scored him one advantage after another. It made Thistlewood want to rage against the machine.

The professor sat there seething, but faking an understanding laugh to appease Laura, and his motivation became clear. As much as he wanted to deny it to himself, he knew the real reason for his involvement in the plot.

He wanted to make a name for himself. He wanted others to study his papers and discuss his intellect. It wasn't about the greater good. It wasn't about country. It was about his deviant, pathological need for recognition.

It was a godless epiphany that initially took Thistlewood by surprise. Had he really done this because of his ego? Had he devolved into a homegrown terrorist because his mother didn't breastfeed him and his father never played catch? Suddenly the room was spinning, and it was he who needed the cool cloth and painkiller. Almost as quickly as it began, the spinning stopped and Thistlewood again focused his attention on the screen in front of him.

It was better to push aside his Freudian rationale and instead focus on the task ahead. The self-realization was too painful. He could convince himself again that his calling was much higher than that of narcissism.

"The service at Arlington National Cemetery will be historic for a number of reasons," Vickie Lupo said, back on screen now, was framed to the right. The procession video filled the left half. "Only two other U.S. presidents are buried at Arlington. John F. Kennedy was laid to rest there in 1963 and William Howard Taft was buried there in 1930."

"She didn't mention Wilson," chimed Thistlewood. "He's not buried at Arlington. But while she's giving a lecture, she might as well mention Wilson."

"Why?" Laura was feeling better. She was sitting up and had removed the cloth from her head.

"He's the only other dead president not buried in his home state. He's buried at the National Cathedral."

"Where are the non-dead presidents buried?" She giggled.

"Funny." He wasn't laughing.

Lupo was again replaced with a full screen shot of the procession. Hundreds of people were lining the streets as the president's casket passed. "And as for President Foreman, he will be buried near the Lockerbie Memorial. It's one of twenty-five monuments and memorials at the cemetery."

"What's the point of this?" asked Thistlewood rhetorically. "Are we watching *Jeopardy*! now?"

"The Lockerbie memorial is officially known as the Pan Am Flight 103 Memorial Cairn. It was built with 270 blocks of red Scottish sandstone, one for each of the victims of the 1988 terrorist bombing of that plane." Lupo was affecting a softer tone, intended to convey empathy. "It is amazing to think," Vickie Lupo said, histrionic now, "that in just twenty-four hours from now, our president, Dexter Foreman, will be buried alongside those important, historic Scottish stones. Let's pause to think about that."

Thistlewood thought about how wrong she was. He thought about how different the world would be in those twenty-four hours. He imagined how his own monumental place in history would change in two full sweeps of the mantle clock. It chimed and a sardonic smile stretched across his face. It was almost tea time.

CHAPTER 12

Ings chose to ride the tour bus, rather than drive his own car or take a taxi, to avoid easy identification by security. He hoped being part of a large group of bag-toting tourists would help ease his entry and egress.

"Arlington Mansion and two hundred acres of ground immediately surrounding it were officially designated as a military cemetery June 15, 1864, by Secretary of War Edwin M. Stanton," the bus narrator said.

The bus passed through Memorial Gate and turned right onto Schley Drive. Ings shifted uncomfortably in his seat and pressed his left foot against the backpack. He could feel the sweat forming under his armpits.

"And here we are passing the monument for President and Justice William Howard Taft." The narrator's voice was deep and without accent. "President Taft was interred in Arlington National Cemetery March 11, 1930. His widow, Helen Herron Taft, was buried beside him May 25, 1943. Following the president's interment, the War Department placed an order for a headstone with the Vermont Marble Company."

Ings watched as they drove by the fourteen and a half foot tall monument. He looked at the small Arlington Cemetery map the tour guide had given him when he boarded the bus. The lettering was too small for him to read.

The bus made a left onto Sherman Drive, another left onto Sheridan, and then slowed in front of a small circle to the right.

They were in front of the memorial to President John F. Kennedy and his brother Robert F. Kennedy.

"From here you may visit the Kennedy family gravesites," the narrator offered as the tourists stood from their seats. "And a short walk to the northeast will put you in front of Arlington House and the Robert E. Lee Memorial. Please feel free to explore the immediate grounds and meet back here at the bus in twenty minutes."

Ings reached down to pull the backpack up onto the seat next to him, slinging one of the straps over his right shoulder as he stood. He carefully filed into the line of tourists and stepped off of the bus and out into the cemetery.

He looked at the map again, and though he still couldn't read it precisely, Ings had a sense of where he needed to go. He walked purposefully to the northeast with a small group interested in foregoing the Kennedy plots to see Arlington House.

The group stopped at the house; Ings kept trekking. He passed the Civil War Unknowns Monument and found himself back on Sherman Drive. Walking north across the Chaffee parking lot he could see the Pan Am Flight 103 Memorial Cairn straight ahead. To its left was a barricaded area that Ings assumed was reserved for President Foreman's funeral.

The drunk carefully and inconspicuously trudged up to the memorial and stood a foot from it, admiring its height. It stood slightly taller than a basketball hoop. From a plaque on its side, Ings read the inscription: "IN REMEMBRANCE OF THE TWO HUNDRED SEVENTY PEOPLE KILLED IN THE TERRORIST BOMBING OF PAN AMERICAN AIRWAYS FLIGHT 103 OVER LOCKERBIE, SCOTLAND 21 DECEMBER 1988 PRESENTED BY THE LOCKERBIE AIR DISASTER TRUST TO THE UNITED STATES OF AMERICA".

Ings pulled the backpack from his shoulder and placed it on the ground in front of him. He knelt and carefully unzipped the small front pocket, pulling out the small card containing the number for the Nokia cell phone attached to the explosives in the larger portion of the backpack. He stood, slipping the card into his pocket, and picked up the backpack.

Ings looked over his shoulder toward the parking lot, and to his left at the area readied for the next day's funeral, before placing the backpack down at the base of the cairn.

Ings slowly backed away and then turned to quickly cross the parking lot, and it never occurred to him how ludicrous it was to do what the knight had asked of him. It also didn't cross his mind that he'd been set up. Not even when he heard someone calling his name from behind him.

"Mr. Ings?" The man's voice was forceful. "Mr. James Ings?"

Ings resisted the reflexive urge to turn around at the mention of his name. He kept walking.

"Mr. Ings," the voice was strong but wavering as the man began to walk hurriedly behind him. "Please stop sir. I think you've left your bag."

Ings glanced to his right, and saw a second person coming toward him, a uniformed security guard. The man was moving at a pace somewhere between a jog and a run. Ings quickly looked away from him and to his left toward the Guard B Comfort Station. There was another guard moving directly toward him. Ings knew he was in trouble.

"Mr. Ings," the voice behind him said, louder, closing in on him, "you left a bag at the Memorial Cairn. I'd like to talk to you about it."

Ings looked over his shoulder at the Good Samaritan guard and saw the man with his weapon drawn. He was not returning the backpack. For a moment he thought about pulling out his cell phone and detonating it, but by the time he'd fully contemplated the idea, he was caught.

Guards from either side of him grabbed at Ings' arms and pulled him to the ground as he passed the Old Amphitheater at Sherman Drive. His face hit the gravel and dirt and the wind rushed from his chest. He lay on the ground, arms behind his back, considering how quickly the men had descended upon him.

"Mr. James Ings?"

"Yes?" Ings grunted and he felt the cold metal of handcuffs clipped to his wrists. His thumbs were held against the small of his back.

"You have the right to remain silent, Sir."

That's when he got it. The clue was there from the minute he'd pressed pause on his DVR a couple of hours earlier. But he'd never bothered to ask the question. The knight had set him up and tipped off the authorities.

"Did you get a phone call?" Ings asked as two of the guards yanked him to his feet. "Did someone call you and tell you I was here?"

"Something like that," one the guards said as the men started escorting Ings back toward the nearest guard house. "How did you know?"

Ings decided to exercise his right to silence.

"How did you know?" the guard repeated, tugging on the cuffs, and Ings almost lost his balance as he trudged forward.

Ings thought about whether or not to blow the plot by ratting out the knight. It would be a fair turn. But what good would that do?

He knew that their plan was in jeopardy, that a diversion may be the only way to fool the feds, given the possibilities of what they might know. There were always necessary sacrifices in war.

Revolutionary martyr Major General Joseph Warren sacrificed his life at the battle of Bunker Hill. A single father of four, he died from a musket ball to the head a full year before the colonies declared their independence. It was his calling. And this was to be the drunk's calling. The knight was asking him to be General Warren. Lost on Ings was the reality that he'd been duped by someone he believed to be a trusted friend.

But he would not talk; he would not risk the plot. He knew deep down that Sir Spencer believed he was the only one capable of the task.

The professor wouldn't have the stomach for it; the artist was nearly as weak; the A.G. was AWOL; Sir Spencer couldn't do it. Ings was the only one capable.

Instead of answering the guard, Ings thought of Neal Peart and awkwardly crooned, "*Though his mind is not for rent, Don't put him down as arrogant. His reserve, a quiet defense. Riding out the day's events.*"

* * *

Matti searched Davidson's journals, speed reading much of the scribbled text. She ran her finger down the center of each page as her eyes flitted from left to right, focusing mostly on nouns and verbs. Flipping page after page, she could not find any information about which of the conspirators would place the calls to trigger the phones. Davidson didn't list any phone numbers.

She knew the phones would utilize one of two types of cellular network technology. They would either rely on Global System for Mobile Communications (GSM) or Code Division Multiple Access (CDMA). GSM was the worldwide standard for cellular data transmission. CDMA was more popular in the United States. Matti remembered from some of her studies for previous NSA analyses that more than a billion people utilized GSM. A quarter of that number used CDMA. But because CDMA was more widely used in the U.S., the chances of the Daturans using that type of technology were more likely.

Additionally, third generation, or 3G, networks used CDMA because of the additional bandwidth for data transmission. She also knew that CDMA was used in a lot of military applications, which included anti-jamming and secure communications.

Matti knew if she couldn't stop the Daturans from placing the calls to detonate the bombs, her only alternative was to prevent the calls from connecting. She needed a computer. She didn't have time to go home or find an internet café.

Looking around the coffee shop, she fixed her eyes on the grubby, FHM transfixed college student. At his feet was an unzipped backpack that revealed a laptop computer. It would do.

Matti pinched her cheeks with her thumbs and forefingers and licked her lips. She stood to adjust her assets and then walked with purpose to the unshaven misogynist. He refined his posture and snapped shut the magazine as Matti approached his table. He pulled an ear bud from his right ear and then rubbed his chin.

"Hi there," Matti said, placing her palms on the table and leaning in slightly.

"Hey," he smiled. "What's up?"

"Yeah," Matti rocked back and forth on her Gore-Tex Merrells, "I hate to ask this, but I really need to get online, and I noticed your laptop..."

He was polite beyond what she had expected. "No problem. It's got a Wi-Fi card. There's free Wi-Fi here. It's fully charged. You should be good to go." He reached down to pull the computer from his bag. "How long do you need it?"

"Ten minutes?" Matti reached for the computer. "Maybe fifteen?"

"That's cool." He tried to smile and rubbed the scruff on his chin again. "Whatever you need." He was watching her denim clad hips sway gently back and forth as she walked.

"Twenty minutes tops," Matti called as she walked back to her seat, looking at him over her shoulder. "I promise." She blinked quickly two or three times before turning her head and retaking her seat across the room. Matti liked her newfound sexual confidence. If the NSA could use it to their benefit, so could she.

"I'll be here!" He waved at her, replaced the ear bud, and reopened the magazine.

Matti was the one now oblivious to the activity around her. She navigated the coffee shop's Wi-Fi network and connected to the internet. She used the search engine task bar at the top right of the screen to speed up her efforts.

She typed "cell phone jammer" into the small text box and hit enter on the keyboard, watching intently as the results populated the screen. She picked a random link that appeared to have relevant information and started reading.

She learned the Vatican had installed cell phone jamming technology for the papal conclave to choose the new pope in 2005. They were trying to prevent anyone from leaking information to the outside world about the balloting process.

She also learned that the British government considered a mobile cellular security bubble to accompany President Bush during a visit to London in 2003. The bubble never materialized, but it would not have been unprecedented had it happened.

Jamming cell phone signals was relatively easy, Matti deduced. And she learned that frequency jamming devices were readily available on the internet. They cost as little as $300. Matti didn't have time to consider that.

She also read about a military technology that could wipe out all combatant radio or cellular transmissions. It was called WolfPack and was deployed in the air through an unmanned system. According to the Department of Defense, WolfPack could deny an adversary use of its communications while not interfering with friendly military and commercial radio communications.

That wouldn't work. If she couldn't even get her boss to listen to her, she certainly couldn't rely on anyone at the Pentagon to take her call. And if they did, she knew they wouldn't act quickly enough.

Then she came across an article from the *Register*, one the world's largest online technical publications. It was from February 2008 and was titled, *Taliban Demand Nighttime Cell Tower Shutdown*. Reporter Lewis Page wrote that the Taliban was threatening to attack mobile phone companies in Afghanistan unless cellular signals were stopped at night. According to Page, hardline Islamic militia believed that cell towers were being used to locate and track Taliban gunmen. Matti now had her plan.

She quickly searched for a website that could map the cellular towers closest to the Capitol. Finding one pretty easily, she identified a host of towers within close proximity. There were five towers along K Street, northwest of the Hill; one at the Benning Power Plant east of the Capitol; one at the Metro Police Station on Indiana, northwest of the Capitol; and another half dozen were dotted south of the Potomac in northern Virginia. While there were thirty-eight cell phone towers and antennas in the District, she needed to focus on a small area closest to the Capitol. Matti decided to narrow her search to the towers along K Street.

Given what she knew about where the Daturans lived, worked, and tended to gather, she figured that the call would be coming north and/or west of Capitol Hill. That wasn't a given, but she had little with which to work and even less time in which to do it. Using the touchpad on the laptop keyboard, she zoomed into the map of the tower cluster and found one on 13th Street, NW belonging to AT&T.

"GSM," she mumbled. She took a calculated guess that it wouldn't be the right tower given the carrier's technology, and she moved to the tower on M Street.

"T-Mobile," she noted. It was one of only two towers held by that company. "Probably not..." That left three likely towers in Matti's mind: one on L Street, one on DeSales, and one on K Street. All three towers were on leased space atop privately owned buildings. Matti made mental note of the three addresses for the towers. They weren't far apart. She might have time to get to all three of them if she hurried.

"Hey," she called over to the college student.

"Yeah?" He was already looking at her when she called to him.

"How do you want me to close out of your computer?" She'd already erased her browsing history from the laptop's memory.

"Just take it back to the homepage and leave it on," he said, trying ineffectively to appear blasé.

"Will do," she nodded. "I'll be finished here in a second."

She used the touchpad to guide the cursor to the task bar atop the screen and clicked on the home button. The screen went blank as it reverted to the preset home page in the computer's browser. The website PLAUSIBLEDENIABILITY.INFO popped onto the screen.

"Does everybody read this ridiculous site?" she muttered to herself. "It's so crass." She looked across the room to see the site's intended demographic staring at her unapologetically. She turned her attention back to the screen.

The large red, black, and blue banner across the top of the page forced Matti to refocus her eyes. And even then she still wasn't clear on what the headline meant.

"MAN ARRESTED FOR DROPPING BOMB BAG AT ARLINGTON!"

What?

She maneuvered the touch pad and clicked on the headline. A news page appeared with few details.

"EXCLUSIVE! PDINFO has learned that security at Arlington National Cemetery has arrested a 62-year-old man in connection with a suspicious device believed to be an explosive. The man was arrested after a tip call and was taken into custody without incident. We're not sure if the man knew he'd be blowing up people who are already dead. Developing...."

They're diverting attention, she thought. *They know that we know what they're doing.*

Her eyes darted back and forth, not focusing on anything particular as she processed what was happening.

At least they THINK they know what we know.

* * *

"James has been detained," Sir Spencer announced, enjoying the double meaning of the turned phrase. He stood behind the bar, fixing himself a scotch. Edwards and Thistlewood sat across from him, half-expecting he would pour them a shot each. He didn't.

"What do you mean *detained*?" Thistlewood snapped. "I thought we were all supposed to be here."

"Yeah," chimed Edwards, "and where's Bill? Is he out?"

"He is." The knight had his back to the men as he replaced the bottle on the shelf behind the bar. He turned to them as he wiped his hands on his jacket.

Thistlewood noticed that the coat was a thousand dollar Brooks Brothers Golden Fleece Black Watch Smoking Jacket. And it looked somewhat ridiculous.

"Back to Jimmy," Thistlewood redirected, "where is he?"

"He's detained," repeated the knight as he took a sip and then pursed his lips at the cheap sweetness of the drink. "That is to say, he's been arrested."

"What?" Both men said in unison, nearly leaping over the lacquered rosewood.

"Calm down," the knight said dismissively. "It's part of the plan, my good men."

He was playing with them as he had for years, only now he could tell they were cognizant of it. He could sense their distrust of him and their sudden wariness.

"The plan," he continued as he turned his back to them again, searching for a finer bottle from which to drink, "is to take power. The way to do that is to upset the succession. The way to do *that* is to affect our fantastic plan. And none of those wonderful things would be possible without James' sacrifice today." He pulled a large brown decanter from the top shelf. It was a bottle of Cutty Sark Golden Jubilee. He spun back to the rosewood bar and poured a glass.

"I think I can also speak for George here," Thistlewood said, thumbing his left hand at Edwards, "in saying that we're *both* lost."

The knight put his right hand in the waist pocket of the smoking jacket and sipped from the glass. "Mmmm...oak, I think."

Edwards was tired of Sir Spencer's gamesmanship. Enough was

enough. "Sir Spencer, could you please enlighten us as to what's going on? We're at the zero hour here. The casket is nearly at the Capitol and the guests are in the rotunda." He pointed to the television mounted on the wall behind the knight and above the bar. The sound was muted, but they could see the gathering crowd inside the Capitol and the procession's proximity to it. They were maybe an hour away from detonation, and the knight was playing with their heads.

"I took a calculated risk, good men." Sir Spencer licked his lips and leaned onto the bar surface with his palms pressed flat. "As we discussed at the opening last night, we do not know what the feds know and what they don't. I felt as though a last minute diversion might tip the scales back in our direction, and so I sent James on a mission."

Just then, Edwards noticed a "BREAKING NEWS" graphic flash across the television screen behind the bar. He grabbed the remote to his left, turned off the mute and turned up the volume.

"We have breaking news from Arlington National Cemetery, the site of tomorrow's funeral for President Foreman," newscaster Vickie Lupo's voice said as her large head filled the screen. She held a piece of paper in front of her, alternating glances into the camera and at the script as she read the news. *"We have confirmed authorities have arrested a man on suspicion of placing a bomb near the site of the funeral."* Lupo leaned into the camera and presumably adlibbed, *"This is amazing people. I cannot believe someone would be so foolish as to try this right now."*

Edwards and Thistlewood glanced away from the screen briefly to look at the knight, who was indifferently downing another shot of the Cutty Sark Jubilee. The men returned their attention to the television.

"We understand from sources," Lupo was saying, reading from the notes in front of her, *"the man left a bag or backpack of some sort near the Pan Am Flight 93 Memorial Cairn, and we are told authorities were tipped off to the bomb threat by an anonymous caller."*

Edwards looked back at Sir Spencer again, who raised his glass in offer of a toast and grinned, obviously acknowledging the "calculated risk".

"I still don't understand," Thistlewood said, shaking his head and flailing his arms. Unable to sit still, he looked like a hyperactive child an hour overdue for his Ritalin dose. "What is going on here? I thought you said everything was good? Now Bill is out – whatever that means – Jimmy is behind bars, and we preemptively tried to bomb a graveyard?"

"Good man," the knight said calmly, looking directly at the professor, "plots are living, breathing organisms, and ours is healthy. But given the aforementioned events of last night, we needed an insurance policy. I asked James to perform the task because I trust him."

The knight was standing with his arms folded across his chest. He sounded affable, but his body language suggested a defensive posture. "The man has kept stolen explosives in his freezer for years on my behalf," Sir Spencer went on. "He's cleaned money for me when it was needed, and he was jolly good at keeping secrets. I knew I could trust him to deliver the device and not speak a word about it to anyone."

"But you had him *arrested*," countered Thistlewood.

"Did he know you were setting him up?" Edwards asked, beginning to wonder about his own safety.

"That's a question of perspective," the knight said coyly. He looked at his watch. It was getting late.

Before either of the men could ask for a clarification, he held up the index finger on his right hand while pulling his phone out of the smoking jacket's left hip pocket. "I need to send a text." He thumbed a message into the phone's keypad and hit send.

* * *

Bill Davidson sat in his office with a resignation reserved for men who never had anything to gain. His destiny, he'd determined, was not what he'd hoped. Falling short of every expectation throughout his life, Davidson knew he was of little use to anyone.

He swung the chair around so as to close and lock his office door before spinning back to face his desk. He powered down his computer and clicked off the small lamp to the right of the flat panel monitor.

Facing the embarrassment of a hooker's death, a plot to blow up the Capitol, and promise unfulfilled, he opened a drawer on the left side of the desk and pulled out a small shoebox.

Davidson had kept the box and its contents in the desk drawer for more than a year. Until now, however, he'd never found the right time to employ it. There was always more he hoped to do. Always another sunrise.

He opened the box and removed two airplane sized bottles of Beefeaters Gin, a gallon-sized plastic baggie, a large rubber band, and a small bottle of pills. The pills were Amobarbital, a prescriptive barbiturate given to Davidson when he'd suffered from a short-term bout of insomnia.

Davidson had taken two antihistamines ten minutes prior. He sighed and uncapped the pill bottle, dumped half of the remaining amount into one of the airplane bottles to dissolve them, and shoveled the other half into his mouth. He uncapped the second bottle of gin and washed them down then stood from his chair to pull a framed photograph from the wall. He sat down again and looked at the picture. It was his favorite snapshot of himself with his father. They were smiling. Their arms were slung around one another. Davidson couldn't remember where the picture was taken, only that he liked it. He took another deep breath against the growing lump in his throat and placed it face down on the desk in front of the computer.

He lifted the remaining airplane bottle and swigged the gin/Amobarbital cocktail. Then, with tears welling in his eyes, he took the unzipped plastic bag and pulled it over his head. He stretched the rubber band to fit onto the bag and then around his neck.

Sitting in the office chair, he could feel the condensation of his breath on the inside of the bag. He could smell the gin and taste the remnants of the pills on his tongue and roof of his mouth.

As the realization of the finality of his decision took hold, he started breathing more quickly. His heart was pounding harshly against his chest. The fog inside the bag made it hard for him to see beyond his nose.

He wondered why he hadn't chosen a gun. It would have been faster and maybe painless. He'd seen how quickly his girl had dropped lifelessly to the floor the night before.

But this was appropriate, almost poetic, in its form. A life that slowly disintegrated into worthlessness was slowly, quietly snuffed. Whoever had read his tea leaves as a young child, had interpreted them incorrectly, he decided. He began to feel dizzy and disoriented. His breathing slowed. His last conscious thoughts were of what the knight had told him in their final conversation.

"You wanted so badly to become something you were never really capable of becoming," Sir Spencer had said. Davidson knew the man was right.

He thought he might vomit, but the urge subsided, and he felt a wave of calm pass through his body. His eyes fluttered and he gasped as he passed out. Five minutes later, Bill Davidson was dead. The sadness and the potential were gone.

* * *

Matti's attention was distracted as her cab pulled up outside of the Norfolk Southern offices at the corner of 15th and K Streets. The building sat in a high rent area of the District not far from the White House and next to McPherson Square.

She'd been there before with her father. Not long after his admission about her mother's drug use, he'd come to visit her. She'd given him a tour of the city she called home. They'd talked around her mother, neither of them really wanting to go there.

But as they'd walked up to the statue of the Union general who'd died in the Battle of Atlanta, her dad made an effort.

"I'm to blame," he'd said. He didn't need to qualify it. Matti knew what he meant.

"No you're not," she'd said. "I am."

"What?" he had asked, quite confused.

"I could have saved her," Matti had said as she ran her hand along the smooth granite of the statue's pedestal. "If I'd put the pieces together of who she was, I could have saved her. And if I'd been able to solve what really happened the night she died, I could have saved you."

Her father had pulled his hands to his face and cupped them over his mouth. Above his fingertips, his eyes welled. He'd shaken his head.

"It wasn't your job to save anyone." His voice was shaky and the words warbled from his lips almost unintelligibly. Matti hadn't believed him then.

But now she thought he was right. Maybe she was crazy to think she could save *anyone*.

As the cab parked at the curb, Matti refocused on the job at hand. She looked out the window at her stop. Atop the building was a cell tower that stretched one hundred and seventy feet from the ground. Matti asked the cabbie to wait for her as she scooted from the backseat.

"The meter is running," he mumbled.

"That's fine." She shut the door behind her and walked to the main entrance of the large stone building. Underneath the address placard was the nameplate for a California based law firm whose D.C. offices were inside.

She approached the seven-story building and faced a set of three double doors, each of which was adorned with the words "Southern Railway" atop their frames. She chose the center set of doors and entered, finding herself in the lobby. Matti was flying by the seat of her twenty-nine dollar pants.

She cleared her throat and tried to sound authoritative as she addressed a blazered security guard. "Sir, I need to speak with whomever is in charge of the cellular tower atop this building, please."

The guard, a middle aged man with close cropped hair and a walkie-talkie, assessed the woman in front of him. She was wearing a sweatshirt and denim jeans.

"Why is that, ma'am?" he asked. His hand slid down his side to the top of his two-way radio.

"It is a matter of national security, sir, and it is urgent."

"Do you have any identification, ma'am?"

The woman seemed a little off kilter to the guard. He took her Maryland driver's license and a green NSA identification badge. He studied the badge, flipping it over to look at the back, and then compared the name with that on her driver's license.

"Hang on a minute." The guard walked over to a small desk with a telephone and pulled the receiver to his ear.

Matti could see he was speaking with someone but couldn't decipher what he was saying. She saw him pull a pen from his breast pocket and write on a pad of paper while cradling the phone in the crook of his neck. Matti braced herself for an argument when he put down the phone and walked back to her, still holding her identification badge and driver's license.

"Ma'am," he handed back her IDs, "I don't know that we can help you. If you need help with the cellular tower, you'll need to talk with the Atlanta office. I've written a contact name and number here for you."

"That's not gonna be sufficient," Matti said, standing her ground. "I need to talk with someone here. Who's your supervisor?" "Just a minute, ma'am." The guard mumbled into his two-way radio and within seconds an older man in the same company blazer appeared. He approached Matti with his hand extended.

"Hello, sir." Matti shook his hand. "I need to talk with someone who controls the cell tower atop this building. I may need the reception and transmission interrupted. Can you help me?"

"I sure can," the man said, seeming nice enough. His bald head reflected the light from the chandeliers above him.

"Great!" Matti was surprised but relieved. "So I—"

"If you can show me a court order."

"What?"

"If you want to alter or record the transmission of the cell tower, the Atlanta office has already informed me you need a judge to sign off on it."

Matti didn't have a court order. She couldn't *get* a court order. There was no time. And she couldn't waste any more of her energy here; she had two more places to visit.

All she needed to do was get the right tower to shut down. Two out of three was better than none, and she knew the more time she spent arguing with the security guard, the less time she had to better her odds. The seemingly impossible task was Matti's only chance of stopping a catastrophic attack. The FBI might think it had the plot thwarted, but if what Davidson had told her was true, the feds were wrong.

"Fine. I'll go elsewhere." Matti nodded at the men and turned to leave. She didn't see them radio the office and ask that Metro Police be called.

CHAPTER 13

Secretary of Veterans Affairs John Blackmon was glad to miss the memorial service. He wasn't much for saying goodbye. It was just as well he was the designated successor. From the back of his Town Car he was watching the proceedings with passing interest.

Of more concern to him was whether or not he'd be able to catch his flight to Florida in time to arrive for a late dinner. If he had to be in any 'undisclosed location' for the day, it might as well be on South Beach. Blackmon liked the nightlife there and was a fan of The Clevelander, a hip Ocean Drive hotel, restaurant, and bar with the classic South Beach art deco décor.

The small hotel, with only sixty rooms, provided him with enough privacy and security that he needn't worry about too many prying eyes. He liked the backstage rooms that had direct elevator access to the disco and sundeck. After the week he'd had he needed the break. Thankfully the Secret Service okayed the location, with the caveat he not go bar hopping until after the president's interment at Arlington, to which he'd agreed.

Though the short ride from his office on Vermont Avenue to Reagan National airport was usually quick and painless, the traffic detours and congestion from the memorial made the trip a bit lengthier, even with a police escort.

Blackmon checked his cell phone for messages he might have missed but found none. He leaned forward and turned up the volume on the television. Vickie Lupo was talking. The video on the screen showed the inside of the Capitol Rotunda.

"The Rotunda," she opined, *"is essentially full. It is a grand and yet sad sight to see our nation's leaders gathered in one place for such a somber occasion. The last time so many of these men and women were together was for what turned out to be President Foreman's final State of the Union address."*

Blackmon checked the web browser on his phone and noticed the headline about an arrest at Arlington National Cemetery. "Freakin' nut cases," he mumbled.

"The State of the Union speech, as a quick aside" Vickie *droned, "is modeled after the British Speech from the Throne. That, of course, is delivered by the reigning monarch. Now, as you might remember, President Foreman gave what many critics considered a fantastic speech that night. It deviated sharply from the typical guns and butter diatribe we usually get from the commander-in-chief. It sounded more like a stump speech. And yet, what so many pundits concluded, it was delivered by a man who was running for nothing but the betterment of the nation. And as we await the arrival of the president's casket at the Capitol and continue to show you pictures of the procession, we want to also replay some of the president's more salient points that night. Take a listen.:*

"We have reached a crossroads in this nation..." The right half of the screen replayed the president's address, while the left half showed live video of his casket nearing Capitol Hill. *"And we must ask ourselves, at what cost do we define patriotism? Are we patriots when we buy foreign goods over ones made here in the United States? Are we patriots when we ship jobs overseas to ease our bottom line? What about the hiring of illegal immigrants when hardworking citizens cannot find work? Or when we refuse health care to people because they have preexisting conditions or because their insurance isn't good enough? Are we patriots then? And are we patriots, my fellow Americans, when we buy gas guzzling, carbon emitting, eight cylinder SUVs?*

"I am not here to judge. You did not elect me to do that. And I think most of us believe the only judge is a power higher than us all. But I believe there comes a point when patriotism crosses a line into treason. When the goal becomes pursuit of the dollar alone and when the betterment of the few outweighs the health of the collective, then we all cease to be patriots. And we

all become traitors. When we cannot find the appropriate balance between capitalism and social well-being we are no good to anyone, and we desecrate the memories of the men and women who have fought to keep us free.

"So I ask this collection of fine, democratically elected leaders to choose the side of patriotism. Join me, please, in the fight for what is just and for what will better the lives of our children. This is our crossroads."

Secretary Blackmon remembered that address well. He was in the room, sitting between the Secretary of Energy and the Secretary of Education. There was electricity in the room. It was the first time Blackmon really felt the president's cult of personality.

He remembered looking past the president as he spoke, watching for the Speaker of the House. Even she, he thought, was moved by the president's words as she listened to them hang in the air of a joint session.

It didn't matter. Less than a year later Foreman was dead and the partisan bickering had not stopped. Few measures made it through both houses of Congress without so many compromises and addendums they became worth less than the paper upon which they were printed. Maybe, if things fell the right way, he'd be in charge. And he could deliver a speech that really did affect change.

Blackmon sighed and looked at his watch. He checked his phone again for any messages.

* * *

Matti looked at the meter in the front seat of the taxi. It was nearing the amount of cash she had in her pocket.

"Do you take credit cards?"

"I like cash," the cabbie grumbled without turning around to look at her. He glanced at her in the rearview mirror.

"But do you accept credit?"

Yes," the man admitted, "but I like cash. Can you tip me in cash if you pay credit?"

"Sure thing," Matti said agreeably. She needed the man's help to get her through the difficult traffic. Catching a cab had been tough enough. The last thing she needed was to get ditched and have to find another one.

After navigating closed streets and detours, the cabbie turned right onto DeSales Street and pulled to the curb on the side of the Mayflower Hotel. Matti saw the building she needed across the street. She scurried out of the cab quickly and again asked the driver to wait.

This building was between Connecticut Avenue and 17th Street NW just a block west of the National Geographic Society Building. Matti crossed the street and found the entrance locked. A guard buzzed her in and she pulled the door open to a small lobby. There were a couple of high back leather lounge chairs, a bank of flat panel televisions on the wall, and a small security desk.

On the televisions Matti could see news coverage of the presidential funeral procession. It appeared as though the pall bearers were carrying the casket up the Capitol steps. On one of the screens Matti could see the inside of the Capitol Rotunda full of people. They were standing and awaiting the casket's arrival. She didn't have much time and she knew it.

"May I help you?"

The woman behind the desk was dressed in a dark blue cardigan, standard issue for the building's hired security.

Matti tried a softer approach than the unsuccessful one she'd attempted at the first stop. "I need some help." Matti handed the woman her driver's license and her NSA ID badge without the woman having to ask for them.

The guard was comparing the two cards side by side. "What do you need, Ms. Harrold?"

"I need to speak with whoever is in charge of the cellular tower on top of the building."

The tower here was taller than the one atop the Norfolk Southern building. It rose one hundred and ninety-three feet from the street. Because of that, Matti thought the chances of this being the right tower were greater than the first.

"Hold on a moment," the woman picked up a phone and dialed a three digit extension. Matti could hear the line ring and then someone answer on the other end. She was anxious. There was little time left.

The woman was looking at Matti's green NSA card, running her fingers through the attached beaded chain. "This is security on the first floor. I have a woman here who is representing the National Security Agency. Her name is Matti Harrold." The woman paused to let the person on the other end of the line speak.

"She says she needs to speak with someone who deals with the cellular tower on top of the building."

Another pause before the woman looked up at Matti.

"Ms. Harrold," she asked, "what is your question regarding the tower?"

"I need you to shut it down."

"She needs us to shut it down," the woman repeated in the same tone Matti employed. The voice on the other end of the line said something quickly and then the woman behind the desk hung up the phone.

"I'm told you'll need to speak with a gentleman in our New York office. I spoke with the engineering department here and they cannot help you."

"What if I had a court order?"

"*Do* you have one?" the security guard asked without shifting in her seat. She raised the eyebrow above her left eye.

"No." Matti took her ID cards and turned to leave. "Thanks anyway."

She pushed her way through the glass door and back out onto DeSales. The driver was sitting behind the wheel waiting for her. She crossed the street and jumped back into the cab.

"I've got one more stop to make," she informed him. "I need to get to 1828 L Street as fast as you can get there."

The man turned to look at her as if she were asking for the moon. He placed both hands on the wheel and sat there. Then he pointed at the meter. The fare was close to a hundred dollars.

"You have enough cash for big tip?" "Yes," Matti assured him. "Big tip. Just get me there."

The driver dropped his right hand onto the gear shift and put the cab into drive. He punched the gas and pulled out into traffic. As he turned left onto 17th Street, NW, a pair of Metro police cars and a black Chevy Impala sped onto DeSales and parked. Two officers from each vehicle quickly hopped onto the street and to the building Matti had just left.

* * *

The Secretary of Energy was never one to turn down an opportunity for television face time. There was a running joke amongst the network correspondents who covered Energy: The three most dangerous places in the world were Iraq, Afghanistan, and between the good secretary and a television camera.

The only issue for the secretary was finding a place from which to be the on-air analyst for the president's memorial service. The network execs didn't want him in the studio because they wanted it to appear as though he was "in the mix" somewhere in Washington. There was also the concern among network brass that having a much older statesman next to the relatively young anchor in the studio might diminish the journalist's credibility.

There weren't many independent broadcast studios available on such an important news day, but fortunately for the network, longtime friend Bill Davidson had come through. He'd learned about the conundrum and had offered the studios at Hanover.

The secretary was somewhat surprised he'd not seen the former Attorney General milling about since his arrival at the institute an hour earlier. He assumed Davidson was busy with other work and didn't make much of his absence.

The studio's technician was helping the secretary get settled in his chair while adjusting the lighting.

"Mr. Secretary," he asked, "could I get you to stand? I need to clip this earpiece to the back of your jacket."

"Sure thing," he laughed. "I'm an old pro at these things. What's that called? An IBF?"

"IFB sir," the technician smirked at the secretary's back. "Close enough."

The technician then took a lavaliere microphone and clipped it to the right lapel of the secretary's jacket. He noticed the dark blue fabric was thick and well stitched. The thin pinstripes matched at every seam. The technician knew good clothing when he saw it.

"Nice jacket, sir," he said. "A fine fabric."

"Thanks, young man." The secretary ran his palms along his temples, coiffing his thick white hair. He looked like a hairspray model. "It's from the Executive Suit line over at The Custom Shop on Connecticut Avenue. One hundred percent wool with a high twist weave. Really comfortable. Nicely tailored, I think. I've bought a lot of suits and shirts from them. Been going there a long time. They've got a shop in Houston I used to frequent when I lived there."

He spoke in fragments, perfect for television news punditry. His affability belied just how anxious he was.

"We have a few minutes before they come to you, Mr. Secretary," advised the technician. "So you have some time to relax here. Just remember to turn off your cell phone before you're on air."

"Thanks," the secretary nodded and adjusted his tie. He'd forgotten about his cell phone. He needed to check it. "My phone is over there with my briefcase. Could you hand it to me?"

The technician fetched the phone and gave it to the secretary before returning to the task of light adjustments. The cabinet member's white hair was causing a glare.

The secretary checked his phone and found a single text message. He pressed a button to open the message and then read it:

"Urgent u call now. B4 u go on the air."

The text ended with a ten digit number to dial. The sender information was restricted. That wasn't unusual in Washington – everybody's number was restricted. The secretary looked at his watch again and figured he had time to make the quick call.

He looked at the phone number to remind himself of the numbers and then entered them one by one into his phone. He pushed send and placed the phone to his ear. He heard it ring once.

Then everything around him exploded.

The resulting pressure wave knocked him unconscious instantly. He was thrown backward from the stool and through a bookshelf on the opposite end of the studio. The 55-year old man sustained fatal internal injuries even before the blast sent shards of metal, glass, wood, and drywall through his fine high twist weave wool suit and into his body.

The room collapsed around him and the technician. The technician suffered an instantaneous concussion, even before any external injuries. His orbital sockets blew; his lungs collapsed. And then both men's bodies virtually disintegrated in the ensuing heat and flames.

Unbeknownst to anyone but Sir Spencer Thomas, the Secretary of Energy received a text instructing him to call the Nokia 6210 phone attached to a piece of 6"x6" plywood and a chunk of Semtex. It was the explosive hidden inside The Thoreau collection in the closet that shared a wall with the studio.

Bill Davidson had unwittingly aided the plot by placing the bomb and then inviting the secretary to use his studio for the memorial coverage. Only in death had Davidson lived up to the potential for which Sir Spencer once thought him capable.

As he had with Jimmy Ings, the knight had played the former A.G. perfectly. Never once did he let on what Davidson's true role in the plot would be. He led Davidson to believe his worth was his connection to the current administration; that he could provide valuable timing and location information. That was far from the truth of it. Sir Spencer was rarely close to the truth.

The path was cleared for a single successor to the presidency. The plot was working.

* * *

At 2100 Pennsylvania Avenue, NW, The Cato Street Pub was exactly a mile from the Hanover-Crown Institute. When the Semtex exploded the men felt the ground shudder. All three initially held onto the rosewood bar to steady themselves. The bottles on the bar rattled and a photograph of Tom DeLay fell to the floor, breaking the thin black frame.

Sir Spencer grabbed the throat of the Cutty Sark to keep it upright. "That was Bill," he said impassively, "and the Secretary of Energy."

George Edwards knew to what Sir Spencer was referring, given that he'd handed Davidson the hidden explosive the night before. He knew one of the cabinet members was also a target. The knight's unaffected declaration didn't surprise him. Art Thistlewood, on the other hand, became unhinged.

"What do you mean, 'That was Bill and the Secretary of Energy'?" Thistlewood said in a horrible affected British accent to mock the knight. It sounded at once Jamaican and Irish, but it wasn't the Received Pronunciation.

"That was one of our four explosives, good man. One at the aforementioned Arlington, two in the casket, and one at Hanover-Crown."

"We blew up the Institute?" Thistlewood said incredulously. "With Bill inside?"

"Yes." The knight took a drink directly from the Jubilee decanter. "And don't forget the good secretary."

Thistlewood turned to Edwards with a look of both confusion and disappointment.

"I gave Bill the bomb," Edwards admitted. He shrugged his shoulders as if to suggest it was no big deal. "It was stashed in some books I borrowed from him."

The professor was sweating now, his face red, and a full blood vessel was throbbing along his neck. "I don't understand this. Why was I not told?"

"You were busy shagging the mortician's daughter," the knight countered. "If you'd not been so content to tell the same party joke repeatedly whilst having a litany of May December romances, perhaps I'd have divulged more than you needed to know. But you weren't, so I didn't. I involved you to the extent to which you were needed. The same holds true for our good men Bill Davidson and James Ings. They too knew only what they really needed to know."

"What about George here?" "What doesn't he know?"

"George here," the knight looked at Edwards and then back at Thistlewood, "he doesn't know who the sixth is. I haven't told him."

"Really?" Thistlewood persisted.

"Really, Arthur." The knight was weary of placating the puerility of his minion. "Understand you got out of this exactly what you wanted. You came to me wanting a change. You wanted to make a difference. You, in your tenured ivory tower, complained about the proletariat not getting enough cake from the bourgeois. I gave you the power to make that difference, to eat from the cake, and to affect a regime change in the most powerful country on earth." He sighed. "And yet," he continued, "it wasn't enough. We are on the precipice of accomplishing the impossible. We are set to do with six men what empires and fuhrers could not do with gargantuan armies, and it isn't enough for you."

The knight moved around from behind the bar and stepped to within a foot of Thistlewood. "That is because this was never about patriotism for you. This was never about a better country, my good man."

The knight was seething now, and spitting as he spoke. Drool hung from his lower lip. "This was always about *you*! It was about Arthur Thistlewood The Enlightened. And that is why I could not trust you. You never thought about what you had to lose. You only dreamed of what you had to gain. That is the difference between you and George here."

Before the professor could react there was another loud noise that startled the men. They turned in the direction of the sound to see the large, solid wood red doors fly from their hinges into the room and slide onto the floor.

Standing in the doorway was a cadre of FBI special agents with their weapons drawn. They were yelling instructions at the men and inching forward as they surveyed the hickory walled space for surprises.

In the chaos, the three Daturans raised their hands and dropped to their knees. They knew better than to fight. Arthur Thistlewood urinated in his pants and was forced to lie in the small pool of it on the floor.

"It's over, gentlemen," one of the agents said as he stood over the knight, the professor, and the artist. "You are all under arrest by the authority of the United States Department of Justice. You have the right to remain silent. You have the right to an attorney..."

"Spare me the Miranda, good man," the knight spewed defiantly from the floor. He'd underestimated both the feds' knowledge of their plot and of their ability to act quickly. He knew he'd pay dearly for that miscalculation. But good attorneys could work miracles, and they still had the sixth Daturan. He licked his lips and tried to crane his neck upward to look the lead agent in the eyes. "You're already too late. *A Deo Et Rege.*"

* * *

The third tower, rising two hundred feet from the ground, was the tallest of the three structures Matti targeted to shut down. It stretched skyward from a two hundred and sixty thousand square foot office building on the corner of 18th and L Streets. The building's exterior was alternating panels of glass and black powder coated steel. On its ground floor were a Corner Bakery Café and a Fitness First Health Club. It was a beautiful expanse of a building.

Matti looked at it through the window of the cab before opening the door. She started to get out, and glanced at the sun visor above the front passenger seat. Tucked between the visor and the roof of the cab was a large, legal-sized manila envelope. She had an idea.

"May I borrow that?" she asked the driver.

"What?"

"The envelope? May I borrow the envelope? I'll bring it back."

"Big cash tip?" He wasn't joking.

"Big cash tip." She sighed. "Huge!"

The cabbie reached to his right and leaned forward to grab the envelope. He slid it through the small slot between panels of Plexiglas separating the front and back seats of the cab. Matti thanked him and slid out of the car onto the sidewalk. She could hear the screams of emergency sirens a block south on K Street, a lot of them. Was she too late already? She determined they were heading west toward Georgetown and away from the Capitol and was momentarily relieved. Then she looked to the west and saw a thick black plume of smoke pouring into the sky above the low horizon of buildings. Something had happened. She couldn't worry about it now.

Matti had the taxi wait for her while she jogged through the double set of automated sliding chrome and glass doors. She was losing time.

Straight ahead was a trio of cylindrical brushed nickel planters. They were fluted at the top and held tall, wispy green palms. To the left was the black granite security desk, adorned with a pair of small floral arrangements.

Sitting behind the desk was yet another security guard. He was looking down, reading a paper. As Matti approached, she pulled her cell phone from her pocket and put it to her ear. The manila envelope was tucked under her arm.

"Yes, Mr. Secretary," she said loudly enough to break the guard's train of thought and draw his attention to her. "I am here now. I have the court order, sir. We should be fine." She paused. "No sir, I don't think armed agents are necessary. I imagine the good people here will cooperate without any issues." She paused again as she leaned on the granite. "Yes sir. I will inform you as soon as it's done and I will use a secure line." Matti pushed a button on the phone, placed it on the granite ledge and curled her lips into a smile.

"Sorry about that," she said. "My name is Matilda Harrold." She flashed the green NSA badge and pulled the envelope from under her arm. "I'm with the National Security Agency and I have a court order here. I need to talk with whoever controls the antenna on the top of this building."

The man sat slack jawed. He fumbled for the phone while keeping eye contact with the imposing but beautiful woman in front of him. He wasn't moving quickly enough.

"Immediately sir." Matti looked down her nose at the man while she leaned in.

"Yes, ma'am," the guard nodded and picked up the receiver. He dialed an extension and then nervously asked for a supervisor and the person in charge of the tower.

"Thank you," Matti winked at the man condescendingly. She was inwardly surprised at her playacting. She was good.

A woman appeared from behind Matti. "May I help you?"

"Yes," Matti again held out her NSA badge, "my name is Matilda Harrold. I am with the National Security Agency. I have a court order here for access to the cellular transmissions from the top of this building."

"What is this about?" The woman glanced at the envelope under Matti's arm but did not ask to see it.

"Given the sensitivity of the issue, I can't go into detail," Matti replied, thinking on her feet. "But I will tell you that because of the president's memorial service at the Capitol, we have intelligence that suggests we temporarily halt cellular reception in the area."

The woman didn't seem convinced. "We haven't received any prior notice of this."

"Neither did I," Matti wasn't lying. She held up her finger and pulled her phone from the desk. "Hang on a minute. My phone is buzzing. I'm getting a call." Of course, the phone hadn't rung or buzzed, but neither the woman nor the guard questioned her about it. They were caught in the vortex that Matti Harrold had become.

"No, Sir," she answered. "They've not cooperated yet." Matti glanced up at the woman and bit her lip nervously. "No sir, I don't..." She paused for effect, as though the imaginary caller was interrupting her. "Really, sir..." Matti dramatically pulled the phone from her ear as though the caller had raised his voice in anger. Then she put it back to her ear and nodded before putting her hand over the phone. She looked at the woman.

"This is the Undersecretary and he asks if you can't cooperate, he'll need to speak with your supervisor immediately. I would suggest against that. Can you help me?"

The woman folded her arms and bit the inside of her cheek. She wasn't sure what to make of Matti Harrold, but she didn't think shutting down the tower for a few minutes would cause much harm. The FCC probably wouldn't even know about it. On the other hand, if she failed to comply, and national security was at stake, the consequences could be far greater.

"Okay," she relented. "Tell the Undersecretary we'll comply."

"Good choice," Matti took her hand from the phone and told the imaginary caller all was good. "Give me a fax number, and I'll have the department fax over your copy of the court order. It's under seal at the moment, but should be released once the memorial is over."

Matti knew the lie was a gamble. If the apple bottomed woman knew anything about the law, she'd call her bluff and demand to see the contents of the manila envelope. Incredibly she didn't.

"I'll take care of the tower. We'll shut it down for the remainder of the memorial and then we will flip it back on. John here will get the fax number for you." The woman disappeared into a small hallway at the opposite end of the lobby.

Matti turned back to the guard and, borrowing a pen, jotted down the fax number for the building. She scribbled the digits on the back of the envelope. She couldn't believe her ploy had worked.

Granted, the chances of the bomb-triggering phone call coming through the tower atop the L Street building were small, but getting one tower shut down at least lessened the likelihood of the plot being successful. She'd done everything she could do. Now she just had to wait.

Matti noticed a small 13-inch television on the guard's desk. The sound was off but Matti could see the memorial was underway. Speaker of the House Felicia Jackson was at a lectern speaking. The news coverage cut between shots of her talking and of the audience. There was an occasional shot of the First Lady and of various cabinet members. The Rotunda was packed. Then it appeared as though people were getting up from the seats and walking toward the exits. The speaker was no longer at the podium. Something was happening.

Across the bottom of the screen there was text crawling from right to left:

Explosion at Hanover-Crown Institute in Georgetown. Unknown number of dead and injured. Authorities will not confirm if explosion is accidental or if it is connected to earlier arrest at Arlington National Cemetery. Capitol Rotunda under immediate evacuation...Developing...

Matti couldn't believe what she was reading. The incidents had to be connected. She wondered if Bill Davidson was dead. Was he the bomber or was he a target? Matti's mind was spinning with the possibilities and the repercussions.

"Do you want to listen?" the guard asked politely. "I can turn up the volume for you."

"Yes," Matti responded without taking her eyes off of the small screen, "Thanks." She began to pray for divine intervention as she half-listened to the speaker addressing the memorial. Matti told herself again she'd done everything she could do.

"This is a live feed we are watching of the president's memorial service. And it appears as though the hundreds attending are being ushered quickly out of the Rotunda by Capitol Police. At least I think they are Capitol Police. There may be Secret Service involved too."

Matti watched confused as people began to move from their seats in the Rotunda. Who had ordered the evacuation? Did her superiors believe her theory? Was the evacuation merely a precaution? The video switched from the interior of the Capitol to the exterior. The scene unfolding on the television screen looked to Matti as though it was straight from an action movie. There were men and women, dressed in suits and dresses, running down the eastern steps and onto the Mall. They looked frightened. It reminded Matti of the scenes of lower Manhattan as the towers fell.

The news anchor wasn't offering much insight about the explosion at Hanover and Matti turned her attention from the television. She looked to her left toward the front entrance of the building where she saw four uniformed police officers exiting their cars at the sidewalk just behind her cab. Standing with them was her supervisor.

CHAPTER 14

John Blackmon sat in his stone leather seat next to the wet bar aboard a Lear 35 at Washington Reagan National Airport. He had chartered the flight and footed the $7,000 bill himself. Three Secret Service agents sat in the seats behind him. One aide sat in front of him, next to the bar.

"How quick is the flight?" he asked the aide.

"Right at two hours, Mr. Secretary. The trip is right at 800 miles from here to Miami International. "

Blackmon nodded. He sat back and thought about what lay ahead for his nation.

It was a country that, for a long time, he believed was heading in the wrong direction. There were too many taxes with too few services. Immigrants and welfare recipients seemed to get more from the system than hard-working college graduates. It wasn't fair.

Despite it being outside of his purview as Secretary of Veterans Affairs, he'd often challenged the president on policy decisions far outside of his bailiwick. He questioned monetary policy. He argued over HUD funding and immigration reform. There were times he acted as though he was the Secretary of Commerce in the midst of cabinet meetings.

A lot of beltway insiders were certain Blackmon wouldn't last a second term. In an effort to reach out to all political mindsets, President Foreman kept Blackmon on board, making a concerted effort to pull Blackmon more closely into the inner circle of the White House. It was a genuine effort at consensus building.

Blackmon saw it as an act of war. As he saw it, the more closely the president held his enemies, the more control he had over them.

So when Blackmon's longtime supporter, Sir Spencer Thomas, suggested to him they could eventually effect change as long as he played the game, the Secretary of Veterans Affairs eased his pursuit of policy change and instead took the president up on his offer of friendship. And when the vice president was diagnosed with a non-operable malignant brain tumor, the talk began that Foreman might eventually nominate Blackmon to the number two spot.

Serendipity was at work. Within months, they would be a heartbeat away from the presidency. Foreman's popularity and the other party's disorganization assured he would be a shoe-in at the next general election. Or, if Foreman's popularity waned, Sir Spencer was certain there were other measures they could take.

Then the unthinkable happened. The vice president hung on for months with the help of experimental drugs, and after his death the nomination process stalled for weeks. And Foreman dropped dead before Blackmon could assume the vice presidency.

If the aneurism had waited to pop just a day later, Blackmon would likely have ascended to the throne without even trying.

He was crushed. But then his friend, the knight, proposed an outlandish plot, suggesting Blackmon file suit to stall the installation of the Speaker of the House. While the courts hammered out the constitutional questions, the knight assured the secretary they could figure out a way to take control regardless.

The secretary was not a huge fan of violence, but it was what it was. He was happy to do his part if it meant becoming the leader of the free world.

He reached into his coat pocket and pulled out a small piece of paper about the size of a business card. On it, the knight had written a ten digit number.

Blackmon picked up his cell phone from his lap and pressed the numbers one at a time. He took a deep breath and pressed SEND.

He looked out of his window toward the National Mall. He waited. Nothing.

"Mr. Secretary," the flight attendant was standing in front of him. She was girl next-door-cute. "Could you please turn off your phone until we're in the air? We're ready for take-off."

He nodded at the flight attendant and held up his index finger, asking her to wait just a moment. This was a charter flight; she could play by his rules.

Blackmon checked the series of numbers and realized he'd misdialed. Quickly, while smiling wryly at the attendant, he dialed the correct series of numbers and pressed send. He pulled the phone to his ear and heard it ring once.

* * *

Matti walked quickly from the lobby security desk to the chrome and glass sliding doors at the building's entrance.

"Let me explain," she began, addressing her boss. He was closest to her as she rushed to the sidewalk. The Metro police officers were leaning up against the taxi. "Arlington was never the target. It's the Capitol. They're trying to blow up the Capitol with everyone inside. I've got the proof, sir. A stack of journals is in the trunk of the taxi here." She motioned to the cab. The driver had gotten out of his seat, opened the door, and was standing against his car in the street, concerned he might not get paid. He was smart enough not to say anything yet.

"The bombs are triggered by cell phones. I've targeted a handful of towers and attempted to get the owners to shut them down to prevent the detonation calls from connecting." Matti was speaking quickly and was losing her breath. She was afraid her boss would use the slightest pause to interrupt her.

"I convinced the people here to shut down the tower on top of this building until the memorial service is over. It's a shot in the dark, sir. But I am hopeful the call connects through this tower and the attack is stopped." Matti glanced over the supervisor's shoulder and could still see a black column of smoke rising in the distance. "Well, at least I was hoping to stop the attack at the Capitol." She followed the smoke upward as it turned to gray and dissipated. She thought about Bill Davidson, wondering if she'd failed him. She worried she'd failed her country.

Matti was certain she'd ruined her career.

"We know," her boss responded, uncharacteristically

sympathetic.

Matti's eyes narrowed. "I'm confused, sir."

He stepped closer to her and lowered his voice. "After your little escapade last night, the FBI determined you needed to be watched. They've been following you, with my knowledge, since you left headquarters. We know you went to the Hanover Institute. We know you went to the coffee shop. We knew, before your cabbie did, where you were headed. We weren't sure of the order of your stops. But we knew."

"How did you know where I'd be going?" Matti slipped her hands into the front pockets of her jeans and wrapped the fingers of her right hand around her cell phone. "Were you tracking me through a cell locator?"

"No." He shook his head. "Remember the guy with the computer in the coffee shop?"

"Yeah."

"He's one of us. Well, he's FBI. He was a tail. When you asked to use his laptop, it worked out perfectly for us. He quickly checked your keystrokes and the sites you visited. We knew you were looking for cell towers and we knew which three addresses you'd highlighted."

Matti felt silly for not having known the scruffy college student was an agent. Then again, he wasn't sporting a high end handbag like the woman at the art opening.

"We knew you were onto something," he admitted. "My superior wanted me to give you a long leash. I wasn't convinced, but we couldn't follow official protocol on this."

"What about Arlington?"

"That came as a surprise. We didn't expect it. When Metro police got an 'anonymous call', they alerted Arlington. Arlington, in turn, notified the FBI. The backpack bomb was set to trigger with a cell phone. It's disarmed. The man arrested was Ings. He didn't give any good intel. But with a sudden knowledge of the bomb's makeup and the information you were gathering, we felt confident the Daturans would similarly trigger any subsequent attacks."

"What happened at Hanover?"

"We couldn't coordinate the shut off quickly enough."

"So....?"

"So they blew it up."

"Is Bill Davidson dead?"

"We think so. He never left Hanover after you did. The Secretary of Energy was also killed. Though we don't know who triggered the bomb, we believe he was targeted because of his position in the line of succession."

"What happens now?"

"We're confident from the make-up of the backpack bomb that whatever is in the casket will not detonate as long as cell transmission is blocked. Even if someone tries using a satellite phone to trigger the bomb, the receiving phone is a cell. It won't work. With the help of several cell phone carriers and a federal magistrate, we've begun to shut down all cellular communication in the Metro region. We were too late with the coordination to prevent what happened at Hanover. But we think the threat is contained."

He spoke too soon.

Matti felt the ground shudder and heard a loud explosion. She was disoriented, not sure what had happened. As she got her wits about her, she looked in the direction of the Capitol and saw smoke pluming upward into the sky.

Matti looked back at her boss. He was pale and stared at the smoke with the same disbelief Matti imagined her face had conveyed just seconds before. Even the cab driver was distracted from his fare. He couldn't take his eyes off the smoke.

Matti's boss dialed his phone, attempting to ascertain exactly what had happened but he couldn't get a signal.

She stepped next to her boss and leaned against the car. His eyes searching the sky in disbelief, he put his arm around her and they watched the blackness fill the sky. Matti was exhausted. She replayed the last three days of her life, the rules she'd broken, the instincts she followed and those she ignored. She felt lightheaded. How could she have betrayed her beliefs for good and ultimately fail, while at the same time, a vile group of men could hold true to their foul beliefs and succeed? Matti finally understood there was no black and white. Right and wrong were not mutually exclusive. Everything was in the eye of the beholder.

She realized then her mother's death was just an accident. She realized at that moment she couldn't have saved either of her parents.

In the distance she could hear sirens.

Maybe she was never meant to be the hero.

* * *

Within a millisecond of the explosion, and for a moment thereafter, the heat inside the Capitol Rotunda reached 6900 degrees Fahrenheit, two-thirds the surface temperature of the sun. At detonation the Semtex instantaneously transformed into high pressure gas which expanded rapidly into a blast wave. The pulse of that wave resulted in what explosives experts called *brisance*. It shattered all material within the immediate range of the blast, exerting a force on anything in its outward path that equaled fifteen times Earth's gravity.

The pressure of the blast then reversed itself and morphed into the final phase of the explosion, the blast wind, which moved at a rate of one thousand yards per second until it hit the walls of the Rotunda. The length of the explosion from beginning to end was ten milliseconds.

Atop the rotunda, two hundred sixty-nine feet above the Capitol's east front plaza, the fifteen thousand pound Statue of Freedom stood proudly since 1863. Its bronze classical female figure held a laurel wreath of victory and protective shield in one hand, the hilt of a sheathed sword in the other. Her fringed robe was secured with a brooch inscribed with the letters "U.S." Within seconds of the explosion, she lay in pieces on the ruptured Rotunda floor. The cast-iron globe upon which she had long rested was snapped. The encircling words *E* and *Pluribus* were separated from *Unum*.

All thirty-six windows surrounding the dome were shattered. The sandstone walls extending upward forty-eight feet from the rotunda floor and the separating Doric pilasters were crumbled such that the fireproof cast iron upper half of the walls collapsed upon them. Each of the eight niches, containing large scenes depicting the Revolutionary War and early exploration were unrecognizable as small fragments of the canvasses smoldered amidst the rubble.

The statues and busts lining the walls were reduced to large chunks of marble. Vinnie Ream's Lincoln and Houdon's Washington were indistinguishable from those of Garfield, Grant, or Hamilton. The gold replica of the original Magna Carta, a gift from the British government in 1976, melted from the explosive flash of heat.

There was a large thirty foot wide hole in the floor where President Foreman's casket was perched upon the catafalque. He would have no burial at Arlington.

After the dome collapsed onto itself, what had been the 1.3 million cubic feet of the Rotunda was silent. There were no screams or calls for help, no moaning or crying.

Nobody within the immediate blast range survived the percussive wave. If the pressure didn't crush their bodies or the gases ravage their lungs, the heat, shrapnel, and debris finished them.

George Edwards had guessed correctly. Three bricks of Semtex *were* enough. In the confined space of the Capitol Rotunda they had accomplished exactly what the Daturans had hoped they would. The damage to the dome itself was as great as any one of the six conspirators could have imagined.

* * *

The eight seat plane picked up speed as it moved down the runway. Its thirty-six foot wingspan sliced through the air almost silently. From his window, John Blackmon had seen the large flash and a column of thick black smoke from the east end of the National Mall.

The secretary felt a simultaneous rush of excitement and disbelief. It had worked. The knight was right. All of the players had performed their roles perfectly. The Daturans had succeeded where Al-Qaeda had not. They brought down the Capitol and with it the incestuous breed of legislators and lobbyists who had, for far too long, corrupted the Republic.

Now they could control the nation's future. They could return it to the path of controlled spending and relative pacifism. It was a dream realized. He could now be the face of a revolution. He would be the Washington or the Jefferson of the 21st century. The nation would return to its intended roots where citizen representatives could serve the greater good. The government would again be of the people and for the people. It was a new day.

Blackmon began to process the work he had ahead of him. He could picture his inauguration in his head. It would be a small affair, in the White House. Family, friends, close associates, cabinet members.

Wait! he thought. *The cabinet is gone. I'll have to replace all 14 of them plus me!* He began making mental notes of who might be best to head the different departments. He'd have to move quickly with the transition. Congress, or what was left of it, would rubber stamp anyone he picked if he issued the nominations quickly. They'd back him without pause as they had for George W. Bush after 9/11.

He'd need to pick a new vice president, have to find a chief of staff. There was so much to do, and he already felt behind schedule. It was invigorating, this newfound power. He was the leader of the free world. Blackmon knew it likely the rest of the Daturans might end up in prison, but they'd never connect him to the plot. They needed him to run the country so that their dreams of a more perfect union could be realized. That was the beauty of the plan. Despite his vocal protest to the contrary in his meetings with Sir Spencer, Blackmon knew he had the most to gain and so little to lose.

Of course he'd have to leave Miami as soon as they landed there. He'd probably be shuttled around to various hidden locations until the Secret Service could assure his safety. Once he returned to Washington he'd have to play martyr and savior all at once. That would be a daunting and politically tricky task. The secretary knew of only one man who'd pulled that off successfully and he had a virgin mother. However, he'd have the bully pulpit. And that ultimately was worth the test.

Blackmon felt the slight push of takeoff press him against his seat and the plane lifted into the sky. The sixth Daturan leaned his forehead against the window next to him and watched the black pillows of smoke rise into the air, inwardly smiling at what he'd done to better his country.

* * *

Felicia Jackson could taste the grass in her mouth. It was earthy and ripe. She tried spitting it out as she rolled over onto her side and faced the Capitol. She closed her eyes and opened them again, hoping that would erase the image. It did not. She was lying on the ground roughly one thousand yards from the flags encircling the Washington Monument and could smell the acrid smoke rising above her.

She winced at the sting in her nostrils and tried to pull herself to her knees. Her left shoulder ached and her left ankle throbbed. Her heels were on the ground next to her where she'd dropped them when the Capitol exploded.

"Are you okay, Madam Speaker?"

She looked up and squinted at one of the men on her security detail. His voice was muffled and was difficult to hear against a high pitched tone resonating in her ears.

She was disoriented by her senses flooding back to her all at once.

"Are you okay?" The man reached down and helped her sit upright. "Can you hear me?"

"A little," she was speaking much more loudly than was necessary. But the blast had temporarily muffled her hearing. Felicia scanned the scene in front of her. There were dozens of people, if not more, lying or sitting on the damp ground of the National Mall, all of them blown off of their feet by the explosion.

The closer the people were to the Capitol, she noticed there was less movement among those on the ground. They were hurt or dead.

How could this have happened? Who had done this?

Through the fog in her head, Felicia couldn't decide what incensed her more; the attack or her lack of knowledge that it was imminent.

One moment she was delivering the political equivalent of a eulogy and the next her security detail was literally carrying her from the Capitol. In the confusion she saw others scrambling to make their way from the Rotunda and out of the building. She'd never heard the warning or the order to leave. It all happened too fast.

As she moved hurriedly past the Grant Memorial, she saw some wading through the reflecting pond on its western side. They were splashing and falling down as they pushed through the water. There were those moving faster than her as she reached the National Gallery of Art buildings. There were those who'd run out of steam and were huffing as far as they could away from the Capitol. What took six minutes felt like an instant.

When she was maybe a half mile from the building and halfway to the Washington Monument, she felt a shove across the full of her back, was pushed forward, and fell. At first she thought someone had thrown her to the ground. And then she realized it was the blast of the bomb. She felt the earth rattle as she planted her face into the ground. Digging her fingers into the dirt, feeling it collect under her nails, she turned her head to the left, too disoriented at first to process it. In the distance, framing the Mall, she could see the façade of The Hirshhorn Museum.

The Hirshhorn was home to artist Auguste Rodin's most famous public sculpture, "The Burghers of Calais". It told the story of six men expecting death at the hands of King Edward III during the Hundred Years War. The work depicted the men in various states of despair after losing the battle and before they learned their lives were to be spared by the Queen. Felicia loved the piece. It meant to her that women ultimately control the fate of men. It was a self-serving interpretation. In this case it was right.

As she would soon learn, the line of succession was saved because a woman named Matti Harrold had a gut instinct and had followed it. She'd been thrown into an impossible situation under false pretenses and succeeded. She'd gone against every instinct to gain and act on viable intelligence. Without Harrold's fortitude, everyone in the Capitol would have died. Instead, the 29-year-old's persistence had saved dozens if not hundreds of lives.

Felicia would learn the mid-level NSA analyst was as unlikely a hero as anyone. But to Felicia Jackson, that's exactly what Matti Harrold was. It was black and white.

CHAPTER 15

Sir Spencer rubbed his bruised wrists as he stepped into the ten by ten room. They ached from the metal handcuffs employed to bring him from his cell at the United States Penitentiary Lee in Jonesville, Virginia. The guard had tightened them a notch beyond comfortable.

The knight was dressed in khaki scrubs, the standard issue for pre-trial detainees. He'd asked for a burgundy ascot to complete the ensemble. The intake guards weren't amused.

In front of Sir Spencer was a small table with plastic chairs at either end, and in one of those chairs was the man who he was paying eleven-hundred dollars per hour.

Sir Spencer plopped into the chair, licked his chapped lips and closed his eyes. "Where do we sit, good man?"

The door to the small room slammed shut, a guard visible through a small window.

The defense lawyer, Braxton P. Mayhew, tugged at the cuffs on his suit coat and cleared his throat. His voice was soft, almost a whisper. "Believe it or not, we are in good shape."

"How do you mean?" Sir Spencer eyed the pick stitching on the lawyer's lapel. He imagined just three billable hours would pay for a jacket of such quality.

"Before we get into any of that, I need to counsel you on your behavior here," Mayhew advised.

"Do tell, good man," Sir Spencer said, swallowing against the dryness in his throat.

"Do not talk to other inmates."

"I'm in solitary."

"Do not talk to family members, or anyone who visits you. The conversations in the visitation room are frequently recorded and used as evidence."

"I've no family nor expected visitors."

"Okay, good. With that out of the way, let's talk about the others." Mayhew folded his hands on the table and leaned in as he spoke, looking Sir Spencer directly in the eyes.

Sir Spencer nodded, acknowledging the importance of what his lawyer was about to tell him.

"Jimmy Ings isn't talking," Mayhew began. "He's too loyal to you, despite whatever happened at Arlington. And much of the physical evidence points to him. The explosives, the meeting place, pretty much everything has his hands on it."

Sir Spencer ran his tongue across his teeth. "As it was intended to be."

"Secretary Blackmon has also retained counsel and isn't speaking," said Mayhew. "He's in a federal facility in Miami. I don't expect him to be an issue."

"Nor do I," said Sir Spencer. "He's the only one who blew up the Capitol."

"Bill Davidson—"

"Is dead," Sir Spencer cut in.

"Art Thistlewood is squealing like a pig," Mayhew continued. "He's spilling everything he knows."

"I should have purchased the yacht," the knight lamented.

"What do you mean?"

Sir Spencer shook his head, his eyes looking somewhere beyond the walls of the holding cell. "Thistlewood often said that if we ever got caught doing something illegal, *conspiring* with ill intent, that I'd have to purchase him a large yacht to keep him quiet. He loved the Chesapeake, and fancied himself a finer man than he was."

Mayhew didn't know how to respond, so remained quiet.

"Needless to say," the knight went on, his gaze returning to the lawyer, "I thought he was joking."

"It's not a problem," Mayhew said.

"What's not a problem?" Sir Spencer shifted his wait in the

small plastic chair.

"Thistlewood," Mayhew clarified. "We have people who can neutralize the threat."

"Ha!" laughed the knight. "I assumed we did. If you'd told me we didn't, I'd have neutralized *you* and found someone else."

"So that leaves young George Edwards," said the lawyer. He wasn't amused by Sir Spencer's threat, so he pressed forward. "And he could be tricky."

"How so?"

"My contacts within the bureau tell me there may be credible surveillance linking you to Edwards; photographs, phone recordings.

"Not an issue," Sir Spencer shook his head. "It's circumstantial and, given that Edwards is a United States citizen, the eavesdropping might be illegal. There's so much NSA backlash, I'm confident you'll get it tossed."

"There's another problem with Edwards."

"Which is?"

"We don't know where he is at the moment." Mayhew shifted in his plastic seat.

"Come again?" Sir Spencer's eyes narrowed.

"Well," Mayhew cleared his throat again, "you're each being held in separate locations."

"So?"

"Ings is the Arlington County Jail," Mayhew answered. "They've sent Thistlewood to the Big Sandy facility in Kentucky. You're here at Lee."

"Then where is Edwards?" asked the knight. "Any fool with an iPhone and a wireless connection can find federal prisoners."

"Sir Spencer," the lawyer's tone was sharper and frustrated, "I am aware of that. I know how the system works and how it doesn't work."

"Not well enough," Sir Spencer chided before licking a bleeding crack on his lower lip.

"They're using a pseudonym," said Mayhew. "They've disguised his identity."

"Why would they do that with him and not with the others?"

"There could be a host of reasons," shrugged the lawyer. "Other than Davidson, who's dead, he was the most well-known among you. His art sells for ridiculous sums of money and is likely to sell for even more now. It could be that. Or..."

"Or what, Mayhew?!" Sir Spencer slammed his fists onto the table. The lawyer jumped back in surprise.

"Or, since he knew everything you knew, they're protecting him from you."

"Hmmm..." The knight released his fists and stretched his fingers on the table. He closed his eyes and leaned back, a smile worming across his parched, bleeding lips. "That's a fascinating prospect. It's one I didn't expect. But I find it fascinating nonetheless."

Mayhew sat forward, his eyes on the knight's fingers and then the small tendril of bright, freshly oxygenated blood finding its way to Sir Spencer's chin.

"Do you know what I dislike most about being in federal custody?" Sir Spencer asked.

"What?"

"The cuisine," Sir Spencer said, opening his eyes. "I have a strong distaste for what passes as food here."

The lawyer leaned back in his seat but said nothing.

"This morning they served eggs, which I can only assume were conceived from powder, and a sausage link that was more than likely not meat intended for human consumption," the knight exhaled. "What I wouldn't give for a frittata, potatoes, and a bellini."

"Sir Spencer," Mayhew said, "I really think—"

"Ah-ah-ah!" Sir Spencer held up his hand, silencing the lawyer. "Let me think about the bellini." He closed his eyes again and slowly inhaled. He puffed his cheeks, as if savoring the bittersweet taste of nectar and champagne.

"You say to me," Sir Spencer said, without opening his eyes, "that George Edwards knew everything I did. You say that they are protecting him from me. I find that fascinating."

"You said that already." Mayhew checked his watch. They were running out of time and his client was pontificating. "We don't have time—"

"Do you know why it's fascinating?" the knight interrupted.

"Why?"

"Because George Edwards certainly did *not* know everything I knew. He does not *know* everything I know. And because, you think they can protect him from me?"

"I'm just saying that—"

"I led a self-loathing band of misfits to murder hundreds of people when one assassination would have accomplished the same result. I manipulated cabinet members and the former head of the Department of Justice to betray their instincts and destroy a powerful symbol of democracy. I put a bullet into a perfectly beautiful courtesan. Do you really think anyone can protect George Edwards from me?"

The silence was interrupted by the clang of the door opening, followed by a sour faced guard walking to Sir Spencer's side of the table.

"You're done for now," the guard grunted. He turned to Mayhew. "He's done for now."

"Remember what I said about unnecessary discussions," Mayhew reminded him as he stood.

Sir Spencer smiled as he stood and adjusted his scrubs. "I do think we'd be better served by you remembering what *I* said, good man."

EPILOGUE

"If men were angels, no government would be necessary."
--James Madison

Felicia rubbed her right hand along the chest of drawers just to the right of the fireplace in the White House Map Room. Her fingers stopped at a medicine chest sitting atop it. She touched it lightly and smiled at the irony.

The small box was believed to have belonged to James Madison. It was one of the few surviving items of the White House fire during the War of 1812. Now the box was in *her* house. A precious item from the collection of the man whose constitutional arguments had put her inauguration in doubt now sat in *her* Map Room.

Above it, on the wall, hung a small portrait of Madison. She would replace it with the portrait of another president. Maybe it would be Roosevelt, who used the ground floor space as a situation room during World War II. It was his use of the room for that purpose that gave it its current name.

Perhaps she'd hang Coolidge's portrait in Madison's place. He'd used it as a billiards room during his administration.

Or maybe she'd hang the visage of Barack Obama. He'd retaken the oath in this room after Justice John Roberts flubbed the oath on the steps of the Capitol the day before.

There was time enough for picture hanging. There were more important things to which she must attend. The first order of business was placing her right hand on the bible and taking the oath.

After John Blackmon was arrested on the tarmac at Miami International Airport, the Supreme Court refused to hear his lawsuit. It saved the Constitution and her chance at leading what everyone still considered the free world. She rubbed her shoulder, thinking about the attack.

Ninety-eight people died in the explosion, including twenty-six members of Congress; two cabinet members were among the thirty-five badly wounded. Felicia couldn't understand what would drive people to such violence. She didn't understand the motivation behind extremism. The irony of that thought was lost upon her as she glanced again at Madison.

Turning toward the center of the room she looked at the small group gathered for her moment. There were elected and appointed officials, family, and a few friends who she'd invited for the occasion. There was one television camera that would broadcast the induction live to the world. The White House photographer was checking light levels so that he might record the event for posterity and every internet website imaginable.

In the corner of the room, near the map cabinet, stood a beautiful young woman who Felicia did not recognize. She'd been talking to an older man in a cheap suit who'd just left her to take his seat. Felicia slipped her hand from the chest of drawers and walked to the stranger, extending her hand.

"Felicia Jackson," she offered as she approached. "Thank you for being here." Her left eyebrow was raised as if to ask, "And you would be...?"

"Madame Speaker," the woman took her hand firmly. "Thank you for the invitation. I'm Matti Harrold."

Matti was wearing a blue sleeveless, cowl neck wrap dress from Banana Republic. She'd paid seventy dollars for it. And while she thought a presidential inauguration might call for something more expensive, she'd spent her mad money on the outfit for the art opening and had had to make do with the clothing in her closet.

"Matti?" Felicia looked surprised. "You look wonderful."

"Thank you." Matti looked at her feet, blushing slightly. "That's very kind."

"I invited you here," Felicia continued, "because I wanted to thank you for your heroism."

"It's my job." Matti smiled. Her lips curled upward without revealing her teeth. "And I didn't stop the attack."

"You went above and beyond your job."

The women were still locked in a handshake, which didn't feel awkward to either of them. Felicia pulled Matti a step closer to her and then put her left hand on Matti's right. "Had it not been for your tenacity more people would have died."

Matti nodded and exhaled. The praise was more uncomfortable than the prolonged handshake.

"I would like to offer you a position in my White House." Felicia searched Matti's face for a response.

Matti was floored. In less than a week, she'd gone from mid-level NSA analyst to potential White House staffer. Bizarre. She wasn't sure what to think or how to respond to the offer. She blinked nervously. It was hot in the room. Matti was uncertain whether the heat was from the number of people in the room or from her own discomfort. She waved her hand in front her face but didn't respond immediately. Felicia could sense Matti's hesitancy.

"I am asking you to be a part of my team, Ms. Harrold," Felicia clarified. "You will have a very important advisory role in my administration."

"Why?" was the best Matti could muster.

"You are clearly a patriot, Matti. I need patriots. I need people I can trust. I want instinct and guts over intellectual and gutless. We have plenty of the latter in Washington. I need more of the former."

"I'm not sure..." Matti was afraid the speaker had misread her. She worried that luck and timing had given Speaker Jackson the wrong impression of her capabilities.

"I know it sounds trite, Matti, but your country needs you. And from what I have read about you, *I* need you. You saved my life and the lives of hundreds of other good Americans."

In what was both a rare moment of public emotion and a politically calculated move, Felicia pulled Matti close to her and hugged her. Matti paused awkwardly, and then she gently wrapped her arms around the speaker's back, patted her and then pulled apart.

"Okay, Madame President," Matti relented. "I accept."

"Excellent!" Felicia placed her hands on Matti's bare shoulders and squeezed. "Now go grab a seat."

Matti nodded and noticed the thirty other people in the room were seated. She located an armless chair in the back row and sat next to her father. She felt the eyes of cabinet members and the first family following her as she walked. It was both exhilarating and embarrassing. She knew they'd witnessed the speaker's hug. So had her dad.

"What was that about?" he asked. He was wearing his best suit and Matti thought he looked handsome. He'd complained about having to wear church clothes.

"She offered me a job," Matti whispered into her dad's ear. She wanted to say more. She wanted to tell him how much she loved him and how much she missed her mother.

Matti wanted him to know she'd forgiven her mother. She was letting go. Instead she lifted his hand and pulled it onto her lap. She squeezed it.

He nodded and then leaned into her.

"You know," he was speaking just above a whisper, "I sleep okay now."

Matti turned to look at her father. He was smiling. She smiled back and tightened her grip on his hands.

"Me too," she whispered.

The room quieted and the camera operator indicated the room was live on television. The Chief Justice took his place in front of the fireplace on the western side of the room.

Felicia Jackson, in a black silk dress with white pearls, stood opposite him with her right hand on her family's large King James Bible. It was black with gold trim. She raised her left hand and her mind drifted to the moment she stood in the halls of the Capitol looking up at Washington as he took the oath.

Her husband held the bible in his palms and looked at his wife with great pride. He knew what this moment meant to her. He imagined what it could mean for the nation if she chose to put the people above her own ambition. He knew his wife well and accepted her for her faults, as he knew she did for him. He looked down at the $1,100 python covered platform taper toe pumps she purchased for the event and chuckled at the ridiculousness of it all. The gray, brown, and white diamond patterned shoes with red leather soles were out of character for her. They were out of place for such a solemn, momentous event in the life of the nation. But *he* thought the shoes, covered with the skin of a deadly, life-crushing snake, the most appropriate apparel choice anyone in Washington had made in decades.

"Please repeat after me," began the justice, without noticing the shoes. "I, Felicia Baines Jackson, do solemnly swear..."

Matti shifted in her chair quietly. She watched the speaker become president from a vantage point reserved for those at the highest levels of power.

"...that I will faithfully execute the office of President of the United States."

Matti wondered what was in store for her now. Her job, her career, and her life were as uncertain as they'd ever been.

These were uncertain times in her country. The nation could spin down so many possible paths. There was no salve for the pain inflicted on a grieving electorate.

"And will to the best of my ability..."

It was not an overstatement, Matti thought, to suggest that democracy, freedom, and the essence of what the founding fathers had promised were in the balance with a new leader. It was frightening for the daughter of a football coach.

"...preserve, protect and defend the Constitution of the United States."

It was overwhelming for a girl who excelled with order and purpose. Yet Matti found herself pushing past the chaos. Sitting in a place where presidents played pool and a world war was won, she cued up a rare calm.

Matti stood and applauded as President Jackson shook the Chief Justice's hand.

ACKNOWLEDGEMENTS

Without my wife, Courtney, you wouldn't be reading this book. Her encouragement and gentle nudging are what have kept me writing and, in the case of SEDITION, helped shape a much better narrative. Our children, Samantha and Luke, are the world's finest cheerleaders, even if neither of them can do a Russian split.

My thanks to the team at Post Hill Press, in New York and in Nashville, for their confidence in trust in me and their outstanding efforts in bringing this story to a wider audience.

I also am grateful for the masterful editing of Felicia A. Sullivan. She improved the story and made my writing the best it could be. I owe her a gazillion dollars...or a yacht.

Jason Farmand has my utmost gratitude. His cover design rocks.

The pages of this book are filled with the seemingly endless hours of research used to create a realistic, plausible (though unlikely) plot. I relied, in part, on the expertise of others who include Joel Androphy, Guy Womack, and Trek "Thunder" Kelly. I thank each of them for their help.

Thanks also my wife Courtney, Curt Sullivant, Don Eaker, and Lisa Brackmann. They are the beta-readers who waded through the early drafts and gave me constructive critique.

Lisa, Bob Morris, Graham Brown, and Steven Konkoly are all wonderful, successful authors. Their help in navigating this "author thing" has remained invaluable.

To my parents, Sanders and Jeanne, my siblings Penny and Steven, and my in-laws, Don and Linda Eaker, thank you for your support and endless viral marketing efforts on my behalf.

Finally, to you the reader, thanks for reading the book. Regardless of your politics, I hope you saw past the party lines, and understood this is a book about patriotism, about democracy, and about what one will do to protect what's most important.